Fatal

Vengeance

Part II of the Fatal Trilogy

A fictional story about the boomerang effects of getting even at all costs. Guy Simmons finds himself protecting his siblings, Alex, Dana, and Cassie, from the pitfalls of life. In addition, he is tasked with taking care of his stepmother, who is battling breast cancer. Unfortunately, Guy has his own set of problems when his perfect marriage to Regine Croswell-Simmons falls apart. A culmination of murder, lies, and deception become the central theme as Guy and his family members seek vengeance on one another's behalf. The question of *'Who did it?'* leaves you in suspense until the very end.

Other Novels by Dorothy J Morris

Fatal Rebounds

Part I of the Fatal Trilogy

Fatal Blow

Part III of the Fatal Trilogy

Coming Soon!

Library of Congress Control Number (LCCN): 1-543310751

Fiction: Contemporary and Mystery

ISBN: 978-0-9836488-0-2

Published by:
Dorothy J Morris
www.dorothyjmorris.com
contactme@dorothyjmorris.com

Printed in the USA

First Edition - Paperback and Electronic

Acknowledgements

Thank you God, for giving me the desire to write and use my vivid imagination. The positive feedback I received from my first novel has inspired me to continue my writing journey. I am blessed to have the best friends (too numerous to list) and co-workers (Social Security Administration) in the world.

I would be remiss in not mentioning the biggest influences in my life. *Gone but not forgotten*: my mother, Maggie Burger Johnson is responsible for my spiritual foundation; my father, Corrie Johnson Sr. contributed to my ability to tell a colorful story; my big brother, Corrie Johnson (Bam) Jr., made me believe that I can achieve anything through hard work and determination; and my grandmother, Ida Mae Burger encouraged me to let go past hurts so I can look forward to a brighter future.

I cannot forget the special men in my life, who have always been there to give me professional or personal guidance. Thank you Andrew Morris (my hubby and honey-pooh bear) for accompanying me to my book signings and events. Peter and Nathan Johnson (brothers); Tavarus, Christopher, Nate, and Kelvin (nephews); Carl Thornton (father-in-law), Gus Mackey, Errol Simmons, Abdul Giwa-Osagie, Bernard Hill, Esset Tate, Ronnie Lockhart, Willie Banks, Chip Mitchell, Morris Sessomes [Thanks for enhancing my website, and for providing your creative input. You are a genius!]; James Robert Burger, Jackie Burger, Robert Kirkland, Heath Kelly, Tom and Wilford Morris (brothers-in-law), Teddi Robinson, and Sidney Monroe. They say behind every good man, there's a good woman and that woman just happens to be *moi* (LOL!)

A special thank you to the ladies who have encouraged me to continue my writing journey: Cassandra Johnson (sister), Carolyn Simmons, Lizzie Johnson, Rosa Mackey, Ms. Jay (mother-in-law); Gracie Kennedy, Shebby Flemings, JerryAnn Lowsman, Cheryl Morris; Emma Simmons, Rosa Mackey, Donna Giwa-Osagie, Leslie Watley, Leslie West, Peaches Paige, Karen (Icetea) Johnson, Joyce Franklin, Earlene Whitworth-Hill, Ernestine Braswell, Mary Steward, Joyce Hodges-Johnson, Renita McKall, Tatia Little, Colleen Cates, Georgiana Hamlin, Lavern Monroe, Shana O'Neal Robinson, Sandra Fowlks (also known as Saja Bo Storm, author of the Twisted Trysts series), Sybil Imani, Alora Walker, Stacey Syes, Juanita Carter, and all of my relatives (*too numerous to name*). Thanks for letting me bend your ear (or both ears, in most instances).

Fatal Vengeance could not have been possible without feedback from my silent readers: Victoria Mackey, Nicole Morris, Keirra Kennedy (daughters); Marcia Wagner, Marissa Turner, Carolyn Simmons, Heath Kelly, Willie Banks, Joyce Franklyn, Lareda Kellam, Theresa Webster, Marchand Bey-McQueen, Felicia Boatwright, Gekia Gant, Monique Johnson, and Wanda Russell. Thank you for providing invaluable feedback after reading the rough drafts.

A special thank you to those who contributed to Fatal Vengeance book cover: Nikkea Smithers, author of eleven published novels, President of "Readers with Attitude" book club, and editor/illustrator (www.nikkeasmithers.com); Juan Stevens, professional photographer (www.juanstevens.com); Kionne T. Agent, fashion model, actress and poet (www.kionnetagent.com); Michael T. Reeves, model and entrepreneur; and Renee Hoyt, model and actress.

To all readers, in general, thank you for spreading the word about the Fatal Trilogy. I am overwhelmed by your love and support. I hope this book will inspire you to read Part I *Fatal Rebounds* (if you have not done so already) and Part III *Fatal Blow,* which will be released in the very near future.

.

This book is dedicated to my beloved parents, Corrie and Maggie Johnson.

I miss you so much.

Chapter 1

Fire and Desire

*J*eanine Benedict was the previous owner of Trowne Key Estates, a multi-million dollar company comprised of five-star resort hotels and condominiums around the world. She turned the company over to her stepsons, Guy and Alex Simmons, after she was diagnosed with terminal breast cancer a year earlier. Since that time, her youngest stepson, twenty-four-year-old Alex Simmons was tasked with overseeing the full operations of Trowne Key Estates. Jeanine had made it abundantly clear to the entire staff that all major decisions had to be approved by Alex.

The change in leadership did not bode well for fifty-year-old Sidney McKinley, Trowne Key's Chief Executive Officer. He did not respect Alex as his leader. In fact, Sidney made it his mission to make Alex's new role as President an extremely difficult task.

One morning, they met in the conference room with six other Senior Executive staff members, to address the impact of the weakened economy. "I think if we downsize management," Alex explained while distributing supportive documentation, "we can survive the economic crisis and still stay afloat."

Sidney sat next to Alex, staring straight ahead. "Mr. Simmons," he interjected with an air of superiority, "this company will not survive with fewer managers. We should consider merging with Centennial Resorts."

With squinted eyes, Alex looked at Sidney sideways. Instinctively, he suspected his CEO of wheeling and dealing behind his back. "Explain how a merger would benefit this company," Alex countered in a harsh but controlled tone.

Arrogantly, Sidney turned up his nose at Alex before addressing the staff. "Centennial has earned an excellent reputation for providing quality service, and they have a good standing in the hotel industry. A merger would likely boost our revenue."

Alex slouched in his chair and looked at Sidney with slanted eyes. After deep thought, he asked, "What does the owner of Centennial have to say about this merger deal?"

"Let me handle all the details," Sidney replied with a smug grin. "I'll keep you posted on my progress."

Unbeknownst to Alex, Sidney had already discussed the merger proposal with Bryce Jennings, the CEO and owner of Centennial Resorts. He wanted to make sure the ten million dollar side-deal he made with Bryce was ironed out beforehand. Sidney had also planned on resigning from Trowne Key Estates immediately after the merger deal went through. He relished the idea of making Alex his scapegoat.

In a foul mood, Alex realized Sidney had managed to undermine him in front of his staff, again. After looking around the conference room, he noticed the staff seemed entertained by the tension between him and Sidney. "Everyone out!" Alex sharply ordered, as he sat up in his chair.

As if on cue, the staff scrambled to exit the room. When Sidney stood up to leave, Alex asked him to remain seated. The room was cleared within seconds.

After the conference room door closed, Alex turned to Sidney, and asked, "What is your problem?"

"*Me?*" Sidney stressed with his hands pointing at his chest. "I don't have a problem."

Drumming his fingers on the conference table, Alex thought it was a good idea to clear the air, once and for all. "Ever since I arrived at Trowne Key," he stated in a measured tone, "you act like you have an issue with me. So I ask again, what is your problem?"

"Mr. Simmons," Sidney replied in a condescending manner, "I've been with this company before you were born, so I know a little more than you will ever know about Trowne Key Estates." He paused, before adding, "Mrs. Benedict has always trusted my judgment. Remember, she promoted me to CEO prior to her departure."

"But *I'm* the one in charge!" Alex barked. "And don't you forget it!" He felt his blood pressure rise. Sidney's flippant attitude was getting on his last nerves.

Amused by Alex's explosive reaction, Sidney continued in his *'better than you'* attitude. "I can assure you that every decision I make is in the best interest of this company."

"You mean every decision *I* make!" Alex angrily retorted.

"Mr. Simmons," Sidney said with a wide grin, "for some reason, you seem unsure of yourself." Laughing inside, he took pleasure in rattling his employer.

"Listen to me, *asshole*!" Alex shouted with fire in his eyes. "I don't care how long you've been with this company. If you ever use that tone with me again, you will be out of a job!"

Sidney bit his tongue, fearing Alex would follow through with his threat. He exhaled as he stood up to leave. Then he casted his eyes downward, before asking, "Will that be all?"

Alex gathered his paperwork before he looked at Sidney with a straight face, and said, "Do not make any decisions without my approval. Am I clear?"

Sidney's face turned red in response to Alex's backlash. Under his breath, he muttered, "*Idiot,*" as he rushed out of the conference room, slamming the door behind him.

Alex slumped back in his chair, realizing he and Sidney may never see eye to eye. They bickered over everything, from business deals to office supplies. Alex was looking forward to a reprieve in the comfort of his office.

Walking out of the conference room, Alex stopped by his secretary's desk, which was situated in front of his office. Seeing his new secretary's smiling face seemed to bring balance to his workday. "Hello Maria," he greeted with a warm smile. "Do I have any messages?"

Maria batted her eyes and smiled before responding. "Nada, Señor Simmons."

Alex glimpsed at the way Maria ogled him with her big brown eyes and vivacious smile. Two months earlier, he had interviewed twenty-seven-year-old Maria Gomez for the secretary position. He was instantly impressed with her level of professionalism. However, for the past two weeks, he had noticed a dramatic change in her behavior. Maria was unusually flirtatious and frisky. She had also started throwing hints that she wanted him, sexually.

After Alex walked into his office and sat behind his desk, Maria followed after him, twisting her hips for added effect. She stood in front of Alex, striking a pose with her hands on her hips. "Señor Simmons," she purred, "is there anything I can do for you?"

"Not at this time," Alex said, as he looked up from the file he was reviewing.

Swiping her dark brown highlighted hair to one side, Maria asked, "Are you sure?" Her question had a sexual undertone.

Alex ignored Maria's gestures as he turned on his computer. "I'll let you know if I need anything," he replied, keeping his eyes focused on the monitor.

Put off by Alex's dismissive response, Maria returned to her desk with a pouty face. Seconds later, she cracked a smile when she thought of a plan to seduce her boss. She sprayed on some perfume, then retrieved a compact mirror from her purse and applied red lipstick. "Alex Simmons," she said to her reflection in the mirror,

9

"you don't know what you're missing. When I get through with you, you're going to kiss the ground I walk on."

After unfastening the first two buttons of her white silk blouse, Maria grabbed a handful of paperwork from her desk before returning to Alex's office. "Señor Simmons," she said after gliding her tongue across her upper lip, "I forgot to give you your messages."

Alex smiled as he held out his hand. He knew Maria was lying, but he was enjoying every minute of her charade.

Caught in her lie, Maria added to it. "Oh...um," she stammered, unprepared for Alex's reaction. "I left them on my desk."

Smirking, Alex sat back in his chair, and crossed his hands on the back of his head.

As she turned to leave, Maria purposely let the paperwork she was holding slide out of her hands. "Oopsie daisy!" she sang out, as she turned to Alex with a wide grin. "I'm so clumsy, papí." Her motions were slow and deliberate as she bent over in her black tight-fitting pencil skirt, to retrieve the scattered papers. Then she turned in Alex's direction to reveal her busty cleavage. Out of the corner of her eyes, Maria caught Alex gawking at her chest.

Regaining his composure, Alex cleared his throat and sat erect in his chair. "Do you need any help?"

While still bent over, Maria looked at Alex and smiled. "No thank you, papí." She picked up the last piece of paper, stood up, and straightened her skirt. "Um, I guess that's everything, huh?"

"I guess so," Alex said, as he turned toward the ringing phone.

"I'll get that," Maria insisted, as she lunged toward the phone on Alex's desk.

Alex held up his hand to stop her, after noting a familiar number flashing on his caller ID. He picked up the phone on the third ring. "Hello, Prettyface. How are you?"

Maria's smile turned upside down after guessing Alex's girlfriend, Rhaunda Coleman, was the caller. She stomped out of his office, quietly closing the door behind her.

Rhaunda blushed in response to the pet name Alex had given her two years earlier. "Hi Alex, I'm calling to ask if we can go out to dinner tonight."

"Not tonight," Alex firmly replied. "I have a business meeting."

"Who is she?" Rhaunda accused, automatically assuming Alex was cheating on her.

Alex remained tight-lipped. He wondered if Rhaunda was referring to the girl he was with the previous night.

Rhaunda bristled after acknowledging Alex's silence. "Did you hear me?!" she shouted over the phone.

"Yes," Alex muttered under his breath. He had a feeling he was in a no-win situation.

"I'm tired of this crap!" Rhaunda exclaimed. "You think I'm stupid. I know you're cheating on me!"

Alarmed by Rhaunda's outbursts, Alex sat up on the edge of his chair, and said, "I have no idea what you're talking about."

"You're lying!" Rhaunda snapped.

"If I am cheating," Alex said with an attitude, "it's your fault. I asked you to marry me, remember? But you said *no*. What do you want from me?"

Rhaunda frowned. "How can I marry an unfaithful man?"

Alex exhaled. He did not have the heart to tell Rhaunda he was tired of her stance on remaining celibate until marriage. "Face it Rhaunda," he said after a short pause, "your father is the real reason you won't marry me."

"Could it be that he knows you're a cheater?" Rhaunda rebuffed, trying to hold back tears.

Alex shook his head. "No, it's more than that. One day, you will have to choose between me and your father."

Rhaunda began crying in response. Her voice trembled when she spoke. "I... shouldn't have...to choose."

"You're right. I'm sorry." Alex was kicking himself for being insensitive.

"I love you, Alex," Rhaunda professed between sniffles. "I don't want to lose you."

"I love you too, but I have needs." At that very moment, Alex was thinking about Tina Turner's number one hit: *What's Love Got to Do With It.*

Drying her eyes, Rhaunda knew what Alex was hinting. "I told you we have to wait until we're married."

"I gotta go," Alex spouted out of frustration.

"But Alex...."

Alex interrupted Rhaunda, and said, "Maybe you should go on with your life." His voice was filled with anger. "I don't have time to wait on someone who needs their daddy's approval to be with me. Forget about us. It's over!" he announced with conviction, before slamming the phone on its cradle.

In deep thought, Alex sat back in his chair, rubbing his temples and thinking about Rhaunda. From the beginning, he thought she was special. He was particularly in awe of her beauty. She weighed one hundred eighty-five pounds and stood five feet, seven inches tall. Her sultry dark brown eyes sparkled against her yellow complexion and black curly afro. Even though she had the perfect shape, Rhaunda wore blouses and dresses that covered her cleavage, and long skirts and loose fitting slacks that downplayed her curves.

Alex admired Rhaunda for always putting God first in her life. However, he acknowledged her religious beliefs had wreaked havoc on *their* relationship. His thoughts were interrupted when his cell phone rang. "Hey Guy, what's up?" he answered, after noting his older brother's name flashing on the caller ID.

"I'm okay," Guy said, sounding upbeat. "I need you to stop by the house this evening."

"Sure, is everything okay?"

"Everything's fine. I just need to discuss some things with you."

"Okay, I'll be there."

When Alex was on the phone with Rhaunda, Maria had returned to her desk and pressed the conference line and the mute button, to listen in on their conversation. A wicked smile had crept across Maria's face, after she heard how her boss had ended his relationship with his girlfriend. This revelation made her plan to seduce Alex that much easier.

As soon as Maria stood up to return to Alex's office, Sidney appeared at her desk. "How can I help you Mr. McKinley?" Her question was rushed and impatient.

Frowning, Sidney was taken aback by Maria's attitude. "Will you see if Mr. Simmons is available?" he firmly requested.

"He's in a meeting at this time," Maria lied, making sure Sidney did not disrupt her plans. "Is there anything I can do for you?" she asked in a hurry.

"Please relay a message to Mr. Simmons."

Maria retrieved her pen and notepad from her desk to transcribe the message. Her eyes shot up at Sidney, as she asked, "What is it?"

Sidney frowned. "Mr. Simmons and I have a meeting with Bryce Jennings tomorrow afternoon."

Maria looked up from the notepad after transcribing the message. "Is that it?" she snapped.

Sidney nodded. He made a mental note to tell Alex about Maria's rude behavior.

"I'll be sure to inform Señor Simmons," Maria said, before she strolled in Alex's office. "Señor Simmons, Mr. McKinley asked me to relay a message to you."

Alex thought Maria was toying with him again, until he saw the slip of paper in her hand. "Thanks," he said, as he took the note from her extended hand.

Maria smiled as she walked around Alex's desk and stood close to him. "I think I know what's troubling you."

"What are you talking about?" Alex asked with an arched brow.

With no shame in her game, Maria pulled up her skirt, revealing her pink lace panties. Then she leaned over and whispered in Alex's ear, "I can make you feel real good, papí."

"This is inappropriate behavior!" Alex protested, pushing Maria away from him. His eyes briefly veered to the opened door. "Not here," he mumbled, feeling weak and vulnerable.

Picking up on Alex's half-hearted response, Maria smirked as she stood up and pulled her skirt down. Then she stared Alex down like a piece of meat. "What if you meet me at my place tonight?"

Alex stared at Maria in disbelief. "Aren't you still married?"

"Yes," Maria nonchalantly replied, "but my husband has issues."

Alex shrugged his shoulders. "I'm sure your husband wouldn't want you sleeping with your boss."

Maria bit her bottom lip as she hungrily looked into Alex's eyes. "But I need you in the worst way, papí. I promise we'll be alone. My husband works the nightshift."

Thinking with the wrong side of his brain, Alex grabbed a pen and sticky note from his desk. "What's your address?"

"One-two-two-zero Northwest Twenty-First Avenue," Maria quickly noted. After Alex jotted down her address, she said, "Papí, I need you to ring my bell."

Alex laughed at Maria's corny statement. "Okay, you got me. I'll be there tonight."

"Awesome, papí!" Maria replied with glee. "I look forward to seeing you later." Her eyes nearly popped out of its sockets when she noticed the bulge in the crotch of Alex's pants.

Pulling his chair closer to his desk, Alex attempted to hide his mishap. "Uh...me too," he muttered.

Maria put her hand over her mouth to stifle her laughter. Then she immediately returned to her desk. Two weeks earlier, someone had offered her ten thousand dollars to seduce Alex. Since that time, she had been pulling out all the stops. Maria was looking forward to fulfilling her part of the bargain.

Chapter 2

More Money, More Problems

*A*t twenty-nine, handsome debonair Guy Simmons and his beautiful sophisticated wife, Regine Croswell-Simmons, had the perfect marriage. With combined assets worth millions, they lived in a beautiful mansion located in a private gated community in Clearwater, Florida. Less than a year after marrying, they had a beautiful baby boy, Kevin Charlie, nicknamed KC. Both Guy and Regine were proud of their one and only child, who seemingly made their lives complete.

However, Guy had a lot on his plate. He was busy running his own company, Calvent Lucent Technology, and assisting his brother, Alex, with complex issues involving Trowne Key Estates. Outside of work, he was also raising his twin sisters, Dana and Cassie, and taking care of his stepmother, Jeanine Benedict, who was battling breast cancer.

A year earlier, Jeanine had refused further chemotherapy treatments, so Guy had convinced her to move in with him and Regine, to look after her. The doctor had told Guy and his brother that there was still hope for Jeanine. He had also explained that there was a new drug, Humercin, which could possibly stop the cancer growth, or cure the cancer altogether. However, the drug had not been approved by the Food and Drug Administration, and was still in the testing phase in London.

Jeanine had played a vital role in Guy and his siblings' lives, after their parents died ten years earlier. Even though she resented the fact that their mother was her husband's mistress, she loved the children as if they were her own. She was on the phone talking to Sidney McKinley, Trowne Key's CEO, when Guy walked into her bedroom, to check up on her. Upon seeing him, Jeanine covered the mouthpiece of the phone with her hand, and said, "Good morning, Guy. Don't leave. I need to talk to you."

Guy nodded as he strolled in the room, while Jeanine resumed her phone conversation with Sidney. At sixty-two, Jeanine bore a youthful appearance. Guy noted her skin was blemish and wrinkle free, and she looked as beautiful as the day he first met her. Though, he was concerned about her physical condition. She had lost a lot of weight, and her ability to take care of herself was limited.

"How's everything at Trowne Key?" Guy asked, as soon as Jeanine hung up the phone.

Jeanine paused before responding. "Considering Alex's limited experience, the company is doing quite well."

"So why do I hear concern in your voice?" he asked, after noting Jeanine's solemn expression.

"Sidney told me Alex has changed. He's become cocky and arrogant."

Guy walked over and sat on the edge of Jeanine's bed. Then he lightly placed his hand on top of hers. "Mom, Alex is young," he acknowledged in a soothing voice. "He'll be fine."

"I know," Jeanine thoughtfully replied. She smiled while eyeing Guy's black blazer and gold tie against his white ironclad dress shirt. "I see you're off to work."

"Yes, I have a meeting this morning. Is there anything I can do for you, before I leave?"

"No, I'm fine. I appreciate everything you've done for me."

Guy smiled. "I couldn't have done it without your help."

Jeanine assumed Guy was talking about her past actions when she had hired a private investigator to secretly watch over him and his siblings when they were younger. She had even threatened violence, to protect them. "I know my actions were extreme," she said with a slight nod, "but I couldn't live with myself if something had happened to any of you. I'm not as strong as I used to be, so *you* have to protect this family at all costs."

Scrunching his brows, Guy looked into Jeanine's eyes with deep concern. "I don't understand what you mean."

"Some people are willing to do anything to gain financial wealth," Jeanine explained, "even if it means resorting to the unthinkable. You have to keep a close eye on everyone in this family, especially the twins. When it is discovered that Dana and Cassie are heirs to the Toils and Day Paper Company, some people will try to lure them in different directions. You have to make sure they're always protected, and they surround themselves with positive people."

Guy nodded. "I understand."

"I'm glad you do, because you also have to look out for your brother. Alex has a lot of growing up to do. Make sure he doesn't fall prey to women who could potentially put him in harm's way."

"You don't have to worry about Alex," Guy commented with a light chuckle. "He's not serious about anyone."

"That's what I'm afraid of," Jeanine replied with a grim outlook. "One of these days, Alex is going to come across the wrong woman, who won't tolerate his indiscretions. So it's up to you, to make sure Alex sees the error of his ways. Now, before it's too late."

"I'll do my best."

"Do more than your best," Jeanine insisted. "You have the financial means to make it happen."

Guy leaned over and kissed Jeanine on the cheek. "You have my word," he said, as he looked into her eyes. "Have a nice day. Call me if you need anything."

"That won't be necessary," Jeanine coyly replied, "especially since you hired Mimi to take care of me."

Guy grinned. "I expect nothing but the best care for my beautiful mother. I love you."

Jeanine beamed after hearing Guy's heartfelt words. "I love you too, son."

Six months earlier, Guy had hired Mimi Kirkland to take care of Jeanine. Childless and unmarried, Mimi came highly recommended by Sidney McKinley, Trowne Key's CEO. She migrated from London to take care of Jeanine without reservations. They had effortlessly bonded, and acted as if they had known each other their entire lives.

After Alex got off work, he climbed into his brand new yellow Lamborghini, en route to Guy and Regine's home. His car was one of many extravagant toys he had purchased as a young millionaire. Alex could have easily afforded a mansion in the suburbs, but he opted for a three-bedroom condominium in a lush landscaped waterfront community in Tampa Bay, Florida.

Alex's condo screamed bachelor pad. He had it decorated with large dark brown furniture and expensive pictures. To heighten the sexual encounters with women he invited to his home, he had the walls and the ceiling in his bedroom covered with huge mirrors and centered around his king size bed.

Immersing himself in his newfound wealth, Alex started engaging in the *Tiger Woods* phenomenon. He treated sex as if it was air to breathe. Unlike Tiger, Alex did not use his money or power to attract women. He did not have to. Women were blown away by his tall muscular physique, beautiful brown eyes, and charming demeanor. Even his swagger was tantalizing.

Alex was attracted to a certain type of woman. He preferred married women, or women who were in committed relationships. He told his sex partners he was not looking for anything serious. Of course, his partners did not know about his steady relationship with Rhaunda Coleman.

As Alex drove up the sprawling driveway of Guy and Regine's home, he spotted his brother outside waiting for him. He thought something was wrong after parking his car. Swiftly, he climbed out of his car and darted toward Guy, panting. "Is everything okay?"

"Everything is fine," Guy said with assurance.

Still perplexed, Alex stood back and pensively stared at Guy, before asking, "What's going on? Is Mom okay?"

Guy smiled as he gently squeezed Alex's shoulder. "Calm down, Alex. Mom is fine. I just wanted to catch up with you. How are things going at Trowne Key?"

Alex frowned. "Sidney's a pain in the butt," he spouted. "Otherwise, everything's fine."

"Good to hear that. Let's go inside so we can talk."

Every time Alex came over to visit his family, he was reminded of the severity of Jeanine's health. He wished he could do something to repay her for making their lives better.

As they walked up the pathway, Guy noticed Alex's gloomy expression. "Don't worry. Mom is getting the very best of care."

Alex smiled. "Thanks for looking after her."

"It's my honor," Guy said, smiling with pride. "I don't know what our lives would have been like if it weren't for her."

"I know," Alex replied with a thin smile. On a lighter note, he asked about his sister-in-law. "Is she here?"

"Yes, Regine should be here. I haven't seen her yet. I arrived a few minutes before you pulled up."

When Guy unlocked the front door and walked in the house, his two-year-old son ran toward him with outstretched arms. "Hi Daddy!" KC happily squealed.

"Hey there!" Guy cheered, as he picked KC up and lightly threw him in the air. "How's my little man?"

KC giggled as he held out his teddy bear. "Kiss him, daddy!"

Guy kissed the bear, then tickled KC.

KC roared with laughter, while squirming around in Guy's arms. Alex stood in the back-ground, grinning.

Seconds later, Guy put KC down and watched him run toward his toys, which were scattered all over the living room floor. As if on cue, Regine appeared from the kitchen and smiled upon seeing Alex and Guy. She hugged and kissed her husband. Then she turned to her brother-in-law and gave him a hug. "How are you, Alex?"

Alex smiled. "I'm hanging in there. I'm proud of you sis. I heard you just opened another restaurant in Tampa."

"Thank you," Regine humbly replied. "It's been a busy year."

Last year, Regine had opened her first cuisine restaurant in St. Petersburg, Florida. Soon after, she opened another restaurant in Orlando, Florida. She had quickly earned a reputation for operating one of the finest five-star restaurants on the East Coast.

"Are you staying for dinner?" Regine asked Alex.

Alex shook his head. "No, but I'd appreciate it if you can fix me a plate to go."

Regine smiled. "Sure, no problem."

Looking around, Alex found it odd that neither of his sisters were present. "Where are the twins?"

"They're in the family room," Regine answered. "I'm glad you're here. I think you and Guy should talk to them."

Alex frowned as he looked at Guy for clarification. "Talk to them about what?"

Guy chuckled as he turned to Alex. "I think Regine is referring to the birds and the bees."

Earlier, Regine had recruited Guy to talk to the girls, after her failed attempt the previous night. Dana had walked out of the room laughing, and Cassie looked at her like she was a ghost.

"But they're only sixteen," Alex countered.

Regine turned to Alex with a smirk on her face. "They're almost seventeen. I think you can teach them a lot about what type of guys to avoid," she teased. Regine was aware of Alex's playboy antics.

Alex ignored Regine's snide remark as he walked over to his nephew, who was sitting on the floor playing with his toys. He squatted down next to KC, and patted the top of his head. "How's my nephew?"

KC looked at Alex and smiled. "Look, Uncle Alex," he said, as he held up a yellow remote control car, which was the exact replica of Alex's Lamborghini.

"One of these days," Alex said as he eyed the remote control car he had special made for KC's second birthday, "I'm going to buy you a car like this one."

"No you're not," Regine playfully protested.

Alex looked at KC and smiled. "As long as I'm living, my nephew will get anything his heart desires."

"We'll see about that," Regine offhandedly replied. "In the meantime, you and Guy need to talk to the twins. They're older now. Dana is boy crazy, and Cassie...well Cassie is shy." She stopped short of telling Alex that Cassie was possibly having an identity crisis.

"Come on, Alex," Guy interjected. "Regine is going to nag us until we get this out of the way."

18

Chapter 3

Unfaithfully Yours

*T*wenty-four–year-old Rhaunda Coleman was at work, at her father's church, when Alex hung up on her. Fuming mad, she slammed the phone on its cradle. Then she began crying as it dawned on her that Alex had ended their two-year relationship.

Her secretary, an older gray-haired lady, walked into Rhaunda's office after hearing whimpering sounds. "Ms. Coleman," she said with deep concern, "are you okay?"

Tears streamed down Rhaunda's face as she nodded "yes" without verbally responding.

"Ms. Coleman, are you sure you're okay?" the secretary asked again. When Rhaunda did not respond, she walked out of the office, closing the door behind her. Then she picked up the phone and called Rhaunda's father, Pastor Thomas Coleman.

The pastor was in the temple rehearsing his sermon when the secretary called and told him Rhaunda was crying and upset. He had already figured his daughter's disposition had a lot to do with Alex Simmons. He told the secretary he was on his way to see about Rhaunda.

Rhaunda pulled a tissue from its holder and dried her eyes, after deciding she should try to go and talk some sense into Alex. She stood up, grabbed her car keys and purse, and headed for the exit.

Before she reached for the doorknob, her father, who stood five feet, five inches tall and weighed two hundred pounds, rushed through the door. Huffing and puffing, he peered at his daughter with his beady little eyes, which stood out against his fair complexion and plump face. "And where are you going?!" he barked.

"I'm going out for a little bit," Rhaunda murmured, after blowing her nose with tissue. "I have to take care of some business." She felt guilty for not being completely honest with her father, but she knew how much he detested Alex.

Pastor Coleman's baritone voice permeated her office, when he shouted, "Does this have anything to do with that boy?!"

"Dad," Rhaunda said while averting her eyes downward, "I don't know what you're talking about." Her response matched the way she felt, weak and timid.

Pastor Coleman frowned. "You know exactly what I'm talking about. Alex Simmons has proven to you, time and time again, that he cannot be trusted. What further proof do you need?"

"But dad...."

Her father held up his hand to silence Rhaunda. "Alex Simmons is not the man for you. I'm more familiar with *his kind* than you think."

"What do you mean?" Rhaunda asked with furrowed brows.

The pastor ignored his daughter's question, figuring it would be too painful to tell her the truth about his own indiscretions. "You need to get on with your life," he firmly stated. "God has a better man, and a better plan for you."

"I suppose you're right," Rhaunda conceded, but her heart quickly flipped-flopped. Alex was her one and only boyfriend. She was in-love with him, and love conquered all. Unfortunately, Rhaunda's overprotective father had made it impossible for her to date anyone, besides Alex. Her father was also the reason why she chose to remain a virgin until marriage.

After looking into Rhaunda's sad eyes, the pastor hugged and kissed his daughter on the forehead. "The sooner you get Alex out of your system, the better."

"I know," Rhaunda muttered, as she walked behind her desk and sat down.

Satisfied he had gotten through to his daughter, the pastor briefly looked at his watch. "Now I'm going back to the temple. Are you going to be okay?"

Rhaunda nodded. "Yes, Daddy."

The pastor phoned his wife, Elizabeth, as soon as he left Rhaunda's office. It bothered him that Alex was still causing his daughter grief. "It looks like Alex and Rhaunda are at odds again," he said, as soon as Elizabeth answered his call. "Honey, you need to convince Rhaunda that she's better off without him."

"I've been trying," Elizabeth pointed out. "Rhaunda is in-love. What do you want me to do?" she asked, sounding defeated.

"Try harder!" the pastor demanded, before disconnecting the call. He was furious with Alex, but more furious with himself for not being able to protect Rhaunda from guys like Alex.

Elizabeth flinched at the sound of the dial tone. She concluded Rhaunda's infatuation with Alex Simmons was causing a rift in her *perfect family* image. Elizabeth and her husband were the same age, had the same fair complexion, and were about the same height. They seemed happy and in-love after forty years of marriage.

Rhaunda was their only child. For most of their daughter's life, Elizabeth and Thomas had worked hard to keep personal matters private and out of public scrutiny. They had sheltered Rhaunda, and made sure her upbringing was centered on church and worshiping God. They had even sent their daughter to an all-girls school for most of her life. Their biggest regret was when they had honored Rhaunda's request to go away to graduate school in Miami, Florida, where she met and fell in-love with Alex Simmons.

When Rhaunda broke up with Alex in graduate school, she had a nervous breakdown. Elizabeth thought, with time, Rhaunda would have bounced back to her usual self. Instead, she noticed a significant change in her daughter's behavior. Rhaunda had become a recluse, shunning the few friends she had, and lashing out over insignificant issues.

Soon after, Elizabeth took Rhaunda to a doctor for depression. It was more serious than she thought. She had planned on keeping Rhaunda's diagnosis a secret. In the interim, Elizabeth had convinced her daughter to move back home, and work for her father as the church event planner. She was hopeful after her daughter and Alex reunited a year after the breakup in graduate school.

Elizabeth was in the kitchen slicing up chicken cutlets when her husband called. Angry with Alex for causing her daughter misery, she stuck the knife into the wooden cutting board with vigor, as she shouted aloud, "Alex Simmons! You will not get away with this! I'm getting ready to make your life a living hell!"

Two weeks earlier, Elizabeth had followed Alex's secretary, Maria Gomez, for a week before she approached her in a quaint little Caribbean restaurant in downtown Tampa. Maria was sitting alone eating lunch, when Elizabeth walked up to her table.

"Hi, are you Maria Gomez?" Elizabeth asked with a wide grin, pretending to be excited to see her.

Maria looked up and wiped her mouth with her napkin before she spoke. "Do I know you?"

Elizabeth answered Maria's question with a question. "Do you work for Alex Simmons?"

Maria raised a brow. "Yes," she confirmed while nodding.

"Good," Elizabeth happily stated. "May I sit and talk to you for a little bit?" She did not wait for Maria's response. Elizabeth sat at the table, making herself a force to be reckoned with. "Well, let's get started," she suggested with clasped hands, while resting her elbows on the table.

Maria sat back in her chair with her arms folded. "Who are you?" she asked, hinting she was annoyed with Elizabeth's presence.

Smirking, Elizabeth sat up on the edge of her chair, and said, "That's not important. How long have you been working for Alex Simmons?"

Maria tensed up as she gazed at Elizabeth in disbelief. "I don't know you," she offered with an attitude.

"What if I pay you for your answers?" Elizabeth boldly replied, as she slid a hundred dollar bill across the table.

Smiling inwardly, Maria grabbed the money and answered Elizabeth's previous question. "I've worked for Mr. Simmons for a month and a half."

"So," Elizabeth continued, "Do you find him attractive?"

Maria could not help but smile. Secretly, she was smitten with her boss. "Señor Simmons looks *muy bueno*," she declared, dreamily.

From the little Spanish Elizabeth learned in college, she knew Maria found Alex to be very attractive. She eyeballed Maria before probing further. "So you like him, huh?"

Maria's eyes lit up as she bore a sly grin. "That man knows how to rock my world!"

Elizabeth chuckled, feeling confident about her plans to give Maria an offer she could not refuse. "Have you tried seducing him?"

"I'm a married woman," Maria countered with a scowl on her face.

After sizing Maria up as a money-hungry tramp, Elizabeth knew this woman could be easily swayed. She smiled, before asking, "What if I made you an offer you can't refuse?"

"What do you mean?" Maria asked with a questioning gaze.

"What would you do if I gave you ten thousand dollars?"

Maria grinned, while imagining how she would spend the money. "Well," she slowly replied, "that depends on what I have to do to earn it?"

Elizabeth leaned over the table and spoke in a soft but clear voice. "Lure Alex over to your apartment and make love to him."

Mentally, Maria questioned this woman's angle, but cherished the idea of making love to her boss.

"Can you handle that?" Elizabeth asked, after sensing Maria's reluctance.

Maria eyed Elizabeth with suspicion. "Why are you doing this?"

Elizabeth smiled. "I made a bet with one of my girlfriends that Alex could easily be enticed by beautiful women."

Maria blushed. She assumed Elizabeth had just given her a compliment.

"Well?" Elizabeth persisted.

Maria thought about her financial situation before responding. "I think I can do it. My husband works the night shift, so it should be no problem. When will I get the money?"

Elizabeth knew Maria and her husband were in dire financial straits. She discovered Maria's husband had been laid off for several months before he got his recent job as a security guard. With a big smile, Elizabeth pulled an envelope out of her purse and handed it to Maria. "This is a little incentive. You'll get the full ten thousand after you've fulfilled your part of the bargain."

With apprehension, Maria took the sealed envelope, then looked at Elizabeth, and asked, "How will *you* know if I followed through on my end?"

Elizabeth bore a mischievous grin. "Trust me, I'll know."

"How can I reach you?"

After handing Maria a business card with a cell number written on it, Elizabeth grabbed her Coach bag and stood up to leave. "Call me when you've lured Alex to your apartment," she ordered, before walking away from the table.

Maria frowned, wondering how or if Elizabeth knew where she lived. She was beginning to second-guess her decision, but her doubts disappeared after she opened the envelope and removed the cash. Her eyes glistened at the sight of ten one-hundred dollar bills.

Chapter 4
Reality Bites

*T*hree months shy of seventeen, Dana and Cassie Simmons had developed into two beautiful young ladies. They were both five feet, seven inches tall, weighed one hundred and ten pounds, and were shaped like models. Their green eyes were prominent against their very light complexion and lightly freckled face. Both had shoulder-length, naturally curly, light-brown hair. Dana wore hers straightened, parted down the middle and flipped under. Cassie preferred updos, typically ponytails.

Although they were identical twins, their style of dress drastically differed. Dana was a girlie-girl, sporting the latest fashions and trends. She never left the house without lip-gloss and bold colored eye-shadow. Cassie, on the other hand, opted for jeans and sneakers. She despised makeup. Even their attitudes were on opposite ends of the spectrum. Dana was loud and out-spoken, whereas Cassie was conservative and quiet.

In the family room, they were engrossed in a reality show on TV, until Guy and Alex entered the room. Dana sucked her teeth and rolled her eyes, detesting her older brother's presence.

Guy ignored the scowl on Dana's face as he walked into the family room with ease. He guessed Dana was still upset with him for not letting her have a boyfriend. He stood six four and weighed one-hundred eighty pounds. Guy was physically fit and extremely handsome. His height and deep voice commanded the twins' attention. "Girls, we need to talk."

Twisting her mouth and rolling her eyes, Dana glared at Guy with contempt. Cassie, on the other hand, stared at her brothers with a blank expression.

"Can't this wait?!" Dana snapped.

"No!" Guy yelled back, as he turned off the TV with the remote control. "This is important."

Alex frowned as he eyed Dana. "Will you chill out?" He could not believe she was outright disrespecting Guy.

Dana crossed her arms and stuck out her bottom lip. Now she was furious with Alex for chastising her.

"You girls are getting older now," Guy explained, as he looked at both Dana and Cassie. "Boys are only after one thing. They will lie and tell you they *love you* just to get between your legs."

Dana chuckled. "I just know you're not going to talk to us about the birds and the bees," she remarked with an attitude.

"Yeah," Guy muttered, "something like that." He knew Dana was determined to do what she wanted to do, with or without his permission.

The twins were still virgins, but Dana enjoyed watching her brothers squirm. "All I can say," she teased, "is you're a day late and a dollar short."

Alex's eyes shot up as he turned to Dana. "What do you mean?" He could not imagine his sisters having sex at their age.

Snapping her fingers in the air, Dana continued with her snippy attitude. "I'm saying, *you're too late.*"

Alex gasped. He was temporarily rendered speechless.

Guy wondered if Dana was hinting that she was having sex, or was she just toying with him. "Do you have any questions for me?" he asked, after a short pause.

"Nope!" Dana sharply answered.

Growing tired of Dana's obnoxious outbursts, Guy continued with caution. "We have another matter to discuss. Mom thinks I should take measures to protect you girls."

"Why?" Cassie asked. "We're not in any danger."

Realizing this would be a delicate topic, Guy sat between Dana and Cassie on the sofa before asking, "Did you know that you and Cassie have a different father from mc and Alex?"

"Come on," Dana chided, "we're not stupid. It didn't take a rocket scientist for us to figure that out."

Turning to Guy, Cassie asked, "Who is he?" She had always hoped her father would show up one day to claim her and her sister.

"His name is Bobby Toil," Guy slowly answered. "He died when you were younger. His father, your grandfather, owned the Toils and Day Paper Company. Before your grandfather died, he listed you girls in his will. At twenty-one, you will receive your inheritance, as long as you continue your education in college."

"Are you serious?" Dana asked, as she sat up on the edge of the sofa.

Guy nodded in affirmation.

"How much money?" Dana probed. "Is it Paris Hilton money?"

"Yes," Guy confirmed with a slight nod.

Dana was excited but Cassie's glimmer of hope was shattered. She barely remembered her mother, who died in a car accident when she and her sister were four-years-old. Now she had to accept the news of her father's death. It was too much for her to bear.

Guy sighed. "Now you know why mom is worried about you girls," he said, as his eyes shifted from Dana to Cassie.

Dana sucked her teeth. "I think Mom is being paranoid."

"You're probably right," Guy thoughtfully replied, "but we shouldn't take her advice lightly. I'm going to hire a bodyguard for you girls. He'll be on-call every time you leave the house."

Dana stood up, twisting her neck back and forth. "We don't need a bodyguard!" she exclaimed. "We're old enough to protect ourselves."

"Dana!" Alex scolded. "You don't know what's at stake."

"I want Guy to stop treating us like kids," Dana complained.

Guy stood up to face Dana. "I love both of you," he said, briefly turning to Cassie. "I would die if something ever happened to either of you."

"Oh, whateva," Dana sassed. "I can't wait until I turn eighteen, so I can get out of this house!" she screamed, before stomping out of the family room and running upstairs to her bedroom.

Guy turned to Cassie and noted sadness in her eyes. "Do you have any questions for me?"

Cassie shook her head, affirming she did not. She was troubled over the news of her father's death. With her eyes fixed to the floor, she stood up and headed upstairs to her bedroom.

After Cassie left the room, Alex turned to Guy, to address his concerns. "I think you should have held off on telling them about their inheritance."

"Alex, I thought about this long and hard. I wanted to make sure the twins understood why a bodyguard is necessary."

"I suppose you're right," Alex determined. "I'm going to head home."

"Why don't you go say 'hello' to Mom?"

Tears welled up in Alex's eyes at the thought of seeing Jeanine. The last time he saw her, she was frail and using a walker to get around the house.

"Mom loves you," Guy egged on. "She's not going to be around much longer."

Alex nodded. "You're right," he said, after deep thought. "I'll go see her. Slowly, Alex walked toward Jeanine's bedroom, while Guy stayed behind. He knocked on her door, which was cracked open. "Mom, it's me, Alex."

"Please come in," Jeanine replied with enthusiasm. She sat up in bed when Alex opened the door and walked in.

Alex bore a nervous smile as he walked over and kissed Jeanine on the cheek. "Hi Mom."

"Hi, Alex," Jeanine said in a hoarse voice. "I'm so glad you came to visit me."

Holding back tears, Alex pulled up a chair and sat next to Jeanine's bed. He noticed her pale complexion had turned ash gray, and her eyes were yellow and glassy.

"Alex," Jeanine weakly said, "I was always worried about your brother, but I never thought I had to worry about you."

Perplexed, Alex's eyes widened. "What are you talking about?"

"So far, you've been lucky," Jeanine explained. "You've managed to get yourself out of some sticky situations." She bore a thin smile before continuing. "There's a thin line between love and hate. If you don't settle down, you will regret it."

"I don't know if I'm ready to settle down," Alex acknowledged, after concluding his relationship with Rhaunda was all but over.

Jeanine forced a smile. "I know. Just be careful. When a woman is emotionally connected to a man, sometimes there's a strong passion that drives her to do the unthinkable." When she stretched out her hand toward Alex, he placed his hand on top of hers. "I love you," she softly professed.

Alex smiled, feeling her love. "I love you too."

"Be careful."

"I will," he said with a slight nod.

Satisfied she had gotten through to Alex, Jeanine rested her head on her pillow. Then she closed her eyes and drifted off to sleep with a heavy heart.

Guy strolled into Jeanine's bedroom shortly afterward. Then he stood in the background, resting his hand on the back of Alex's shoulder. "Did you get a chance to talk to her?"

"Yes, a little bit," Alex stated without taking his eyes off Jeanine.

"She's worried about you."

"I know," Alex said, as he stood up to leave Jeanine's room. Guy followed Alex into the kitchen.

Regine smiled when Alex walked into the kitchen. "Here you are," she said, as she handed him a wrapped plate of filet mignon, roasted potatoes and steamed vegetables.

"Hmmm," Alex said, after sniffing the top of the plate. "It smells good. Thanks sis."

Regine nodded and smiled. "Anytime."

"I'm headed home. I'll talk to you later."

Guy followed Alex outside to his car. "It was good seeing you," he said, as he embraced his brother.

"Same here," Alex said with a warm smile. "You take care of yourself." He opened his car door and climbed in before turning to Guy with a smug grin. "I might have a little snack waiting for me later on."

Shaking his head, Guy was put off by Alex's remark. "Man, you need to slow down before someone gets hurt."

Alex laughed in response. "Come on, Guy. Lighten up."

"What about Rhaunda?" Guy asked, curious to know where she fit in Alex's life.

Alex became serious at the mention of Rhaunda's name. "That's my boo. If I get married, she'll be the one."

"Well," Guy sternly said, "treat her with respect and stop messing around."

"Don't go there," Alex said, as he held up his hand.

Guy put his hands in his pockets, thinking of a way to reason with Alex. "I'm really surprised you didn't learn anything from my past mistakes. I almost lost Regine, chasing behind another woman, remember?"

"Yeah, I remember, but Regine accepted your marriage proposal, Rhaunda rejected mine." Alex was clearly bitter.

Guy did not know how to respond, so he remained quiet.

Alex thought about the recent conversation he had with Rhaunda over the phone. He regretted the way he blew her off. After putting on his shades, Alex started his car engine before turning to Guy. "Why are you questioning me about my life, anyway?"

"I care about you."

"This doesn't sound like you. Where is all of this coming from?"

"I've been thinking about your safety, that's all. You need to slow down before someone gets hurt."

"Nothing is going to happen to me," Alex replied, before throwing his gear in reverse. "I'll stop by next weekend."

Guy nodded. "Okay, be safe."

Chapter 5
Poison

*A*lex thought about calling off the arrangement with his secretary, but he wanted to relieve some tension. The ordeal with his sisters had him on edge. During the drive to Maria's apartment, Alex thought about his break up with Rhaunda. He wished things could have turned out differently. After parking his car, he strutted up the path to Maria's front door, feeling weary.

"Hello Alex," Maria cooed in a seductive voice, after she opened the door, revealing her million-dollar smile. "I'm so glad you made it."

Alex smiled as Maria opened the door wider, motioning for him to step inside. Rhaunda had become a non-issue, when Maria stood before him in red bikini panties, a red sheer bra, and red six-inch stiletto heels.

Teasingly, Maria placed her index finger on the tip of her tongue and looked at Alex with sultry eyes. "You see something you like?"

"Wow," he spewed, while inspecting Maria's curvy body. With a big grin, he walked past her, looking around the apartment. "Are you sure it's okay for me to be here?" he asked, as he loosened his tie and pulled off his jacket.

"Yes, I told you that my husband works at night. Please have a seat and make yourself comfortable. I have to make a quick phone call."

"Sure," Alex said with a sly grin. "Take your time."

Maria went to her bedroom and dialed the number of the person who promised to make her ten thousand dollars richer. She grew excited after Elizabeth answered on the first ring. "He's here," Maria said in a hushed voice.

"Good!" Elizabeth happily replied.

Maria glanced at the closed bedroom door before asking, "When will I get the money you promised?"

"Call me tomorrow, sweetheart," Elizabeth said in a syrupy voice. "I'll let you know where we can meet up."

As soon as Elizabeth disconnected the call, she called her daughter using the latest voice over technology to disguise her voice. "I'm calling to tell you that your boyfriend is up to no good," she vented with disgust. "He's at his secretary's home right now." Elizabeth gave Rhaunda the address before she ended the message.

Then she called Maria's husband at his job to inform him of Maria's impending sexual encounter with Alex.

After drenching herself in perfume, Maria returned to the living room with a big grin on her face. Her eyes zoomed in on Alex's hairless, six-pack chest. "Take off your pants and boxers," she demanded with a light giggle. "I want to see what I'm working with, papí."

Without further probing, Alex complied with Maria's request, then followed her into the bedroom and sat on her bed. He stared at Maria's tanned legs as she slipped out of her shoes. Suddenly, Alex was taken by surprise when Maria leaned over and smothered him with kisses. He had easily succumbed to her robust energy, whiffing her perfume as he planted small kisses along her neck.

"Wait," Maria insisted, as she stood up, pulling away from Alex's embrace. She closed the bedroom door to capture the full essence of the candlelit room, then turned to Alex with a wide grin. "I have something to show you."

When Maria removed her bra and revealed her perky thirty-eight double-Ds, Alex moaned with delight. "What else do you want to show me?" he asked with a wicked smile.

Maria smiled. "Papí, I have the biggest surprise for you," she said, before she pulled off her panties, spread her legs, and placed her hands on her hips. "You like?"

"Hmmm," Alex groaned, as he hungrily eyed Maria's shaved cherry jubilee. "I like."

Suddenly, Maria jerked her head toward the bedroom door. She heard movement coming from the living room.

Alex's eyes grew bigger as soon as he heard noises on the other side of the bedroom door. "Who is that?" he asked, his voice was filled with fear.

"Shhh," Maria fearfully warned, placing her forefinger over her lips. "I think it's my husband."

"Are you serious?" Alex asked in disbelief, but did not wait for a response. Quickly, he stood up and looked around the bedroom for his clothes. Then he panicked after realizing he left his clothes in Maria's living room.

Understanding Alex's dilemma, Maria ran to the bedroom closet, grabbed her husband's robe, and threw it in his direction. "You have to get out of here!" she screamed, as she rushed over to the window and threw it open.

Alex rushed to put on the robe and bolted toward the window. He barely had his head out of the window when Maria's husband, Armando, rushed in the bedroom with fire in his eyes.

"What in the hell is going on in here?!" Armando hollered with venom spewing from his mouth.

Maria's voice trembled. "Armando…papí…let me explain," she urged, trying to think of a plausible reason for Alex's presence in their bedroom. She could not understand why Armando was home from work so early, since he worked at night.

Alex struggled to squeeze through the small bedroom window, without success. His heart was pounding in overdrive when he dropped to the floor and slowly turned around.

"Who in the hell are you?!" Armando barked, before taking a closer look at his wife's employer. He instantly recognized Alex from when he picked up Maria from work one day. "I can't believe this crap!" he shouted, as he turned to Maria with a scowl on his face. "You're screwing your boss?!"

With pleading eyes, Maria reached for Armando, pulling on the shirt tail of his uniform. "Papí, we didn't do anything."

Bitter and heartbroken, Armando pushed Maria away from him. "You're a selfish, no-good, scandalous slut!" he proclaimed with malice in his heart. Tears burned the back of Armando's eyes as he glared at Maria. "I have given you everything you have ever asked for, and '*what do you do?*' you go and screw your boss!"

With caution, Alex interjected himself with a wave of his hand. "Um…I'll leave you two, to talk about this in private," he stammered, as he tried to walk around Armando.

Armando shoved Alex backward. "You're not going anywhere!" he shouted at the top of his lungs, while rubbing his fists for full effect. "You need to learn a lesson about sleeping with another man's property!"

Quivering from fear, Alex turned to Maria for help. In response, she pleaded with her husband. "Papí, please let him go."

"After I get through with him," Armando grumbled, "I'm going to deal with you next." Moving at the speed of lightning, he turned to Alex and punched him in the stomach.

Alex keeled over, feeling the stinging pain in his abdomen. He braced himself as he stood up, only to receive Armando's fist to his right eye. He fell backwards, rolling off the bed and onto the floor with a loud thump.

"Get up!" Armando demanded, as he towered over Alex and pulled him up by the robe. He drew back a tight fist, ready to pummel Alex's face but stood still after hearing commotion in the front of the apartment.

Bracing himself, Armando watched in fear as three strange men bum-rushed the bedroom. "Who in the hell are you?!" he asked the men, while keeping a firm grip on Alex.

"Your worst nightmare!" the leader of the pack threatened. "Let him go!"

Armando released Alex, then held up his hands to surrender. "I…don't…have a problem…with you," he stuttered.

"And as of now," the leader stressed, "you don't have a beef with Alex either." Then the leader threw Alex his clothes, which were retrieved from the living room, earlier.

Quickly, Alex slipped on his shirt and pants while Armando stood in one place, stunned.

"You know what he did with my wife?" Armando asked the leader.

"I think we can guess," the leader stated with a light chuckle, "but you put your hands on the wrong man this time."

Armando raised a brow, as he asked the leader, "What is it to you?"

The leader faced Armando without flinching. "Let's just say, if you put your hands on *Alex Simmons* again, you will regret it."

Armando was rendered speechless. Common sense told him these men meant business. His tough stance from earlier, all but disappeared.

Unsure of what to do next, Alex looked at the leader of the pack for guidance.

"Get the hell out of here!" the leader yelled at Alex.

Alex put some pep in his step as he collected the rest of his belongings. Then he turned to the leader, and muttered, "Thank you," before rushing out of the apartment. Swiftly, he ran to his car like his life depended on it. Then he drove home like a maniac. He banged on the steering wheel out of frustration. "Why did I do it?!" he asked himself, while wiping sweat from his forehead. "I should have known better!"

Alex was so busy trying to get away from the scene, he did not notice Rhaunda's SUV parked behind his Lamborghini. She ducked down as Alex sped out of the apartment complex. Feeling sucker-punched, Rhaunda sat up in her car with tears drenching down her face. This, she thought, was the final straw. She was tired of Alex's unfaithfulness.

As soon as Alex got away, Maria turned to the men with terror-filled eyes. "Armando is going to kill me," she stated with trembling lips. "Please take me with you."

The leader of the pack looked at Armando, who bore bloodshot eyes, before he turned to Maria, and said, "Gather as many clothes as you can, and put them in one suitcase."

Armando went ballistic. "She can't go!" he hollered out. "You can't take her! My wife is my property!"

The leader shot daggers at Armando, as if daring him to say another word. It worked, because Armando shut his mouth and stepped back.

"I'm ready," Maria stated, as she snapped her suitcase shut and grabbed the handle.

"Maria," Armando begged, "please don't go."

With deep regret, Maria turned to face Armando, and sincerely stated, "I will always love you." Then she picked up her suitcase and rushed out of the bedroom.

Six months earlier, Maria had relocated from Puerto Rico to Florida to be with Armando. Their living arrangements were not what she had expected. She quickly discovered Armando was barely making ends meet, and he had a hard time keeping a steady job. She loved her husband but determined it was not enough for her to stay with him.

After Maria left, the leader turned to Armando, and said, "In case you get any wise ideas to come looking for your wife, or Alex, you might as well plan your funeral."

Armando stood still, until the men exited the room. As soon as the front door closed, he rushed to the phone in his bedroom and called his friend, Philipo Rijos. "I have a problem," he said in a hurry.

"Talk to me," Philipo urged while driving.

After a short pause, Armando said, "I caught Maria with her boss."

"That doesn't surprise me," Philipo replied with a light chuckle. "I told you she was a *slut* when you married her."

Armando was offended by his friend's remarks but quickly recovered. "Can you help me get her back?" he asked in an almost pleading voice.

Philipo shook his head, laughing. "Why are you calling me?"

"He threatened me."

"Who?"

"Maria's boss, Alex Simmons. The man she cheated on me with." Armando did not know the names of the men who threatened him, so he lied.

Philipo chuckled. "You've got to be kidding."

"I wish I was."

"Why did he threaten you? Maria's your woman."

"He wanted her for himself. He threatened to kill me if I tried to go after her."

In response, Philipo pulled over to the side of the road and parked his car. "Where can I find this guy?" he asked in a husky voice.

Armando was relieved Philipo had finally taken him seriously. He gave his friend the little knowledge he knew about Alex. "How soon can you get to him?" Armando inquired.

"You want him dead or alive?"

"I don't care."

"Where is she?"

"With him." Armando continued the lie, hoping this piece of information would help his cause.

Philipo frowned. "Maybe he did you a favor."

"Never mind that!" Armando retorted. "I want my wife back!"

"I'll call you after I look into this matter."

"Thank you," Armando said with relief. He knew Philipo to be a man of his word. They were childhood friends, but chose different paths in life. Philipo engaged in criminal activity, whereas Armando struggled to become a productive citizen.

Chapter 6

A Woman's Worth

Guy was jolted awake early the next morning, sweating profusely. He had dreamt Dana and Cassie had disappeared, and there were no clues of their whereabouts. Even though Guy had already made arrangements to hire a bodyguard, he could not shake the feeling that something bad was going to happen to the twins.

Unable to sleep, Guy got out of bed and went into the kitchen, where he found Dana and Cassie heading out the side door. They were on their way to the bus stop. "Good morning, girls," Guy said, trying to sound upbeat. "How do you feel about me taking you to school today?"

Rolling her eyes, Dana put her hand on her hip and twisted her mouth. "That's not necessary," she sassed.

Guy's left jaw twitched, before he said, "What if I say, you don't have a choice?"

"What's the big deal?" Dana questioned, as she folded her arms.

Exhaling, Guy walked over to the kitchen counter to fix himself a cup of coffee. "Things are going to be different from now on," he said, as he poured coffee into a mug.

"Why?" Cassie asked with raised brows.

Guy took a sip of coffee before responding. "Because I have to protect you and your sister."

Dana chuckled as she threw her book bag over her shoulder. "Guy, you're tripping. We'll see you after school." She turned to Cassie and tugged on her arm. "C'mon, let's go before we miss the bus."

When they walked out the door, Guy was torn over whether he should have been more forceful with Dana. Deciding to take matters into his own hands, he walked into his office and phoned his best friend, Big Mike, whom he had befriended in college.

As sole owner of a reputable private investigation firm, Big Mike was partly responsible for uniting Guy and his siblings with their stepmother over a year ago. He had also forced Guy to realize Regine was a good woman.

Guy smiled when Mike answered on the first ring. "Hi Mike, how's it going?"

"I'm fine, buddy. How are you?"

"I'm hanging in there. The twins are getting older, and I'm worried about their safety."

Big Mike nodded. "I take it they're the reason you called."

"Yes, I was wondering if you could recommend someone to watch over them for me."

"Sure. Do you want a bodyguard, or do you want someone watching them from afar?"

"I prefer a bodyguard. I know my request may seem a little extreme, but you can't imagine what I'm going through."

"It's better to be safe than sorry," Big Mike replied with understanding.

Guy smiled. "I'm glad you feel that way. How soon can you send someone over?"

"Tomorrow morning."

"Good, I'll keep a close eye on them until then. Thanks for looking out."

"No problem."

After Guy hung up the phone, he returned to his bedroom and sat on the side of the bed, rubbing his temples. He tried to shake off the bad feeling he had about the twins, to no avail.

Seconds later, Regine woke up and noticed her husband was unusually quiet. "What's the matter, honey?"

Not wanting her to worry, Guy turned to Regine and smiled. "I love you, baby. You are more beautiful today, than the day we first met."

"Okay, what do you want?" Regine teased with soft laughter.

"Nothing," Guy said, before he leaned over and kissed his wife on the cheek. "You are the love of my life."

Regine smiled. "I know it's six months away," she bashfully stated, "but how do you feel about jump-starting our three-year anniversary?"

Guy's cheeks flushed as he bore a wide grin. "That sounds like a plan." He took off his silk black boxers while looking into Regine's big brown eyes. He loved everything about his wife, including her curvy body and smooth chocolate complexion. Guy was still in-love after all this time, and wanted to show it by satisfying Regine's mind, body and soul.

"Don't you have to work today?" Regine inquired, while lightly chuckling.

Gently, Guy kissed Regine on the lips, then looked into her eyes. "Not before I make sweet love to my wife." With precision, he removed Regine's negligee, then hungrily kissed her breasts.

Regine moaned with pleasure as Guy smothered her with kisses.

She touched his manhood, while slipping her tongue into his mouth. "Ooh, baby," she cooed, "I need you. I love you."

Guy smiled as he crawled on top of Regine, and entered her cream pie with great anticipation. "I love you more," he whispered in her ear, as they made sweet love.

Thirty minutes later, both Guy and Regine shivered with delight. Their lovemaking was intense but satisfying. Shortly after, Guy rolled over and got out of bed. "I'm going to take a quick shower," he said, as he turned to Regine with a warm smile. "Why don't you take the day off?"

Regine smiled. "I just may do that." Feeling rejuvenated, she curled up in bed and closed her eyes.

Guy kissed Regine on the cheek before climbing out of bed to dress for work. Next, he walked into his son's room and found him sound asleep, holding his toy robot in his hand. After kissing KC on the cheek, Guy grabbed his briefcase and headed for work. He relaxed a little, knowing the twins would soon have a bodyguard that would protect them at all times.

Chapter 7
Balancing Act

*A*fter the incident with Maria and her husband, Alex had taken three aspirins and downed them with three shots of Hennessy before crashing on the sofa. He had drifted off to sleep dreaming Armando had killed him. Alex prayed that if he woke up, he would change for the better. Suddenly, he had a new respect for life, and women.

Alex woke up the next morning with a major hangover. He drove to the office in a lethargic state, wishing he could have taken the day off. However, he and Sidney had an important meeting with Bryce Jennings, the owner of Centennial Resorts, and he would not miss it for the world. Alex was mentally prepared for his meeting, but could not help but think about the altercation he had with Maria and her husband, Armando, the night before.

Upon arriving at the office an hour late, Alex contacted the temp agency for a new secretary after noting the vacant desk in front of his office. His mind drifted back to Maria and her husband but his thoughts were interrupted when his office phone rang. The caller ID showed an unfamiliar number.

"Hello Alex," the caller said, as soon as he picked up the phone.

Alex gasped. He was caught off guard upon hearing the caller's voice. "Uh, Maria," he stammered, "what a surprise."

"I need money," she pleaded. "My husband cleaned out my bank account."

Unnerved by Maria's phone call, Alex sat back in his chair, grunting. "That's not my problem."

"Don't be like that, Alex. Your men dropped me off at the airport, and bought me a one-way ticket to Puerto Rico. But I need some money. I only need enough to get on my feet and start over."

Alex guessed Maria was referring to the same men who helped him escape from Armando. "How much do you need?" he inquired in a huff. He thought Maria was trying to make *her* problem his.

"Ten thousand dollars." Maria figured Alex owed her that much. She could not believe that Elizabeth, the woman who had arranged for her to seduce Alex, did not fulfill her part of the bargain.

Alex whistled after pondering Maria's request. "This sounds like extortion to me."

"It's not like I asked you for a million dollars!" Maria snapped.

Alex determined the sooner Maria was out of his life, the better. "Fine, how should I send the money?"

Exhaling, Maria was relieved Alex had honored her request. "You can wire it to San Juan, Puerto Rico, through the Western Union."

Alex checked his watch before responding. "I'll wire the money to you today, but I don't want to hear from you ever again. You need to get on with your life, and put all of this nonsense behind you."

"You heartless bastard!" Maria shouted, trying to hold back tears. "You came to my apartment, remember?!"

"First of all," Alex retorted, "you asked me to! Secondly, I don't recall forcing you to drop your panties."

"Just send me the damn money!" Maria demanded, before she hung up on him.

Shaking his head, Alex was stunned by his former secretary's reaction. He said to himself, *"She put herself in this situation, and now she's blaming me."*

After grabbing his car keys, Alex figured he had enough time to wire the money before his meeting with Bryce Jennings.

Returning to the office an hour later, Alex found Bryce Jennings sitting in the reception area. He had remembered Bryce's face from the profile on Centennial Resorts' website. "Mr. Jennings," he greeted with an extended hand, "it's so nice to meet you. I'm Alex Simmons, president and owner of Trowne Key Estates."

"The pleasure is all mine," Bryce said, as he shook Alex's hand.

Alex glanced at his watch before turning to Bryce. "I thought our appointment was this afternoon."

"Yes, it is," Bryce confirmed. "I got out of my morning meeting early, so I thought we could meet now, if it's not too much trouble."

"No it isn't," Alex admitted, before he turned and noticed his new secretary sitting at Maria's desk. She looked to be in her late fifties. "Ms. JoAnn Leigh?" he questioned, to be sure the temp agency sent him the right person.

"It's nice to meet you," JoAnn said, as she smiled and extended her freshly manicured hand.

"Same here," Alex said, as he smiled and shook her hand. "Please hold all calls, until after the meeting with Mr. Jennings."

JoAnn nodded. "Yes, sir."

Alex smiled as he turned to Bryce. "Can I get you coffee or anything?"

Bryce shook his head. "No, I'm fine."

"I'm going to get a few things from my office, and we'll meet in the conference room in a few minutes."

"No problem, take your time." Bryce thought to himself, *Alex Simmons, you have no idea what's in store for you.*

At thirty years old, Bryce had done quite well for himself. He resurrected Centennial Resorts after the original owner, his stepfather, died of a heart attack during bankruptcy proceedings. That was five years ago. Since then, Bryce used his stepfather's old contacts and their money to create an empire, making Centennial Resorts a highly regarded competitor. The merger deal with Trowne Key Estates was part of his elaborate plan to dominate the hotel and resort industry.

Fifteen minutes later, Alex reappeared from his office and escorted Bryce to the conference room. "Please have a seat," he insisted, pointing to the chair next to his.

"Thank you," Bryce said, as he sat down. Then he looked around the conference room before turning to Alex. "Where is your CEO, Sidney McKinley? He's the one who arranged this meeting."

Alex also thought it was strange that Sidney was not present for the meeting. Normally, Sidney was the first to arrive and the last to leave. "I'm not sure," he said, after checking his watch. "It's still early. I'm sure he'll be here any minute. Would you rather wait until he gets here?"

Bryce swatted at the air. "No, that's not necessary."

Over the next hour, Bryce talked to Alex about his company and its many accomplishments over the past five years. Then he retrieved a document from his briefcase, and handed it to Alex. "This is what I'm proposing."

While reviewing the merger proposal, Alex's eyes grew bigger when he looked at the number of zeroes behind the dollar symbol. Bryce was offering to buy into Trowne Key Estates for fifty million dollars.

"I must say," Alex finally said with surprise in his voice, "this is a very lucrative offer."

"I knew you would see it that way," Bryce replied with confidence. "How about it? Can we seal the deal?"

"I have to run this by my brother first."

Bryce raised a brow. "Your brother?"

"Yes, he's part owner of Trowne Key Estates, but I'm sure he will be impressed."

"Good," Bryce said with a wide grin. "Now that we're done with business, do you have some time to go out for brunch?"

Alex checked his watch before responding. "Sure, let me inform my secretary. There's a nice bistro not far from here."

Bryce smiled. "It sounds like a plan."

Suddenly, the conference door opened. It was Sidney McKinley. "I'm sorry I'm late," he said, as he rushed into the room with a stack of paperwork. "I didn't know we changed our meeting time."

"We started early," Alex explained.

"Please accept my apology," Bryce interjected. "I arrived an hour early."

Sidney walked over and took a seat next to Bryce. "No problem. I worked out the figures for the merger proposal."

"That's not necessary," Alex said, as he held up his hand. "Bryce has proposed a very lucrative offer. We just have to wait and see how Guy feels about it."

Sidney was flustered. He became so angry his voice trembled. "Sir...Mr. Simmons," he stuttered, "you don't...understand."

Alex stood up and walked over to Sidney. "As of now, I'll be overseeing the merger deal. Bryce and I are stepping out for brunch."

"Can I go with you?" Sidney asked, turning to Bryce for a response.

Briefly, Bryce glanced at Alex before answering Sidney. "Maybe next time," he mumbled.

Sidney's mouth flew open to speak, but nothing came out but hot air.

This was a first for Alex. He had never seen the speechless side of Sidney. "We're just going out for brunch," he reiterated, to lessen the tension in the room.

"Okay," Sidney replied, while gazing at Bryce with questioning eyes. "Call me if you need anything."

"Will do," Alex said, as he and Bryce stood up to leave the conference room.

Dumbfounded, Sidney remained seated. He grimaced when Bryce walked by him with a smirk on his face.

Six months earlier, during a conference for hotel executives, Bryce had approached Sidney with the merger deal in mind. "You know," he said to Sidney, "I was wondering if you'd be interested in going into business with me, as my partner."

"Partner?" Sidney asked in disbelief.

"Yes, I'm thinking about expanding my company. With a partner like you, we could dominate the hotel industry."

Sidney exhaled. He was unable to believe his ears. "Are you serious?" he asked, after pondering Bryce's proposal.

Bryce nodded his head before divulging his elaborate plan to take over the hotel industry. The merger deal would be a major part of the scheme, except Alex would not be signing a merger contract. Unknowingly, he would be signing a contract that would give Bryce full ownership of Trowne Key Estates.

Initially, Sidney was repulsed by the idea, but his hatred of Alex permeated his thoughts. Also, unbeknownst to Jeanine, Sidney had resented the fact that she did not give him the opportunity to be part owner of Trowne Key Estates, prior to her departure. He looked around to see if anyone else was in earshot before responding. "What if the owner does not agree with your plan?"

"That's why I need you. If you can convince Alex Simmons to meet with me, I'll handle the rest."

Shaking his head, Sidney was overcome with doubt.

"What if I gave you ten million dollars, in addition to partnership?" Bryce asked, after noting Sidney's uneasiness.

Sidney's eyes almost popped out of their sockets. "Uh... uh...um...wow," he stammered.

"So do we have a deal?"

"I still don't know how you plan on getting away with this."

"Just leave all the details to me. I promise, you won't regret your decision."

Sidney pondered his decision before responding. "I'll do it," he firmly replied, figuring he had more to gain by dealing with Bryce.

Bryce nodded his head. Internally, he was gloating over the idea of using Sidney to get to the bigger fish. Afterwards, he would have no use for Sidney.

Looking back, Sidney wondered if Bryce was genuine. He was torn between telling Alex about Bryce's scheme, or accepting Bryce's ten million dollar bribe. When he thought about it, Sidney had a much better deal without any conditions. He could have easily resigned from Trowne Key Estates, and received a severance package worth five million dollars.

Unfortunately, Sidney had allowed greed to take over when he sided with Bryce. At present, he was worried about whether Bryce would renege on his offer. He acknowledged it was too late to undo his actions.

During brunch, Bryce and Alex acted as if they had known each other their entire lives. They drank Mimosas, while chatting about the nuances of their respective businesses. Their conversation was light, until Bryce revisited the merger deal.

"Can I ask you a question?" he asked, as he leaned toward Alex. "Is there a reason you have to get your brother involved?"

"I told you, my brother is part owner of Trowne Key Estates. I cannot make a move without his approval."

"I see," Bryce said, pondering Alex's comments. Up to this point, he thought Alex was the sole decision maker.

"Don't worry," Alex said with assurance. "My brother has a lot on his plate, but he's also a clever businessman."

Bryce chuckled. "It's no pressure. Just make sure he knows we stand to make a ton of money with the merger deal."

Alex nodded, agreeing with Bryce's analysis. Prior to their meeting, he had his accountant crunch some numbers, and was amazed at the many benefits the merger deal would yield. "I promise. I'll talk to him soon."

Bryce smiled. "I'd appreciate it. Time is of the essence."

Chapter 8

Love is Blind

For the past two weeks, Dana and Cassie had grown accustomed to having a bodyguard around at all times. Billy Hampden was not what they had expected. Although he stood six four and weighed over three hundred pounds of pure muscle, Billy was a big teddy bear when it came to the twins. He was extremely accommodating, and gave them more freedom than their brothers.

In addition to protecting the twins, Billy was also a mentor to Malik Mitchell, a seventeen-year-old kid from Tampa, Florida. Billy met Malik through the Big Brother program, administered by the YMCA. They had quickly bonded, becoming good friends. After learning Malik did not have a male role model, Billy had inserted himself into his young friend's life as much as possible. He had promised Malik he would always be there for him as long as he stayed on a straight and narrow path.

Six months earlier, Malik had gotten into trouble with the law. He was with three other young men on a street corner selling drugs. They were arrested and thrown in jail. However, Malik was released on his own recognizance, but the other young men remained in jail. They were repeat offenders. Since it was Malik's first offense and he was only sixteen at the time, the judge mandated that he join the Big Brother program.

One day, Malik's high school counselor phoned Billy and told him he needed to come to school right away. Billy wondered what prompted the phone call, especially since Malik had not been in trouble for the past six months.

Twenty minutes later, Billy met with the school counselor, and was disappointed to learn that Malik had been suspended for five consecutive days. He found Malik standing outside waiting for him.

"What happened at school?" Billy asked, after Malik climbed in the front passenger seat of the limo.

Malik heatedly spouted, "I ain't gon' let nobody try me! Dude rolled up on me, and I had to do what I had to do."

Billy pulled onto the highway before glancing in Malik's direction. "So fighting was your only solution, huh?"

"No!" Malik exclaimed. "But it was the only one I used. Man, I'm not going to stand there and get beat down. I ain't no punk!"

Billy shook his head. He was clearly disappointed. "When are you going to learn that fighting should be the last resort?"

Malik chuckled. "Yeah, right." He concluded it was pointless to try and explain to Billy that fighting was the only resort, especially in his neighborhood. Fifteen minutes later, he realized they were not headed to the YMCA. "Where are we going?" he asked, as Billy drove across the highway, en route to Clearwater, Florida.

"I have to make a stop, to pick up my clients."

"Clients?" Malik asked, looking surprised.

"I'm a bodyguard, remember?"

Malik nodded. "That's straight. You make a lot of money?"

"I make enough to get by." Billy briefly turned to Malik, and asked out of curiosity, "What are your plans for the future?"

"I plan on making a lot of money," Malik replied, while nodding and rubbing his hands together.

"How?" Billy asked, as he glanced at Malik.

Malik sat up with his chest poked out. "Don't worry about all that," he stated, while nodding his head. "I got a plan."

"I hope you're not thinking about selling drugs. If you do, you will end up in one of two places."

"Where's that?" Malik asked with wide eyes.

"In jail or six feet under."

"I hear you," Malik mumbled.

Billy pulled in front of Dana and Cassie's high school minutes later. Before he got out of the car, he turned to Malik, and warned, "Do not say anything to my clients. Do you understand?"

Malik brushed off Billy's concerns with the wave of his hand. "Sure, man, whatever. Go handle your business."

Minutes later, Billy returned to the limo with the twins on each side of him. He opened the back passenger door and closed it after Dana and Cassie climbed in.

By the time Billy got behind the driver's wheel, Malik was drooling and breaking his neck to see through the dark tinted window glass that separated the back passenger seats. He was blown away by Dana's green eyes and long legs.

"What's the matter with you?" Billy asked, after noticing the way Malik was straining to look at his clients through the heavily tinted glass.

Malik turned to Billy with excitement in his eyes. "Man, you didn't tell me she was *fine*."

Billy smiled. "Who?"

"The one in the mini skirt."

Billy buckled his seatbelt before responding. "Oh, that's Dana, and her twin sister, Cassie."

"C'mon Uncle Billy, introduce me."

"No Malik," Billy said, before starting the ignition. "That's not a good idea. I was hired to protect them."

Malik frowned. "From who?"

"Anyone that poses a threat."

"Unc, you know I ain't no threat."

Billy drove onto the highway, mulling over Malik's request. "If Dana is interested," he reasoned, "I'll introduce you."

"When?" Malik asked, as his heart fluttered from anticipation.

"I'll ask her after I drop you off."

Malik grinned. "Straight. Thanks Unc."

After pulling up in front of the YMCA, Billy watched Malik unbuckle his seatbelt and climb out. Then he leaned over, and said, "Stay here, until I come back for you."

Malik did not hear Billy's instructions. His mind was preoccupied with Dana. "Unc, you gon' do that, right?"

Billy nodded. "I haven't forgotten. Just stay out of trouble."

Malik stood back and smiled as the limo drove off. He could not see through the heavily tinted passenger windows, but was hoping Dana would notice him.

When Billy dropped off the twins in front of their home, he told Dana that Malik was interested in meeting her.

Dana smiled in response.

"Well?" Billy asked, probing for an answer.

"Sure," Dana answered. She was also smitten with Malik. She thought he was attractive in his baggy khaki pants and white T-shirt, which was loosely hanging on his skinny body frame. Dana especially liked the way Malik's dark chocolate skin glistened in the sun. Even his midnight eyes and sexy smile melted her heart.

When Billy returned to the YMCA to retrieve Malik, he told him Dana had agreed to meet him. "But there's a catch," he quickly added.

"What's up?" Malik asked with raised brows.

"Dana cannot have a boyfriend." Billy repeated what Guy had told him the first day he showed up for work. "Do you understand?"

Malik nodded. "That's cool. Unc, check this. Let me open the door for them the next time you pick them up from school."

"Sure," Billy agreed. "You can ride with me tomorrow."

Based on Malik's wide grin, Billy thought introducing Malik to Dana was not a bad idea after all.

The next day, Malik rode in the limo with Billy to pick up the twins from school. When Billy escorted Dana and Cassie out of the school building, Malik opened the passenger door with a wide grin. His gold teeth sparkled like a ray of sunbeams.

Dana's heart fluttered when she saw Malik. Far from being shy, she introduced herself first. "What's up?" she asked, sounding hip.

"What's up with you, Shorty?"

Since they were the same height, Dana was amused by her new nickname. "I asked you first," she said with an attitude.

Malik smiled. "Maybe we could go get something to eat, to talk about it. Are you down with it?"

"I don't know," Dana replied with reservations. My brother...."

"I already know," Malik interrupted. "Uncle Billy said we have to see each other on the down low." Then he turned to Cassie, and asked, "You think you can keep a secret?"

Shrugging her shoulders, Cassie said, "I don't care."

"Cool," Malik remarked, before turning to Dana. "Y'all feel like pizza?"

Cassie remained silent while Dana bore a wide grin. "Sure," Dana agreed with a nod.

It was Billy's idea to take Dana, Malik and Cassie to the pizza parlor. He wanted to give them time to get acquainted before taking them home.

Over pizza, Malik asked Dana, "Do you like taking risks?"

"Yeah," Dana answered, trying to pretend as if she was down with whatever.

"Peep this," Malik said, after biting into a slice of pizza. "If I get ahold of some transportation, can you sneak out of school?"

Dana looked to Cassie, who shook her head, disapprovingly. Then she turned back to Malik with a wide grin. "Sure, I think I can make it happen."

"Cool, give me your number, so I can call you later on."

After going through her book bag, Dana pulled out a piece of paper, wrote down her cell number, and handed it to Malik.

Malik glimpsed at the paper and smiled. "Thanks, Shorty."

Billy smiled as he looked at the exchange between Dana and Malik. He knew he had to work hard to ensure that Guy never found out about Malik. Otherwise, he could find himself out of a job.

Chapter 9
Crushed

*A*fter Rhaunda caught Alex fooling around with his secretary, she was determined to get him out of her system. She had been down this path before. She knew, with time, she would eventually get over Alex. Rhaunda had resisted the urge to contact him. It also helped that her parents kept her busy with church duties.

Despite Rhaunda's efforts to downplay her emotions, her mother, Elizabeth, had noticed a significant change in her daughter's behavior. She entered Rhaunda's bedroom and found her in bed staring at the ceiling. "Honey, are you okay?"

Rhaunda did not look at her mother when she responded. "Not really," she dryly admitted, "but I will be."

"Do you want to talk about it?"

Rhaunda shook her head, while her eyes remained focused on the ceiling.

"Honey, I'm here, if you need someone to talk to."

Rhaunda turned to her mother with tears in her eyes. She was choked up when she finally spoke. "I'll…be okay."

"Is this about Alex?" Elizabeth knowingly asked.

"I don't…want to talk about him."

Elizabeth sighed. Her daughter was hurting and there was nothing she could do about it. "Do you feel up to going to church tonight?" she inquired, hoping to get Rhaunda's mind off Alex.

"I'm fine. I just want to be alone."

Elizabeth walked out of Rhaunda's bedroom, closing the door behind her. During times like this, she thought Rhaunda needed a friend. She went downstairs to her husband's office, to call Alecia Kellam, her daughter's best friend.

Elizabeth met Alecia when she visited Rhaunda in graduate school. At first sight, she concluded that Alecia had a colorful personality. She also believed that Alecia could help Rhaunda get over Alex.

"Hello," Alecia answered on the first ring.

"Hi Alecia, this is Rhaunda's mother. I'm calling to see if you would be interested in relocating to Florida."

Alecia frowned. "I don't know, Mrs. Coleman. Tampa is not my cup of tea."

"Please consider it. Rhaunda could use a friend right now. Besides, there are so many opportunities here," Elizabeth added, to persuade Alecia. "Why don't you come to Tampa for a couple of weeks, to see how you like it?"

Alecia twisted her mouth, pondering Elizabeth's question. "I'll think about it."

"You can stay here at the house with us, if you prefer," Elizabeth persisted.

Alecia giggled at the thought of staying with Rhaunda's family. "Okay, Mrs. Coleman, I'll think about it. But if I relocate to Tampa, I'm getting my own apartment."

Elizabeth's eyes lit up with glee. "That sounds wonderful! I'll see you soon."

"Uh, Mrs. Coleman?"

"Yes, Alecia. What is it?"

"Are Rhaunda and Alex still dating?" Alecia asked, trying not to let on that she was interested in Alex.

"I don't think so. Why do you ask?"

"I was just curious, that's all."

"I see," Elizabeth slowly replied, thinking it was peculiar that Alecia had asked about the status of Rhaunda and Alex's relationship.

"It may take a while," Alecia said after pondering her decision, "but I think I can convince my father to help me relocate." She smiled at the thought of seeing Alex again.

"Come as quickly as you can," Elizabeth pleaded.

After Elizabeth hung up the phone, her mind was in overdrive thinking of ways to comfort Rhaunda. In deep thought, she walked into her bedroom with droopy shoulders.

Her husband, Pastor Coleman, was in bed reading the bible when his wife walked in their bedroom. "How is she?" he asked, after closing his bible.

Sitting on the foot of the bed, Elizabeth turned to her husband with sadness in her eyes, and weakly said, "I'm not sure."

The pastor put his bible on the nightstand, climbed out of bed, and walked around the bed to sit next to Elizabeth. "Honey, try not to worry," he said, as he wrapped his arm around her. "Maybe this is a wake-up call for Rhaunda."

"I know," Elizabeth affirmed, "but she's in pain, and I can't help her."

"Just being here for her is enough. You'll see, the sooner Rhaunda gets over Alex, the better off she'll be."

Elizabeth nodded. "I hope you're right." She hated to admit it, but she did not think her daughter would ever get over Alex.

Pastor Coleman embraced and kissed his wife on the forehead. "Honey, lie down and get some rest. Things will get better, you'll see."

Elizabeth rested her head on the pillow and covered herself with the blanket. She could not go to sleep, because she was worried about her daughter. When she paid off Alex's secretary, Maria Gomez, to seduce Alex, she had hoped her actions would have helped Rhaunda. She now realized they may have backfired. Elizabeth had parked her car several yards away, when Alex ran out of the Maria's apartment and darted past her daughter's SUV. It tore her apart to see Rhaunda crying in agony.

Alecia gloated after disconnecting the call with Rhaunda's mother. She felt hopeful that Rhaunda would finally leave Alex alone, so she could have him all to herself. Alecia had been trying to get Alex's attention, without success. She had even showed Rhaunda proof Alex was cheating on her.

More determined than ever, Alecia set her plan in motion to capture Alex's heart. She was hopeful that her father, Dr. Eldridge Kellam, would give her the money to relocate to Florida. Picking up the phone, she called his office in London.

Dr. Kellam was worth millions, after he and his staff developed the cure for stage IV breast cancer. When his wife was diagnosed with breast cancer a decade earlier, he had put all his money and energy into finding a cure. She died six months before he was able to complete his research. However, Dr. Kellam was not deterred. Five years after his wife passed away, he had stumbled onto the cure. Shortly after, the doctor opened his own pharmaceutical company. In the process, he spoiled his one and only daughter rotten.

"Dad, I need money to relocate to Tampa," Alecia said, after her father answered her call.

"Why?" Dr. Kellam asked out of curiosity.

"Rhaunda is my nearest and dearest friend," she stressed with a happy-go-lucky voice. "Maybe I could help out at her father's church."

"Are you serious?" he asked, after pondering Alecia's sudden interest with wanting to help out at anyone's church.

"It's just a temporary plan." Alecia said with a wide grin. "That is, until I can find my true passion. I hope you don't mind me working."

Dr. Kellam chuckled. "Certainly not. I think it's a great idea. I've always been fond of Rhaunda's father. Pastor Coleman is an honorable man. When do you want to leave?"

Alecia quickly said, "Next month, if possible."

"Fine, make the arrangements, and I'll pay for everything. I'll send a check to the pastor's church tomorrow, as a token of my appreciation."

Alecia jumped for joy while balancing the phone to her ear. "Thanks Daddy!"

Dr. Kellam smiled. "No problem. I want you to be a productive citizen. Working at the church will put you on the right path."

Alecia smiled in response. She had no intentions of working for Pastor Coleman, or hanging out with Rhaunda.

Up until three months ago, Alecia had traveled all over the world, and had an interesting social life. The men she dated were not the type of men she would ever introduce to her father. They were typically struggling artists or writers, working odd jobs here and there, to make ends meet. However, once they were in Alecia's company, they never had to worry about money or going hungry. She took care of her men, often dolling out cash allowances.

Alecia had also spent excessive money on herself, as if it was an endless supply. One day, she was in for a surprise during one of her shopping sprees in Paris, France. The cashier was ecstatic after she rung up Alecia's order, twenty-five thousand dollars in designer clothes and shoes.

Suddenly, the cashier's excitement dissipated after sliding Alecia's Visa card through the credit card machine. "I'm sorry, ma'am," the cashier said to Alecia, "your credit card has been declined."

Alecia chuckled. "Darling," she said with an air of superiority, "you are mistaken. You need to swipe the card again."

The cashier did as Alecia suggested and came up with the same results. "Do you have another card?" she asked in a neutral tone, even though she was put off by Alecia's snobbish attitude.

Alecia became indignant. "Let me talk to the owner!" she barked.

"I am the owner." The cashier's response was laced with contempt. "Now, if you don't have another card, I will gladly cancel this sale."

Alecia looked at the customer standing behind her and chuckled. "I'm sure this is all a misunderstanding," she explained to no one in particular, as she pulled out another card.

The cashier swiped the alternate card, then she became furious when INSUFFICIENT FUNDS flashed on the credit card machine. "I suggest you come back when you have sufficient funds," the cashier stated, as she returned the card to Alecia.

Embarrassed, Alecia huffed and puffed as she stormed out of the store and headed for the bank. After consulting with the bank's president, Alecia learned that she was denied access to her money. She pulled out her cell phone to call her father. "Dad, what's going on?"

"I froze your accounts," Dr. Kellam firmly stated. "You're acting like money grows on trees. You are to return home immediately."

"But dad...."

"No buts," Dr. Kellam interrupted, before hanging up on her.

Soon after, Alecia had returned home from Paris, believing her father would lift the freeze on her accounts. To her dismay, her father had put her on a stringent budget. Alecia was given two thousand dollars a week to spend at her leisure. Though, she complained after receiving her first allowance. "Dad, how can I survive off so little money?"

"You will survive," Dr. Kellam replied with indifference. "Maybe you should think about finding a good husband."

"All guys are jerks!" Alecia emphatically replied.

Dr. Kellam sighed. "Whatever happened to Alex Simmons? You used to talk about him all the time. I hear he's worth millions."

"He is?" Alecia asked in disbelief.

"Yes, he and his brother are the new owners of Trowne Key Estates condominiums and resorts," he said with a slight nod. "Alex Simmons is the type of man I'd like to see you marry some day; not the idiots you've been fooling around with."

"I didn't know you felt that way."

Dr. Kellam smiled. "I only want the best for you. Whomever you end up with, I'll be happy as long you're happy."

Alecia never forgot her father's desire for her to marry Alex, but knew he would have a fit if he found out she was relocating to Tampa just to be with him. Though, once she captured Alex's heart, she was certain her father would be proud of her. But first, she needed to know what she was getting herself into. She went on the internet to find out as much information as she could about Alex Simmons. She also decided to rely on a very reputable investigation firm Beaming with delight, Alecia was planning on making Alex Simmons the center of her universe.

Chapter 10

Fireworks!

Malik felt like he struck gold when he met Dana. It had been two weeks since they started seeing each other, but he thought it seemed like a lifetime. Although he was seeing other young ladies, Malik was enamored with Dana. He liked her spunkiness and her willingness to prove herself. He called her Saturday evening after fantasizing about what it would be like to make love to her. "Hey Shorty, can you meet me tonight?"

"Are you crazy?" Dana asked with wide eyes. "My brother would kill me."

"C'mon Shorty. I'm feeling you."

"I don't know," Dana replied, shaking her head. Her body said *yes* but her mind said *no*.

"What? You scared?"

Dana frowned. "Scared of what? I'm not afraid of anything."

"Now that's my girl. I'll pick you up tonight at eleven."

"You have a car?" Dana asked with raised brows. She was used to Billy escorting them everywhere.

"Nah. I'll ask my friend if I can borrow his car."

"Alright," Dana agreed, deciding to take a risk. "I'll meet you near the entrance of the driveway." She thought that it would be a safe enough distance from the mansion, to keep from getting caught. After disconnecting the call, Dana went to her sister's room and knocked on her door. "Cassie, I need to talk to you."

"What is it?" Cassie asked, after she opened her door.

Dana walked in her sister's room, closing the door behind her. She turned around, and confessed in a hushed voice, "I'm going to sneak out of the house tonight, to be with Malik."

Cassie frowned. "Guy is going to have a fit if he finds out."

"I know, but I have a plan. I just wanted you to know who I'm with, in case I end up missing," Dana added with soft laughter.

"That's not funny!" Cassie spouted.

"Geez, Cassie. I was just kidding."

"You know Guy checks on us at night," Cassie pointed out. "He's going to notice when you're not there."

Dana smiled as she thought of a solution. "I'm going to prop up my bed with pillows, to pretend it's me."

"What if he calls out your name?"

"He'll assume I'm asleep," Dana answered.

Cassie shook her head. "I don't think you should go."

"My mind is made up. Please don't tell Guy."

Cassie sighed. "I hope you know what you're doing."

"I do." Dana stood up to leave her sister's room. A couple hours later, she waited until everyone went to bed before she changed her clothes and crept out of the house through the side door. She ran down the driveway toward the waiting car. Her eyes lit up as soon as she spotted Malik sitting behind the steering wheel of an older model Chevrolet. "Where are we going?" she asked, as soon as she climbed into the car.

Malik smiled as he drove onto the highway, heading to Tampa. "First, we're going to get a bite to eat. Then we can go spend some quality time together at a spot not too far from where I live."

Dana smiled. "That sounds like fun!"

"You down with it?" Malik asked, hoping Dana got the hint that they would be doing more than just cuddling.

"Yes, I'm down with it," she slyly replied. She knew what Malik was hinting. Ever since they met, Dana had planned on losing her virginity to Malik. She had dreamt of making love to him in a candlelit room, with rose petals scattered over the bed and soft music playing in the background.

Grinning from ear to ear, Malik drove into a parking space in front of McDonalds. After ordering their food, they sat at a corner table in the back of the restaurant. They shared a big Mac and a large order of fries. Both were excited to be in each other's company. "So Shorty," Malik said, "tell me about yourself."

"What do you want to know?"

"Everything. What about your parents?"

Dana's eyes began to water. "My parents died," she softly whispered.

"Damn, Shorty. Sorry to hear that."

"It's okay, I barely remember them. I was very young when they died."

Malik reached over and placed his hand on top of Dana's. "We have a lot in common. My mom died six years ago. I live with my foster mom and six other kids."

"I didn't know that." Dana's heart went out to Malik.

Malik looked into Dana's eyes and smiled. "We have each other, and that's all that matters." His comforting words made Dana feel at ease.

"Let's get out of here," Malik said, "and go to the spot I was telling you about."

Thirty minutes later, Malik drove in front of the apartment complex, where he lived. He guided Dana to a vacant apartment that he sometimes used to escape the drama at home. He guessed Dana was a virgin, but was not turned off. In fact, Malik liked the idea of being her first. He could have sex with any girl in his neighborhood, but sex with Dana would be special, or so he thought.

Dana hesitated when Malik opened the front door.

"What's the matter?" he asked, after noting Dana's apprehension.

"I don't know about this," Dana timidly admitted.

After opening the door wider, Malik grabbed Dana's hand and guided her inside the apartment. "Baby, you're safe with me."

Dana wrapped her arms around her body as she looked around the cold apartment. She felt grimy all over. "I have money," she said, hoping Malik would change his mind. "We can go to a hotel."

Malik frowned. "What's the matter? You think you're too good to be in my neck of the woods?"

"No, that's not it," Dana lied. But deep down, she thought she made a mistake by coming here with Malik.

"C'mon, Shorty," Malik said, while wrapping his arms around her hips and squeezing her buttocks. "I think you need to chill out and relax. I'll be gentle with you."

Dana bore a nervous smile, before she said, "Okay, I trust you."

After clearing the debris in the middle of the floor with his feet, Malik retrieved a blanket out of the bag he brought with him and spread it across the hardwood floor. Then he pulled out a tea candle and lit it with a lighter.

Peering at Dana with a mischievous grin, he removed his clothes and sat on the blanket. "C'mon baby," he cooed while stretching out his hand to Dana. "Don't leave me hanging."

"Do you have a condom?" she asked, trying to delay the inevitable.

Malik snickered. "What do you know about condoms?"

Placing her hands on her hips, Dana bounced back to her usual sassy self. "Enough to know I don't want to get pregnant," she said, trying to act tough, but her heart was beating like a drum.

Malik leaned over and retrieved a condom from his bag. He held it up before putting it on his manhood like a pro. "See, Shorty, I got you covered. Now come over here and stop trippin'."

Taking her time, Dana took off her clothes and sat down on the blanket next to Malik. She tried to cover her breasts with her arms, but Malik was assertive, pulling her closer to him. Then he planted small kisses along her neck and lips before inserting his tongue in her mouth.

"What are you doing?" she asked, struggling to pull away from Malik's embrace.

"Trust me," Malik insisted, "I got you."

Slowly but surely, Dana surrendered to Malik's touch. She felt warm and bubbly inside. Though, she prayed her first sexual experience would be fast and painless.

Five minutes later, her wish had partially come true. The sex was quick but painful. Soon after, they turned away from each other, and fell asleep. It was in the middle of the morning before Malik realized the time had slipped by. He checked his glow in the dark watch before shaking Dana awake. "Shorty, hurry up and get dressed," he ordered, as he stood up and put on his clothes. "I gotta take you home."

"Why?" Dana asked, after opening her eyes.

"It's getting late. I have to take you home before your brother finds out you're gone."

Suddenly, Dana became conscientious of her nakedness, so she pulled the blanket over her body. "What time is it?"

"Three o'clock."

"Oh shoot!" Dana went into panic mode. She quickly dressed and met Malik at the door.

On the drive home, Dana remained quiet while Malik did all the talking. "So babe, you like the way I laid it on you?"

Dana looked at Malik, frowning. "I don't ever want to go back to that apartment."

Maneuvering the car onto the highway, Malik glanced at Dana, before asking, "Why?"

"Because I deserve better," Dana griped.

Sucking his teeth, Malik shook his head. Dana's uppity attitude was getting on his nerves. "Well, I don't have money to spend on a hotel."

"I told you, I have money."

Malik looked at the gas gauge. It was less than a quarter tank full. "Well if that's the case, I need money to fill up this car."

Without prompting, Dana dug in her purse and retrieved her wallet. Malik's eyes grew big when Dana pulled out her prepaid debit card. "*Damn* baby, how much is on that card?"

"Enough. My brother deposits my allowance on my card every week." Dana did not think it was necessary to tell Malik that she had over a thousand dollars at her disposal.

Surprised by this revelation, Malik peered in Dana's direction, and asked, "Are you serious?"

Dana nodded yes.

Dollar bills flashed in Malik's eyes as he pulled into the nearest gas station. "We can go to a hotel the next time. Alright?" he asked, knowing Dana would be footing the bill.

"Okay." Dana was satisfied with Malik's response. She extended her card to him, to pay for the gas.

"I think I'm gonna make you my girl," Malik said, before climbing out of the car to pump the gas. "How do you feel about that?" he asked, as he turned to Dana.

Dana smiled. "I'd like that." In that instant, she had fallen head over heels in-love with Malik. When he climbed back in the car, she cuddled up next to him, feeling his warmth.

Like clockwork, Guy woke up late at night, to check up on the twins. He went to Cassie's room first, and was satisfied when she responded. Then he knocked on Dana's door. When he did not get an answer, he turned the doorknob and walked into her bedroom. It looked like Dana was in bed, but he became suspicious after noticing an odd-looking shape bundled in her bed with a blanket thrown across it.

He walked into Dana's room and called out her name. When he did not get an answer, he pulled the cover from over the bundle. Totally pissed, Guy returned to Cassie's room and knocked on her door. "Open the door!" he shouted.

Cassie knew Dana was busted. She got out of bed, and opened her door. "What is it, Guy?"

"Where is your sister?! he demanded to know.

"I don't know," Cassie lied.

"I believe you do," Guy accused. "Is she with a boy?"

Feeling pressured to answer him, Cassie nodded, confirming Guy's suspicions.

Frowning, Guy asked, "Who is he?"

"I'd rather not say," Cassie replied, briefly averting her eyes away from him.

Guy shook his head in wonder. "Go back to sleep," he said, as he turned away from Cassie. Boiling over from anger, he walked downstairs and headed outside. He had planned on waiting on the front porch until Dana came home.

As Malik neared Dana's home, he turned off his headlights before pulling into the sprawling driveway. He thought he was being discreet. However, his efforts proved fruitless after the porch lights came on, revealing Guy's presence.

Guy felt rage building up from the pit of his belly, when he spotted Malik and Dana coasting up the driveway.

Dana shuddered when she noticed Guy. "Malik," she fearfully said while grabbing his arm, "you can drop me off here."

"You sure?" Malik asked, detecting fear in Dana's voice.

"Yeah, I'll see you tomorrow."

Dana jumped out of the car and bolted for the front door. When she tried to pass by Guy, he grabbed her arm, forcing her to turn around and face him. She was shaken by her brother's touch. "What?" she asked. Her question was filled with guilt and shame.

Fearing he was on the verge of slapping the crap out of her, Guy released his grip. "I'll deal with you later." Then he rushed over to the car, reached through the window and grabbed the collar of Malik's shirt. "If I catch you over here again," he said through gritted teeth, "I will kill you." Snapping back to reality, Guy let go of Malik and backed away from the car.

Sweating bullets, Malik nodded, threw his car in reverse and backed out the driveway, burning rubber as he sped away.

Guy turned back toward the house, then rushed toward the front door. Before he reached the doorknob, Regine walked out of the front door, closing it behind her. She put her hands up to block him from entering the house. "No Guy, you are too angry to deal with Dana right now."

"Dana has crossed the line!" Guy sharply proclaimed. "Tonight was the final straw!"

"I know," Regine said in a soothing voice, "but yelling at her may make things worse. Dana's young. She's going to make mistakes. Leave her alone for now. You can talk to her tomorrow."

Guy was upset, but realized Regine was the voice of reason. "Fine!" he conceded, still overcome with rage.

Regine grabbed Guy's hand and walked with him in the house. She knew her husband would not get any sleep tonight, but hoped he would be more levelheaded in the morning.

The next morning, Dana woke up early. She walked into the kitchen, and found Guy drinking coffee and reading the newspaper. "Good morning Guy," she softly said.

Still wired up from last night, Guy looked up from the newspaper. "Good morning," he mumbled.

Dana fidgeted with her hands, not sure what to say next. She dreaded being on Guy's bad side. "I'm sorry about last night. It won't happen again."

Guy slammed the newspaper on the table, then glared at Dana with disgust. "You're damn right it won't happen again!"

"But I love him," Dana replied in her defense.

"What do you know about love?"

"It's no different from the love you had for Justina."

Guy grimaced. He never expected Dana to rehash his past. Undoubtedly, he had been in love with Justina Reyes, his wife's best friend, a couple of years ago. "She was a mistake," he said, after a short pause.

"You asked her to marry you, remember?"

"Yeah, I remember, but it was a mistake." Guy vividly remembered when Justina rejected his proposal, but had asked to keep the engagement ring. He felt hurt and used. "I don't want you to repeat my mistakes," he thoughtfully added.

"We're in-love," Dana explained.

"Why?" Guy asked, not expecting an answer. "Because you had sex?" He shivered at the thought. "That's not love, that's lust." His voice softened, as he said, "Please promise you will never see this guy again."

"I can't," Dana honestly replied. "I know what I'm doing."

Guy sighed. He knew he could not win this argument with Dana, so he asked, "What's his name?"

"Malik Mitchell."

"How did you meet him?"

"At school," Dana lied. She knew Guy would fire Billy if he ever found out he had introduced her to Malik.

"Where does he live?" Guy probed.

Dana felt hopeful when she answered. "He lives in Tampa."

Grunting, Guy paused before he spoke. "Promise you won't go out with him again." He noticed Dana's hesitance, before adding, "At least, until you're seventeen."

"I promise," she said, after crossing her fingers and mentally calculating the number of days and weeks left before her seventeenth birthday.

Smiling, Guy was satisfied with Dana's response. "You know I love you, right?"

Dana smiled. "I love you too."

Chapter 11

Scared Straight

*A*lex and Bryce had been hanging out at different clubs and bars for the past three weeks. Everywhere they went, people assumed they were brothers. They were both handsome, rich, and had the same height, body build, and cocoa complexion. Alex and Bryce were also magnets for the ladies.

Earlier, they had played a game of golf on the Tampa Bay golf course. Then they met up at a bar in Y'bor city, a square mile of clubs and bars in downtown Tampa. Bryce figured the time they spent together would put him one step closer to his goal. After ordering beers, Bryce was tempted to ask Alex about whether he mentioned the merger deal to his brother. He did not want to appear too anxious, so he decided to keep the conversation light and personal.

"Can you tell me about yourself?" Bryce asked.

After taking a sip of beer, Alex put the mug on the table before he turned to Bryce, and asked, "What do you want to know?"

"It's already a well-known fact that you're a ladies' man," Bryce stated with a light chuckle.

Alex cracked a smile. "I think I can say the same for you." Since their first meeting, he learned that his new associate was considered one of the most eligible bachelors on the Gulf Coast.

Bryce snickered. "Okay, I'm an open book."

"What do want to know about me?"

"About your parents."

"My parents?" Alex asked, as he looked at Bryce with questioning eyes.

"Yes, I'm curious to know about the culprits who raised a fine young man, such as yourself."

Alex pondered Bryce's compliment before recounting a glimpse of his past. "My parents died in a car accident several years ago. My stepmother became a permanent fixture in my life long after they passed away."

Eager for more information, Bryce leaned closer to Alex. "Tell me about Mrs. Benedict."

"What do you want to know?"

"How is she?" Bryce asked out of curiosity. Thanks to Sidney, he was abreast of Alex's entire family.

Alex became choked up, thinking about Jeanine's medical condition. "She's okay, considering…."

Bryce held up his hand. "I understand if you don't want to talk about her."

Alex nodded. He appreciated Bryce's thoughtfulness.

"So, Alex," Bryce said to change the subject, "have you ever thought about settling down?"

"Yeah, but I don't know if that's going to be happening anytime soon."

Bryce sipped his beer before responding. "Didn't you tell me your brother, Guy, had a wife?" he asked, after remembering what his hired henchman dug up on Guy.

"I believe so," Alex confirmed with uncertainty. He did not recollect divulging any information about Guy and Regine. He figured the beer must have had an effect on his memory.

Bryce said, "Maybe *you* should settle down and get married."

Alex shook his head, mulling over Bryce's suggestion. "I don't know about that. I broke up with my girlfriend," he confessed with his head held low. "I doubt if she would even talk to me."

"You never know, until you try."

"Maybe you're right," Alex said, after pondering Bryce's suggestion.

When the waitress refilled their drink orders, Bryce held up his mug of beer and waited for Alex to do the same. "To love, peace and happiness."

"Here, here!" Alex cheered, clicking his mug with Bryce's.

After they left the bar, they went their separate ways. Alex climbed into his car, smiling and feeling good about his friendship with Bryce. Pulling out onto the highway, Alex noticed a car following him. He thought it was a coincidence, so he kept driving.

Fifteen minutes later, Alex looked in his rearview mirror and noticed the same car on his tail. He was unable to make out the driver, but remembered Maria's husband, Armando, had threatened to kill him. Putting the pedal to the metal, Alex maneuvered his Lamborghini in and out of traffic, exceeding one hundred miles per hour. He breathed a sigh of relief after dodging the other car. Though, Alex was unable to shake the feeling that Armando was serious about killing him. His hands were shaking as he picked up his cell phone to call his brother.

Guy was in his home office when the phone rang. He had just gotten home from work. "Hello."

"Hi Guy," Alex said, unable to calm his nerves. "I'm on my way over. I need to talk to you."

Alarmed by the trembling sound of Alex's voice, Guy asked, "Is everything okay?"

Alex glanced in the rearview mirror before responding. "I'm not sure," he whispered.

Guy's brows wrinkled. "What do you mean, 'you're not sure?'"

"I'll explain it when I get there."

After disconnecting the call, Alex reflected on another life-threatening incident he had encountered in graduate school. At the time, he and Rhaunda were dating but things fell apart when she caught him having sex with Cyprus Wilson, a gorgeous blue-eyed blonde, who attended the same school. Even though he was butt-naked, Alex tried to run after Rhaunda, but Cyprus' boyfriend, Danny DeSoto, showed up and blocked his path.

Alex was trying to figure out how to get around Danny in one piece. "It's not what it seems," he weakly stated, after looking into Danny's blazing eyes.

Danny's nostrils flared as he approached Alex, and threatened through clenched teeth, "I'm going to kill you!"

"Wait! Let's talk about this!" Alex shouted with a pleading voice. He covered his private area with one hand, and reached out to Danny with his free hand.

Suddenly, Danny hunched low and flipped Alex over on his back. He straddled Alex, then repeatedly punched him in the face with both fists.

Alex buckled under, grunting with each blow. He looked to Cyprus for help, but she quickly dressed and rushed out of the bedroom. She was thrown off balance when she bumped into a well-groomed older black man, who was tall, big and muscular.

"Uh, excuse me," Cyprus said to the man, before grabbing her car keys and sprinting out of her apartment.

The man rushed into the bedroom and found Danny pummeling Alex's face into the floor. Then he grabbed Danny under his arms and pulled him away from Alex.

While the man held Danny at bay, Alex hurriedly stood up and put on his boxer shorts and pants. He was grateful to the stranger for intervening on his behalf.

Danny's heart was beating out of control when he turned to the man, who continued to block his path to Alex. "I'm going to kill him!" Danny threatened.

"No you're not," the man warned in a stern voice.

"You can't stop me!" Danny screamed.

The man pulled out his gun and held it in Danny's face. "Oh yes I can," he firmly stated. "If I find out you hurt Alex in any way, consider yourself dead. Got it?!" the man barked, before pushing Danny out of the bedroom.

Unfazed by the man's threat, Danny stood in the door entrance and formed an L-shape with his thumb and index finger. He pointed his index finger toward Alex and mouthed, "You're dead," before rushing out of the apartment.

The man took note of Danny's gesture out of the corner of his eyes. Then he grabbed Alex's hand to help him to his feet. "Are you okay?"

Wincing from pain, Alex stood up halfway with his hands over his stomach. "Yes," he muttered. "Who are you?"

The man put his gun in his holster before responding. "Let's just say someone who has your best interest at heart." He refused to tell Alex he was hired to protect him.

For a few seconds, Alex squinted his eyes at the man. He wondered if they had crossed paths in the past.

The man looked at Alex and shook his head. "You need to slow down with women, though. Someone is liable to get hurt."

"She came on to me first," Alex defensively replied.

"Alex, you don't have to always take the bait."

Still in pain, Alex mustered the strength to stand up straight. "Yeah, I know. Thanks for looking out. What's your name?" It did not escape Alex that the man had mentioned his name a couple of times.

On purpose, the man ignored Alex's question. "I don't think that guy is going to be bothering you any time soon."

"Are you sure?" Alex asked with uncertainty.

"I'm positive," the man said, before he left Alex standing in the middle of Cyprus' bedroom. After walking out of the apartment, he retrieved his cell phone from his pocket and flipped it open. "There's a problem," he said to the person on the receiving end. "Alex put himself in a compromising situation. He was caught with a young woman, whose boyfriend seems *hell-bent* on seeking revenge. You want him dead or alive?"

"Dead," the person said, before disconnecting the call.

Alex was relieved when Danny did not follow through with his threat. Though, he found it strange that both Danny and Cyprus had seemingly disappeared.

After graduate school, Alex and Rhaunda had made amends. He had even asked her to marry him, but she rejected his proposal. Rhaunda had also requested that they take things slow. Alex had agreed to Rhaunda's terms, but later discovered they were not compatible. However, the recent incident with Maria's husband, prompted Alex to second-guess his decision to break up with Rhaunda. The saying, opposites attract, quickly came to his mind.

Alex missed Rhaunda, but thought her message was loud and clear when she refused to accept his phone calls. He assumed she did not want anything to do with him.

After pulling into Guy and Regine's driveway, Alex was ready to spill his guts. He was in trouble. He needed his brother's help. When Alex knocked on the door, Guy greeted him with a warm hug.

Earlier, Guy had spotted Alex's car on the surveillance monitor in his office. He instantly noticed his brother's frazzled appearance. "Alex, are you okay?"

Taking a deep breath, Alex walked through the front door with a heavy heart. "I think someone is following me."

Guy closed the door, before asking, "Why do you think that?"

Alex briefly averted his eyes toward the floor. "I think it has something to do with what happened to me a couple of weeks ago."

Guy crossed his arms and shook his head. "This has to do with a woman, right?" he asked, but already knew the answer.

"But it was different this time," Alex explained.

"How so?"

"The woman's husband threatened to kill me."

Suddenly, Guy felt a set of eyes on his back. Turning around, he spotted Mimi dusting the mantel a couple of feet from the foyer. "Alex, let's go to my office, for some privacy."

After they walked into the office, Guy closed the door behind him, and asked Alex, "Do you know the guy that threatened you?"

"It was Maria's crazy husband," Alex said, as he sat in the chair in front of Guy's desk.

With raised brows, Guy walked around his desk and sat down. "Is she the same Maria you hired a couple of months ago?"

Alex nodded his head, confirming Guy's suspicions.

Guy closed his eyes for a few seconds, trying to refrain from yelling at Alex. "What were you thinking?" he asked in a controlled but harsh tone.

"I…wasn't," Alex stammered, still shaken up. "There…were… these guys that rescued me."

Leaning toward Alex, Guy probed further. "Did you get their names?"

"No."

"What did they look like?"

"They were all big and buff. One of them knew my name." Then Alex explained how Maria lured him over to her apartment.

Cupping his chin, Guy pondered Alex's dilemma.

Alex sat on the edge of his chair, feeling uncomfortable with Guy's silence. "I didn't tell you this before," he said with caution, "but I had a similar altercation in graduate school."

"What happened?"

"Well, it involved this girl name Cyprus Wilson. Her boyfriend went ballistic when he caught us together. He threatened to kill me, but a man came from out of nowhere and rescued me."

Surprised by this revelation, Guy's mouth flew open in response. "Are you serious?" he asked in disbelief.

Alex nodded in affirmation. "No telling what would've happened if the man had not shown up."

Guy nodded as he picked up the phone and called Big Mike. "We have a problem," he said, as soon as his friend answered.

"What's going on?" Big Mike asked, detecting urgency in Guy's voice.

Guy was getting ready to respond but paused, when he looked up and noticed Regine standing in the door entrance. "I'll put Alex on the phone," he said to Big Mike, "and let him tell you." After Guy handed the phone to Alex, he stepped outside his office, closing the door behind him.

"Hon'," Guy said to Regine, "do you need me for anything?"

"No, Mimi told me Alex was here, and looked a little distraught. I wanted to see if he was okay."

"Everything's fine," Guy assured her, as he walked with her to their bedroom. He thought this was a great opportunity for Alex to talk to Big Mike, in private.

While Alex was in graduate school, Big Mike had gotten him out of a jam from being a potential suspect in an assault and battery case against Guy's ex-girlfriend, Justina Reyes. Alex wanted to kill Justina for coming between Regine and Guy.

With reservations, Alex put the phone to his ear. "Hi Mike."

"Hi Alex, how are you holding up?"

"I'm okay, considering."

"Talk to me," Big Mike insisted.

Alex sighed before explaining everything he had told Guy about Maria and her husband, Armando. He also told Big Mike about his past situation with Danny DeSoto, in graduate school.

"Can I be frank with you?" Big Mike asked, after digesting everything Alex had told him.

Alex said, "Sure."

"Lately, you've been in some pretty sticky situations," Big Mike stated, while measuring his words. "Your brother is worried sick about you."

"I know," Alex admitted. His voice was filled with shame and remorse.

Cutting to the chase, Big Mike said, "I was there when you had an altercation with your secretary's husband. I didn't tell Guy because he has enough on his plate, dealing with your sisters and stepmother."

Alex's jaw dropped from shock. "How did you know I needed help?"

"A while ago, your brother asked me to keep a close eye on you."

"He did?" Alex asked in disbelief.

Big Mike nodded. "Yes. I was about to intervene when Maria's husband came home, but two black sedans pulled up. You ran out of the apartment minutes later."

Alex went blank. He was still stuck on the revelation that Guy had asked Big Mike to watch over him. "How long have you been following me?" he asked, after snapping out of his spell.

"Not long."

Alex needed clarification, so he asked, "Was it recently?"

"Yes. I was following you earlier today. I'm sorry I scared you."

"Oh, wow," Alex muttered.

"Guy was worried about you. It was a good thing I followed you, especially in light of the incident you encountered three months ago."

Alex frowned. "Three months ago?"

"Does Andrean Walker ring a bell?"

Alex held his head down in shame as he remembered being in a hotel with the sexy former cover girl model. Andrean's husband busted through the door with a gun, and found them in bed together.

Andrean jumped out of bed and covered herself with the blanket. "Baby, it wasn't me," she said to her husband, while pointing to Alex, who was completely naked. "He made me do this."

Alex could not believe Andrean threw him under the bus. What made the situation worse was that her husband believed her. Alex froze in place when Andrean's husband aimed the gun at his head.

Coincidentally, a strange man barged into the hotel room, accusing Andrean's husband of sleeping with his wife. That strange man was a private investigator and one of Big Mike's employees.

Forgetting she was caught up in her own web of deception, Andrean became furious as she turned to her husband. "What?!" she screamed. "I can't believe you have the audacity to be mad at me, when you're screwing around on me!"

"Let me explain," her husband lamented with a shaky voice. "I don't know what this guy is talking about," he said, while pointing the gun to the floor and reaching out to his wife with his free hand. He had forgotten Alex was there.

Andrean was not having it. She slapped her husband in the face with vigor and hatred. In response, he blocked his face, pleading with her to believe him. With all the drama going on, Alex and Big Mike's employee slipped out of the room, undetected.

Alex held the phone to his ear, shaking his head in disbelief. "You were there?" His voice was riddled with shock and awe.

"No, it was one of my employees. You were very lucky in that instance."

"Thanks for looking out," Alex said, after realizing Big Mike had saved his life.

"No, you should thank your brother. Guy would probably die if something ever happened to you."

Alex regretted taking Guy through so much. He was overcome with guilt.

Big Mike said, "Think about it, Alex. "You have a good life. Don't blow it over sex."

Chapter 12
Call of Duty

*W*hen Guy returned to his office, he closed the door and retrieved the phone from Alex's extended hand. "So Mike, what do you think?" he asked, as he held the phone to his ear.

"I'm not sure," Big Mike honestly replied. "I'll send one of my employees to see if Maria's husband still poses a threat. I'll also find out what happened to Danny DeSoto, the kid Alex had an altercation with in graduate school." He paused, before asking, "Do you think your stepmother hired someone to watch over Alex? You know, the way she did with you."

"Why do you think that?"

"Alex told me strange men showed up out of nowhere to save him. They also knew his name. I'm sure they didn't pull his name out of thin air. I think you should ask your stepmother if she knows anything."

Guy turned his back to Alex and lowered his voice. "If my mother wasn't involved, Alex's safety is the last thing I'd want her to worry about."

Big Mike sighed. "I understand. I can't tell you what to do, but one day you're not going to be around, and Alex is going to have to learn the hard way."

"I know," Guy continued in a hushed voice, "but while I'm alive, I'm going to do everything within my means."

Big Mike knew it was senseless to debate Guy, especially when it came to his siblings. "I should have some definitive answers regarding Armando Gomez and Danny DeSoto soon. In the meantime, you should talk to Alex about settling down."

Guy turned around to face Alex before responding. "I'll do that. Thanks for everything."

"No problem. Do you want me to continue following Alex?"

In light of Alex's emotional state, Guy figured Alex was scared straight. "No," he said, after deep thought. "I don't think that's necessary."

After Guy hung up the phone, he thought about giving Alex advice about women and relationships, but changed his mind once he took note of the worry lines on Alex's forehead. "So Alex, how are things going at Trowne Key?"

Alex was relieved Guy had changed the subject. With relaxed shoulders, he sat up on the edge of his chair. "Everything's fine," he said, trying to sound upbeat. "I met with Bryce Jennings earlier today. We played golf and later on, we met up and had a few drinks."

With squinty eyes, Guy tapped into his memory bank. "Isn't he the owner of Centennial Resorts?"

Alex nodded. "Yes."

"Why are you hanging out with him?"

Alex thought this was a good opening to tell Guy about Bryce's merger proposal. "He wants to invest in Trowne Key for an unbelievable price," he said with excitement in his eyes.

Guy sat in his office chair, pondering Bryce's request. "Alex," he said after a short pause, "how much do you know about him?"

"He's seems legit," Alex said with confidence. "Bryce is offering twenty-five million for a joint investment opportunity with Trowne Key."

With bulging eyes, Guy whistled as he sat up on the edge of his chair. "That's a nice chunk of change. What's the catch?"

"He wants fifty percent ownership of Trowne Key Estates."

"No deal," Guy firmly replied.

"But Guy...."

"Again," Guy interrupted, "no deal. Mom told me Trowne Key stays in the family. Our family," Guy added for emphasis.

"Can you at least think about it?" Alex asked, hoping to persuade Guy.

"I'll think about it," Guy said, to appease his brother. Though, he was certain that he would not change his mind.

Biting his bottom lip, Alex figured it was pointless to try and force Guy to agree with the merger deal. He checked his watch before he stood up to leave. "I think I'm going to head home."

"Why don't you consider staying here? There's plenty of room."

Alex thought about Guy's request, but after talking to Big Mike, he believed he was not in danger. "Thanks for the offer, but there's no place like home."

Guy nodded. "Okay, be careful."

Mimi walked into Jeanine's bedroom minutes after Alex left. She wanted to tell Jeanine what she had overheard. "Hello Mrs. Benedict," Mimi said, after closing the door behind her. "How are you feeling?"

"I'm fine. Who was that at the door?" Jeanine asked, remembering she heard the door chime throughout the house, earlier.

"That was Mr. Alex Simmons," Mimi replied, as she grabbed the water pitcher from Jeanine's dresser, and filled an empty glass with water.

"Is everything okay?" Jeanine asked. .

Mimi gave Jeanine her pain pills and some water to wash it down before responding. "It seems that Alex has gotten himself into a little trouble with his secretary's husband. I believe he said his name was Armando Gomez. But don't worry, Alex told Guy that some strange men rescued him." Mimi recited what she had heard while standing next to Guy's office, eavesdropping.

Jeanine turned to Mimi with fear in her eyes. "What else did you overhear?"

Mimi looked at the closed door before turning back to Jeanine. "Guy expressed his concerns after Alex told him he met someone named Bryce Jennings, who happens to be the owner of Centennial Resorts."

"Why was he concerned?"

"I didn't get a chance to hear his explanation."

Suddenly, Jeanine became alarmed by this revelation. She touched Mimi's hand. "Dear," she said in a raspy voice, "give me some privacy. I need to make a phone call."

As soon as Mimi walked out of the bedroom and closed the door behind her, Jeanine picked up the phone and called Trowne Key's CEO. "Hello Sidney," she said in a barely audible voice.

"Hello Mrs. Benedict. How are you feeling?"

"I've had better days, but enough about me. I received information that Alex has been socializing with the owner of Centennial Resorts. His name is Bryce Jennings. Do you know anything about him?"

Sidney broke out in a cold sweat upon hearing Bryce's name. "Well...uh...he seems nice."

"You know what I mean. What does he want with Alex?"

"I'm...not sure," Sidney nervously replied. "Have you spoken with Alex?" He asked more for his benefit, than Alex's.

"Not yet. Listen Sidney, I need you to call me if you hear anything unscrupulous about this Bryce Jennings."

"Will do." Sidney exhaled after disconnecting the call with Jeanine. He felt like his scheme with Bryce was falling apart. He was disappointed when Bryce called and told him Alex did not sign the contract for the merger agreement, even though he assured him that it was just a matter of time.

Unable to get any answers from Sidney, Jeanine dialed a number she remembered by heart. "Hi Tim. How are you?"

"Mrs. Benedict!" Tim Carter bellowed with excitement in his voice. "It's so good to hear from you."

Tim viewed Jeanine as more than his former employer; she was like family. He would do anything for her. Tim had even come out of retirement to be her private investigator, once again.

"Did you get a chance to check up on Alex for me?"

"Alex is fine," Tim said with assurance. "He was in a little trouble a couple of weeks ago, but his life is not in danger."

"What happened?"

"I'll spare you the details. Let's just say, Alex escaped another problem."

Jeanine frowned. "It had to do with his secretary, right?"

"Correct," Tim confirmed, wondering how Jeanine found out about Alex's secretary. "Maria Gomez's husband is not going to be a problem."

"How do you know?"

"Have I ever let you down?"

Jeanine smiled. "No you haven't." She distinctly remembered the times Tim had carried out her wishes, in respect to her stepchildren. In one instance, Guy's uncle, Nate, had roughed him up the same day he graduated from high school. Jeanine had instructed Tim to make sure Nate never put his hands on Guy, again. Tim had hired a couple of thugs to beat the crap out of Nate. Nate survived the attack, and never posed a problem for Guy or his siblings, again.

"I need one more favor," Jeanine said, before disconnecting the call.

"What is it?"

"See what you can find out about Bryce Jennings. He's the owner of Centennial Resorts."

"I will call you as soon as I find out anything."

"Tim, I appreciate you looking after Alex for me. I never thought he would repeat his father's mistakes. The old saying, *'like father, like son'* rings true," Jeanine stressed, between coughs.

Tim gripped the phone, fearing the worse. "Mrs. Benedict!" he called out. "Are you okay?"

"Yes, I'm fine," Jeanine said, breathing hard from anxiety. "Did you ever find out what happened to the young man Alex had an altercation with in graduate school?"

"Danny DeSoto?"

Jeanine nodded. "Yes."

"I'm afraid I haven't been able to locate him. I can only guess, but maybe Danny decided to cut his losses and move on."

"I hope you're right, but continue searching."

"I promise."

Considering Jeanine's terminal condition, Tim wanted to fulfill her every wish, even if it meant resorting to the unthinkable. Two years earlier, she had asked him to keep a close eye on Alex in graduate school. He was near the scene of the crime when Danny DeSoto jumped on Alex. He was about to intervene when a strange man rescued Alex. Afterwards, Tim had searched high and low for Danny DeSoto, without success.

After Tim hung up, Jeanine became overwrought with worry over Alex's safety. Alex had become what Jeanine dreaded the most - *a full-fledge womanizer.* "God, protect Alex," she muttered, before closing her eyes and dosing off to sleep.

Minutes later, Guy walked into Jeanine's room to check up on her. He was almost brought to tears when he noticed the phone dangling from her hand. She was seemingly motionless. "Mom?" he softly whispered. When she did not respond, Guy panicked and called for Mimi.

Within seconds, Mimi appeared in Jeanine's room and ran to her bedside. "Mr. Simmons, is everything okay?"

Guy pointed to Jeanine. He was choked up and unable to speak.

Mimi rushed to Jeanine's bedside, to check her vitals. Five seconds later, she smiled as she turned to Guy. "Mrs. Benedict is sedated. I gave her medication earlier to help her rest."

Guy exhaled, breathing a sigh of relief. "Please stay with her at all times." He walked away from Jeanine's room, emotionally drained.

Chapter 13

When It Rains, It Pours

*A*rmando was devastated when Maria left him. He went through her things and found an envelope full of money hidden in the bedroom closet. He became enraged when he counted one thousand dollars in ten one-hundred-dollar bills. Instantly, Armando assumed Maria had gotten the money from Alex Simmons. When the phone rang, he almost broke his neck trying to answer it. It was his friend, Philipo, whom he had not heard from since Maria left him.

"Is he dead?" Armando asked, automatically assuming Philipo knew he was referring to Alex Simmons.

"I have bad news for you." Philipo's voice was void of the enthusiasm Armando wanted to hear.

Armando scrunched his forehead, as he asked, "What's going on?"

"Alex is off limits."

"What! Why?!" Armando yelled.

Philipo sighed. "It's a long story," he simply replied.

"Fine!" Armando shouted. "I'll go after him myself."

Shaking his head, Philipo somberly replied, "I was afraid you would say that. You've been warned," he added before disconnecting the call.

Enraged, Armando hung up the phone and grabbed his gun from the top dresser drawer in his bedroom. After loading the gun, he grabbed his car keys and headed out the front door. He was on his way to Alex's office to kick his butt.

Suddenly, Armando noticed a car following him. When he slowed down, the car slowed down. The same thing happened when he sped up. He wiped the sweat from his forehead as he tried to swerve in and out of lanes to get away from the mysterious car.

Twenty minutes later, Armando was still looking over his shoulder, hoping to get away from the car that was following him. He was not successful. Believing he would be safer in a crowded area, Armando turned into the Wal-Mart shopping plaza and drove into a parking space near the store entrance. His plan did not work.

When Armando climbed out of his car, a mysterious man punched him in the face, knocking him to the ground. "I see you don't take no for an answer," the man said, as he aimed the gun at Armando's head.

Armando threw up his hands to surrender. His eyes grew bigger after realizing it was the leader of the pack. The same man who had threatened him earlier and intervened on Alex's behalf.

"Wait!" Armando begged for mercy. "Please don't do this! I promise. I won't go near Alex. You have my word."

"Too late," the man said, as he fired his silencer three times, then he stepped back as Armando fell backwards into his car with blood splattered all over his face and shirt. The man quickly propped Armando behind the steering wheel of his car. Then he used a towel to cover Armando's face. Even though the parking lot was crowded, no one heard or saw the killing. Armando's body was not discovered until the next morning.

Philipo had played a minor role in Armando's demise. He loved his friend but was more loyal to his employer. However, he had refused to pull the trigger, opting to be the getaway driver. With tunnel vision, Philipo sped away from the crime scene. If he had looked back, he would have spotted Tim Carter, Jeanine's private investigator, following him.

Earlier, Tim followed Armando until another car cut in front of him. He pulled back but continued to discreetly follow Armando into the Wal-mart parking lot. He parked his car several yards away, and was stunned after witnessing Armando's execution.

Chapter 14
Born this Way

*T*hroughout high school, Cassie felt awkward and out of place. Unlike Dana, she had fewer friends and was routinely excluded from parties and other social gatherings sponsored by her peers. Playing soccer was the only thing that brought balance in her life. She was a good player, scoring most of the goals in each game.

One day, Cassie was in the locker room after soccer practice, sitting alone. Suddenly, she felt a pair of eyes staring at her. She turned in that direction and spotted her coach, Mrs. Whitmore, who bore a scowl on her face.

"Cassie!" Mrs. Whitmore hollered. "After you get dressed, meet me in my office, pronto!"

Thrown off by the coach's demeanor, Cassie feared she did something wrong. She took her time getting dressed, ignoring her teammates' questioning gazes. As soon as she opened the door to the coach's office, the air stood still around her. She was surprised by Mrs. Whitmore's angry demeanor.

"Have a seat!" Mrs. Whitmore sharply ordered.

Cassie slowly walked into the coach's office and sat in the chair across from her desk. "Mrs. Whitmore, I didn't do anything," she said in her defense.

"Not yet," the coach said in a condescending manner. "Some of your teammates told me they feel uncomfortable around you."

Dumbfounded, Cassie sat on the edge of her chair, seeking clarification. "I don't understand what you mean."

"Don't play dumb with me!" Mrs. Whitmore yelled with an attitude. "This is a respectable school, and we don't have room for *your* kind."

"My kind?" Cassie quizzed, as her right hand flew to her chest.

"Lesbians! Dykes! Or whatever you call yourselves!" the coach shouted with venom spewing from her lips.

Choked up over the name calling, Cassie's eyes began to water. "But…I didn't do…anything…."

"Don't deny it!" the coach cut in. "I caught you red-handed, looking at my girls in that way. You better be glad you're one of my best players. Otherwise, I would've kicked you off this team a long time ago. So from now on, you cannot go into the locker room, until the other girls are fully dressed. Do you understand?"

As tears rolled down her face, Cassie tried to make sense of the coach's allegations but came up empty. Before she walked out of the office, the coach shouted, "I will be notifying your parents!"

Cassie did not bother telling the coach her parents were deceased. She figured the coach would eventually find out Regine and Guy were her legal guardians. She went home and started locking herself in her bedroom.

Everyone, except Guy, had become concerned with Cassie's strange behavior. Guy figured her behavior was related to teenage drama. However, Regine was determined to find out what was going on with Cassie. She walked upstairs and knocked on Cassie's bedroom door. "Cassie, honey," she said through the closed door, "are you okay?"

Dana heard Regine call out her sister's name even though her door was closed. After deep thought, she opened her door and peered out of her bedroom, which was next to her sister's. "She's not going to answer you."

"Why not?" Regine asked, as she turned to Dana with a raised brow. "Is there something I should know about your sister?"

Dana shrugged her shoulders. "Beats me," she said, before she returned to her bedroom, closing the door behind her.

Sighing, Regine knocked on Cassie's door again. "Cassie," she said loud enough to be heard through the door, "if you ever need someone to talk to, I'm here for you."

Regine felt hopeless as she went in search for Guy. She found him in his office. He was on the floor with KC, stacking ABC blocks. She smiled as she looked toward heaven and thanked God for her miracle baby.

"Hi honey," Guy said, after spotting Regine at the door entrance. "Is everything alright?"

"I'm fine," Regine solemnly replied.

Detecting concern in his wife's voice, Guy quickly stood up and approached her. "What is it, honey?"

Regine tightened her lips. She was not sure how to address her concerns. "When was the last time you spoke with Cassie? For the past two days, she's been locked up in her bedroom."

Guy sat back in his chair, pondering Regine's question. "I guess a couple of days ago. I don't think it's a big deal. You know how flighty teenagers can be."

"But Cassie has changed since she started high school."

"Every kid endures peer pressure," Guy thoughtfully explained. "It's nothing to worry about. This is Cassie and Dana's junior year in high school, so they might be getting a little pressure from young men."

Regine averted her eyes away from Guy, as she muttered, "I don't think that's Cassie's problem."

"Why did you say that?"

"Cassie's been acting strange, that's all. She didn't even go to her junior prom."

Guy shrugged his shoulders. "So what, I didn't either."

"Maybe you're right," Regine determined. "I'm going to the kitchen to prepare lunch. You know where to find me."

After Regine left, Guy wanted to see for himself if Cassie was fine. "Come on little man," he said as he picked up KC and placed him on his hip. "We have to go see about your Auntie." Guy knocked on Cassie's bedroom door, and said, "Open up. "I need to talk to you." He frowned when Cassie did not respond. When he knocked again, he received the same response.

Guy walked away from Cassie's door believing Regine's concerns might have merit. He went to the kitchen to talk to his wife about seeking professional counseling for Cassie.

Cassie assumed Regine and Guy had received the coach's phone call. Too ashamed to face them, she stuffed a few things in a duffle bag and opened her bedroom window. She decided to run away. She stopped in her tracks when she heard another knock at the door. "What now?" she asked herself, agitated by the attention she was receiving. "Why can't they leave me alone?"

"It's me," Dana said in a hushed voice, but loud enough for Cassie to hear her. "Open the door."

Stumped, Cassie remained in one place.

Dana turned the knob but the door was still locked. "Please Cassie; open the door so we can talk. I know what happened at school. Your secret is safe with me."

With reservations, Cassie threw her duffle bag in the closet before she opened the door, to let her sister in.

"You don't have to worry about Guy and Regine," Dana explained, as she walked in Cassie's room and closed the door behind her.

"What do you mean?" Cassie asked. Her heart skipped a beat while awaiting Dana's reply.

Dana flopped down on her sister's bed before stating, "I picked up the phone when your coach called, and pretended to be Regine."

Cassie breathed a little better, knowing Dana had intercepted the coach's call. She walked to her bed and sat next to her sister. "The coach thinks I'm a lesbian."

Affectionately, Dana wrapped her arm around her sister's waist, before asking, "Are you?"

"I don't know."

Dana smiled. "If you're gay, I'll still love you."

"I feel like a freak," Cassie declared, as tears burned the back of her eyes.

"There's nothing wrong with you," Dana said with assurance. After deep thought, she thought of a solution to help her sister. "How do you feel about going on a double date with me?"

"I'm not even sure if I like boys," Cassie thoughtfully admitted.

"I know, but have you tried going out with one, or kissing one, or having one hold you in his arms while whispering *I love you?*" she asked with dreamy eyes, as she playfully tooted her lips and kissed the air.

Cassie laughed softly before she turned serious. "You think it's possible to let a boy get that close to me?"

"You never know," Dana said, as she stood up to leave. "Billy is on his way to pick me up, then he's going to swing by to pick up Malik. We're going out to get a bite to eat. Do you want to go with us?"

Without Guy's knowledge, Dana continued to see Malik behind his back. Cassie had agreed to keep her secret.

"No, I'd rather go to the library."

"Fine, Billy can drop you off along the way. We'll just tell Guy we're going to the library."

Cassie nodded, agreeing with Dana's plan.

Dana smiled. "Let's get out of this room before Regine and Guy starts worrying about both of us."

After Cassie dried her eyes, she followed Dana out of the bedroom. Silently, she prayed Dana's plan would work.

Regine and Guy were discussing Cassie but stopped talking, after they heard someone approaching the kitchen. They smiled when they saw the twins.

"Hi Cassie," Guy greeted with a wide grin.

"You had us worried," Regine stated.

Bashfully, Cassie said, "I'm sorry for the way I've been acting."

Overprotective of Cassie, Dana stood next her sister and held her hand. "She's dealing with a lot of stress at school, that's all."

Guy looked at Cassie with concern. "We're here if you ever need someone to talk to."

"I'm glad you said that," Dana interjected, "because Cassie and I are going on a double date next week, and we'd like your permission."

"Correction," Guy countered, "you're going on your first date when you turn seventeen."

"Fine," Dana replied with an attitude, "but we'd like to go without our bodyguard."

Guy sat up on the edge of the chair with slanted eyes. "You can go," he firmly stated, "as long as Billy goes with you."

"It's not fair!" Dana hollered for dramatic effect.

"That's the only way!" Guy retorted.

Dana frowned. "It's not necessary!" she exclaimed. "You're still treating us like we're kids!"

"Guy," Regine interjected, "do you really think it's necessary for Billy to go with them? The girls will not be alone. They'll have their dates to protect them. Besides, they can always call us if something happens."

"I'm not going to change my mind," Guy said to Regine, before turning to Cassie. "Who's this guy you're going on a date with?"

Dana spoke up for Cassie. "I'm going out with Malik, and Cassie is going out with his friend."

"Dana, you know how I feel about Malik," Guy grimly replied.

"Oh Guy!" Dana whined. "Malik is not a bad person."

Guy did not want to argue with Dana, so he lowered his voice. "After you graduate from high school and go off to college, what is Malik going to do?"

Dana shrugged her shoulders. "I don't know. I guess he'll get a job."

"As what?" Guy sarcastically inquired. "A street pharmacist?"

Regine lightly elbowed Guy. "Dana," she interrupted, "Guy was just kidding. What he wants to know is do you see yourself with Malik when you go off to college?"

"I'm not sure," Dana replied with shrugged shoulders. "It's not like we're getting married anytime soon." Rolling her eyes, she turned to Cassie, and said, "Let's go upstairs and get dressed. Billy will be here soon."

"Where are you girls going?" Regine asked.

"To the library," Dana and Cassie said in unison.

Regine smiled. "Okay, have fun."

As soon as Dana and Cassie left the kitchen, Regine turned to Guy with a frown on her face.

Perplexed, Guy asked, "What?"

Regine shook her head. "What are you trying to do? Make sure she stays with Malik?"

"You know I don't like him with my sister. Now Dana goes and pairs off his friend with Cassie."

"At this rate, you're going to give Dana to Malik with a big red bow tie wrapped around her head."

"I know what you're saying," Guy grumbled, "but I don't like him."

Regine shook her head. "Mark my words. If you continue to express your disapproval, you will ensure that Dana stays with Malik, whether you like it or not."

"Over my dead body," Guy muttered to himself.

Throughout the day, Guy could not get Malik Mitchell out of his thoughts. He had a feeling Malik was bad news, so he phoned Big Mike to initiate an investigation.

"Are you sure this is a good idea?" Big Mike asked. "I've known Dana since she was a little girl. She has always been strong-willed."

Guy nodded. "I'm sure."

"Okay, give me a few days, to see what I can find out."

"Thanks Mike. I appreciate it."

Next, Guy contacted Billy.

Billy flipped his phone open after noting Guy was the caller. "What's going on?" he asked, after looking over at Malik and Dana eating their subs.

Guy cut to the chase. "Billy, Dana met this guy named Malik Mitchell. I don't want her anywhere near him."

"Sir, uh…may I ask why?" Billy nervously inquired.

"He's bad news."

"I understand," Billy said, assuming it had something to do with Malik bringing Dana home at two o'clock in the morning, a month earlier. He was shocked when Malik told him Guy had threatened him. After disconnecting the call, he trotted over to the table to break up Malik and Dana's happy union. "We have to go."

"Come on, Billy," Dana spouted. "Can we stay a little longer?"

"Okay," Billy conceded after being taken in by Dana's pleading eyes, "but we have to leave in fifteen minutes, not a minute longer."

Dana and Malik smiled in response.

On their way to pick up Cassie from the library, Malik sat in the front of the limo with Billy while Dana sat in the back passenger seat. Billy thought it was best to tell Malik what Guy had told him, in private. "Malik, Dana's brother does not want you to see her anymore."

"I know," Malik mumbled.

"Don't worry," Billy said with assurance, "there are plenty of other girls out there."

"Unc, I'm feeling Dana."

Billy shook his head. "Maybe in a few years, her brother will have a change of heart. "In the meantime, you need to concentrate on getting an education first. When do you plan on going back to school?" he asked, after remembering Malik had not returned to school ever since he was suspended two months earlier.

"I'm never going back!" Malik replied with conviction. "I have my own hustle going on."

Billy tightened his lips in an attempt to measure his tone. "What are you talking about?"

Realizing he may have said too much, Malik decided to change the subject. He did not want Billy to know he was back on the street corner selling drugs. "I'll think about going back to school, a'ight?"

"No slang," Billy chided. "We made a deal, remember?"

"Sorry about that, Unc."

"How is your foster mother treating you?"

"You know how it is. She wants me out of her house."

"You can stay with me," Billy volunteered.

"Don't worry, Unc. I have a place to stay."

Billy peered at Malik with raised brows. "Come again?"

"My homeboy, Sapp, found a place for me to stay. You met him a couple of weeks ago."

"Yes, I remember him." Billy stopped short of telling Malik that he had doubts about Sapp. He was puzzled over how Sapp had appeared out of the blue and became Malik's friend. "Make sure you give me your new address so I can stay in touch with you."

"Fo' sho'."

"Malik!" Billy scolded with a frown on his face   .

Malik laughed, knowing his slang language was annoying Billy. "I mean, for sure," he mocked.

Billy glanced at Malik and smiled.

"Will you give me time to say good-bye to Dana?"

"Sure." Billy pulled his car over on the side of the highway. Then he waited for Malik to get in the back of the limo with Dana before driving onto the highway.

"Hey baby," Malik said, after closing the door behind him.

Dana smiled. "What are you doing back here?"

"I have something to tell you." Malik held Dana's hands while he told her he could not see her anymore.

"Why?"

"Your brother is trippin'."

Dana knew it would come to this. She was at a loss for words. In response, Malik embraced her, holding her close to him. "Don't worry," he said with confidence, "I'll find a way to come and see you when I get my own car. I promise, a'ight?"

Dana was doubtful as she nodded her head. The only thing she knew for certain was that she loved Malik, more than life itself.

When Billy pulled in front of the library to retrieve Cassie, Malik returned to the front passenger seat. Instantly, Billy noted the sadness in his young friend's eyes, but there was nothing he could do or say to make the situation better. During the drive to Malik's home, they did not exchange their normal rapport. Even more disconcerting, Malik climbed out of the car without uttering a word.

Chapter 15

Redemption

*A*lex thought his sexual adventures with various women would satisfy his needs, but he felt a hole in his heart. Lately, Rhaunda had weighed heavily on his mind. He could not deny that he still loved her. The more he thought about it, the more he realized Bryce's advice about settling down and getting married made sense.

In hindsight, Alex recognized his break up with Rhaunda was hasty. He knew he had hurt her feelings, and was hoping she would forgive him. After deep thought, he called the local florist to order a bouquet of roses. Then he asked the florist to add a note that read: *I'm sorry. Please forgive me. Love, Alex.*

Satisfied with the first step to win Rhaunda's heart, Alex perused through his cell phone and deleted the phone numbers of every woman he was intimate with. Next, he boxed up everything that reminded him of different women he had been with throughout most of his young adult life. "Rhaunda, baby," Alex said to himself, "I'm not going to give up until I make you my wife."

Alex called Rhaunda's home number, and was surprised when her father answered his phone call. "Hello Pastor Coleman."

"What in the hell do you want with my daughter?!" the pastor shouted, after detecting Alex's voice.

"I…uh…," Alex stuttered, "I need to talk to Rhaunda."

"No you don't!" the pastor sharply rebuffed.

Alex felt uneasy. He was unsure of what he could say, to appease Rhaunda's father. "I'm sorry…."

Pastor Coleman interrupted Alex, shouting, "Rhaunda is off limits!" He hung up the phone, believing he had gotten rid of Alex.

Swallowing hard, Alex understood the pastor's anger. For some reason, he thought it would be best to talk to the pastor in person. Bravely, he appeared on Pastor Coleman's doorstep thirty minutes later. He was determined to make amends with Rhaunda.

Pastor Coleman grunted when he opened the door and noticed Alex standing there with a bouquet of flowers. "What do you want?!" he snarled. "I thought I made myself clear!"

"Yes sir, you did," Alex confirmed, his voice was filled with fear. "Um…but um…I need to talk to you."

"There's nothing to talk about!" the pastor sharply announced.

Alex was getting ready to return to his car when he heard someone coming up from behind the pastor.

"Thomas!" the pastor's wife called out from the background, "Who are you talking to?"

The pastor glared at Alex, before answering, "No one."

Elizabeth came to the door with a plastered smile. Then she greeted Alex with exaggerated enthusiasm. "Hi Alex! It's so good to see you. Come on inside."

"He's not welcome in my house!" the pastor exclaimed.

Elizabeth ignored her husband as she opened the door wider for Alex. Her eyes and smile were filled with excitement but deep down, she wanted to kill him for hurting her baby. "Are those for Rhaunda?" she asked, after noting the bouquet in Alex's hand.

"Yes, ma'am," Alex answered, while glimpsing at Rhaunda's father.

With reservations, the pastor stepped aside.

Pretentiously, Elizabeth hugged and kissed Alex on the cheek. Then she grabbed his hand and guided him through the foyer. "Have a seat in the guest room. I'll let Rhaunda know you're here."

"Okay," Alex said, as he shifted his eyes to the pastor.

Frustrated with his wife's dismissive attitude, the pastor shook his head as he turned and darted toward the library room.

"Mr. Coleman!" Alex called out. "I would like to talk to you."

Pastor Coleman stopped in his tracks, before he slowly turned around to face Alex. "What do you want?!"

"I'm sorry for everything," Alex admitted with sincerity. "I want to do right by Rhaunda. I love her."

The pastor approached Alex with narrowed eyes. "Your actions speak otherwise."

"I'm ready to settle down. I want to ask you for Rhaunda's hand in marriage."

Angry beyond comprehension, Pastor Coleman strolled over to Alex, stood in front of him, and sternly asked, "What makes you think I would give you my approval to marry my daughter?"

"I know I messed up," Alex said, as he briefly held his head down. "This time, things are going to be right between us."

The pastor folded his arms, mulling over Alex's comments. "Considering your track record with other women," he made clear to Alex, "I have a hard time believing you."

Alex's eyes grew bigger. It dawned on him that his affairs with other women were well known, seemingly to everyone, even though he tried in vain to be discreet.

"Oh, I know all about you," the pastor replied, after gauging Alex's surprised reaction. "My private investigator gave me a full report of your perverted flings with other women."

Exhaling, Alex realized he was exposed. "Let me show you I'm a changed man."

The pastor was in deep thought as he cupped his bearded chin. Seconds later, he looked at Alex with a wide grin. "I know what you can do to make this right."

"What is it?" Alex quickly asked. "I'll do anything."

Grunting, the pastor was doubtful of Alex's stance. "If you can remain faithful to Rhaunda for six consecutive months, I'll give you my approval to marry her. Otherwise, you must leave her alone for good. Deal?" the pastor asked, as he held out his hand.

Nodding his head, Alex thought the ultimatum seemed reasonable. "Deal," he said, as he shook the pastor's hand.

Pastor Coleman turned and walked away with a look of satisfaction. He knew it would be a matter of time before Alex failed the test, miserably.

Elizabeth despised Alex but knew he was the only person capable of bringing sunshine in her daughter's life. She put her ear to Rhaunda's bedroom door before knocking. "Rhaunda, honey, Alex is here to see you."

Rhaunda lifted her head from her pillow, and asked, "What does he want?"

Slowly, Elizabeth opened Rhaunda's bedroom door and walked in. "Honey, things are not always as bad as they seem," she explained in a soothing voice. "Why don't you go and hear him out?"

"Mom, Alex is not serious about committing to me, or any woman for that matter."

Sitting on the edge of Rhaunda's bed, Elizabeth explained, "Alex is young and dumb. When he gets older, he's going to realize you're priceless. Trust me, I've been in your situation," she added, as she gloomily turned away from her daughter.

Rhaunda sat up in bed, frowning. "What are you saying, Mother?"

Elizabeth averted her eyes downward before responding. "Life has a way of taking you by surprise."

"What do you mean?" Rhaunda asked, seeking clarification.

Elizabeth sighed. "Your dad had an affair. After I found out, I gave him an ultimatum. That's when he woke up and realized he was about to lose me."

"Mother, when did this happen?"

With a thin smile, Elizabeth continued, "I left your father long before you were born. It was the hardest thing I ever had to do, but I needed my sanity. Eventually, he decided our marriage was worth fighting for."

Rhaunda was dumbfounded. Throughout her entire life, she thought her parents were exceptional, and her father was always faithful to her mother. Unfortunately, her mother's confession did not alleviate her doubts about Alex. "I don't know if I could ever trust Alex again."

Elizabeth smiled, lightly touching Rhaunda's shoulder. "I have a gut feeling Alex is serious this time. Some people call it intuition, but I say *'it's God's way of speaking to you.'* Everyone deserves a chance to redeem themselves. Go see what Alex wants. If your gut feeling tells you it's not going to work, walk away from him and never look back."

"I suppose you're right, Mom," Rhaunda thoughtfully replied. "I'll go downstairs to see what he wants."

"That's a great idea," her mother said with a wide grin.

Elizabeth had pegged Alex as a *playboy* from the very beginning, and did not think he was right for her one and only child. Though, she could not deny that Rhaunda loved Alex. So she decided to give Alex another chance, for her daughter's sake.

Minutes later, Alex spotted Rhaunda walking downstairs. He immediately stood up and rushed to her side. "These are for you," he said, as he held out the bouquet of red roses.

Rhaunda took the bouquet and smelled the roses. "Thank you."

Smiling, Alex grabbed Rhaunda's free hand. "I'm sorry about everything," he acknowledged, while looking into her eyes.

"Alex, I've been thinking," Rhaunda said, after a short pause. "I don't think things are going to work between us."

Clasping his hands around her waist, he softly said, "I messed up. I promise, if you give me a chance, you won't regret it." His voice was filled with sorrow.

"Alex, we've been down this road before. I don't think we're right for each other."

Is this déjà vu? Alex silently asked himself. He shook his head, wondering how he ended up in his brother's shoes. To convince Rhaunda he was sincere, Alex dropped to his knees and held her hands. "Please…let me make it up to you."

Alex's response was new to Rhaunda. "Are you sure?" she asked with a raised brow.

"I've never been more certain of anything in my life. I need you."

After a short pause, Rhaunda looked in Alex's eyes. She believed he was sincere. "Okay, I'll give you another chance."

"Are you serious?" Alex asked with excitement in his eyes.

Rhaunda nodded. "Yes, but I don't want to go through the rest of my life, worrying about whether or not you're committed to me. I refuse to share you with another woman."

"I want you, and only you," Alex reiterated, as he stood up and gave Rhaunda a warm embrace. Then he smothered her with kisses.

"Whoa, what are you doing?" Rhaunda asked, as she pulled away from his embrace.

Alex chuckled. "I'm sorry. I got carried away."

Bashfully, Rhaunda looked downward before gazing into Alex's eyes. "Now what?"

"Let's go out and celebrate a new beginning. I made reservations for us at your favorite seafood restaurant."

"Skinners?" Rhaunda asked in surprise.

Alex smiled. "Yes."

"Oh, thank you," Rhaunda replied with high spirits. "Let me go get dressed."

While Alex returned to the sofa, Rhaunda ran upstairs, accidentally bumping into her mother.

"What's going on?" her mother asked.

"Oh Mom!" Rhaunda boasted. "Alex and I decided to make things right."

"I'm so happy," Elizabeth said, as she embraced Rhaunda and kissed her on the cheek. "I pray things work out between you two."

"Me too, Mom."

Rhaunda dashed upstairs to get dressed, while her mother invited herself to sit next to Alex on the sofa. "Alex," Elizabeth said with a warm voice, "I'm so glad you made a wise decision to pursue Rhaunda."

Alex grinned. "I am too. She's a sweet girl."

"Lean over," Elizabeth requested with a wicked grin. "I need to whisper something in your ear."

Looking at her with slanted eyes, Alex thought it was a strange request. Slowly, he leaned over, turning his ear toward her face.

Elizabeth's voice was soft and clear, as she threatened, "If you hurt my baby again, I will kill you." Then she backed away and looked at Alex with a big smile on her face. "You kids have fun tonight, okay?"

Alex looked at Elizabeth with fear in his eyes. For the past six months, he had been threatened by several people, but Rhaunda's mother had taken him by surprise. Alex was more afraid of her than anyone else. He stood up after he saw Rhaunda bouncing down the stairs.

"I'm ready!" Rhaunda shouted out with glee.

Alex was blown away by Rhaunda's beauty. She looked glamorous in her black knee-length dress and diamond necklace.

Looking at her daughter with sparkling eyes, Elizabeth stood up and gloated. "You look absolutely heavenly, darling."

Rhaunda smiled. "Thanks mother."

Turning to Alex with a sly grin, Elizabeth said, "Don't forget what I told you, sweetie."

"Okay," Alex muttered, avoiding Elizabeth's piercing gaze. He walked to the front door with Rhaunda on his arm. After they climbed into his car and buckled up, Rhaunda turned to Alex and asked, "What was my mother talking about?"

"She told me to make sure you had a good time," Alex lied.

"Awww," Rhaunda cooed, "she's so sweet."

Alex thought, *If only you knew.* "I'm thinking about going back to church," he said, to change the subject.

Rhaunda's mouth flew open. She tried to conceal her shock. "What's the catch?" she asked seconds later.

"I'm doing this for me," he truthfully admitted.

"I'm happy you made the right decision. Would you like to come to church with me?"

After dealing with Rhaunda's parents, Alex did not think that was a good idea. "No, I'd rather go to my own church."

"I guess it doesn't matter where you fellowship," Rhaunda determined. "As long as you go, that's what counts."

Alex glanced at Rhaunda and smiled. "I'm glad you agree."

Rhaunda said, "We're having a revival service at my church in a couple of weeks. Would you like to come with me?"

"What about your father?"

Rhaunda chuckled. "My father is not God."

"What if I meet you there?" Alex asked, trying to see as little of Rhaunda's parents as possible.

"That's fine with me."

Alex backed out of the driveway, vowing to change for the better.

Chapter 16

Sophisticated Seventeen

*W*hen the clock struck one second after midnight, Dana merrily ran into her sister's bedroom and turned on the light. Then she started jumping up and down with glee. "Cassie, we're free!" she bellowed with great enthusiasm. "We're finally free!"

Cassie yawned as she opened her eyes to find out why Dana was in her room shouting. Before her sister disrupted her sleep, she was dreaming about her biological father, and what would it have been like if he was still alive. "Simmer down, Dana," Cassie urged. "You're going to wake up everyone in the house."

"Aren't you excited?!" Dana asked, as she danced and swung her hands from side to side. "We are finally free!"

"You are so crazy," Cassie teased, laughing hysterically. "You're acting like we just escaped the slave plantation."

"But we did!" Dana cheered, as she bent down to hug Cassie. Then she stood back up and started doing a freaky dance. A few minutes later, Dana flopped on the bed next to her sister, and cooled herself off by flapping her hands back and forth. "Are you up for shopping today?" she asked, breathing hard from dancing. "We have to get ready for our dates, remember?"

Cassie was afraid to let on that she was nervous about going on a date. Though, she was grateful to Dana for putting an end to all the rumors at school about her being gay, especially since her sister told everyone about her big date with Malik's friend. Even the soccer coach, started treating her better. Ultimately, the gossip stopped, but it did not stop some girls from looking at her sideways.

While mulling over Dana's question about going shopping, Cassie considered backing out on her date, but knew her sister would nag her until she finally gave in. "We'll go shopping," Cassie dryly announced, "but I'm picking out my own clothes."

"But *I* pick your clothes for your date," Dana countered. "Agreed?" she asked with bright eyes.

Shaking her head, Cassie frowned as she thought about the skimpy outfits Dana wore. "I don't know," she glumly replied.

"Will you trust me?" Dana asked, after sensing Cassie's hesitance. "In order for you to be attractive to boys, you have to show a little skin."

Admiringly, Cassie looked at her sister. She wished she was as strong and vivacious as Dana. "Okay, you win," she conceded, knowing her sister would not accept *no* for an answer. "But I'm not showing too much skin."

"Cool," Dana said, as she stood up, resumed dancing, and starting singing, "Heyyy... hooo...heyyy...hooo...."

Upon hearing the commotion, Guy got out of bed and followed the noise to Cassie's bedroom. "What's going on in here?" he asked, after he walked in on Dana goofing off.

"Seventeen! Seventeen!" Dana repeatedly sang at the top of her lungs.

Guy stood back and chuckled. "Okay, okay, settle down."

"You know what this means?" Dana asked Guy, as she twirled her neck back and forth.

"No," Guy said with folded arms.

"Cassie and I are going out on our first double-date, remember?"

"Oh brother," Guy lamented, as he turned around and returned to his bedroom.

Regine woke up as soon as her husband returned to bed. "Guy," she groggily said, "Is everything okay?"

"The girls think they're free to do whatever they want to because they're seventeen."

"They're in for a rude awakening," Regine light-heartedly replied. "This is just the beginning."

"That's what I'm afraid of," Guy grumbled, before cuddling up next to Regine. He thought to himself, *This is one more thing I have to worry about.*

When Dana and Cassie returned from shopping, Regine greeted them at the door with a wide grin. "Are you girls ready for your first double date?"

"Yes we are," Dana happily announced.

Regine noticed Cassie did not respond. She turned to her and asked, "How do you feel about going on your first date?"

Cassie shrugged her shoulders. "I don't know," she said with indifference.

Regine's maternal instincts kicked in, detecting Cassie's un-easiness. "Don't feel pressured to go out if you don't feel like it."

"She's fine," Dana intervened. "Cassie is just nervous, that's all."

"What time are you girls leaving?" Regine asked, to change the subject.

"At seven," Dana answered.

Regine looked at her watch before responding. "It's almost six o'clock," she pointed out. "Make sure you girls take your cell phones with you."

"I never leave home without it," Dana sassed, as she held her pink and lightly glittered iPhone in the air.

Regine chuckled. "Okay, smarty pants."

Dana and Cassie giggled as they ran upstairs to get dressed.

After getting dressed, Dana strolled into Cassie's bedroom and noticed that her sister was in her walk-in closet getting dressed. "C'mon, Cassie!" she urged, as she banged on the closet door. "We don't have all day."

"Okay!" Cassie shouted from inside her closet. Seconds later, she walked out, fully dressed in the outfit Dana had personally selected for her. Cassie was speechless as she looked at her reflection in the full length mirror.

"You are beautiful!" Dana beamed, as she walked around Cassie, analyzing her work of art.

Cassie frowned, clearly put off by Dana's compliment. "But I look like you," she unhappily announced.

With a wide grin, Dana stood next to Cassie in the mirror. "I know you do," she laughed. "We're twins, silly."

Exasperated, Cassie turned to Dana with a pouty face. "You know what I mean."

"Cassie, you can't attract boys in baggy jeans and oversized sweatshirts." Dana was happy she had convinced Cassie *not* to try on her new outfit in the store.

"But this is too much skin," Cassie whined, as she stood in the mirror trying to adjust her short skirt.

"Stop complaining," Dana said, after she applied more lipstick in the full length mirror. "Your date is going to be blown away when he sees you."

Looking in the mirror once more, Cassie regretted letting Dana talk her into wearing a short floral skirt and matching halter-top. She even appeared uncomfortable in her three-inch strapless sandals, another one of Dana's suggestions. Though, she had stopped Dana from applying bold-colored makeup on her face. She opted for clear lip-gloss and light powder, instead. Taking a deep breath, Cassie braced herself for what she presumed would be an awkward evening. She followed Dana downstairs where they were greeted by Guy and Regine.

"Wow!" Regine stated with surprise in her voice, after admiring Cassie's new look. "You look different."

Guy looked Cassie over, and frowned when his eyes landed on the length of her mini skirt. "Cassie, you need a longer skirt."

"No she doesn't," Dana defensively answered for her sister. "Come on Guy, give us a break." Hurriedly, she grabbed Cassie's hand and dragged her out the front door to greet their dates. Dana was happy she had talked Guy into letting her and Cassie go on a date without Billy, their bodyguard.

Dana's heart fluttered when she saw Malik waiting for her by his new car, a spruced up sixty-seven Mustang. She wondered where he had gotten the money to pay for it, especially since he did not have a job.

Shortly after, Guy had followed the twins outside. He looked at Malik and shook his head in disgust. Then he looked at Sapp and noted he sported the same street clothes Malik had on.

Sapp extended his hand and introduced himself. "Hello, sir, I'm Sapp Burger."

Guy noted Sapp sounded articulate, and seemed to be more polished than what his baggy jeans and oversized t-shirt portrayed him to be. "Hi, I'm Guy, the twins' older brother," he broadcasted, shaking Sapp's extended hand.

"It's nice to meet you," Sapp said with a warm smile.

"Same here," Guy said with slight nod. Then he turned to Malik, and firmly instructed, "Make sure you have them home by ten." His voice was void of enthusiasm.

Malik nodded as he opened the door for Dana.

Dana instructed Cassie to sit in the backseat with Sapp, while she sat up front with Malik. When Cassie climbed in the backseat, she stared straight ahead, avoiding Sapp's watchful glare. Dana was right; Sapp was blown away by Cassie's beauty.

To break the ice, Dana looked back at Cassie, and asked, "You remember Malik, don't you?"

"No, I'm afraid not," Cassie lied, remembering she did not like him. She believed Malik was only with her sister for her money.

Chuckling, Malik glanced back at Cassie while backing out of the driveway. "Girl, stop playing like you don't know me."

"So Malik," Dana interjected, "where are we going?"

"We can go to your favorite restaurant, and maybe afterwards, we can go to the club."

"But we're not twenty-one," Cassie blurted out.

"Malik hooked us up." Dana smiled as she turned to Cassie and handed her an ID card.

Cassie looked at the photo on the ID card and frowned. "Who is this white girl?"

"You, for tonight," Dana explained with light laughter.

Malik also laughed. "Why are you trippin'? You're half-white. You might as well use that half to your advantage."

Shooting daggers at the back of Malik's head, Cassie crossed arms in a huff. She was clearly offended by his remarks.

Sapp did not like Malik's comment either, especially since he had the same light complexion as the twins. Noticing the scowl on Cassie's face, Sapp gently placed his hand on her thigh. "He's just kidding," he said, to excuse Malik's behavior.

Cassie snapped her head in Sapp's direction, and barked, "Get your hand off of me!"

"Uh…my bad." Sapp held up his hands, playfully surrendering.

Cassie rolled her eyes and moved closer to the door. She stared out of the window, pretending as if Sapp did not exist.

Thirty minutes later, the clan walked into Dana's favorite Italian restaurant. They opted to dine at a corner table. Dana and Malik were hugged up next to each other, while Sapp and Cassie sat across from them looking awkward.

"So," Sapp said as he looked at Cassie, "what do you do for fun?"

"I play soccer."

Sapp smiled. "That's cool. What are your plans after you graduate from high school?"

"Go to college." Cassie provided short answers on purpose.

"Is there anything else you like to do for fun?" Sapp probed.

"Nope." With another short answer, Cassie had hoped Sapp would get the message, and leave her alone.

Sapp had a feeling Cassie was going to be short with him all night. Bewildered, he looked to his friend for an answer but Malik shrugged his shoulders.

The clan placed their dinner order and ate in silence. Thirty minutes later, Sapp wiped his face, placed his napkin on the table and stared at Cassie with a nervous smile. He was trying to find a way to break the ice between them.

Cassie spotted Sapp watching her from the corner of her eyes. He made her so nervous, she was unable to digest her food properly. She pushed her plate to the side, indicating she was through with her meal.

Dana intervened after noting the awkward exchange. "Cassie loves sports," she said to Sapp, "especially football."

Sapp turned to Cassie, and asked, "Who's your favorite team?"

"The Miami Dolphins," Cassie answered with a twinkle in her eye.

Sapp smiled. "Personally, I like the Baltimore Ravens."

Cassie balked at Sapp's preference. "You've got to be kidding!" She perked up as she ranted about the Ravens losing streak and comebacks over the past three years.

"Wow, you know a lot about football," Sapp indicated, sounding impressed. "Maybe we can go to a game together."

"Yeah, maybe," Cassie shyly replied.

The camaraderie around the table was nice and pleasant. That was, until Malik started talking about money. He turned to Cassie with a knowing smile. "Dana told me y'all gonna be getting your inheritance when y'all turn twenty-one."

"Yeah man," Malik boasted to Sapp, after Cassie did not respond. "Dana told me their grandfather owned the Toils and Day Paper Company."

Surprised by this revelation, Sapp's head snapped in Dana's direction. He personally knew the company Malik mentioned was worth billions. Out of curiosity, he asked Dana, "Who is your father?"

"Bobby Toil," Dana answered. "But my sister and I never met him. Our brother told us he's deceased."

"See man," Malik cheered as he turned to Sapp with excitement in his eyes. "We're sitting up here with two gold-mines."

Shaking her head, Cassie was fuming mad when she turned to Dana with a scowl on her face.

In response, Dana turned to Malik with an attitude. "Why did you have to bring that up? I told you about that in confidence."

Malik swatted at the air, diminishing Dana's concerns. "Baby, don't get all testy. We're just making small talk."

Dana rolled her eyes skyward.

"But since we're on the subject," Malik said with a smirk on his face, "I think we should live together when you go off to college."

"I don't think so," Dana countered. "You have to be enrolled in college to live on campus."

"You can live off campus with me," Malik smoothly replied. "Just tell your brother to get you an apartment in one of those high-class ivory castles," he added, envisioning a life of luxury. "What's more important?" he asked, after noting Dana's silence. "Making me happy, or making your brother happy?"

Dana looked into Malik's eyes and chose her words carefully. "I have to do well in college in order to get my inheritance. That is one of the stipulations."

"Stipulations!" Malik repeated with hearty laughter. "Look at my girl, using big words on a brotha."

"Malik, why don't you come to school with me?" Dana asked, hoping he would consider.

"Baby, I'm not smart like you," Malik reasoned. "Besides, don't you need a high school diploma first?"

Getting serious, Dana turned to face Malik. "I've been meaning to talk to you about that."

"About what?" Malik questioned with an attitude.

Dana glanced down at her drink before responding. "About returning to high school."

"Don't!" Malik scolded. "School ain't for a brotha like me."

Dana said, "My brother is going to trip when he finds out you dropped out of high school."

"So don't tell him," Malik bluntly replied.

Dana twisted her mouth, before asking, "What are you going to do when I go off to college?"

"I'll be around," Malik said with assurance. "I'm not going to let you go like that. Just know, wherever you go, I'll be close by." Then he looked at Dana with a big grin, before kissing her on the cheek. "Baby, stop sweatin' the small stuff. We gon' be alright."

Suddenly, Dana felt someone staring at them from the corner of her eyes. She looked over and saw two girls she recognized from her high school. Her eyes zoomed in on Tabatha Williams, who sported a gay pride insignia on her shirt.

"You have a problem?" Dana asked Tabatha with an attitude.

"No, do you?" Tabatha countered, her tone was harsh.

When Malik looked to see who Dana was talking to, he did not expect to see Tabatha, who was glaring at him while massaging her fists. He averted his eyes, figuring Tabatha was still brooding over the altercation he had with her sister a month earlier. In one of his drug induced rages, Malik had beaten her sister up, and gave her two black eyes. He was relieved Tabatha's sister refused to file domestic charges against him.

Dana rolled her eyes at Tabatha as she turned to Malik, and asked, "What is her problem?"

"Chill out," Malik pleaded with Dana. "Just ignore her."

"I don't know why she's looking at me like that," Dana snapped, "but she's about to get slapped."

"Damn Dana!" Malik shouted. "I said chill out."

With narrowed eyes, Dana looked at Malik, and asked, "Do you know those dykes?"

Cassie cringed at the sound of that derogatory word, while Sapp looked on in silence.

Malik was going to lie but thought the truth sounded better. "Yeah, I know Tabatha, and her girl, Sammie."

"How do you know them?" Dana asked with crossed arms.

"We go way back from the hood. Let's get out of here and hit the club," Malik said, as he stood up to leave. Then he made a gesture for Sapp to pick up the tab.

As if on cue, Sapp left a one-hundred dollar bill on the table. Everyone, except Dana, stood up and followed Malik to the exit.

Dana took her time walking by Sammie and Tabatha's table with slanted eyes and a chip on her shoulder. She wondered if there was something more going on between Tabatha and Malik.

"She has no idea who she's dealing with," Tabatha said to her friend Sammie, who was sitting directly across from her.

"Don't worry," Sammie assured Tabatha, "she's the type of female that got to learn the hard way."

Tabatha nodded. "Yeah, that's if she lives long enough to tell her side of the story."

Chapter 17

Hot Pursuit

*F*or the past two weeks, Alex and Rhaunda were seemingly in-love, and committed to working things out. Rhaunda was beginning to believe Alex was sincere about hanging up his playboy card. For the first time in their relationship, Rhaunda was truly happy. She loved Alex with all her heart, and was ready to become his wife.

Alex was also feeling good about the progress he had made to mend their relationship. He was surprised Rhaunda's parents warmed up to him, but wondered if they were genuine. He knew they did not trust him to be faithful to their daughter, so he made a concerted effort to avoid being in compromising situations with beautiful women.

When Alex returned home from work one day, he was stumped to find a beautiful chocolate Nubian princess standing in front of his condo. He climbed out of his car with apprehension. "Hello," he said, as he approached the strange but familiar-looking woman.

Alecia Kellam was wearing a sleek black tight-fitting dress, an over-sized floppy hat tilted to one side, dark brown sunglasses, and diamond-studded stiletto heels. She looked like a professional runway model, ready for a photo-op for *Cover Girl* magazine. She greeted Alex with a warm smile. "Hi handsome."

Alex looked around to see if Alecia was, indeed, talking to him. "Do I know you?"

Grinning, Alecia removed her hat and sunglasses, to give Alex a clear view of her face. "I'm Alecia Kellam, Rhaunda's best friend. You remember," she said with soft laughter. "We attended graduate school together."

Alex shook her hand, then squinted his eyes as if remembering. He instantly recognized the one and only Alecia Kellam. She was the same woman who tried to hit on him in graduate school. "I remember you," he dryly said. "What can I do for you?"

"I just relocated to Tampa," she happily announced, "and was wondering if you could give me a *personal* tour."

"Come on, now," Alex light-heartedly said, "you know I can't do that. Besides, Rhaunda is your best friend."

"I know," Alecia cooed, as she twirled her long black, curly hair and batted her big Diana Ross eyes. "But I was hoping we can be discreet."

"Like sex buddies?" Alex teased with nervous laughter.

"Sounds good to me. How about it?" Her question was seductive and tempting.

Looking around, Alex wondered if he was being pranked. "You've got to be kidding," he said, as she turned to face Alecia.

"Do I look like someone who plays games?" she asked, but did not wait for a response. "I like you. I've always liked you."

Without further thought, Alex flat out said, "I don't think so. Tell Rhaunda I'll see her at the revival service tomorrow tonight." He unlocked his door and walked inside, closing the door behind him. He did not think twice about Alecia and the little stunt she tried to pull.

Stunned, Alecia returned to her car feeling deflated. Things were not working out as she and Rhaunda's mother had anticipated. When she relocated to Tampa, Elizabeth assured her that Alex and Rhaunda were no longer an item, and had even convinced her to pursue him.

Alecia sat behind the steering wheel of her car, thinking about Alex's plan to go to Rhaunda's church for the revival service. Bells and whistles went off in her head as she retrieved her cell phone from her purse and dialed Rhaunda's house number.

Grimacing, Alecia was put off when Rhaunda's father answered her call. "Uh...Mr...I mean Pastor Coleman, how are you?" she asked, remembering the last time she had asked, the pastor had given her a mini sermon.

"Is this Alecia?" Pastor Coleman enthusiastically inquired.

Alecia rolled her eyes as she bore a plastered smile. "Yes, sir."

Ever since Alecia's father donated ten thousand dollars to Pastor Coleman's church, the pastor had bent over backwards to be extra nice to her.

"How's your father?" the pastor probed.

Alecia eased out onto the highway before stating, "He's fine. He told me to tell you hello." Alecia flat out lied for reasons unknown to her. "Is Rhaunda there?" she asked, to cut the conversation short.

"Yes she is. Hold on." After the pastor called out for Rhaunda, he returned to the phone. "Alecia, it was good talking to you. Hopefully, you can make it to the revival service tomorrow night."

"I wouldn't miss it for the world," Alecia stressed with excitement.

"Dad, I got it," Rhaunda interrupted, after she picked up the phone in her bedroom,

"Alecia," the pastor said before disconnecting the call, "remember what I told you. Let me know if you need anything."

Rhaunda waited until her father hung up the phone before she greeted her friend. "Hi Alecia. I haven't heard from you in a while."

Alecia rolled her eyes skyward. She thought if it weren't for Alex, Rhaunda would never hear from her. "I'm sorry, I've been busy unpacking. You know how it is."

"I thought you were serious about coming to church, and giving your life to the Lord."

"Yes I am, which is why I'm calling."

"Really?" Rhaunda asked with an arched brow.

"Yes!" Alecia cheerfully replied with a plastered smile. "I've been thinking long and hard lately about my relationship with God," she deceitfully replied. "I personally think the Lord has answered *your* prayers."

"What do you mean?"

"You told me every time we spoke, you were praying for me. So, your prayers have been answered."

"Praise the Lord!" Rhaunda rejoiced. "We have a revival service tomorrow night. Would you like to come?" she inquired, hoping Alecia was committed to giving her life to the Lord.

Alecia drove into the parking space in front of her apartment building, before asking, "Are you sure I won't be imposing?"

"Not at all," Rhaunda answered. "I can pick you up if you prefer."

"I'd appreciate that," Alecia stated, while balancing her cell phone to her ear. "I've never been to a revival service. What should I expect?" she asked, as she climbed out of her car and bolted upstairs to her apartment.

While Rhaunda gave her the long spiel about the traditions of a typical revival service, Alecia unlocked her front door, strolled into her apartment and headed for her bedroom. Then she stepped out of her shoes, threw her purse on the dresser, and sat on her bed.

"I'll pick you up at six," Rhaunda stated, after hearing silence on the other end of the line.

"Thanks, I'll see you tomorrow."

After disconnecting the call, Alecia turned on her Bose stereo system in her bedroom and started playing her favorite song, "I'm Going to Make You Love Me" by Diana Ross and the Supremes. Then she laid across her bed and started thinking about the day she and Alex would be together. "Alex Simmons!" she sang aloud, while squeezing her pillow. "I'm going to make you love me!"

Alecia had traveled all over the world, and had everything her heart desired, but she wanted Alex. She was mesmerized by his good looks and charm. The word *sexy,* she determined, was synonymous with Alex Simmons. When she found out he and Rhaunda were dating again, she could not believe it. She thought to herself, *Why should Alex settle for Ms. Goodie Two-shoes, when he could have someone experienced like me?*

After Rhaunda hung up with Alecia, she felt good about the prospect of seeing her friend again. They were the same age, but their lifestyles drastically differed. Whereas Rhaunda was extremely religious and conservative, Alecia was a free spirit, often sleeping with different men on a whim.

Despite their differences, Rhaunda had given Alecia the benefit of the doubt. She was an optimist, who believed everyone was capable of changing *with God's help.* Because of her strong relationship with God, Rhaunda had dismissed Alecia's unsolicited advice, when she had called her last month to discuss Alex's rendezvous with his secretary, Maria Gomez.

"Alex is a playboy," Alecia had explained over the phone. "You need to wake up and smell the coffee. A man like Alex has needs. If you don't provide them, someone else will."

Rhaunda was crushed, but wanted to believe Alex was nothing like Alecia portrayed him to be. She wondered why she had bothered calling Alecia in the first place, especially since her friend had always spoken negatively about Alex.

Chapter 18

See Your True Colors

Entering the club first, Malik started dancing and moving to the hip hop music, blaring from the surround sound speakers. Dana laughed at Malik's footloose antics, while Sapp and Cassie shook their heads in disbelief.

"Oh, that's my song!" Malik excitedly shouted, as he grabbed Dana's hand and headed to the dance floor. "C'mon baby, let's dance!"

Cassie and Sapp stood near the entrance staring at each other, before averting their eyes to the dance floor. After an awkward moment of silence, Sapp turned to Cassie, and asked, "Would you like to dance?"

"No," Cassie simply replied.

"Are you sure?" Sapp prodded.

"I don't dance," she lied. In fact, Cassie loved dancing, especially in the privacy of her bedroom. She was nervous because she had never come close to being within inches of the opposite sex.

Sapp said, "You sure you don't want to give it a try?"

"Uh...um....," she stammered, "maybe we should sit this one out."

"Why? I have on deodorant," Sapp teased, as he lifted his arm and pretended to sniff.

Cassie giggled in response.

Sapp smiled. "Would you like a drink?"

"Sure."

In silence, Sapp guided Cassie to a vacant table where they sat across from each other. Minutes later, a waitress came to their table to take their drink orders. Sapp ordered two beers for both of them.

Cassie held up her hand, as she proclaimed, "I don't drink."

"Just take a sip," Sapp insisted. "You might like it."

The waitress returned to the table with two bubbly beers. When she placed a mug of beer in front of Cassie, Sapp urged her to try it. She took a sip, but the frown on her face spoke volumes.

Sapp laughed in response. "Okay, I'll order you a coke."

"I'd appreciate that," Cassie said, as she pushed the beer aside.

Several minutes later, Malik and Dana appeared at their table drenching in sweat. Dana sat down next to Cassie, and grabbed a napkin off the table to wipe the sweat from her forehead. Also exhausted from dancing, Malik flopped down in the chair next to Sapp.

"Ya'll not gonna dance?!" Malik jovially asked Cassie and Sapp, while bopping his head back and forth to the sound of the music.

"Nah man," Sapp replied, as he shook his head. "I can't get Cassie on the dance floor."

Dana playfully nudged Cassie's shoulder with hers. "Go on Cassie. Show Sapp some of your moves."

"She can dance?" Sapp asked in disbelief.

"Not only can she dance," Dana boasted, "but she was in a step-dance class a couple of years ago."

Cassie's eyes grew bigger, realizing there was nothing she could say to counter the truth.

"C'mon, Cassie," Dana urged, "give him a chance."

Sapp held out his hand for Cassie's. "Trust me," he insisted, "it'll be fun."

After extending her trembling hand to Sapp, Cassie allowed him to guide her on the dance floor. She stood motionless, while Sapp threw his hands in the air and started gyrating. His dance techniques were so good, the other dancers formed a circle around him, cheering him on.

Feeling numb, Cassie stood in one place. She wondered if everyone could see how uncomfortable she was on the dance floor.

"Come on, Cassie," Sapp encouraged as he bumped her hip with his, "show me what you're working with."

Coincidentally, Cassie started moving her hips from side to side. Then she began shaking her body, losing control to the groove of the beat. She was so involved in her dance moves, she did not notice the crowd forming around her. Sapp stood back with a look of amazement before he joined the crowd cheering Cassie on.

When the fast song went off and a slow love song came on, Cassie stopped in her tracks. She was unsure of what to do next.

"Come on," Sapp said after sensing Cassie's uneasiness, "let's sit this song out."

"Thank you," Cassie softly said, after breathing a sigh of relief.

Sapp smiled after observing her reaction. "You've never been out with a guy before, have you?"

Caught off guard by his question, Cassie stepped away from Sapp, and asked with a trembling voice, "What are you talking about?"

"Nothing," Sapp answered, feeling as though he was losing his way to Cassie's heart. "Let's enjoy the night."

Cassie stopped in her tracks, unable to form an adequate response. "I'm going home," she finally announced, before rushing toward the exit.

"But wait!" Sapp called out from the dance floor. "Why are you leaving?!"

Cassie did not look back. She was determined to get as far away from Sapp as she possibly could.

When Dana spotted Cassie heading out of the club, she stood up and ran after her. "Cassie!" she called out. "Where are you going?!"

Glancing back at Dana, Cassie simply said, "Home."

"Why?" Dana whined. "Aren't you having a good time?"

"This was a mistake."

"What was a mistake?" Dana asked. Then she became frustrated when Cassie remained quiet. "Talk to me," she insisted.

Choked up, Cassie tried to hold back tears, with little success. "I'm not attracted to him," she admitted, as tears rolled down her face. "Why me, Dana?" she cried out.

"It's going to be okay," Dana said, as she hugged her sister. "I'll go tell Malik to take us home."

"No, that's not necessary," Cassie replied, trying not to sound like a party-pooper. "Go back inside, and have a good time."

"Are you sure?"

Cassie nodded, then flagged down the first taxicab that drove up in front of the club.

Shortly after, Sapp walked out of the club and spotted Cassie getting into the cab. He approached Dana, and asked, "What's wrong with her?"

"Nothing," Dana offhandedly replied. "Let's go back inside. I think I saw one of my girlfriends I can introduce you to."

Sapp stood still, frowning. "Did she leave because of me?"

Dana turned to Sapp and smiled. "It has nothing to do with you. It's complicated."

When Dana and Sapp went inside the club, Dana spotted Malik ordering more drinks. She exhaled as she approached the table. "Malik, don't you think you've had enough to drink?"

"Chill out!" Malik demanded, slurring his words. "You're *my* woman! Know your place!"

Dana rolled her eyes as she turned to Sapp. "Come on, Sapp. I want to introduce you to my girlfriend."

After making the introductions, Dana rejoined Malik, who had just downed three shots of Grey Goose. She noticed he was becoming louder and more obnoxious by the second. When he asked for a refill, she became worried. Once before, she had witnessed how liquor had turned Malik into a violent person.

"Babe," Dana pleaded, as she tried to take the shot glass out of Malik's hand, "I think you've had enough."

Malik turned ice cold before exploding. "What in the *hell* are you doing?!"

Dana placed her hand on top of his. "Malik," she said with caution, "please take me home."

Suddenly, Malik slammed the shot glass on the table, drew back his fist and punched Dana in the face with all his might. He stood back and gloated as she fell out of her chair and onto the floor. She struggled to get up, but the stinging pain from Malik's fist left her temporarily immobile. Covering her face with her hands, Dana began crying, nonstop.

Sensing all eyes were on him, Malik was suddenly remorseful. He knelt down beside Dana, rubbing her shoulder. "Baby," he whispered, "I'm sorry."

Dana pushed Malik's hand away, yelling, "Don't you dare touch me!" She struggled to gather her bearings as she stood up and rushed toward the exit.

Malik tried running after her, but Sapp grabbed him.

Effortlessly, Sapp contained Malik, as he was much bigger and stronger. "Man, let her go!" he insisted.

"Get off of me!" Malik shouted. "That's my woman!"

Determined to keep Malik away from Dana, Sapp grabbed his friend around the waist, and would not let go. "At this rate," he struggled to say, "you're going to lose her. Let her go."

"Damn!" Malik exclaimed. "That's my meal ticket. I need to make things right," he stressed, trying to pull out of Sapp's grasp.

Sapp shook his head. "Not tonight. You need to go home and sober up, first. I'll drive you."

Malik had known Sapp long enough to realize he would not take *no* for an answer. He felt as if he had known Sapp his entire life. Sluggishly, he retrieved his keys from his pocket before handing them to Sapp. When Malik took a step forward, he lost his balance, crashing to the floor.

Sapp put one of his arms around Malik's shoulders, and the other around his waist to help him stand up. Suddenly, Malik broke free of Sapp's stronghold, and rushed to the restroom. The liquor had taken a toll on him.

Quickly, Sapp followed Malik to the restroom. He wondered if Malik would ever get his act together. He walked into the stall and noticed his friend over the toilet, vomiting. Disgusted, Sapp grabbed two paper towels and handed them to Malik. "Come on, man," he urged, "let's get out of here."

Sapp drove Malik to his apartment in silence. Then he had to practically carry him upstairs, which was on the second floor. Sapp unlocked the door and turned on the lights, then nudged Malik in the direction of the sofa.

"I need to talk to Dana," Malik slurred, before collapsing on the sofa.

"No," Sapp countered. "You need to stay home and sober up. You're in no condition to drive. I'm taking your keys with me, just in case."

Malik did not hear Sapp. He had drifted into a deep sleep. Within minutes, he was sprawled out on the sofa, snoring.

Sapp left Malik's apartment, reflecting on their friendship over the past couple of months. He was getting tired of watching after his friend, always having his back. Sapp had contemplated telling Malik's father, Abdul Mitchell, he was tired of being an *undercover* bodyguard.

When Sapp first arrived in Tampa several months earlier, he was surprised to find Malik living in a vacant, run-down apartment. At the time, Malik was also selling drugs for a local drug dealer, and engaging in street fights.

Sapp had approached Malik as he was walking out of his apartment. "Yo man," he said trying to sound hip, "I'm looking for an address. Can you help me out?"

Quick to take advantage of a money-making opportunity, Malik held up five fingers as he requested five dollars in return for the information.

Sapp smiled as he pulled out a twenty-dollar bill and handed it to Malik. "Keep the change."

Smiling, Malik took the money and stuffed it in his pocket. "Okay, what address are you looking for?"

On purpose, Sapp looked above Malik's head, across the apartment complex. "Never mind, I see the address I was looking for," he lied.

Malik chuckled. "You know I'm not giving you your money back."

Sapp cracked a smile. "No problem, I'm hungry. You want to go get a bite to eat?"

"Yeah, I'm down," Malik quickly agreed. "You buying?"

Sapp smiled, admiring Malik's hustle. "Yes, I'm buying."

During lunch, Sapp had discovered it would be easy to lure Malik with money. He had given his new friend an offer he could not refuse. He had agreed to lease an apartment for him, and for every dollar Malik made on the streets, Sapp had agreed to pay him the same amount to stay off the streets.

When Sapp got involved with Malik, he never thought things would turn out so badly. He witnessed how *'the love of money'* changed Malik, and not for the better. After Malik started drinking and doing drugs, Sapp knew it would be a matter of time before his new friend got into trouble with the law.

Unlike Malik, Sapp was accustomed to an enriched lifestyle. He had come from a privileged background, thanks to his grandparents. After high school, he went to Harvard to pursue a degree in Criminal Law. During his senior year, he was required to write a thesis, so he decided to write about a world he was unfamiliar with; the drug and gang world, which was how he got involved with Malik.

A friend had introduced Sapp to Chico, a die-hard criminal, who in turn, had introduced him to Abdul Mitchell, which happened to be Malik's father. Sapp had lied when he told Abdul he was in dire need of money, and wanted to work for him. Initially, Abdul had rejected the idea, but after thinking of how Sapp could benefit him, he hired him on the spot.

Abdul thought Sapp and Malik were the same age, so he paid Sapp to discreetly look after his estranged son. Though, Sapp was actually twenty-two years old, a fact he failed to disclose to his new boss. Sapp figured his youthful appearance got him the job. Abdul told Sapp to help Malik wherever there was a need. Money was never an issue. Whatever Malik wanted, Sapp gave it to him, courtesy of Abdul. Sapp figured that was the problem.

Sapp had called Abdul two weeks earlier, and told him Malik had started drinking and doing drugs. But, Abdul had assured Sapp that it was just a phase. Sapp did not agree. He was concerned that someone was going to get hurt behind Malik's violent outbursts. In light of the recent incident, Sapp made one promise to himself: *Malik will never get another opportunity to put his hands on Dana again.*

✸

Scared and embarrassed, Dana ran out of the club to get away from Malik. To her amazement, a cab pulled up in front of her as if on cue. "You called for a taxi?" the cab driver with a foreign accent inquired.

Without answering the cabbie's question, Dana climbed into the backseat.

"Where to?" the cabbie asked, as he turned to face Dana.

To delay confronting Guy, Dana leaned over and told the cab driver to take her over to her friend, Pam Dixon's house. Using her cell phone, she called Pam and told her that she was on her way. She knew her friend's parents were not home. Pam's father had moved out of the house several months ago, and her mother worked the graveyard shift at the hospital as a nurse.

Still feeling the sting from Malik's fist, Dana retrieved her compact mirror from her purse to look at her face. She started crying at the sight of redness around her jaw, which was visible on her very pale complexion. Dana tried to conceal the red mark by applying a ton of facial powder, to no avail.

"Oh God," she sobbed, "how am I going to explain this to Guy?" She sat back in the cab, reflecting on why she decided to stay with Malik, since this was not the first time he hit her.

When they first met, Malik had told Dana about his life growing up without his father. He had also told her that his mother was a prostitute and up until he was eight years old, she would take him with her to hang out in the lobby of the hotel while she satisfied her Johns. One day, Malik's mother never returned to the lobby to retrieve him. He became worried, so he notified the hotel clerk. The clerk called the room his mother had checked into, but there was no answer. So she asked Malik to wait in the lobby before she went to his mother's room to find out what happened.

After knocking, the clerk unlocked the door with the master key, and was shocked to find Malik's mother sprawled out on the floor, lying naked and bloodied. Immediately, she rushed back to the lobby and dialed nine-one-one. The police and ambulance workers had stormed the hotel within minutes. Hopelessly, Malik watched the paramedics wheel his mother's lifeless body out of the hotel. He had never gotten over that moment, or the fact that the police never found his mother's killer.

Every time Dana told Malik she was ending their relationship, he would tell her the same sob story. Feeling guilty, she would repeatedly give him chances to make it right between them. However, this recent incident had Dana doubting his sincerity. She knew Malik's life had taken a turn for the worse when he started drinking, excessively.

During the ride to Pam's house, Dana was unsure if she should break up with Malik. She loved him in spite of his violent temper. When the cab driver parked in front of her friend's house, she paid the driver, then called her sister's cell phone. "Hi Cassie, I called to see if you made it home."

"Where are you?" Cassie whispered.

Dana frowned. "Why are you whispering?"

"Because I'm in the garage, waiting for you," Cassie explained, ducking down on the side of Guy's Mercedes Benz. "Guy and Regine don't know I'm home."

Perplexed, Dana asked, "Why not?"

"Because I don't want them to know I arrived home without you."

Dana exhaled with relief. "I'm right around the corner, at Pam's house. Can you come over here?"

"I'm on my way."

Five minutes later, Cassie appeared at Pam's doorsteps. She was happy to see her sister, but freaked out when she saw Dana's face. "What happened?!"

Dana covered the bruise with her hand. "I fell down," she lied.

"Stop lying!" Cassie shouted. "How dare Malik put his hands on you! I'm going to kill him!"

"Calm down," Dana insisted, looking around to see if anyone could hear them. She was relieved Pam had gone to sleep early. "Come inside and be quiet."

"Fine," Cassie said as she sauntered through the front door, "but whatever you have to say, won't change my mind about that idiot. Malik is such a coward. I wonder if he would ever hit a real man."

With her eyes glued to the floor, Dana pondered Cassie's comments. She knew her sister was right about Malik, but realized they had more pressing issues. "We have to call Guy and Regine, to tell them we're here."

"I'll call them," Cassie volunteered.

Dana was relieved. She knew Guy would not believe her if she had called. Lately, Guy had caught her in so many lies, even Dana could not believe some of the stuff she came up with.

Cassie used Pam's house phone to add legitimacy to their whereabouts. As soon as her brother answered, she said, "Hello Guy, I'm calling to let you know we're okay."

"Where are you girls?" Guy asked, as he looked at the grandfather clock on the wall in the living room. "You should have been home an hour ago."

"I know," Cassie conceded, "but we ran into Pam. She agreed to give us a ride home, so Malik wouldn't have to drive so far." Cassie's lie sounded believable.

"Are you on your way home?"

Cassie bit her bottom lip while she thought of a good response. "If you don't mind," she finally said, "we'd like to spend the night with Pam. She's right around the corner."

Guy paused before responding. "Why can't you come home tonight?"

"We wanted to spend some time with Pam. Her mother is here," Cassie added, to give more credence to her lie. "You want to talk to her?" she egged on, hoping her bluff did not backfire.

As Cassie had suspected, Guy looked at the caller ID. "No, that's not necessary. I'll see you girls in the morning."

"Okay." Cassie hung up with a look of satisfaction. But when she looked up and saw the red mound on the side of Dana's face, she became angry all over again. Deep down, in the pit of her belly, she wanted to kill Malik.

Chapter 19

Priorities

*A*fter Guy hung up the phone, he felt uneasy. He had a feeling Cassie was hiding something. With the phone still in his hand, he mulled over her explanation for why she and Dana did not come home.

"Was that the girls?" Regine asked, as she turned away from the television. She and Guy were in the living room watching the late night news before Cassie called.

Nodding, Guy put the phone on its cradle. "They'll be home in the morning."

"Why?" Regine asked, as she peered in her husband's eyes for a response.

"They wanted to spend the night with Pam. You know, the young lady that lives around the corner."

"Why didn't they come home?"

"I don't know," Guy nonchalantly replied, not wanting his wife to worry.

Regine used the remote control to turn off the television. "Guy, let's go to bed," she said, as she stood up. Guy nodded as he stood up and walked with Regine toward their bedroom.

Mimi was right around the corner in the kitchen, eavesdropping on Regine and Guy's conversation. She walked into the living room as they were headed to their bedroom. "Mr. and Mrs. Simmons, are Dana and Cassie okay?" she asked with deep concern. "I see they're not home yet."

Agitated, Guy looked at Mimi with narrowed eyes. "I appreciate your concern," he said in a stern voice, "but let me worry about Dana and Cassie."

Mimi began wringing her hands. She was unsure of how to respond. "Oh...uh...yes sir," she muttered. "I understand." Promptly, Mimi excused herself and went to her bedroom.

Regine was confused over the exchange between Mimi and Guy. "Why did you talk to her in that manner?" she asked, as soon as they walked into their bedroom. "Mimi was concerned about the twins, that's all."

Guy sighed as he took off his robe. "I just get the eerie feeling that she's too involved in our lives."

Regine frowned. "What do you expect? Mimi is around us twenty-four/seven."

"Maybe I'm just being paranoid."

Regine chuckled as she removed her robe and took off her bedroom slippers. "I tend to agree. Lie down and get some rest."

Guy kissed Regine before they crawled under the covers and snuggled up. Regine had easily drifted off to sleep, but Guy found it difficult to close his eyes. He remained awake, worried about the twins.

The next morning, Regine woke up to find her husband in a deep sleep. She was relieved because she felt Guy tossing and turning in bed all night. She did not want to disturb him, so she quietly got out of bed, to prepare for work. Regine was in her bathroom when she heard her son screaming. She ran into his bedroom and found him bundled on the floor, crying non-stop.

As usual, KC had gotten up early to play with his toys. He felt a sharp pain in his ankle after he fell over his toy truck.

"What's the matter, KC?!" Regine cried out, as she knelt down and gathered him in her arms. When KC pointed, she noticed a huge mound on his ankle. Breaking out into hysteria, Regine hollered for Guy.

Thinking the worse, Guy jumped out of bed and rushed into KC's room. "What's the matter?!" he frantically asked Regine.

Regine pointed to KC's ankle. "He's hurt," she explained with sadness in her voice.

Guy knelt down beside Regine and inspected KC's injury. "I think he sprained his ankle."

"We should take him to the doctor," Regine suggested, as she cuddled KC in her arms.

"It hurt, Momma," KC whimpered, as tears poured down his face.

"I know baby," Regine replied in a soothing voice. "We're going to take you to the doctor, so he can make you feel better."

Guy gently rubbed KC's back as he spoke to Regine. "I think he'll receive quicker care if *you* take him to the hospital. I'm going to stay here and wait for the girls to come home."

"Guy, the girls are fine," Regine countered with an attitude. "*We,* as in you and I, have to take KC to the hospital."

"You go ahead without me," he persisted. "I'll meet you at the hospital later on."

"KC should be your first priority!" Regine shouted with gusto.

"Why are you making a big deal out of this?" Guy asked out of frustration. "It's just a small bruise."

"That's not the point!" Regine exclaimed.

Guy firmly said, "I don't want to argue about this."

Regine shook her head in disgust. "You can't protect the twins from life," she snapped.

"My siblings are my responsibility," Guy pointed out with bass in his voice.

Regine sighed. "Dana and Cassie will be eighteen next year, and Alex just turned twenty-five. When are you going to cut the umbilical cord?"

"You will never understand," Guy mumbled, before stomping out of KC's bedroom.

"Understand what?!" Regine yelled to his back.

Turning around with a scowl on his face, Guy said, "My job is to protect my siblings."

"Guy, trust me. Nothing is going to happen to them."

"Can you put that in writing?"

Blankly, Regine stared at Guy. She was speechless.

"Just what I thought," Guy stated, after Regine remained mum.

"But they're not kids anymore," she made clear. "The girls feel trapped with the bodyguard you hired to watch over them. They need a little freedom. For once, they want to be normal; just like all the other kids their age. If you don't ease up, they will rebel."

Guy was getting ready to respond, but Regine held up her hand to silence him. "I can assure you that Dana will rebel," she emphasized, "more so than Cassie. I know you love the twins. I love them too, but you're smothering them."

Regine sighed after Guy did not respond. "I'll be at the hospital tending to *our* child, if you need me."

Ten minutes earlier, Mimi had awakened after hearing the commotion. Fearing backlash from Guy, she stayed in her room but cracked open her door to hear what was going on. As soon as Regine left for the hospital with KC in her arms, Mimi went to Jeanine's room.

Instantly, Jeanine's eyes shifted to her bedroom door. She was wide awake, finding it difficult to sleep more than three hours at a time. "What is it?" she asked, after noting worry lines on Mimi's forehead.

Before responding, Mimi walked into Jeanine's bedroom and closed the door behind her. She slowly turned to Jeanine with a cold stare.

"Mimi, tell me what's going on," Jeanine insisted, after sensing something terrible had happened.

"Dana...and Cassie," Mimi stammered, "they didn't come home. Mr. and Mrs. Simmons are worried sick about them."

"Oh God!" Jeanine cried out, as her hand flew to her chest. "Are they missing?"

"No, they spent the night with a friend."

Jeanine breathed a sigh of relief as she rested her head on her pillow. "So they're okay?"

"Yes, but Mr. Simmons suspects that they're hiding something."

"Is there anything else I should know?"

Mimi thought about telling Jeanine about KC but changed her mind. She knew Jeanine was crazy about her grandchild, and hearing news of his injury would probably cause her unnecessary grief.

After drilling Mimi for more information about the twins, Jeanine asked her to leave the room, so she could make an important phone call to the Toils and Day Paper Company. She thought it was time for the twins to know their biological father's family. More importantly, she thought the Toils should share the burden of protecting the twins.

Dana and Cassie returned home the next day, in the middle of the afternoon. They crept through the side door and eased the door closed, so as not to alert anyone of their presence.

Fully alert, Guy sat up on the sofa as soon as the twins walked by the living room. "Hi girls. Why don't you sit down and tell me how your date went?"

The twins stopped in their tracks, caught off guard by Guy's presence. "We had a good time," Cassie blurted out, after sensing Dana's nervousness.

"Yeah," Dana added, "we had a good time."

Guy knew when Dana was lying, and this was one of those times. He turned to Cassie, and asked, "Do you want to talk about your dates?"

"No," Cassie said as she grabbed Dana's hand, "maybe later."

When the twins walked past Guy, he became alarmed when his eyes zoomed in on Dana's face. He jumped up from the sofa to take a closer look.

"What?" Dana asked, as she instinctively put her hand over Malik's fist print.

Guy's nostrils flared from rage. "Move your hand!" he shouted.

When Dana removed her hand, Guy's body tensed up. "Who did this to you?!" His voice was filled with fury.

Dana began crying. She was unable to think of a plausible explanation. "We had a little disagreement," she weakly answered.

"We who?!" Guy barked. "Was it Malik?!"

"Yes," Dana softly replied with her head lowered. "It was an accident."

Shaking his head, Guy had a burning desire to punch Malik in the face. "You can't see him anymore!" he ordered. "You understand?!"

Dana attempted to put on a hard stance, but she broke down crying. Her voice cracked, as she stammered between sniffles, "You can't...tell me who...to see and...what to do."

"But Dana," Cassie said as she turned to her sister, "this was not the first time Malik put his hands on you. When are you going to realize your relationship with him is not healthy?"

Guy gasped as he turned to Cassie. "You knew Malik was beating on your sister, and you didn't tell me?"

Cassie froze up like a deer in headlights. She had never witnessed Malik hitting Dana, but assumed he had something to do with the black eye her sister had covered with makeup a couple of weeks earlier. It was the same day Dana had skipped school to be with Malik.

Before Cassie could respond, Regine walked through the front door with KC on her hip. The hospital physician had wrapped KC's sprained ankle in gauze and a snap-on cask. Regine entered the living room, and picked up on the tension in the room. Then she peered at Guy, who seemed like he was on the verge of exploding.

"Guy," Regine said in an almost pleading voice, "whatever it is, we'll talk about this later. Now is not a good time."

Guy turned to Dana with a scowl on his face. "You are not to see Malik anymore," he firmly repeated, "and I mean it! You don't know anything about *that* character."

"I know he loves me," Dana replied with conviction.

"Love doesn't hurt," Cassie interjected.

Dana turned to Cassie, and asked out of spite, "What do you know about love? You don't even like boys!" she shouted, before barging upstairs to her bedroom, slamming the door shut.

After Dana ran upstairs, Guy turned to Cassie, and asked, "What is your sister talking about?"

Cassie lowered her head. "I...don't...know," she stuttered. She felt deflated, wishing she could crawl under a rock.

Guy exhaled. He was unsure what Dana was implying about Cassie, but he did not think twice about it. He was still upset with Malik for putting his hands on Dana. Forcing himself to change focus, Guy turned to Regine, and asked, "How's KC?"

Regine smiled as she looked at KC in her arms. "He's fine. You were right. KC sprained his ankle."

"That's good to know," Guy said with relief.

When Guy extended his arms toward his son, KC happily went to him. He smiled before kissing KC on the cheek. "I'll take care of him," Guy said to Regine, before he walked upstairs to his son's bedroom.

As soon as Guy walked away with KC, Regine looked at Cassie, then rubbed her shoulder with care. "Do you want to talk about it?"

When Cassie remained silent, Regine suggested that they go to the green room, which was aligned with exotic plants and flowers, to talk in private. She followed Cassie into the green room, and closed the door behind them. "Have a seat," Regine instructed, pointing to the chair by the wall-to-wall glass windows.

Cassie sat on the chaise, looking out the windows, which were in clear sight of Regine's rose garden. "Why do you want to talk to me?" she softly asked, avoiding eye contact with Regine.

"Cassie," Regine said in a caring voice, "I've been noticing some changes in you. You've been quieter than usual. Whatever is troubling you, you can always talk to me. I love you."

Cassie turned to Regine, looking like she lost her best friend. "I love you too," she replied in a soft whisper.

Sensing Cassie's unwillingness to open up, Regine continued, "I've never been the one to beat around the bush, so I'm going to ask you directly. Are you gay?"

Cassie looked down at the floor, and shyly answered, "I don't know."

"Are you attracted to boys?"

"No."

"Are you attracted to girls?"

Cassie's eyes began to mist, and her voice cracked when she finally spoke. "No, I'm...so confused." Squirming in her chair, she grew uncomfortable talking to her sister-in-law.

"God made all of us unique," Regine said, as she leaned over and embraced Cassie. "I'm here for you. No matter what, I love you."

Cassie dried her tears with her hands. "May I be excused?"

Regine smiled and nodded her head.

As Guy headed to KC's room, he was startled when Mimi approached him from behind.

"Mr. Simmons," she said in a hurry, "how's KC?"

Guy was put off my Mimi's presence. He turned around, and said through gritted teeth, "He's fine."

"Is his ankle okay?" Mimi probed.

Ignorning Mimi's question, Guy said, "I'll let you know if we need anything."

Mimi gasped in astonishment as Guy turned his back to her and walked to KC's room. Quickly recovering from Guy's abrupt response, she went to Jeanine's room and explained KC's injury. Jeanine's reaction was better than she had anticipated.

Chapter 20

Lightning Strikes Back

*F*eeling overwhelmed, Guy sat in the rocker with KC in his arms. He was concerned about his son's injury, but he was also focused on Dana, and her recent altercation with Malik. He looked down and noticed his son had fallen asleep. After kissing KC on the cheek, Guy put him in bed, then headed to his office

Sitting at his desk, he carefully reviewed the investigative report Big Mike had given him a couple of days earlier. It outlined Malik's criminal history, current residence and hang out locations. It also provided the names and addresses of all the young women he was dating. It was four pm when he reached for the phone and called his brother.

Alex was at the bar with Bryce Jennings when his cell phone rang. He looked at the caller ID before he answered. "Hey Guy, what's up?"

"Dana's in trouble," Guy blurted out.

Alex turned away from Bryce, when he asked, "What happened?"

"The guy she was seeing beat her up," Guy admitted, still sizzling with anger.

"Are you serious?!" Alex shrieked, as he quickly stood up and walked away from the booth. He went to an isolated area near the restrooms, to talk in private. "When did this happen?"

"Last night," Guy stated.

"Damn! Did you ever tell Dana about Big Mike's investigation?"

A day before Dana and Cassie's seventeenth birthday, Guy was shocked when Big Mike called and told him Dana was dating a *loser*. Even more upsetting, Dana was just one of several girls Malik was seeing. By comparison, Big Mike told Guy that Dana was the smartest, the prettiest and the wealthiest.

Guy sighed as his eyes connected with Alex's. "I was hoping Dana would have been over Malik a long time ago. Besides, you know Dana. If I had told her about the investigation, it could have pushed her closer to him."

Alex did not agree with Guy but kept his feelings to himself. "What's this chump's name again?"

"Malik Mitchell."

"How can I forget?" Alex asked, rolling his eyes. "How do you want to deal with this?"

"I was thinking maybe you and I can pay him a visit."

"I agree."

"Good. I want to make sure this young man understands that if he ever puts his hands on Dana again, he will regret it."

Alex nodded in agreement. "I'm on my way."

Minutes earlier, Bryce had followed Alex and overheard part of his phone conversation. "Is everything okay?" he asked, as soon as Alex disconnected the call.

"I have to go!" Alex said in a hurry, as he rushed toward the exit.

Bryce was concerned about Alex, but for his own selfish reasons. He was disappointed when Alex had told him Guy would not readily go along with the merger deal. But he was not discouraged. Bryce made up his mind to try and get through to Guy, himself. He figured if Guy was anything like his brother, convincing him to agree to the merger deal would be a piece of cake. In the meantime, Bryce hoped that it was not too late to get back in Sidney's good graces, especially since he had ignored his phone calls for the past three weeks.

After disconnecting the call with Alex, Guy dashed to the bedroom to get dressed. He was so focused on dealing with Malik, he walked right past Regine without acknowledging her.

Figuring Guy was up to something, Regine followed him into their bedroom. She became concerned when she saw Guy changing his clothes. "Hon', where are you going?"

"Out." Guy gave her the short answer on purpose.

Leaning against the door with one hand on her hip, Regine waited for Guy to elaborate. After noting Guy's silence, she asked, "Out where?"

Guy sighed as he glanced at Regine. "The less you know, the better. Don't worry, I'll be home soon."

"You're not going anywhere until I get some answers," Regine firmly stated. She was tired of being left in the dark.

Guy ignored Regine as he slipped on his jeans and pulled his sweatshirt over his head. Then he sat down and put on his socks and sneakers.

Regine gripped the doorknob, trying to contain her anger. "Guy, are you listening to me!" she shouted with vigor.

Blankly, Guy stared at his wife, before he said, "This has nothing to do with you."

"What has nothing to do with me?!" Regine angrily questioned. "Why won't you talk to me?"

Rushing to the bedroom closet, Guy opened the door and retrieved a lockbox from the top shelf. He used the key he hid in his wallet to open the lockbox. With care, he retrieved a nine-millimeter gun and a loaded clip.

"Guy!" Regine hollered. "You promised to get rid of that thing!"

He had purchased the gun after Jeanine had warned him to protect his family at all costs. The gun was the first thing that came to his mind.

"I'm going to get rid of the gun," Guy said as he turned to Regine, "after tonight." He tucked the gun in his jacket pocket, then grabbed his car keys. Thinking clearly, he had planned on using the gun to threaten Malik.

"Guy!" Regine barked. "We have a family. What about KC?"

He turned to Regine with narrowed eyes. "Dana is also my family!"

Regine shook her head in disbelief. "So, you're willing to jeopardize our family over a fight between teenagers."

"Just stay out of this!" Guy demanded, as he rushed past her toward the front door.

On the verge of tears, Regine stood in one place, believing her marriage was falling apart. In the eight years she had known Guy, he had never lashed out at her.

Guy was tempted to turn around and apologize to Regine for his hostile reaction, but his anger toward Malik outweighed that option. To avoid arguing, he thought it was best to wait outside for Alex.

Twenty minutes later, Alex pulled up in the driveway. He frowned as he watched Guy climb behind the wheel of his Mercedes Benz.

When Alex remained in one place, Guy reached over, threw the passenger door open, and yelled, "Get in!"

After Alex got in the car and buckled up, he asked, "Where are we going?"

"To the club Malik frequents," Guy answered, after deep thought. Big Mike's investigative report stated Malik hung out at the Roundtree Bar and Club in Tampa.

As soon as Guy walked out of the front door, Regine picked up the phone to call her mother, Sue Croswell-Randolf. She and her mother were estranged for almost twenty years before they rekindled their relationship a year earlier.

"What is it, baby?" Sue asked. Her voice was filled with worry. She had just awakened out of a deep sleep.

"It's Guy," Regine admitted, trying to hold back tears. "I think he's going to do something crazy."

Instantly alert, Sue sat up in bed, giving her daughter her full attention. "Tell me what's going on."

Regine explained the rift between Guy and Dana's boyfriend, then asked, "What do you think I should do?"

"Do you know where Dana's boyfriend lives?"

"Yes," Regine confirmed. Without Guy's knowledge, she went to his office, rummaged through his desk, and found Malik's investigative report. "His name is Malik Mitchell, and he lives in the Kinston apartments. Do you think I should intervene?"

Sue shook her head. "No, that's not a good idea. You have to believe that your husband knows what he's doing."

Regine was choked up as she stated, "I feel like I'm in the dark. I don't know what to do."

"I know, baby," Sue replied sympathetically. Let's pray for your marriage, and for Guy's safety."

After Sue prayed feverishly, Regine felt somewhat better, but knew her mind would not be at ease until Guy returned home. "Thank you, Mom."

"No problem, baby. Try not to worry."

After Sue hung up, she called Regine's father, Kevin. Sue wanted him to stop Guy from doing something he would later regret. "Hi Kevin, it's me, Sue."

Kevin smiled. "Hi Sue, it's good to hear from you."

"I need your help. I believe Guy is on his way to confront his sister's boyfriend."

Kevin frowned. "Which one?"

"Dana."

"What happened?"

"Guy went berserk after Dana's boyfriend hit her."

"What's the boyfriend's name?"

"Malik Mitchell. Regine told me he lives in Kingston apartments in Tampa."

Kevin nodded, remembering Kingston used to be one of his stomping grounds when he sold drugs for a living. "Don't worry. I'll take care of the problem."

"Kevin!" Sue called out, before disconnecting the call.

"What's up?"

"No killing this time."

"You know how I roll," Kevin said, before he hung up the phone.

Sue felt relieved to know Regine's father was involved. Though, she was troubled over her daughter's mental state. After returning the phone to its cradle, she turned to her husband, Richard, with sadness in her eyes.

Lovingly, Richard rubbed Sue's back. He woke up after Sue received Regine's call earlier. "Say the word," he said in her ear, "and I'll do anything you want me to."

Sue smiled, feeling comforted by his words. "You can never return to the United States. I can't take that risk."

"Baby, I will die for you."

"I know, but I'll let Kevin take care of this." Sue knew her husband loved her, and would do anything to make her happy.

"Whatever you decide," Richard said, as he sat up and looked into Sue's eyes, "I'm behind you one hundred percent, even if it means sacrificing my life."

"I know, honey," Sue said, before she kissed her husband on the lips.

Two years earlier, Richard had helped her get even with Justina Reyes, her daughter's best friend. Sue sought vengeance after Justina wreaked havoc on Regine and Guy's lives. But she did not know her husband, a stranger at the time, was paid to make Justina's life a living hell. By the time Sue and Richard found out about each other, he had managed to take everything Justina owned. Unfortunately, his actions had landed him on America's Most Wanted list.

At six pm, Guy and Alex pulled in front of the Roundtree Bar and Club with one target in mind: *Malik Mitchell*. The club scene was what Guy had imagined: a whole in the wall with no security guard in sight. They looked around but did not find Malik. As they were prepared to leave, Alex looked around the bar and spotted a young man who looked to be about Malik's age. "Hi there," he said as he approached Sapp, "do you know someone named Malik?"

With narrow eyes, Sapp looked Alex up and down before responding. "Yeah, I know him. Why do you want to know?"

"We're his girlfriend's brothers," Guy interjected, as he eyed Sapp. "Weren't you on a date with Cassie last night?"

Sapp nodded after recognizing Guy. "Yeah, how's Dana?"

Guy glanced at Alex before turning back to Sapp. "She's fine. So I take it you know Malik put his hands on her. Were you there?"

"Listen man," Sapp said as he stood up to face Guy, "Malik was drunk."

"I know," Guy said, more for Sapp's benefit. "We just need to talk to him, that's all."

"I dropped Malik off at his apartment last night," Sapp explained. "I haven't seen him since."

"Okay, thanks," Guy said, before he rushed to the exit with Alex on his heels.

As soon as they climbed in Guy's car, Alex asked, "Do you know where Malik's lives?"

Guy nodded. He had remembered Malik's address from Big Mike's investigative report.

Twenty minutes later, they were standing outside his apartment door, banging until the hinges shook. But there was no answer. Guy checked the door handle and discovered it was unlocked. Then he looked back to see if anyone was watching, before he opened the door and stepped inside with Alex right beside him.

Alex flipped on the light switch next to the front door entrance, then almost passed out at the sight of Malik's bloody body sprawled out on the sofa. He turned away, covering his nose with his shirt.

Guy took a closer look at Malik's body. "It looks like someone got to him before we did."

In panic mode, Alex's eyes bounced around the apartment, before yelling, "Guy, let's get out of here!"

Standing still, Guy was stunned by Malik's lifeless body.

"Guy!" Alex hollered out. "We have to get the *hell* out of here! The police may be on their way. Let's go!"

Snapping out of his spell, Guy thought about the implications if he and Alex were caught in Malik's apartment. He bolted out of the apartment with Alex on his heels. When Guy climbed behind the wheel of his Mercedes Benz, he did not start the engine right away. He sat there in silence.

Frantically, Alex turned to Guy, and asked, "What are we waiting for?!" His question was filled with fear and anxiety.

"What if they think we did it?" Guy said in an almost hushed voice.

Alex's heart sank as the reality of Guy's question hit him like a ton of bricks.

"We were at the club looking for Malik earlier," Guy acknowledged aloud. "We had asked at least five people if they had seen Malik. Now he's dead."

Sighing, Alex closed his eyes while massaging his temples. After failing to think of a solution, he turned to Guy for answers. "What are we going to do?"

Guy cupped his chin and bit his bottom lip, pondering their dilemma. "We have to go back inside the apartment and remove the body."

"Are you crazy?!" Alex exclaimed.

Guy touched Alex's shoulder as he looked into his eyes. "This is the only way."

"And take it where?!" Alex screamed. His body trembled like an icicle.

Guy rested his elbow on the armrest and placed his hand on his forehead. He was unable to think of a good solution.

"We weren't raised like this," Alex reasoned. "Let's go home."

Nodding his head, Guy started the ignition and drove away in silence. His mind was in overdrive trying to think of a solution to their problem. Forty-five minutes later, Guy drove into his driveway. He knew Alex was freaked out by the night's events. "Are you going to be okay?" he asked as he turned to his brother with genuine concern.

Alex nodded, then checked his watch, before climbing out of Guy's car.

"Yo, Alex!" Guy called out from his car. "What's the rush?"

"I gotta go!" Alex yelled back. He was determined to meet with Rhaunda at the revival service, despite being a couple of hours late.

Guy stared at Alex with questioning eyes.

Cracking a smile, Alex said, "I told Rhaunda I would meet her at her father's church, for revival service."

Perplexed, Guy looked at his brother for clarification.

Alex smiled. "My new friend, Bryce Jennings, thought I should settle down, like you and Regine."

Guy grimaced when Alex mentioned Bryce's name. He did not like Bryce but did not understand why. "Do you want to stop by tomorrow, to talk about tonight?" he asked, choosing to voice his concerns about Bryce at a later time.

Alex thought about Guy's request before responding. "If it's okay with you, I'd like to put what happened tonight behind me."

Guy nodded. "I understand."

After Alex left, Guy remained in his car. He still believed he and Alex should have gotten rid of Malik's body. On a whim, Guy headed back to Malik's apartment determined to follow through with his plans.

Kevin went straight to Malik's apartment, upon arriving in Tampa. In a heavily tinted sedan, he and three of his henchmen waited for Guy. Kevin sat in the backseat, cupping his freshly edged goatee that hinted sparks of gray against his milk chocolate complexion. He was wearing a sharp black two-piece suit and a black godfather hat, looking the role of an American gangster.

As a former drug lord, Kevin was constantly on the move. He never lived in a city or state for more than six months at a time. Though, he was never too far from his four daughters, who lived in different states along the East Coast. Regine, his eldest daughter, had asked him about the whereabouts of her estranged siblings, but Kevin thought it was too dangerous to reveal that information. When Regine's mother, Sue, phoned him earlier, he was relieved to know Regine was safe and unharmed.

After Guy pulled into a parking space in front of the Kingston apartments, he was headed up the path to Malik's apartment. He was startled when Kevin approached him from behind.

"What's going on?" Kevin grumbled.

Guy fumbled for a response. "Oh…hi," he uttered.

Kevin looked at Guy with narrowed eyes. "What are you doing on this side of town?"

Guy winced. He did not anticipate Kevin's question.

"Go on home," Kevin insisted. "I'll take care of Malik."

"How did you know?" Guy said in a soft whisper.

Kevin nodded, before gruffly answering, "I have my sources."

"But Malik is not there," Guy said with the quickness.

"How do you know?" Kevin asked with squinted eyes.

"I was here earlier. I was getting ready to wait for him in front of his apartment."

"No problem," Kevin said after looking at Guy sideways, "we'll stay here and wait for him."

"That's not necessary," Guy quickly replied. "Malik and I were able to resolve our differences."

Kevin raised a brow. "Are you sure?"

"Yes, we're cool," Guy lied, cracking a thin smile.

Twisting his mouth, Kevin narrowed his eyes as he stared at Guy. He knew his son-in-law was lying.

Kevin's silence was making Guy nervous.

"Okay," Guy said to break up the tension, "I'll see you later. You want me to tell Regine you're coming over?"

"No, I just came to town to take care of some business. Tell Regine I'll see her later."

"Will do," Guy said, before he climbed in his car and drove away. On his way home, he was wondering how Kevin knew he would be at Malik's apartment.

Kevin stood in one place as Guy drove away. Despite Guy's assurance, he ordered that his men follow him to Malik's apartment. Armed with their guns, they walked into the apartment, and discovered Malik was nowhere in sight.

Chapter 21

Friend or Foe

With precision, Alecia sat in front of her vanity mirror putting on red blush, two shades of red eye shadow and candy apple red lipstick. Then she stood up admiring her red V-neck, tight-fitting dress in the full-length mirror. "Looking good and feeling good," she said to herself. "When Alex takes one look at me, he's going to be in church heaven."

Puckering up, Alecia blew herself a kiss, then gloated as she turned her body in every angle. She was satisfied with the results of the plastic surgery she had completed two years earlier. She had determined that her booty and breasts implants were well worth the fifty thousand dollar investment. However, her monthly hair extensions were one of her most lavish expenses, which prompted her to beg her father to increase her weekly allowance. Of course, Dr. Kellam granted his one and only child her wish.

Alecia put on her five-karat diamond necklace and matching earrings, then brushed on some facial powder. "Look out Alex," she cheered in the vanity mirror, "before you know it, you will be all mine. Now, if I can just find a way to move Rhaunda out of the picture for good. She's such a silly girl."

Quickly, Alecia slipped on her five-inch stiletto heels after she heard a knock at the door. "Rhaunda," she said, as she opened the door and glanced at her watch. "You're early."

Rhaunda frowned at Alecia's *hoochie-mama* dress and gaudy makeup. "You know we're going to church, right?"

"Yeah, why?" Alecia asked, pretending to look dumbfounded.

"It's nothing," Rhaunda replied, after rolling her eyes.

Thirty minutes later, Rhaunda parked her car near the church entrance. She glanced at Alecia before climbing out of her car.

Alecia took her time getting out of the car. She wanted to be the center of attention, and it worked. After straightening her skirt, she looked up to find the church members gawking at her.

Although embarrassed by the attention they were receiving, Rhaunda introduced Alecia to the church members they passed by on their way inside church. She noticed their reaction to Alecia's getup, and thought, *They're probably wondering why she's dressed up like she's going to a club.*

"Hello ladies," the usher greeted Rhaunda and Alecia at the front door, smiling from ear-to-ear. His eyes zoomed in on Alecia, as he said, "Please follow me. I have the perfect seat for you." He sat them three rows from the pulpit.

After they were seated, the usher winked and smiled at Alecia, giving her his undivided attention. "Miss, is there anything I can do for you?"

"No thank you," Alecia dismissively replied, while turning away from the usher. Sadly, he got the hint that Alecia was not interested in him, and walked away.

Turning side-to-side, Alecia looked all around the church for Alex. Then she turned to Rhaunda with an attitude. "I thought you said Alex would be here."

"That's what he told me," Rhaunda replied, before gazing at Alecia with raised brows. "Why are you asking about Alex?"

Pretending to laugh, Alecia swatted at the air. "I was just curious, that's all."

For a brief moment, Rhaunda mentally questioned Alecia's motives before turning her attention to her father, who had just opened the revival service with a prayer. He was preceded by the choir who sang an old gospel hymn.

Throughout church service, Alecia continued rubbernecking, looking for Alex to walk through the church entrance at any moment. *"Where is he?"* she silently asked herself. Her eyes were so focused on the entrance, she did not hear the pastor's request for all new visitors to stand up and introduce themselves.

Rhaunda lightly elbowed Alecia before she whispered in her ear, "Stand up."

"For what?" Alecia questioned, looking confused.

"You're a new visitor," Rhaunda explained in a soft voice. "You have to stand up and introduce yourself."

Alecia rolled her eyes as she looked down her nose at Rhaunda. "No I don't."

Unable to comprehend Alecia's rebellious behavior, Rhaunda sighed, before asking, "Why did you bother coming to church with me? It's obvious your heart isn't here."

Alecia rolled her eyes, copping an attitude with Rhaunda. "You're the one that kept insisting that I come to church with you. Had I known you were going to have a snotty attitude, I wouldn't have come."

"Do you want to leave now?"

"Yes," Alecia said, as she glanced at her watch. "You didn't tell me we would be in church all night. It's been an hour already."

Rendered speechless, Rhaunda measured her tone and chose her words correctly when she finally spoke. "We'll leave after the choir sings again."

"Fine." Alecia crossed her arms in a huff, as she thought aloud, "I wonder what happened to Alex."

Rhaunda jerked her head in Alecia's direction, and asked, "What did you say?" She heard her the first time, but she thought she was mistaken.

"Oh...um...I mean," Alecia stammered for a response. "I thought Alex would be here by now. Did he tell you that he would be late?"

"I don't recall telling you that Alex would be here. But, to answer your question, I guess he chose to stay home." Rhaunda paused, before continuing, "Why are you asking me about Alex, anyway?"

"It's nothing," Alecia replied, before averting her eyes away from Rhaunda. Seconds later, she noticed her friend staring at her from the corner of her eyes. She stood up to leave, unable to withstand Rhaunda's scrutiny.

"Where are you going?" Rhaunda asked, after Alecia stood up.

Alecia glanced back at her friend with a snippy attitude. "I'll wait for you outside."

Shaking her head, Rhaunda asked herself, "Why did I bother inviting her?" Then she waited until the choir began singing before she stood up holding two fingers skyward to excuse herself. When she walked outside, she was shocked by what she saw. Alecia was standing next to Alex's car, while he remained behind the wheel of his car. They looked too cozy for Rhaunda.

With steam coming from her ears, Rhaunda stomped over to Alex's car with gusto. "Hello Alex," she said with an attitude, "how nice of you to make it."

"Sorry I'm late," Alex said, finding it difficult to get out the car, because Alecia was in the way. "I had some things to take care of back at the office." He thought the truth would have sounded unbelievable.

"That's why you have an assistant," Rhaunda curtly replied.

Turning toward Rhaunda, Alecia folded her arms and snarled at Rhaunda. "Why are you acting childish? Can't you see this man's gotta work?"

"Alecia, you have nothing to do with this!" Rhaunda shouted, followed by a *'don't you dare say another word'* look. "Mind your business, and stay out of mine."

Alecia held her hand up to silence Rhaunda, then she turned to Alex, and asked, "Do you mind taking me home?"

"I don't think that's a good idea," Alex answered, as he looked at Rhaunda to intervene. He could not understand why she was staring at him with her mouth balled up.

"I don't care!" Rhaunda retorted. "Do whatever you want to do," she added, before turning around and walking toward the church.

"But Rhaunda!" Alex called out, as he tried to climb out of his car. "It's not what it seems." When Alecia did not move from in front of his car door, Alex frowned as he looked at Alecia. "Do you mind?" His tone was brash and impatient.

Alecia hesitated before she stepped aside. She wanted his undivided attention. In fact, she had purposely stood in front of Alex's car door to block him from exiting the car.

After Alex climbed out of his car, he ran to catch up with Rhaunda. "Hold up, Rhaunda!" he hollered out. "Let's talk about this."

Angry beyond reproach, Rhaunda spun around and faced Alex with a scowl on her face. "Do me a favor, and drop dead."

"Rhaunda," Alex begged, "I'm sorry I was late. I had to go with my brother to take care of an issue."

"Let me get this right," Rhaunda replied with an attitude, "first you told me you had to stop by the office. Now you tell me you and Guy had something to do. Which lie do you want me to believe? And what is more important than praising the Lord?"

Sighing, Alex briefly averted his eyes to the ground. "I can't tell you," he mumbled, "but one day I will."

Rhaunda crossed her arms and peered into Alex's eyes. "I thought you changed, but I can see that I was wrong about you. I saw you leaving your secretary's house," she sneered. "Maria Gomez, right?"

"That was a mistake," Alex muttered under his breath. "I'm sorry."

"Oh yeah, was Cyprus Wilson a mistake? I'll never forget the way you betrayed me in grad school."

Stumped for words, Alex shook his head in disbelief. He tried to be truthful, but realized Rhaunda was still dwelling on the past.

Rhaunda was fed up with Alex's deception. She glanced over at Alecia, who stared back at her with contempt. "It looks like you have someone waiting for you."

Spinning around, Alex spotted Alecia leaning against his car with a big grin on her face. He turned back to Rhaunda, and asked,

"What can I do to convince you that I have no desire for Alecia, or any other woman?" he asked with sincerity. "I want to be with you, and only you."

"There's nothing you can do. It's over!" As soon as Rhaunda said the words, she instantly regretted it. She walked inside the church and did not look back.

When Alex returned to his car with his head bowed, Alecia smiled at the thought of being left alone with him. "I guess it's just you and me," she pointed out, as soon as Alex climbed into his car. "Instead of taking me home, let's go for a joy ride."

"I'm taking you home," Alex grumbled, before turning on the ignition.

"Okay." Alecia was not deterred by Alex's response. She cheerfully walked over to the passenger door and climbed in, feeling as if she had the upper hand.

"Where do you live?" he grumbled, after Alecia buckled up.

"On the east side."

Thirty minutes later, Alex drove in the parking space in front of Alecia's apartment. He put the gear in park, then noticed Alecia staring at him out of the corner of his eyes. "What is it?" he asked, while staring straight ahead.

In a seductive voice, Alecia asked, "Would you like to come inside?"

Alex grimaced. "No, I don't think that's a good idea."

"But I do," Alecia said, while leaning toward Alex with perched lips. "I promise, you won't regret this."

Pushing Alecia away from him, Alex shouted, "Stop this! Rhaunda and I *are* a couple, whether you like it or not!"

Unfazed by Alex's reaction, Alecia scooted closer to him, and breathlessly said, "I'm not trying to break you two up. I just want us to be friends with benefits."

As soon as Alex got a whiff of Alecia's perfume, his body weakened. Then blood rushed to his manhood when she placed her hand over his crotch. Hot and bothered, Alex stuttered, "I'm not…sure this is…a good idea."

Alecia began nibbling on Alex's ear. "I won't bite," she purred. "How about sharing a drink with me?"

Alex knew he wasn't thinking with the right side of his brain when he agreed to go with her. Once inside the apartment, Alecia poured Alex a shot of vodka, while she fixed herself a glass of water. She opted for water, because she wanted to be alert for Alex later on. Discreetly, she slipped a couple of *"ruffies"* in his drink.

Alex retrieved the drink from Alecia's extended hand and took several sips. He thought the liquor would calm his nerves, but his head was suddenly spinning out of control.

"Now, if you don't mind," Alecia softly cooed, "I would like to change into something more comfortable."

Feeling woozy, Alex slurred, "No, I don't mind. Take your time." He tried to shake off the drowsiness, but everything seemed off balance.

When Alecia came out of her bedroom dressed in red silk lingerie, Alex wiped away the sweat that suddenly appeared on his forehead. "What are you doing?" he asked, his voice was shaky. "You're Rhaunda's friend."

"Rhaunda didn't tell you," Alecia smugly replied as she sat on Alex's lap and wrapped her arms around him, "we share everything." Toying with his tie, she looked at him with a bright white smile. "I happen to know Rhaunda's still a virgin. I also happen to know that a man like you has needs," she added, as she unbuttoned Alex's shirt and rubbed his chest. Then she looked down and noticed the huge bulge in Alex's crouch. "That's not your cell phone, is it?" She laughed while invading Alex's space.

Alex pretended to laugh while peeling Alecia's arms from around his neck. "I gotta go," he weakly replied.

"And miss all of this?" Alecia asked, as she stood up and removed her lace robe, exposing her assets.

Alex fell under Alecia's spell after she removed her bra. The bulge in his pants grew bigger. Smiling, Alecia focused on what was between Alex's legs. "Let's go take care of that," she said, as she grabbed his hand and guided him to her bedroom.

Suddenly, Alex could not talk. The drugs were affecting his brain and free will. Feeling helpless, he stood next to Alecia's bed in a groggy state. Alecia took control by undressing Alex, then easing him down on the bed. "Alex," she cooed as she removed her thong, "how would you like some strawberry cream pie?"

Alex blacked out but his manhood stood erect. With a sheepish grin, Alecia pushed Alex on the bed, then crawled on top of him and rode his pulsating penis like a seasoned jockey. An hour later, she crashed on her pillow, completely satisfied. "Ooh…Alex …baby, you were so big, just like I imagined you would be. Those *ruffies* I gave you worked like magic."

Chapter 22
Duped!

*O*n the middle of the morning, Alex woke up in a daze. He freaked out when he looked over and saw Alecia lying next to him. "Damn!" he muttered to himself. "How in the *hell* did she get here?" He leaned over and shook her awake. "You have to get up and get out of here."

Satisfied from a night of passion, Alecia yawned as she stretched her arms and opened her eyes. "Good morning, handsome," she said with a warm smile. "Last night, you were exactly what I expected."

"Uh, yeah," he stammered, "umm…you have to leave."

"Me?!" Alecia asked with an attitude. "Why are you asking me to leave my own apartment?"

Alex looked around the room and saw pink everywhere. There were pink curtains, a pink bedspread, and even pink carpet. Nervously, he chuckled after it dawned on him that he was not in his own home. He threw back the covers and sprang out of bed looking around for his clothes, which were nowhere in sight.

Alecia was determined to keep Alex with her. She had gotten out of bed earlier, to hide his clothes with the intent of extending his visit. She had also called a twenty-four hour locksmith, to make a copy of his house keys. She figured his key would come in handy one day.

After failing to find his belongings, Alex frowned as he turned to Alecia, and asked, "Where did you put my clothes?"

Pretending to be surprised by his question, Alecia opened her mouth and put her hand on her chest. "You don't remember?" she innocently asked.

"Remember what?"

"You had a little accident," she teased.

Looking crazy, Alex waited for Alecia to elaborate.

"I don't want to embarrass you," she commented while batting her eyes, "but I noticed a wet spot in the crotch area of your pants." She cleared her throat, before she continued, "I take it that you were, shall we say, overwhelmed by my assets." Then Alecia inserted the tip of her index finger in her mouth in a seductive manner.

Alex averted his eyes downward, then looked up after realizing what Alecia was implying. He was embarrassed because he could not remember having sex with her. Shaking his head, he knew he had to leave. Without asking, he searched through her dresser drawers, looking for his clothes.

Discerning Alex's impatience, Alecia quickly came up with a lie. "I put your clothes in the washer last night."

Alex thought Alecia's explanation sounded rational, but he continued to look around the bedroom. "Where are my shoes?"

"I put them in the closet," Alecia said, pointing in that direction.

Alex stared at Alecia with disbelief. "I think I know what you're trying to do, but it's not going to work. I love Rhaunda. What we did last night was a mistake."

Pouting, Alecia rolled her eyes before gazing into Alex's. "How is that possible? All while we made love, you told me that you loved me."

Alex concluded Alecia was delirious. He thought, *There is no way I would ever profess my love for her.* Rushing to the closet, he opened the door and searched high and low for his shoes. Alex turned around and faced Alecia with piercing eyes. "I'm going to ask you one more time," he said in a threatening manner. "Where are my *damn* shoes?!"

Put off by Alex's demeanor, Alecia sat up in bed and crossed her arms. "Why are you acting like that?!" she snapped. As an afterthought, Alecia changed her tone and bore a wide grin, deciding she could get more with honey than milk. "Why don't you come back to bed?" she asked, as she patted her bed. "Let's do a repeat from last night."

Alex darted to the phone on the nightstand next to Alecia's bed, and dialed his cell number. Within seconds, he heard his ring tone coming from underneath the bed. He bent down and looked under the bed, where he found all of his belongings. He grabbed his things and rushed to the bathroom to dress.

Alecia jumped out of bed to go after him, but Alex closed the door in her face. She repeatedly banged on the bathroom door, pleading, "Come on, Alex, don't leave. Why won't you give me a chance?"

"For God's sake!" Alex shouted through the bathroom door. "You're my girlfriend's best friend."

With her back leaning against the bathroom door, Alecia frankly said, "You didn't have a problem with dipping and dabbing before. Or, are you forgetting you slept with Cyprus Wilson in grad school?"

Alex winced in response. His past had come back to haunt him, even though there was no emotional connection to Cyprus Wilson or any woman he slept with, for that matter. "I'm a changed man," Alex tried to convey, as he buttoned his shirt.

"Alex, darling," Alecia said with a wicked grin, "once a dog, always a dog."

"If you feel that way," he griped, "why do you want to be with me?"

Alecia faced the closed door, pleading her case. "We have a lot in common. We're both rich, good-looking, and come from the same pedigree."

"Pedigree?" Alex asked with raised brows.

"Yes, so to speak. We come from old money, money that lasts for generations. I know all about you. I checked you out, personally."

Fully dressed, Alex opened the bathroom door and looked at Alecia with disgust. "You're sick."

"No, I'm not. I'm the type of girl that goes after what she wants, and right now, I have my eyes on you."

"What do you want from me?"

"Your hand in marriage."

"You've got to be kidding," Alex said, as he looked at Alecia as if she had lost her mind. Then he shoved her out of his way and bolted for the front door.

"I'm dead serious!" Alecia yelled at Alex's back. "Have you ever heard of the Kellam Pharmaceutical Drug Company?!"

Stopping in his tracks, Alex turned around and faced Alecia with a bewildered gaze. "Is that the same company that owns the patent for Humercin, the experimental drug that slows or stops the growth of cancerous cells?" he asked, remembering he conducted research on the company after his stepmother's doctor mentioned the drug.

"Yes it is," Alecia said, matter-of-factly. "So far, the drug is in its testing phase, and is only administered in London. But, if you play your cards right, I can make sure your stepmother gets the drug."

Alex was in awe as he cupped his chin, mulling over the possibility of extending Jeanine's life. He looked at Alecia in disbelief. "Can you really make it happen?"

"There is no guarantee that the drug would save her life, but it's worth a try."

When Rhaunda told Alecia about Alex's stepmother being stricken with cancer, she used that piece of information to her advantage. "Now, are you going to take me seriously?"

"What do I have to do?" Alex asked out of curiosity.

"Follow my lead."

"What about Rhaunda?"

Alecia eyed Alex's cell phone in his shirt pocket. "Break up with her, indefinitely."

It was a difficult choice, but Alex loved Jeanine and would do anything to help her. "I'll call Rhaunda when I get home," he said, after weighing his options.

"No! Do it now," Alecia persisted.

"What's the big deal?"

"I need to know if you're serious about us."

Sighing, Alex retrieved his phone out of his shirt pocket, flipped it open, and called Rhaunda. When Rhaunda answered on the first ring, Alex grew nervous. "Hi Rhaunda...um, I've been thinking...."

"I owe you an apology," Rhaunda interrupted. "I never should have turned down your marriage proposal. The truth of the matter is, I was afraid of how my father would feel about you. I let my fear get in the way of my true feelings. I want to make things right between us."

"Are you sure?" Alex asked, to make certain this was what Rhaunda truly wanted. Then he looked up and noticed the scowl on Alecia's face.

"I've never been surer of anything!" Rhaunda blurted out with excitement in her voice. "I'm ready to marry you, even if we have to elope." She became alarmed when Alex did not respond. "What is it, Alex? Did you change your mind about us?"

"No, that's not it. It's just...." Alex struggled for the right words. For the first time in their relationship, he actually saw light at the end of the tunnel. But the light grew dimmer as his new reality set in. "I'm not ready," he finally said, hoping to delay the inevitable.

Rhaunda was choked up, when she asked, "Why not?"

Alex paused before responding. "I have some unfinished business, and it wouldn't be fair to you until there's closure."

"I understand," Rhaunda replied with a soft whisper and a broken heart. "When can I see you?"

"I'll call you."

Unsatisfied with Alex's response, Alecia snatched the cell phone from Alex and closed it. "We had a deal," she said to Alex with an attitude.

In a flash, Alex's business disposition kicked into full gear. "Before I commit," he firmly stated, "I want a contract that states I will comply with your wishes, in exchange for your assurance that my stepmother will be given the miracle drug."

"I can make that happen," Alecia replied with confidence. "When?"

"Tomorrow."

"Fine, I'll contact my attorney today. Anything else?"

Alex pondered Alecia's question before responding. "I need time to talk to my mother's doctor about this drug."

"How much time?"

"Including research," Alex thought aloud, "at least twenty-four hours."

Alecia extended her hand. "Deal?"

Alex left her hanging before he continued, "And another thing, no sex until we sign the contract."

"Are you sure?" Alecia asked in a seductive voice, as she spread her legs apart, tempting to lure Alex with her assets.

"I'm sure." Alex turned and walked out of Alecia's apartment.

Alecia poked out her lips, disappointed by Alex's rejection. Then she smiled as she thought about her future as his wife.

Climbing into his car, Alex's focus was on Jeanine. He prayed this miracle drug would save her life. Making the deal with Alecia, he thought, was like making a deal with the devil. "But this deal is worth the sacrifice," he said to himself, before he called Jeanine's doctor to schedule an appointment. He was relieved when the secretary told him the doctor agreed to see him right away.

Chapter 23
Blood is Thicker

*D*ana began to worry when Malik did not contact her to apologize for mistreating her. "This is not like him," she said in the comfort of her bedroom. She called Malik's cell phone several times, but her calls went straight to his voicemail. As a last resort, she picked up the phone and called Malik's friend. "Hi, Sapp. It's me, Dana."

"Hey Dana, wassup?"

"Have you seen Malik?"

"No, I haven't."

The strange feeling Dana had about Malik became clearer. She did not know what to say or how to feel.

"Are you okay?" Sapp asked, after Dana remained silent.

Dana sighed. "I haven't heard from Malik. I'm beginning to worry."

"Don't worry about Malik. I'm sure he's handling his business." Sapp paused, before he continued, "Dana, maybe you should move on with your life. Malik has changed."

"I know. He's just dealing with a lot of stress, that's all."

"I suppose you're right," Sapp said, after realizing Dana was in-love and there was nothing he could say to make her change her mind about Malik. "I gotta go. I'll talk to you later."

After Dana hung up the phone, she sat on the edge of her bed in deep thought. She decided to go look for Malik. With her mind made up, Dana called Billy, her bodyguard, and asked him to drive her to Malik's apartment. She dressed in a hurry and grabbed her purse before heading toward the front door.

"Where are you going?!" Guy shouted, when he spotted Dana running past him. He had been up all night drinking and pacing back and forth. He could not sleep because he kept having nightmares about Malik's ghost coming back to haunt him.

"I'm going out," Dana said with a snippy attitude.

Guy frowned, suspecting Dana was hiding something. "Out where?"

While casting her eyes downward, Dana thought of a good lie. "Billy is taking me shopping."

"No he's not," Guy harshly stated.

"Why not?!" Dana rebuked. "You can't keep me in this house forever!"

"In this house," Guy firmly stated, "there's no democracy. Go back to your bedroom. I'll tell Billy there has been a change in plans."

"But Guy...."

"No buts!" Guy interrupted. "I'm not going to argue with you about this. You can't leave this house, until I say so."

"I hate you!" Dana yelled, before stomping upstairs to her bedroom.

Although Guy was stung by Dana's hurtful response, he knew he made the right decision. He suspected Dana was going to Malik's apartment. When he turned around, he caught Mimi gazing at him from her bedroom. "Can I help you?" he asked in a harsh voice.

"Mr. Simmons," Mimi said as she approached him, "I can't tell you what to do, but you have to be careful how you talk to Dana."

Guy held up his hand to silence Mimi. "You get paid to take care of my mother," he curtly replied, "not to provide advice. I'd appreciate it if you stay out of our personal family matters."

Mimi lowered her gaze from the sting of Guy's words. "I'm sorry. I was trying to be helpful."

Realizing he had hurt her feelings, Guy touched Mimi's shoulder to comfort her. "I'm sorry for the way I came at you. I know you care about the girls, but there's a lot you don't know."

Mimi was about to respond, but she nodded her head instead. "Is there anything I can do for you?"

"No, thanks for asking."

Guy headed to his office in deep thought. The only thing Jeanine had asked him to do was protect his family. He felt as though he was failing, miserably.

Mimi's heart was weary as she went upstairs to check on Dana. She peered inside her bedroom and found her curled up in bed, crying. "Miss Simmons," she said as she walked into Dana's room and stood next to her bed, "whatever it is, it's going to be okay."

Drying her eyes, Dana looked up at Mimi and shook her head. "Guy has changed," she whined. "I don't think things will ever be the same."

Mimi bore a thin smile as she patted Dana on the shoulder. "He has a lot on his plate. Wait until he calms down, things will get better."

Dana sat up in her bed, when it occurred to her that Mimi could help her. "Will you do me a favor?"

"What is it?" Mimi eagerly asked. She wanted to appease Dana.

"Can you go to my boyfriend's apartment?"

"I have to stay here to take care of your mother."

"I'll take care of her. Do you have any errands to run?"

"Well," Mimi thought aloud, "I have to go to the grocery store."

"Good," Dana said, as she rushed to her dresser and wrote down Malik's address. "Please stop by my boyfriend's apartment along the way. Tell him to call me."

Timidly, Mimi bit her bottom lip as she thought about Dana's request. "Are you sure this is a good idea?"

"Please Mimi," Dana begged. "I need to talk to Malik."

Mimi's heart melted like butter when she looked into Dana's eyes. She nodded her head and smiled. "Okay, I'll leave in a few minutes. Please keep an eye on Mrs. Benedict while I'm gone."

"Sure." Dana hugged Mimi, to show her appreciation. Then she looked her in the eyes, and said, "Please don't tell Guy about my request."

"Okay," Mimi said, after a short pause. "Just do me a favor."

"What do you want me to do?"

"Don't stay mad at your brother. He loves you."

Dana nodded her head. "I know."

As soon as Mimi left the house, Dana strolled into Jeanine's bedroom, and found her sound asleep. She was alarmed at how much weight her stepmother had loss. Suddenly, she became teary-eyed at the notion of losing Jeanine.

Sensing someone was in her room, Jeanine opened her eyes and came to face-to-face with Dana. "Are you okay?" she asked, after looking into her daughter's sad eyes.

With droopy shoulders, Dana walked over to Jeanine's bed and held her hands. "I'm fine, Mom."

Jeanine detected sorrow in Dana's voice, so she asked, "What's the matter?"

Dana lowered her head before answering Jeanine. "I'm fine."

"Why do I get a sense that you're not being truthful with me?"

"It's Guy," Dana softly admitted. "He wants to keep me and Cassie caged up in this house like animals."

"Where do you want to go?"

"I want to see my boyfriend, but Guy won't let me."

"Guy knows what's best for you," Jeanine countered.

"But I love Malik."

"Your brother loves you more."

Dana frowned. "Guy doesn't know Malik like I do."

Jeanine eyed the bruise on the side of Dana's face before responding. "Love doesn't hurt."

Quickly, Dana covered the bruise with her hand. "Malik didn't mean to hurt me," she tried to reason. "He was drinking."

"Drunk or not, a real man would never put his hands on you."

"Mom, you don't understand."

"I know more than you think. Men will come and go, but family is forever," Jeanine stated, before she looked around, expecting to see Cassie. "Where's your sister?"

Dana sighed, averting her eyes skyward. "I don't know, and I don't care," she grumbled.

"Don't ever turn your back on your sister," Jeanine stressed. "She needs you more than you will ever know."

"I know," Dana whined, "but Cassie betrayed me."

"How?" Jeanine asked, but did not wait for a response. "Because she spoke the truth about Malik. Your sister would do anything to protect you."

Frowning, Dana wondered if Jeanine knew what happened between her and Cassie.

"Dana," Jeanine continued, "this house is full of love. Do you realize you're letting one man destroy the bond that you all have? Wake up baby, and realize what's going on around you."

Jeanine's advice resonated with Dana. She knew Jeanine was asking her to choose her family over Malik. It was a hard pill to swallow but she understood Jeanine's request. "Mom, thank you for listening."

"Anytime. Now can you do me a favor?"

Dana smiled, feeling a little better. "Sure, anything."

"Make amends with your sister."

Dana was getting ready to protest, but thought about Cassie's dilemma. "You have my word," she said, after she kissed Jeanine on the cheek. "I'll be back later to check up on you."

Dana went to her sister's bedroom and knocked on the door, to make amends. "Cassie, it's me, please open the door."

Seconds later, Cassie opened the door with a wide grin. "I thought you were mad at me."

"I love you," Dana sincerely admitted. "I can never stay mad at you."

They happily embraced and resumed their normal rapport.

Troubled over the conversation he had with Dana, Guy returned to his office and called Billy.

"Hello, Mr. Simmons," Billy answered after the first ring.

"Hi Billy, I'm calling to let you know that Dana decided to stay home to get some rest."

"Sir, may I ask what's going on? When I spoke to Dana earlier, she was crying."

"It's a long story," Guy dryly admitted.

"Sir, may I ask if this has anything to do with Malik?"

"Why do you ask?" Guy inquired, before firing off the next question. "Have you heard anything?"

Billy hesitated before responding. "Well, I'm the one who introduced Dana to Malik."

"You are?" Guy asked in disbelief. He would have never guessed Billy was associated with the likes of Malik.

"I wasn't sure if you would object, so I asked Dana not to tell you."

"Why in the *hell* did you do that?!" Guy harshly questioned. "It's because of you, we're in this situation!"

"What situation? Is Dana okay?" Billy asked, assuming the worse.

Guy answered Billy with another question. "How well do you know Malik?"

"We met through the Big Brother program. I sort of appointed myself as Malik's guardian; not legally, of course."

"So you and Malik are close?"

"You can say that. Though, I haven't seen or heard from him in quite awhile."

Guy sighed. It never dawned on him that Malik might have family and friends that cared about him. "How much do you know about him?" he asked, after a short pause.

"Malik has had a hard life. His mother died when he was young, and his father has been nonexistent for most of his life. Though, Malik told me his father tried reaching out to him several months ago, but he refused to have anything to do with him."

"Why?"

"Malik is still holding a grudge against his father, for abandoning him as a child."

"Do you know anything about his father?"

"Not much, but he told me his father used to be a professional hit man and was in prison for murder."

Suddenly, Guy's eyes grew bigger upon hearing this revelation. He stood up and started pacing back and forth in his office. "What is his father's name?" he asked out of curiosity.

"Malik never mentioned his name."

"Does his father live in Florida?" Guy anxiously asked.

Billy's antennas flew up during the question and answer session. "Sir, why are you asking all of these questions?"

Guy bit his bottom lip. "I was just curious."

"If you'd like, I can arrange for you to meet Malik."

"That's not necessary," Guy replied, knowing Billy would never see Malik again.

"Malik is not a bad person. I'm trying to talk him into going back to school."

"That's admirable," Guy replied with snippy attitude, after remembering the fist print on Dana's face. "Billy, I'll call you later."

"Okay, let me know if Dana changes her mind."

After Guy hung up the phone, he banged his fist on the desk. He was livid after learning about Billy's involvement. In deep thought, he was massaging his temples with his knuckles when Regine walked into his office. She was wearing a two-piece gray and white pinstripe Kasper suit with matching pumps, and carrying a black briefcase. She frowned when she looked at the worry lines on her husband's forehead. "Honey, what's wrong?"

"It's nothing!" Guy snapped.

Regine dropped her briefcase on the floor and crossed her arms. "How long are you going to shut me out?!"

Guy threw his hands in the air out of frustration. "Regine, please, just leave me alone for now. I have a lot on my mind."

"Fine!" Regine angrily replied. "Continue shutting me out of your life." She picked up her briefcase and stormed out of Guy's office, believing her marriage was on the brink of disaster. She noticed Guy had been acting strange ever since the night he and Alex went looking for Malik.

Still angry, Regine rushed out of the house and climbed in her BMW. Then she turned on her Bluetooth and called her mother, before starting the ignition.

She thought about calling her Grandmother Bessie but decided against it. Regine had forgiven her grandmother for not telling her about her biological father, who had been out of sight for most of her life, but she was unsure if or whether her grandmother had played a role in having her former suitors murdered. Just the idea that her grandmother was involved made her uncomfortable, especially since Bessie was a religious woman.

"Hi Mom, it's me," Regine said, as soon as her mother answered her call.

Sue sensed tension in her daughter's voice. "Hi, baby, are you okay?"

Regine pulled out onto the highway before responding. "It's Guy again. He refuses to talk to me."

"Guy is no different from most men," Sue admitted, trying to make light of Regine's concerns. "Sometimes, you don't know about their problems until they're beyond repair. Be patient with Guy, and realize he has your best interest at heart."

Regine sighed after digesting her mother's advice. "I suppose you're right."

"Cheer up. Things will get better. I promise."

Sue was relieved Regine's father, Kevin, had called her earlier, and told her everything was taken care of with Guy. She wondered what was troubling Guy, this time.

Taking a deep breath, Regine began to relax. "Thanks Mom. You always know what to say, to make me feel better."

"No problem. I never told you this before, but I'm glad you stay in contact with me."

"You're my mother," Regine frankly replied. "What did you expect?"

"Well, I know you're close to your grandmother, so I thought...."

"Mom," Regine interrupted, "I waited all my life to have a relationship with you. I have never stopped loving you."

Moved by her daughter's words, Sue was choked up as tears poured down her face. "You have always been in my heart," she sobbed. "I will always be here for you."

Regine smiled. "Ditto. Now stop crying before you make me cry."

Sue laughed while patting her eyes dry with her fingers. "Okay, we can change the subject. How's KC?"

"His ankle is still sore, but he's fine."

"Give him a kiss for me."

"Will do."

"I love you, baby."

"I love you too," Regine admitted with a warm smile.

A year earlier, Regine and Sue had reunited after being estranged for twenty years. While Sue was strung out on drugs, Regine had grown closer to her grandmother, who showered her with love and advice. At present, Sue was not only living a drug-free life, but she had also become a great wife, mother and grandmother.

Feeling rejuvenated, Regine walked into her restaurant, leaving her personal problems at the front door. She was getting ready to greet her staff when Lamar Green, a potential business investor, walked in behind her, sporting a two-piece navy blue designer suit with matching Stacy Adam shoes. His pitch black hair hinted strands of gray, but did not diminish his youthful appearance. His smile revealed bright white teeth and dimples against his tan complexion. He was sexy, classy, rich and gorgeous.

"Hello Mr. Greene," Regine greeted, while extending her hand.

"You can call me Lamar," he said, as he shook her hand.

"And you can call me Mrs. Croswell," Regine stressed. "My husband would appreciate it."

"Your husband is a lucky man," Lamar said with a warm smile, before checking his watch. "My attorney should be here shortly, to deal with the paperwork."

Regine smiled. "Great. Why don't you make yourself comfortable in my office," she suggested, pointing in the direction of her office. "I'm going to check on my staff."

"No problem, beautiful," Lamar said with dreamy eyes.

Regine laughed at Lamar's compliment, but deep down, she was flattered. She had not received a compliment from Guy in months. Though, she knew she had to keep her rapport with Lamar on a professional level.

Thirty minutes later, the meeting had gone well. Regine determined she and Lamar would work well together. It also helped that Lamar owned several successful restaurants, and knew the full operation of the restaurant business. Regine was looking forward to sharing some of her responsibilities at work, so she could spend more time at home with her family.

Chapter 24

Karma

*A*fter revival service, Pastor Coleman caught a plane to the Virgin Islands, to preside over an all men's retreat. At least, that was the lie he told his wife. Two days later, he returned home with a golden tan. He was thinking about what to tell Elizabeth about his trip as he removed his suitcase from the trunk of his car, and walked up the path to his house.

"Hi honey," Elizabeth said, as she opened the front door and greeted her husband with a hug and a kiss on the cheek. "What took you so long to come home? Your plane landed hours ago."

Avoiding eye contact, he explained, "I had to stop by and pray for Sister Hadly. You know, ever since her husband died, she's been real lonely."

Unbeknownst to Elizabeth, the pastor and Sister Hadly had gone to the Virgin Islands together. He had also driven her home from the airport.

"I hope Sister Hadly's okay," Elizabeth knew the pastor had been spending a lot of time with Sister Hadly. For a fleeting moment, she suspected her husband of having an affair.

"Where's Rhaunda?" the pastor asked, as he looked around, expecting to see her.

"She's upstairs. I think she's still upset with Alex and Alecia."

The pastor removed his jacket and placed his suitcase on the floor, before turning to his wife. "Why is she upset with Alecia?"

"The night of the revival service, Alex took Alecia home. You can probably imagine what happened between them."

"Is she okay?"

"Yes, but I think she's a little heartbroken."

Overwrought with concern, Pastor Coleman walked upstairs to Rhaunda's bedroom and found her in bed. "What's the matter, baby?"

Slowly, Rhaunda turned her head in her father's direction. "It's nothing," she lied, looking as though her world had come to an end.

"Does your disposition have anything to do with Alex?" the pastor knowingly asked.

Suddenly, a river of tears poured down Rhaunda's face. "Dad, why did he do it?" she sobbed.

Pastor Coleman tried with all his might, to constrain his anger. His little girl was in pain, and he wanted to make it right. "Now, now," the pastor said in a soothing voice, as he sat on Rhaunda's bed and embraced her, "it's going to be okay. I'll go talk to Alex."

"You will?" Rhaunda asked in amazement.

"Yes, baby," he said in a soothing voice, even though he knew he was bestowing false hope. He kissed Rhaunda on the forehead. "Lie down and get some rest."

Pastor Coleman stood up and watched his daughter rest her head on the pillow. When she closed her eyes, he rushed out of her bedroom, bumping into his wife.

"Where are you rushing off to?" Elizabeth asked, fearing he was getting ready to do something irrational.

"I'm going to confront that bastard!" the pastor declared.

"No, honey!" Elizabeth protested, as she grabbed her husband's sleeve. "Don't do anything you will regret."

Yanking away from her grasp, Pastor Coleman stomped downstairs, yelling, "That son of a bitch is going to pay for what he did to my daughter!"

Elizabeth ran downstairs after him, shouting, "Rhaunda is a grown woman! She has to learn how to deal with this on her own!"

Ignoring his wife, the pastor grabbed his car keys off the console in the living room before heading toward the front door.

"You can't fight Rhaunda's battles!" Elizabeth yelled, before the pastor opened and closed the door in her face. Her hands flew to her chest as she prayed her husband would not get himself into any trouble.

The pastor drove to Alex's condo like *batman on a mission*. He got out of his car and stomped up the path to Alex's front door. Then he pounded on the door with his fists, as if willing the door to open. Assuming Alex was not home, the pastor returned to his car to wait for him. "That bastard!" he said to himself.

When Alex pulled in front of his condo, he climbed out of his car and walked up the pathway. His heart was aching at the thought of losing Rhaunda, forever. He was caught off guard when the pastor charged at him like a pit bull.

"What's going on?" Alex asked with trembling lips.

The pastor answered Alex's question by grabbing him by the collar of his shirt, then punching him in the face. When Alex fell to the ground, the pastor towered over him and threatened, "This is my last and only warning! Stay the hell away from my daughter!" Satisfied with his actions, the pastor rushed to his brand new Jaguar, and burned rubber as he sped away.

Alex's friend and neighbor, Brian Lancaster, came outside after hearing the commotion. He spotted Alex on the ground, nursing his bruised jaw.

"Who was that?" Brian asked, as he grabbed Alex's hand to help him to his feet.

"Rhaunda's father," Alex mumbled, as he stood up halfway, dusting off his pants.

"The pastor?" Brian asked, after remembering what Alex had told him about Rhaunda's parents a while back.

Alex nodded. "Yeah."

"Wow!" Brian said in surprise. "You have to stop this madness!"

Alex held his head down in despair. "I know, I know...." His heart was still beating rapidly as it dawned on him that he could have been killed.

"What did he say?" Brian probed.

Alex grimaced from pain before responding. "He told me to stay away from Rhaunda."

Brian folded his arms, and firmly said, "I agree with him."

"I know," Alex replied, still hunched over.

"Do you think you need to go to the hospital?"

"No," Alex struggled to say. "I don't think it's that serious."

"You need to go inside and chill."

With his hand over his stomach, Alex opened the door and walked in, closing the door shut with his foot. He leaned against the wall in the foyer for support, then slid to the floor feeling defeated. He wondered if *karma* had anything to do with him getting his butt whipped.

Chapter 25
Inner Turmoil

In a way, Billy understood why Guy had questioned him about Malik. He had hoped to convince Guy that Malik was a good kid. The last time he heard from Malik was a month ago. They met at a local restaurant to talk. Their conversation turned sour when Malik told him that his new friend bought him a car.

"Think about it," Billy said, trying to reason with Malik. "Why is this Sapp person nice to you? What does he want from you?"

"I don't know," Malik answered, clearly frustrated with Billy's questions. "Man, why are you sweatin' me? Sapp is a cool dude."

Billy sighed before continuing. "No one is nice to you without expecting something in return."

"But *you* never expected anything from me," Malik argued.

Shaking his head, Billy was at a loss for words. All he ever wanted was for Malik to get an education, and to steer clear of people that could put him in harm's way.

"Just be happy for me. It's not like I'm out here slanging drugs."

"Fine," Billy conceded, "but what do you do for money?"

Malik smirked. "Sapp gives me cash whenever I need it."

Perplexed, Billy sat back in his chair and paused before responding. "Why does he give you money?"

"Sapp freaked out one day when I told him I was thinking about robbing a bank. He doesn't want me to get in trouble."

"Where is your friend getting his money to give to you?"

"I guess his parents are rich, I don't know," Malik said with shrugged shoulders.

"Do you know anything about him?"

"Sapp relocated here a couple of months ago, and told me he needed a friend."

"You've only known him for two months," Billy said with disbelief, "and now he's your best friend?"

Malik chuckled when he thought about it. "That's cool, ain't it? We just clicked."

"Have you ever met any of his friends and family members?"

"No!" Malik shouted. "I told you he's not from here!" He was tired of Billy interrogating him as if he did something wrong.

Billy held up his hand as a peace offering. "Okay, calm down. Promise me you will go back to school."

"No can do. They don't want me there, and I don't want to be there."

"I thought you would say that," Billy said, as he retrieved a GED book from his briefcase and handed it to Malik.

Malik frowned. "What's that?"

"A test guide. Promise me, you'll study the guide, so you can take the GED exam."

After a short pause, Malik took the book out of Billy's hand, and flipped through it. "Okay, I'll do it," he said, to get Billy off his back.

Billy egged on, "If you pass the exam, you can go to college with Dana."

Malik smiled at that possibility. "That'll be straight!"

Billy smiled. "I take it that you like my idea."

"Man, I said it was straight."

"If you pass the GED, I will personally pay for you to go to college."

"For real?" Malik asked with excitement in his eyes.

"Yes Malik. Just one thing."

"What?"

"Don't drive that car until I find out more information about your friend."

"Billy, will you drop it?!" Malik asked out of frustration. "Sapp is cool with me. You don't have to like him."

"But Malik...."

Malik stood up and grabbed his GED book. "Peace out, man. I'll holla atcha later."

That was the last time Billy saw Malik. Ever since, he had called Malik several times, without success. He did not have the opportunity to investigate Sapp because Dana and Cassie were monopolizing his time. Determined to work things out, Billy headed to Malik's new apartment.

When Billy parked in front of Malik's apartment building, he was shocked to discover policemen surrounding the premises. Then he noticed uniformed officers removing bags from Malik's apartment. After climbing out of his car, Billy walked up the pathway leading to Malik's front door, which was blocked off with yellow tape. Then he looked over and spotted Mimi, Jeanine's caretaker, a couple of feet away. She appeared to have a piece of paper in her hand. Blending into the crowd, Billy stood back and listened as Mimi asked one of the officers what was going on.

"Ma'am," the officer said to Mimi, "do you know the person that lives here?"

"Not really. What happened?" Mimi probed.

"It looks like foul play."

Mimi frowned. "What do you mean?"

"Ma'am, I told you more than I should have. Unless you live here, I'm going to ask you to leave the premises."

"But…." Mimi attempted to ask another question, but the officer turned his back to her. She walked toward a nearby crowd determined to find answers.

Billy observed Mimi walking up to a man in a crowd of ten people. Without being noticed, he moved closer to find out what she was asking the man.

"Sir," Mimi asked the stranger, "do you know what's going on?"

"Oh, you're English?" the man asked, detecting Mimi's accent.

Mimi smiled. "Yes, I am. My friend asked me to come by here and check on her friend, Malik. Do you know him?"

The stranger pointed to Malik's apartment. "He lives in that apartment, but he's been missing a couple of days. Some people believe he might be dead."

"Why do they feel that way?"

"They found blood in his apartment."

"Oh my," Mimi gasped, as her hand flew to her chest.

"Your friend may not be hearing from Malik any time soon."

Mimi shook her head. "That's so sad."

"I know."

After Mimi left the crime scene, she went to the grocery store before she returned home. She was unsure if she should tell Dana about the little information she had learned about Malik, so she went to Jeanine's room first. "Hello Mrs. Benedict. I'm back from the store. Do you want me to fix you something to eat?"

"No, I'm fine," Jeanine said, as she looked at the worry lines along Mimi's forehead. "What's the matter?"

"It's nothing."

"Don't lie to me. Tell me the truth."

Mimi bit her bottom lip. "Ms. Dana had asked me to go to her boyfriend's apartment, to relay a message."

"Well?"

"I couldn't find him. He's missing. A strange man told me he might be dead."

"Did you tell Dana?"

Mimi shook her head. "No. I'm not sure how to break the news."

"You're not to tell Dana what you learned today," Jeanine firmly stated. "If she asks you, simply tell her you didn't find him. It would be the truth. Do you understand?"

Mimi nodded. "Yes ma'am."

Later on, Mimi did as Jeanine had instructed. She told Dana she was not able to locate Malik. Unfortunately, Dana did not take the news well. She came to the conclusion that Malik no longer wanted to be with her.

Billy was heartbroken after he overheard the conversation between Mimi and the stranger. Finding it hard to believe, he returned to Malik's apartment and approached the officer Mimi was talking to earlier. "Can you tell me what's going on?"

"Who are you?" Officer Ratcliff asked, eyeing Billy suspiciously.

"I'm looking for my son, Malik Mitchell."

"Your son?" the officer said in disbelief. He wondered how that was possible, since Billy was Caucasian.

Shaking his head, Billy determined he was dealing with another narrow-minded person. "Yes, I am his legal guardian," he admitted, purposely exaggerating the truth, to get more information.

"Sir, we found blood in his apartment. Once we get the DNA tests, we'll have more answers."

"Blood?" Billy asked in surprise.

"We found some blood on the sofa that may belong to him."

"Were there any signs of a forced entry?"

"No, it looks like someone either had a key, or the door was already unlocked."

"How did you know to come to this apartment?"

"We received an anonymous tip from an untraceable phone."

"Do you have any suspects in custody?" Billy asked, as tears welled up in his eyes.

"Not at this time. If you give me your phone number, we will contact you as soon as we have more information."

Billy gave the officer his business card before walking away from the scene with fire in his eyes. He vowed to find Malik's murderer.

Chapter 26

War of the Roses

*T*hree days later, Rhaunda was still grieving over her break up with Alex. Every morning, she woke in tears, wondering why he did not agree to marry her. She could only guess, but knew his decision had something to do with Alecia. After drying her eyes, she called the one person who might understand her predicament.

Regine was in the green room with Guy when the phone rang. She looked at the caller ID before she picked up the phone. "Hi, Rhaunda. How are you?"

Choked up and holding back tears, Rhaunda said, "I'm hanging in there."

"What's the matter?" Regine asked, sensing something was wrong. She covered the mouthpiece with her hand, and motioned for him to leave the room, so she could talk to Rhaunda in private. Guy nodded, understanding Regine's request.

As soon as her husband left the room, Regine refocused her attention to Rhaunda. "What's wrong?"

Suddenly, tears started pouring down Rhaunda's face. "I think…he had sex…with my best friend," she said between sniffles, "but I don't know for sure."

"Rhaunda," Regine replied in a caring voice, "sometimes you don't need proof. If you believe Alex is cheating, that's all the proof you need."

"What should I do?"

Regine sighed. "You need to move on with your life. If it's meant for you and Alex to be together, it will happen."

"I love him so much," Rhaunda sobbed. "I feel like killing Alex and Alecia for ruining my life."

Alarmed, Regine sat up on the edge of the sofa. "Trust me," she said in an almost pleading voice. "They're not worth it."

Heartbroken and distraught, Rhaunda placed her hand on her chest. "My heart aches," she whispered.

"I know it does," Regine said in a soothing voice. "I was in the same situation not long ago. When Guy left me for my best friend, I thought I would die. But I had to move on with my life. Eventually, Guy opened his eyes and came looking for me. I let him back in my life, but he had to work hard to regain my love. Let me give you a piece of my grandmother's advice: *Let go and let God.*"

Nodding her head, Rhaunda felt somewhat better. "Thank you for listening to me."

"You will be fine," Regine said with assurance. "Use this experience as a life lesson. As soon as you let go of the past hurts, your future will blossom."

"Thank you," Rhaunda replied, while drying her tears.

Regine hung up the phone, feeling Rhaunda's pain. Their conversation had brought back memories of when she was involved in a love triangle with Guy and her best friend, Justina Reyes. She thought it was ironic that Alex was in a similar situation, especially since he had pleaded with her to give Guy another chance.

Her thoughts were interrupted when Guy returned to the green room and sat next to her. He noted Regine's somber mood. "How's Rhaunda?" he asked.

"She's upset," Regine stated, as she turned to face Guy. "You need to talk to Alex. He's getting ready to lose a good girl. Rhaunda doesn't deserve to be mistreated."

"I'll talk to him. What did Rhaunda say?"

"She believes Alex slept with her best friend."

"Wow," was all Guy managed to say.

"I don't understand why he doesn't settle down and marry her."

"Alex proposed to her," Guy said in Alex's defense, "but she said *no*, remember?"

"Yes, I do. But her father has doubts about Alex. You know how important it is for Rhaunda to garner her father's approval."

Guy sighed. "At this rate, I doubt if he would ever approve of Alex."

"Not if Alex continues sleeping with different women. One of these days, he's going to regret it."

Guy slightly nodded, before he said, "That's what I'm afraid of."

Alex's situation forced Guy to reflect on his own past misgivings. He thought he had lost Regine forever when he went after her best friend, Justina. His siblings had stopped speaking to him, and Justina made him look like a straight up fool when he had proposed to her. Not only did she turn down his proposal, but she had asked to keep the engagement ring.

After breaking Regine's heart, Guy knew he could have easily wound up dead at the hands of her father. He was grateful to Kevin for sparing his life, and to Regine, for giving him a second chance.

Rhaunda disconnected the call with mixed feelings. She knew Regine made sense, but the pain was too deep. She picked up the phone and called the culprit behind her pain. "I need to know one thing," she said, as soon as Alecia answered. "Did you sleep with Alex?"

"What if I did?" Alecia snapped.

Rhaunda could not believe her ears, so she asked again. "Did you sleep with Alex?"

Alecia sat up in bed, feeling good about herself. She was cold and heartless. "You did this. I gave Alex exactly what he needed."

Perplexed, Rhaunda put her hand on her forehead as she sought clarification. "What are you talking about?"

"You heard me," Alecia replied with a smug grin. "You didn't want to marry Alex because your father detested him. And, you didn't sleep with him because of your religious beliefs."

"What does that have to do with anything?"

"Alex was acting like a dead man walking," Alecia teased. "How long did you expect him to hold out for you? He's not a practicing priest."

"So you're the answer to his prayers," Rhaunda replied, her voice was laced with bitterness.

Alecia smirked. "Not only am I the answer to his prayers, I'm his savior." She had already gotten what she needed to seal the deal with Alex. Earlier, she had gone to her attorney's office to ask him to draw a contract with Alex.

Tightly holding the phone to her ear, Rhaunda exploded. "You snobbish, arrogant *hooker*!"

Prepared to pay Alex a surprise visit, Alecia stood up and put the contract in her purse before responding. "Rhaunda, I may very well be everything you mentioned, but you should also add that I'm Alex's lover."

"Ooh...you...you..." Rhaunda's lips trembled, as she struggled for a response. She tried with all her might, but could not muster the nerve to call Alecia the one word that suited her.

Alecia giggled at Rhaunda's expense. "Let me help you out," she flippantly insisted. "Are you trying to call me a *bitch*?"

Filled with rage, Rhaunda abruptly hung up the phone and sat on her bed. "I'll fix you!" she screamed aloud, as a river of tears flowed down her cheeks. Though, her tears were a reflection of anger, not sorrow. *"Satan, the devil, you are a liar!"* Rhaunda hollered in vain, as the desire to seek vengeance played tug o'war with her heart.

While Rhaunda was talking to Alecia, Elizabeth was standing outside of her door, eavesdropping. She regretted convincing Alecia to relocate to Tampa. Her plan to rid Alex out of Rhaunda's life had crumbled right before her eyes. With ease, she walked into her daughter's room, and found her crying. "What's wrong, Rhaunda?"

Rhaunda was too upset to respond. She turned away, burying her head in her pillow.

"Baby," Elizabeth cooed, "it's going to be all right. I promise."

Rhaunda's silence spoke volumes.

Elizabeth was tired of seeing her daughter depressed and heart-broken. Too fit to be tired, she stormed out of the house, jumped in her car and headed to Alex's condo. The day before, her husband told her he had kicked Alex's butt but did not kill him. Now Elizabeth was determined to complete what her husband started.

Swerving into a parking space in front of Alex's condo, Elizabeth climbed out of her car without closing it. She was on a mission as she barged up the path to Alex's condo, acting like a mad woman. She banged on Alex's door so hard, the hinges shook. "Open this damn door!" she demanded.

Alex's neighbor, Brian, heard the banging and stepped outside his front door. "Ma'am," he cautiously said, "is everything okay?"

Elizabeth spouted with venom, "Does it look like everything's okay to you?!"

"Uh...no," Brian stammered.

Elizabeth waved her gun toward Brian. "Listen, pretty boy, go back inside to your apartment, and mind your own *damn* business!"

Brian took a step back. He was stunned by Elizabeth's crazed behavior. When he stood still, she slowly approached him with squinted eyes. "What?! You're hard of hearing?!"

"No, ma'am," Brian nervously replied, "but if you don't leave, I'll be forced to call the police."

After considering Brian's threat, Elizabeth backed down, putting her gun in her purse. "Fine!" she barked. "Tell your *little* friend I'll be in touch. He has broken Rhaunda's heart for the last time."

"Rhaunda Coleman?" Brian asked with scrunched brows.

Refusing to provide clarification, Elizabeth firmly said, "Tell your friend I'll be back."

Paying careful attention, Brian watched Elizabeth climb into her car, and leave the parking lot. He feared she might follow through with her threat to kill Alex.

Twenty minutes after her mother left her room, Rhaunda sat up in bed, feeling gloomy. She was distraught by Alecia's spitefulness and Alex's unfaithfulness. Broken hearted, Rhaunda made up her mind to confront Alex, for causing her pain and distress. She retrieved her father's gun, which was stored in a lockbox in his office. Then she bolted out of the house, hopped in her SUV, and put the pedal to the medal. She was driving fast and furious in and out of lanes.

When Alecia sped through a school zone, she was pulled over by a cop. Surprisingly, she was calm when the cop wrote her a ticket and told her to slow down. She was not deterred as she headed to Alex's condo. During the drive, she felt compelled to call his stepmother.

"Hello," Jeanine answered, after Mimi gave her the phone.

"Hello Mrs. Benedict, this is Rhaunda."

"Rhaunda," Jeanine said for clarity. She had met Rhaunda twice, and was still unsure how she felt about her.

"I'm just calling to let you know that your son is a no good, slimy dog."

Jeanine's ears started burning as she sat up in her bed. "Rhaunda, I don't know where your mind is right now," she said in a stern voice, "but if you hurt my child, you will regret it."

Rhaunda cackled. "How can a woman in your condition threaten me?"

"I promise," Jeanine threatened, "even in death, I will haunt you for the rest of your life."

"Yeah, right." Rhaunda hung up the phone when she spotted Alecia driving into Alex's driveway.

After Jeanine heard the dial tone, she handed the phone to Mimi, who was standing next to her bed. "Do not tell Guy about this phone call," she firmly instructed, before the pain medicine kicked in. She decided to deal with Rhaunda on her own terms. Besides, she did not want Guy to worry.

Pounding on the steering wheel, Rhaunda was unable to control her anger. "Damn you, Alex!" she shouted. "How dare you make me look like a fool?!" The yearning for vengeance took over as Rhaunda made a quick U-turn and parked her car around the corner from Alex's condo. She was not thinking straight. Rage had taken over her heart and soul.

Before she climbed out of her SUV, she retrieved the bible from her purse and read a passage from Deuteronomy 32:41, "...I will take vengeance on my adversaries and repay those who hate me." Then she recited the Lord's Prayer as she loaded up the gun and threw it in her purse. *"Vengeance is mine!"* she shouted, as she climbed out of her car and walked briskly to Alex's condo.

Chapter 27

Love Hurts Like Hell!

*A*lex was still sore from the butt-whipping he received from Rhaunda's father, but it did not distract him from trying to help his stepmother. He was relieved when the doctor told him Jeanine would be the perfect candidate for the cancer drug. After hearing this news, he felt a little comfortable with signing the contract with Alecia.

When he returned home, he took a nap, drifting off into a deep sleep. This time he dreamt Rhaunda's father had killed him while he was sleeping with Alecia. Tossing and turning in bed, Alex did not hear his front door open and close. Though, he sensed someone was in his bedroom. He opened his eyes and saw Alecia standing over him, grinning.

"What are you doing here?!" he shouted, as he jumped out of bed, shirtless and in boxer shorts.

"I have my ways," Alecia boldly replied, before shifting her focus to Alex's bruised face. "What happened to you?"

"Forget that!" Alex barked. "How in the *hell* did you get in here?"

Alecia refused to tell Alex she snuck into his condo with a copy of his key. Instead, she held up a document for Alex to see. "I have the contract," she stated with bright eyes. "A deal is a deal."

Suddenly, Alex's anger turned to excitement as he thought to himself, *Mom could possibly live longer.* He loved and admired Jeanine for always being there for him and his siblings. "I have to get dressed," he explained, as he quickly put on his robe.

"Come on, Alex," Alecia grumbled. "Don't treat me like I'm a stranger. Let's celebrate," she said, as she eyed Alex's boxer shorts.

For a split second, Alex pondered Alecia's request. He figured his body was an even trade-off for the drug. Then he looked at Alecia and, for the first time, realized she was absolutely breathtaking. "Okay, let's do this. But first, I need to find a pen."

"Take your time," Alecia suggested, feeling good about this moment. "I need to use your bathroom."

"Sure, it's through those French doors," he said, pointing her in the direction of the master bathroom.

Alecia sashayed in the bathroom and changed into her birthday suit. Then she sprayed mist all over her body for a glowing-effect.

Ready for consensual sex, Alecia walked out of the bathroom in black six-inch stiletto heels.

Alex was sitting on the sofa in the living room reviewing the contract when he spotted Alecia out of the corner of his eyes. He looked up and was shocked to find Alecia stark naked.

"You think you can handle all this?" Alecia seductively cooed, as she leaned against the wall with her legs spread open.

With a smug grin, Alex held up the pen and contract. "After you sign the contract, I can handle anything you want me to."

Alecia rolled her eyes as she grabbed the pen from Alex's hand and scribbled her signature. "Are you happy now?" she asked with an attitude.

Alex looked at the document to verify her signature before responding. "Yes indeed," he said with a wide grin. "I am very happy."

Glad she had finally gotten Alex's attention, Alecia said, "Don't worry about a condom. I'm on birth control."

Shaking his head, Alex explained, "I'd rather be safe than sorry."

"Come on, Alex. It's not like we never had sex without a condom."

Alex emitted a nervous chuckle, as he did not remember their sexual encounter. "Yeah, you caught me off guard the last time. Now I'm thinking rationally."

"Fine," Alecia pouted. "Are you ready?"

"I need to make a copy of the contract first. I'll be back."

Alex stood up and walked into his office, to make a copy for his records. As soon as he placed the contract on the photocopy machine, there was a knock at the door. He did not expect any visitors, so he walked out of his office to see who was at the door. His swift reaction caused the contract to glide to the floor and under the copy machine.

He ignored Alecia, who remained naked in the middle of his living room. "Who is it?!" he shouted, before he made it to the front door.

"It's me, Rhaunda!" she announced with pride in her voice.

"Oh shoot!" Alex gasped with astonishment. "Hold up!"

Alecia frowned. "What does she want?"

"I don't know," Alex said in a hushed voice.

Curious to hear what was going on, Rhaunda put her ear to the door. She heard mumbling sounds on the other side of the door. She wanted to see how Alex was going to explain his indiscretion, especially since he did not have an alternate exit.

"Alecia," Alex continued in a hushed voice, "you have to hide in the closet, in my bedroom."

"Why should I?" Alecia snapped. "She's going to find out about us. It may as well be now."

After focusing on Alecia's naked body, Alex rushed in the guest bathroom, grabbed a bath towel, and extended it to her. "Please," he begged with puppy-dog eyes, "do it this one time. At least until I can talk to Rhaunda in private."

Alecia rolled her eyes and sucked her teeth. "Okay, I'll do it," she hastily agreed after grabbing the bath towel out of Alex's hand, "but why do I have to hide in the closet?"

"Just this one time," he urged with an outstretched hand.

Rolling her eyes, Alecia wrapped the towel around her waist, grabbed her purse and stomped to Alex's bedroom. She opened the walk-in closet door, and was relieved to find a chair. Steaming mad, she slammed the door shut and sat down in a huff.

Seconds later, Alex opened the front door. "Hi Rhaunda," he said, as he peered out of the opening. "I wasn't expecting you."

"I was in the neighborhood," she casually replied, "so I decided to stop by."

"Oh…uh…thanks, for coming by." Alex was surprised Rhaunda was in a jovial mood.

"Is it okay for me to come inside?" Rhaunda asked in a sweet, syrupy voice.

Alex looked back to make sure Alecia was nowhere in sight before he opened the door wider. "Sure, come in," he half-hearted replied, as he stepped aside. "I'm on my way out. I have to go by the office to pick up a package," he added, hoping that she would leave.

Dismissing Alex's lie, Rhaunda sat on the sofa and made herself at home. "I'm not going to stay long. I just need to tell you something."

"What is it?" Alex inquired, as his eyes kept roaming to his bedroom. He was uncomfortable with Rhaunda's surprise visit.

"I can't stand to lose you," Rhaunda declared, as she sat up on the edge of the sofa. "I need you in my life."

"You do?" Alex asked in amazement.

Holding on to her purse, Rhaunda jumped from the sofa and threw her arms around Alex's neck. "Yes, I want us to be together," she said in a breathless voice but excited voice. Her lips were only inches from his. "Will you give us a chance?"

Alex remained speechless as Rhaunda nudged him toward his bedroom by brushing up on him. "And to show you just how serious I am," she said, as she sat on his bed, "I want to give you something special." With a wide grin, Rhaunda unbuttoned her blouse, then leaned back on the bed, seductively biting her bottom lip while gazing at Alex with dreamy eyes.

Eyeing the closet, Alex realized Alecia was listening to their conversation. "Um…Rhaunda…maybe we should wait until we're married," he urged. "I don't want you to do anything you will probably regret."

Pouting, Rhaunda crossed her arms in a huff. "What are you saying? You don't want me?"

"Come here," Alex cooed, as he smiled and held out his hand to Rhaunda. At that moment, his heart yearned for her. He did not want her to feel rejected, again.

Rhaunda held on to her purse as she stood up and slowly approached him.

With dimples flashing in his cheeks, Alex cupped Rhaunda's face and looked into her dark brown eyes. "I want you. No, I need you, more than you will ever know."

Rhaunda smiled. "Baby, I love you too. But I don't want to share you with another woman, especially with Alecia," she explained, before kissing Alex with vigor, and lightly brushing her free hand across the side of his face.

Alex had forgotten about his houseguest as he closed his eyes, kissing Rhaunda back with fierce passion and desire. His body ached for hers as he groaned, loudly.

Listening to Rhaunda and Alex make out, made Alecia sick to her stomach. Her heart was about to explode as she stood up, cracked the closet door open, and witnessed the unlikely lovebirds in action. She thought, *I cannot believe Alex just flipped the script on me! Well, I'll show him!* With her emotions intact, Alecia waited for the right time, to let her presence be known.

Rhaunda was not distracted by Alex's kiss or his roving hands over her back and buttocks. She kept one arm around his waist, then she used her free hand to withdraw the gun from her purse, which hung from her shoulder. Smiling, Rhaunda moved the gun near Alex's face.

Caught off guard by the sight of the gun, Alecia suddenly became concerned about her own safety. She quickly but quietly closed the door. Her heart was beating in overdrive worrying about being discovered by Rhaunda. Quick on her feet, she looked around the closet for a weapon. She grabbed a wire hanger among Alex's suits and shoes, and held it close to her chest. She relaxed a little, believing she was sufficiently armed.

When Alex heard the gun cock, his eyes flew open. He lifted his head and shivered at the sight of the gun. "What...are you...doing?" he asked with trembling lips.

Suddenly, Rhaunda became cocky. "Let's just say, I'm fed up with your crap!"

All the color drained from Alex's face as he took a step back, holding up his hands as if surrendering. "Baby," he stammered with a shaky voice, "let's...talk...about this. You don't...want...to do this," he pleaded, while sweating bullets.

Rhaunda was unmoved by Alex's pleas. She briefly closed her eyes, wondering whether she should follow through with her plan.

Attempting to catch Rhaunda off guard, Alex reached out with trembling hands to wrestle the gun away from her. He was not quick enough. Rhaunda reflexed, then blinked each time she fired the gun.

Within a blink of an eye, Alex fell backwards, hitting his head on the side of his wooden poster bed before crashing to the floor. Blood quickly oozed out of his abdomen. He was rapidly fading away, gasping for his last breath. Seconds later, his eyes rolled to the back of his head, which was severely bruised from the fall.

Rhaunda looked at Alex's seemingly lifeless body, then started shaking, as tears streamed down her face. "Oh God," she cried out. "What have I done?!"

Dropping to the floor, Rhaunda frantically touched Alex's arm for a pulse. Then she became alarmed when she heard whimpering sounds coming from the bedroom closet. After drying her face, she became furious all over again. "Come out, now!" she ordered with her eyes focused on the closet door.

Alecia stopped crying when she heard the directive. She stood still hoping Rhaunda would leave her be. *"What's wrong with her?"* she silently questioned herself. *"She's acting demon possessed."*

"If you don't come out now," Rhaunda threatened, "I will drag you out by your hair weave!"

Alecia dropped the hanger after realizing it could not compete with a gun. She slowly opened the closet door, and came out the closet with her arms wrapped around her shoulders. Her voice trembled, as she begged for mercy, "Please...don't...do this."

"Do what?" Rhaunda asked, as she lifted the gun and pointed it toward Alecia's head. "You did this. You weren't satisfied until you had my man. Now look at what you made me do," she accused, as she waved her free hand over Alex's body.

"Please don't kill me!" Alecia screamed with outstretched hands. Consumed with fear, she did not feel the towel slip from her body and fall to the floor.

After laughing at Alecia's nakedness, Rhaunda shook her head in disgust. "I'm not stupid. Why would I kill you? You're the murderer."

Alecia frowned, as she quietly asked herself, *"Is she serious?!"*

Rhaunda grinned. "You don't think I would kill Alex without a plan, do you?"

Alecia's heart was drumming in overdrive as she tried to figure out Rhaunda's angle. "I thought you loved Alex." Her statement was posed as a question.

"Oh, but I do," Rhaunda proclaimed with a wicked grin. "I love Alex to death! Now I can have him all to myself." She laughed at the thought.

Alecia was on the verge of a nervous breakdown. She wondered what caused Rhaunda to turn into a crazed lunatic. "Just let me go," she pleaded with trembling lips.

"How?" Rhaunda asked, with a sly grin. "Your car is um....how should I put this lightly? Oh, I know....*dead,* just like Alex," she said with venom. "Or, should I say, *burned,* just like you burned me by sleeping with Alex. Or, what about *doomed* like your life will be while rotting in jail."

Alecia gasped. She was unsure of what Rhaunda was hinting.

"Bittersweet, bittersweet," Rhaunda repeated with a smile. She put her free hand on her hip and tilted her head to the side. "I'm going to let you live, and at the same time, let you die slowly, in jail. How awesome is that?" Her question was laced with sarcasm.

Alecia wondered if she should repeat Alex's mistake, by trying to wrestle the gun from Rhaunda.

As if reading her friend's thoughts, Rhaunda said through clenched teeth, "Don't even think about it. You see what happened to Alex."

Crying a river of tears, Alecia thought, *Oh God! This is the devil right here on earth.*

"Shut up that whining, and dry your damn eyes!" Rhaunda demanded. "Now, this is what you're going to do. You're going to go to the phone, dial nine-one-one, and tell the operator you just murdered Alex Simmons. You can tell them it was in self defense for all I care. But, I can assure you that it won't work, especially since you unloaded three bullets, ensuring Alex's death."

Alecia silently asked herself, *"Did I hear her correctly? Rhaunda wants me to call the operator and report that I killed Alex. She has lost her everlasting mind."*

Shaking her head, Rhaunda looked at Alecia's naked body in disgust. "I'm sure the State Attorney will wonder what Alex could have possibly done to make you angry enough shoot him, especially since it's obvious that you were screwing him, earlier."

"It's...not like that," Alecia explained with nervous laughter. "Um...Alex told me you were out of town." She regretted not thinking of a better lie.

Rhaunda placed her right hand over her chest and belted out a weird and obnoxious cackle. "You know what I like about you?" she asked, as she glared at Alecia with hatred in her eyes. "You never pretended to be anything other than a selfish bitch!"

What's up with the cussing? Alecia thought. *I thought Rhaunda was a holy roller, around here toting her bible and acting like she's better than everyone else. I wonder if Alex knew he was dealing with a psycho.*

"Go to the phone, now!" Rhaunda demanded.

Alecia looked at the phone before she turned to Rhaunda, and muttered, "I can't...."

"You can, and you will," Rhaunda said in a manner that did not give Alecia a choice. Then she cocked her gun and twisted her mouth, keeping the target on Alecia's head.

With rattled nerves, Alecia slowly walked over to the phone and picked it up. She paused as she kept her focus on Rhaunda and the gun.

"Do it now!" Rhaunda repeated with force.

Alecia's hands shook as she dialed nine-one-one. Her voice cracked when she finally spoke. "Hel...lo, operator...I...uh...um...um." She looked at Rhaunda from the corner of her eyes, before she continued, "I...um...killed Alex."

Rhaunda waved the gun as a gesture for Alecia to hang up the phone.

Alecia complied, then asked, "Now what?"

"You wait!" Rhaunda barked, before she paid attention to Alecia's birthday suit. "Though, I suggest you put on some clothes. You look like a *killer hooker*," she added with hearty laughter.

Looking down, Alecia felt exposed. Quickly, she covered up her private area with one hand, and used her right arm to cover her breasts.

Throwing the gun in her purse, Rhaunda turned to leave but briefly looked back. "I may pay you a visit in jail," she teased with soft laughter. Then she opened the front door and sprinted down the street to the next block over. Her heart was racing as she opened her car door and sat behind the steering wheel, panting. When she heard the police sirens, she turned the ignition and drove away in a daze.

163

After Rhaunda left, Alecia looked at Alex's body and panicked. "Oh hell no!" she shouted, as she hurriedly dressed. "I'm not going down for this!" Minutes later, she ran out of the front door towards her car, then stopped when she noticed the tires on her car were flat. She was getting ready to run down the street but froze in place, after police cars converged on Alex's property.

One of the policemen yelled over a speaker system, "Stop where you are! Put your hands up so I can see them, and turn around!"

When Alecia complied with the officer's orders, a female police officer approached her with her hand clutched on her gun. "Don't make a move," the female officer warned.

"But I didn't do it!" Alecia screamed. "It was Rhaunda Coleman! You need to check her out! Sh...she made me call the police. I...I didn't kill Alex! I...didn't do it."

The female police officer frisked and handcuffed Alecia, then read her the Miranda rights. "...anything you say or do, can and will be held against you...."

"I told you I didn't do it!" Alecia shouted hysterically, as the female officer shoved her in the backseat of the police car.

Seconds later, several police officers rushed to Alex's condo, and found him sprawled out on the bedroom floor.

After Brian heard the police sirens, he ran outside and was shocked to see them entering Alex's condo. He freaked out when Alex was carried out on a gurney. Remembering Alex's brother, he rushed inside his condo to call Guy.

Chapter 28

Trouble in Paradise

Guy freaked out after he learned Malik's father was a ex-con. He was worried about whether his actions had put his family in danger. His mind kept drifting back to the night he and Alex found Malik's lifeless and bloodied body sprawled out on the sofa. Those images kept him awake at night.

He was in the backyard, sitting on the screened in deck drinking liquor, when Regine opened the sliding door to greet him. "Where are you going?" he asked, after noticing she was fully dressed.

Regine shook her head in disgust when she spotted the half-empty bottle of Hennessy on the table and the glass of liquor in Guy's hand. "I have a business meeting with Lamar Greene."

"Who is he?"

"He's my new business partner. Mr. Greene wants to invest in the new restaurant I'm establishing in Miami."

Guy frowned. "You never told me about him."

"I told you about Mr. Green when I met him a month ago. You don't remember?" she asked in amazement.

For a brief second, he tried but could not recall whether Regine mentioned her business associate. "Well, just make sure you take one of the bodyguard's with you."

"Guy, that's not necessary," Regine grumbled.

"That's the only way you're leaving this house." Guy's response was firm and clear.

"What's going on?" Regine asked, trying to figure out why he was being overprotective. She guessed Guy had hired Big Mike's security firm to watch over his siblings, and had suspected Alex was an unknowing client. Now Guy wanted her to rely on Big Mike's bodyguards to protect her.

Guy sighed. "Regine, you couldn't understand why your parents took drastic measures to protect you against anyone that caused you harm. I couldn't understand their logic either, until now. I'm willing to do whatever it takes to protect my family."

Pressed for time, Regine determined that there was no point in debating with Guy. "Fine," she said, as she turned to walk back inside the house.

"Don't forget what I told you!" Guy yelled loud enough for her to hear him.

Clearly frustrated, Regine stopped in her tracks and turned around. "When is this going to end?"

"What are you talking about?"

"Lately, you've been acting like a raving lunatic, constantly checking doors and getting up to look out the windows like clockwork. Don't you think you're going too far?"

"Until your siblings' lives have been threatened," Guy said in a stern voice, "don't you dare talk to me about taking anything too far."

Flinching, Regine acknowledged that she might have pressed the wrong button. She took a deep breath before responding to Guy in a leveled tone. "I didn't mean to...."

"I know," Guy interrupted, as he stood up and brushed past her. He went to his office, flopped down in his chair and buried his face in his hands.

Fuming mad, Regine followed Guy to his office. She grew concerned after she noticed Guy slouched over in his chair. "Are you okay?"

Guy lifted his head, and answered, "I'm dealing with a lot of stress right now. First Dana, now Alex." He could not get over what Regine had told him earlier, about Rhaunda's desire to kill Alex for hurting her. He had sleepless nights, wondering if she would actually follow through with her threat.

"Why are you worried about Alex? He's a grown man. When are you going to realize you cannot fix your brother's problem with women?"

Nodding his head, Guy tended to agree with Regine.

"Are you listening to me?" Regine asked, after Guy did not respond.

Intuitively, Guy snapped out of his spell and sat up in his chair. "I'm sorry. I have a lot on my mind."

Leaning against the door entrance with her arms folded, Regine said, "I don't see how Rhaunda tolerates Alex's whorish behavior. I guess he has to learn the hard way, like his big brother." Regine knew her last comment was a low blow, but thought it was the only way Guy would listen to reason.

"My job is to protect Alex!" he shouted, as he pounded his fist on the desk.

Regine placed her hand on her hip and responded in kind. "No, your job is to let Alex be a man!"

Guy shook his head. "You don't understand...."

"But I do," Regine countered. "You are so caught up in your brother and sisters' lives, you're forgetting about me and KC."

"What do you mean?" Guy asked, rejecting Regine's analysis. He thought he had given her everything she wanted, and then some.

"I can't live like this. I love you, but it's obvious you have no room for me."

"What are you saying?" Guy asked, as he sat up in his chair.

"I'm getting tired of...." The ringing phone interrupted Regine's response.

Guy answered the phone on the second ring. "Who is this?!" he barked, taking out his built up frustration on the caller.

"Is this Guy Simmons?" Brian curiously asked.

"What do you want?!"

Brian was not sure if he had the right number, so he asked, "Are you related to Alex Simmons?"

"Yes, that's my brother. Who is this?" Guy's impatience with the caller was growing thin. The frown on his face spoke volumes.

"My name is Brian Lancaster. I'm Alex's friend and neighbor."

Guy's frown began to soften. He remembered Alex had told him about his friend, Brian, a while ago. "What can I do for you?"

"I'm afraid I have bad news for you."

Guy became alarmed as he held the phone tightly to his ear. "What is it?"

"Your brother is in the hospital."

"What happened?"

"He was shot."

Guy's mouth flew open as he sat up in his chair. "Where is he?"

"Tampa Bay General."

After hanging up the phone, Guy grabbed his car keys, and brushed past Regine.

"What's wrong?!" Regine shouted, after noticing Guy's reaction.

Guy ignored Regine as he dashed toward the front door.

Regine ran after him and grabbed his hand before he walked out of the front door. "Guy, please talk to me."

After turning to Regine, Guy teared up while trying to get a handle on his emotions. "Alex has been shot."

"Oh, God! No!" Regine cried out, as tears streamed down her face.

Guy embraced Regine, and whispered in her ear, "Alex is going to be okay."

"Let me go with you," she pleaded, still shaken by the bad news.

"No, you stay here."

"I'm going!" Regine replied with force.

Guy knew he could not change her mind, so he hollered for Mimi.

Immediately, Mimi came running downstairs. "Mr. Simmons, you called?"

"We're going to the hospital. I need you to keep an eye on KC, until we return."

"No problem, sir. May I ask who's in the hospital?"

"My brother, Alex. Please do not tell my mother."

"I understand."

Guy looked at his watch, before he added, "Dana and Cassie will be home from school soon. I'll call Billy and tell him to bring them to the hospital."

As soon as Guy and Regine left for the hospital, Mimi walked into Jeanine's room with KC on her hip.

"Bring him to me," Jeanine insisted, even though her voice was barely audible. Her heart melted when she touched KC's face. "He's beautiful."

Mimi chuckled. "And a handful."

Smiling, Jeanine held his hand. "Where are his parents?"

Averting her eyes, Mimi struggled to come up with a good lie. "They…uh…had to go out. They'll be back soon."

Suddenly, Jeanine's eyes flew open when she heard Alex's name on the news station. She focused her attention on the news reporter.

Busted for not being fully truthful, Mimi felt small as she listened to the reporter give an update on the very issue Guy did not want her to tell Jeanine.

"Alex Simmons was shot by a woman named Alecia Kellam," the news reporter stated. "Ms. Kellam has been taken arrested and taken into custody. Mr. Simmons is listed in critical condition. More news to follow."

Jeanine turned to Mimi for answers.

"Mrs. Benedict," Mimi nervously said, "I didn't want to lie to you, but Mr. Simmons told me not to tell you."

"I know," Jeanine replied, while nodding. She knew Guy was trying to protect her. "Please call the hospital to see how Alex is doing."

While balancing KC on her hip, Mimi picked up the phone and called the hospital. After obtaining the information, she slowly put the phone on its cradle. She dreaded telling Jeanine more bad news.

Alarmed by Mimi's reaction, Jeanine asked, "Is Alex okay?"

"He's in a coma."

"Oh God!" Jeanine cried out, as tears poured down her face.

Mimi grabbed a tissue from Jeanine's nightstand and handed it to her. "Mrs. Benedict, please do not worry. Alex is going to be okay."

Jeanine dried her eyes. "I know," she said with a heavy heart. "I just need some rest."

Mimi left the room, closing the door behind her.

Jeanine wanted to go see Alex, but she was too weak to move her limbs. She thought about all the life-threatening situations her stepchildren found themselves in lately, and could not help but feel partially responsible. Ever since she turned the business over to Guy and Alex, making them instant millionaires, their lives have been in utter chaos.

On the way to the hospital, Guy called the hospital and asked to speak to Alex's doctor. He was relieved when the doctor told him that he had successfully removed the bullets, which were lodged between Alex's heart and abdomen. However, the doctor further explained that Alex had lost a lot of blood, and had fallen into a coma following surgery.

After swerving into the nearest parking space, Guy and Regine rushed through the hospital doors, and ran to the receptionist desk, panting. "We're here to see Alex Simmons," he told the receptionist, after showing his ID. "I'm his brother and this is my wife."

The receptionist checked Guy's ID, then looked at her monitor for Alex's name. "He's in the intensive care unit, room three."

Regine and Guy dashed to the ICU where see-through glass encased each room, and white curtains hung in the door entrance, in lieu of doors, to give the patients privacy. Approaching Alex's room, Guy became nervous and quivered at the sight of the white curtain. Noticing Guy's reaction, Regine grabbed his hand to comfort him. She, too, was nervous.

Guy panicked when he stepped into the room where Alex laid still while the oxygen machine pumped air into his heart and lungs. "I was supposed to protect him!" he cried out, as tears poured down his face.

Regine embraced Guy, then she looked into his eyes. "It's not your fault. We have to believe Alex is going to pull through this."

"We all have to pray for Alex," Bryce sadly replied. Sitting in a chair, in the background, he startled both Guy and Regine. Earlier, he told the receptionist he was Alex's brother. He wanted to see for himself that Alex was still alive.

"Who are you?" Guy asked. "Were you with Alex when he was shot?"

Catching on to what Guy was implying, Bryce extended his hand to introduce himself. "I'm a friend of Alex's. I heard he was rushed to the hospital from the news reports."

"You never answered my question," Guy said, after putting Bryce's name with his face. When Alex told him about the merger proposal, he had conducted extensive research on Bryce and his company.

"I'm here," Bryce said after withdrawing his hand, "because I care about your brother."

Guy grunted as he glared at Bryce with contempt.

"We appreciate you coming," Regine intervened after sensing the tension between Bryce and Guy, "but we'd like to be alone with Alex."

"I understand," Bryce said, before he walked past them and out of Alex's room. He silently prayed Alex would come out of the coma soon. Based on his first impression of Guy, Bryce determined that it would be easier to deal with Alex. He was relieved his hired field hand, Philipo Rijos, had called told him Alex was shot.

When Philipo told Bryce about his plan to kill Alex for screwing around with his best friend's wife, he was surprised Bryce told him Alex was off limits. "What is it to you?" he asked Bryce.

"Alex is a part of my master plan," Bryce replied. "Tell your friend that he's not to go near Alex. Otherwise, he won't live to see tomorrow. Got it?"

Philipo nodded. Unfortunately, his best friend, Armando, did not heed his warning. It did not take long for Bryce to order the hit, forcing Philipo to partake in his friend's death. Coincidently, Bryce had instructed him to follow Alex, which was how he found out Alex was shot. As Philipo pulled away from Alex's condo, he thought Bryce would be interested in knowing that his prized possession might be dead.

As soon as Bryce left Alex's room, Detective Tom Hines from the Tampa Bay police department, entered the room.

Sensing someone was behind him, Guy turned around and faced the officer with a bewildered gaze. "May I help you?"

"Yes, are you related to Alex Simmons?"

Guy nodded. "He's my brother."

"I hate to bother you," the detective said, "but I would like to ask you some questions."

"Can it wait?" Regine interjected, annoyed with the detective's presence.

"I wish it could," the detective explained, "but we need to make sure we don't have the wrong person locked up."

"What?!" Regine exclaimed, with a frown on her face. "What is this nonsense about possibly having the wrong person?!"

Guy touched Regine's right shoulder, to get her attention. "Hon', I'll go with the detective. You stay here with Alex." He followed the detective to an empty waiting room.

"Again," the detective said as he and Guy sat down, "I hate to bother you."

Guy held up his hand as a peace offering. "No, it's okay. How can I help you?"

"Do you know Alecia Kellam?"

"No, why?" Guy asked out of curiosity.

"We have her locked up for shooting your brother."

Guy leaned closer to the detective, and asked, "Did she admit to shooting Alex?"

"Yes, but Ms. Kellam explained she had been intimate with Alex, so she had no reason to shoot him."

Guy grunted. "Maybe she's a sick woman, or maybe she snapped after Alex told her he didn't want her."

"We thought about those scenarios, but it still doesn't add up. Ms. Kellam is rich. She could have any man of her dreams. She doesn't fit the profile of a killer," the detective added, after deep thought.

"So what does that have to do with anything?" Guy snapped, slightly annoyed with the detective's analysis.

Detective Hines exhaled before responding. "Ms. Kellam told me your brother's girlfriend, Rhaunda Coleman, shot him, and is now framing her."

"Do you believe her?"

"We have to consider all evidence, including the lie detector test Ms. Kellam insisted on taking."

Guy tilted his head toward the detective. "Well, what were the results?"

"She passed, but with conflicting answers."

"I don't understand."

"The results proved that Ms. Kellam admitted to calling nine-one-one and telling the operator she shot Alex. However, the results also proved that Ms. Kellam told the truth when she stated she did not shoot your brother."

Guy frowned. "That doesn't make any sense. What about the gun?"

"We were not able to find a gun in Ms. Kellam's possession, nor were we able to locate it in your brother's condo."

"That doesn't mean anything. Maybe she left his condo to go hide it, then she came back to see if he was dead."

"We did not find gun residue on Ms. Kellam's hands."

"She could have worn gloves," Guy countered.

The detective nodded, agreeing to that possibility. "We have submitted a court order to search Ms. Kellam's apartment."

"Did Ms. Kellam say why Rhaunda shot Alex?"

"Yes, she stated that Ms. Coleman was not herself."

"Have you interviewed Rhaunda?"

"Not yet. Her mother contacted us, and agreed to bring her in later for questioning."

Guy stood up in a huff. "I don't want her nowhere near my brother!"

The detective took a deep breath before responding. "Because Ms. Coleman has not been charged with shooting Alex, we have no way of controlling her comings and goings."

Guy brushed his hand across his head out of frustration before turning to the detective. "What can I do to stop Rhaunda from coming here to see Alex?"

"You can file an injunction through the courts, but the judge will need justification to impose the order."

"I'm going straight to the courthouse after I leave the hospital."

"That's your best bet," the detective said, as he stood up to leave. "I'll let you know as soon as we have any new evidence."

With a thin smile, Guy shook the detective's hand. "I'd appreciate that."

Chapter 29
Cover-Up

Rhaunda was distraught as she drove away from the scene of the crime. When she neared her parents' home, she was suddenly remorseful. "Oh God!" she cried out. "What have I done?" Her vision became blurred as a river of tears cascaded down her face. By the time she pulled into the driveway, she was weeping, nonstop. She did not notice her mother driving up behind her.

After Elizabeth left Alex's condo, she had returned home to discover Rhaunda was nowhere in sight. She called Rhaunda's cell phone, but did not get an answer. Then she called the church, and was told Rhaunda never showed up for work. Elizabeth had a gut feeling that her daughter's disappearance had something to do with Alex. So she headed over to Alex's condo and watched in horror as Rhaunda dashed out of Alex's front door and sprinted down the street to her SUV. Then she braced herself when Rhaunda sped off, almost colliding with an oncoming car. She was relieved Rhaunda had made it home in one piece.

Elizabeth's heart was beating fast as she unbuckled her seatbelt and rushed to her daughter. "Rhaunda!" she shouted, while banging on the car window. "Open the door!"

Slowly, Rhaunda turned to her mother with misty eyes. She opened her mouth to respond but found it difficult to speak.

"Please baby, open the door so we can talk."

Without saying a word and opting to look straight ahead, Rhaunda pressed the automatic button to the window.

Elizabeth watched the window go down with great relief. She used a soothing and nurturing tone to communicate with her daughter. "Baby, whatever it is, it's going to be okay."

"But Ma," Rhaunda whined as she turned to her mother with wide eyes, "you don't know what I did."

"Whatever you did, it's not as bad as it seems," Elizabeth reasoned.

"But…you don't…understand," Rhaunda stammered as tears flowed down her face. "I just committed…."

"Shhhh…," Elizabeth cautioned, as she put her index finger to Rhaunda's lips. "Whatever you did, God has already forgiven you."

Perplexed, Rhaunda looked to her mother for answers. "How?"

"Because He's merciful," Elizabeth proclaimed, as she opened Rhaunda's car door.

Rhaunda's eyes began to water again, as she softly whispered, "I can go to jail for what I did."

Elizabeth paused as she digested what Rhaunda was hinting. Mentally, she prayed for God to have mercy on her daughter's soul. "Rhaunda, baby, let's go inside and pray. Then you'll be able to erase any memories of today's events."

"How?" Rhaunda asked, wiping away her tears.

"By not talking about it; not even with me. Just pretend like it was a bad dream."

Rhaunda was not sure if this was the right approach, but she trusted her mother.

With nervous jitters, Elizabeth glanced at the driveway. "Come inside," she said as she held out her hand for her daughter, "before your father comes home." In response, Rhaunda grabbed her mother's hand and got out of her car.

Elizabeth wrapped her arm around her daughter's waist and walked with her upstairs to her bedroom. Together, they kneeled down next to the bed and prayed in silence. Afterward, Elizabeth turned to Rhaunda, and said, "I love you. I will never let anything happen to you. Whatever you did, it is in God's hands now. Lie down and get some rest."

Drained and overwhelmed, Rhaunda got in bed and closed her eyes. Though, she found it difficult to sleep.

Elizabeth pulled the blanket over Rhaunda before she walked out of the bedroom and closed the door behind her. Then she rushed downstairs and turned on the television in the living room. Using the remote control, she flipped through the channels until she found the local news station. She sat on the couch as the news broadcaster reported Alecia Kellam was taken into custody for shooting Alex Simmons. Elizabeth waited on pins and needles to hear the news of Alex's condition.

The reporter continued, "Alex Simmons is listed in critical condition. More news to follow."

"Thank God," Elizabeth whispered to herself, relieved Alex was still alive. As First Lady, she prided herself on maintaining a respectable household with a loving husband and daughter. Long ago, she had acknowledged that her and her husband's positions afforded them many opportunities that would be in jeopardy if her family was ever involved in a scandal.

Sighing, Elizabeth picked up the phone in the living room, to call her husband. She feared the pastor would get wind of this news before she had the opportunity to talk to him. She braced herself after he answered her call. "Honey, we need to talk."

"Can't this wait?" he asked, clearly impatient.

"No, this can't wait!" Elizabeth exclaimed. "You need to come home right away!"

Sitting up in his office chair, he asked, "Is everything alright at the house?"

"No," Elizabeth solemnly replied. "It's Rhaunda."

"What about her?"

"Rhaunda and Alex had a little altercation."

"I thought you told me Rhaunda was over that *loser*," he stated, remembering his wife had told him Rhaunda had made up her mind to go on with her life, without Alex. "So what's the problem?"

"Alex has been shot."

"The Lord works in mysterious ways," the pastor replied with a smug grin. "Is he dead?"

"No, but he's in critical condition."

"So why should I care?"

"Rhaunda was there when Alex was shot. You need to come home."

"Oh God!" the pastor gasped. "I'm on my way."

Elizabeth hung up the phone and returned to Rhaunda's room. She knocked before entering. "Honey, are you awake?"

"Yes, mother," Rhaunda confirmed, while facing the wall. She was still shaken up over the scene with Alex.

With a strong stance, Elizabeth walked toward Rhaunda and touched her shoulder. "Alex is not dead, if that's what you're worried about."

"He's alive?" Rhaunda asked, as she turned around to face her mother.

Elizabeth smiled. "Yes, baby, he's alive."

"I thought I killed him," Rhaunda confessed in a soft whisper.

"I know baby." Elizabeth said, as she wiped strands of hair out of Rhaunda's face. "Do not tell anyone else that you shot Alex."

"But I did."

"No you didn't, Elizabeth firmly replied. "Alecia is in custody, not you. She pulled the trigger."

"But she didn't," Rhaunda replied with assurance. "I set her up."

"Good for you," Elizabeth said with a wide grin. "Now your father is on his way home. When he gets here, do not tell him you shot Alex. Understand?"

"Yes, mother," Rhaunda agreed with apprehension.

"Do you still have the gun?"

Rhaunda nodded. "Yes, it's in my purse."

"Give it to me. We need to get rid of it."

"I left my purse in the car."

"Don't worry. I'll go get it. We have to remove the gun residue from your hands. Give me your car keys."

"What are you talking about?" Rhaunda asked, as she sat up and gave her mother her keys.

"If you fired the gun, the residue is on your hands. Don't worry, we're going to wash your hands with my own secret recipe."

In her younger days, Elizabeth was the girlfriend of a professional murderer. Her ex-boyfriend had taught her how to use a gun and get rid of incriminating evidence, including gun residue.

"We have to hurry up," Elizabeth announced, after Rhaunda sat still. "Change your clothes and meet me downstairs. Your father is going to be here any minute. He's going to take us to the hospital to visit Alex."

Rhaunda frowned. "We're going to the hospital?"

"Yes, dear. Like I told you before, you did not shoot Alex, so you have no reason to hide. You and Alex are engaged, remember?"

"We are?" Rhaunda asked in amazement.

Elizabeth smiled. "Yes sweetheart. Your job is to let everyone know it. Alex needs you during a time like this. Trust me, he's going to appreciate your being there for him in the long run."

Perplexed, Rhaunda squinted her eyes, before asking, "Do you want me to be with Alex?"

"I want you to be happy," Elizabeth said, before she walked out of Rhaunda's bedroom, on the way to get the gun. She decided to throw the gun in the lake, not far from where they lived.

After her mother left her room, Rhaunda was beginning to believe that she did not shoot Alex; that it was just a figment of her imagination.

Elizabeth believed her plan would work if Rhaunda followed her lead. She was not about to let Alex throw a wrench in her *perfect family* image. She blamed him for pushing Rhaunda over the edge.

Fifteen years earlier, the doctor had told Elizabeth that Rhaunda would be fine as long as she took lithium for her mental condition. He further explained that any traumatic incident, however, could trigger psychotic episodes that could cause Rhaunda to harm herself or someone else. Elizabeth figured the worst was over, and it was up to her to convince Rhaunda that she was sane and normal.

Chapter 30

Friction

*A*bdul thought it was strange when Sapp did not call him to give him an update on Malik. He had called him several times, but his calls went directly to Sapp's voicemail. Abdul decided to call him from a different phone, and was surprised that his call was answered. "Where's Malik?" he gruffly asked without a formal greeting.

Startled by the sound of Abdul's booming voice, Sapp looked like a deer in headlights. Up until now, he had avoided Abdul's calls, thanks to caller ID. "I…don't…know," he managed to choke out. "I haven't…seen him in…a couple of days."

"I hired you to watch over him. Is there a reason you're avoiding my calls?"

After thinking of a good excuse, Sapp said, "I've been busy."

"Your job is to look after Malik!" Abdul angrily retorted.

On purpose, Sapp had avoided following up with Malik. He was still upset with his friend for putting his hands on Dana. "Malik has been tripping," he stated, putting up a strong front even though he was scared witless. "He's been hanging around the wrong crowd and using drugs."

Abdul's nostrils flared, as he shouted, "What does that have to do with the question I asked you?!"

"I can't control what Malik does," Sapp snapped, "or where he goes, or who he hangs out with." For a split second, he had forgotten he was talking to Abdul, one of America's top-notch criminals.

"That's what I paid you to do!" Abdul barked with venom in his throat. He wanted to crawl through the phone and strangle Sapp. "You have one hour to call me back and let me know my son is safe. Otherwise, I'm coming to Tampa to tear a hole in your *ass*. Got it?!"

Abdul hung up the phone, not giving Sapp the opportunity to respond. He had a feeling Sapp was lying to him, so he contacted his secret informant, Officer Ratcliff of the Tampa Bay police force, to check on Malik. He met the officer several years earlier, during a sting operation. After getting caught in a money laundering scheme, Abdul paid Officer Ratcliff to look the other way.

"You know who this is!" Abdul shouted, after the officer answered his call.

The officer nodded. "What can I do for you?"

"I need you to check on my son." After Abdul gave the officer Malik's name and address, he said, "Do not tell him I'm looking for him. In fact, he should not know I exist."

"I'll call you as soon as I hear something. How much?" the officer asked, hoping to get a hefty sum in exchange for information about Malik.

"You know the deal!" Abdul barked, before disconnecting the call. The officer's question infuriated him. He prided himself on paying off his informants in a timely fashion.

When Sapp heard the dial tone, he jumped in his car and rushed to Malik's apartment. He did not expect to see police cars surrounding the premises. Figuring there was too much heat, Sapp decided to come back later. He turned to leave but turned back when he heard someone calling his name.

"Hey there," Billy said, walking fast to catch up with Sapp. "I thought that was you."

"Hey," Sapp uneasily replied. "How are you?"

Billy briefly turned back to the scene of the crime. "Do you know how this happened?"

Sapp frowned. "I don't know what you're talking about."

Frowning and tilting his head sideways, Billy asked, "You don't know about Malik?"

"Isn't it obvious?" Sapp asked, pointing in the direction of Malik's apartment. "He has gotten himself in trouble with the law. What did he do this time?"

"Malik is missing," Billy weakly replied. "He might be dead."

Sapp stood still. He was temporarily speechless. "How do you know Malik is dead?"

"I spoke to one of the police investigators. He told me they discovered blood in Malik's apartment."

"So, that doesn't mean anything," Sapp replied, dismissing Billy's explanation.

"The investigators are running DNA tests at the lab. They believe the blood belongs to Malik."

"How could they conclude that without running the tests first?"

"I guess they put the facts and the evidence into perspective."

Sapp began to tear up in response. He began shaking before he dropped to the ground, crying.

Billy knelt down beside Sapp to console him. "It's okay," he said, as he embraced Sapp. "Let it all out."

"How could this happen?" Sapp asked between sniffles.

'I don't know, but I aim to find out."

"How?"

"Trust me," Billy said with conviction. "I will find Malik's killer, if it's the last thing I do."

"I don't know what I'm going to tell his father," Sapp said with deep concern.

"Do you know Malik's father?"

"I work for him. He hired me to look after Malik."

Billy's eyes bulged out of his head in surprise. "Well that explains everything," he said, after deep thought. "The car you bought for Malik; was that your doing?"

"No, Malik's father, Abdul, paid for his car. He also paid Malik's rent and gave him an allowance through me."

"Wow," Billy said with disbelief. "Why didn't he do it himself?"

"Abdul told me he tried, but Malik rejected him and anything he had offered him."

"So he used you to get to closer to his son. Did Malik know?"

"No, his father swore me to secrecy. That was the condition for hiring me."

"Are you going to tell his father about Malik?"

Sapp paused as he thought about Billy's question. "I don't know," he finally said. "Abdul is liable to kill me when he finds out."

"Do you have anywhere to hide out?"

Shaking his head, Sapp concluded his life was in jeopardy. He needed an escape plan but was running out of money.

"Why don't you stay with me, until you figure out what to do?"

"I don't think that's a good idea. The people I'm dealing with are dangerous."

Billy rested his hand on Sapp's shoulders. "You will be safe with me."

"Are you sure?" Sapp questioned, his eyes filled with fear.

Billy smiled. "I'm sure."

"Thank you," Sapp said with deep relief.

"You want me to go with you to get your things?"

"No, I'll be fine."

Billy pulled out a piece of paper from his writing pad, and wrote down his address. "I have to go pick up my clients and run a couple of errands, but there's an extra key under the mat in front of my door. You're welcome to make yourself at home. I'll be home later."

Sapp took the paper before he looked into Billy's eyes. "Why are you doing this?"

"Malik was fond of you. I appreciate the way you looked out for him, even though it was your job. He wasn't perfect," Billy added, "but he didn't get into a whole lot of trouble either."

Sapp thought, *If only you knew.* He shook Billy's hand, before turning to leave.

After Billy left Malik's apartment complex, he drove to the twins' school to retrieve them. He was caught off guard when Dana pulled him aside, and asked, "Have you heard from Malik?"

Billy shook his head. "I haven't seen Malik in a while."

Dana eyes began to water, as she admitted, "I'm worried something has happened to him."

Billy tightened his lips. He was unsure if he should tell Dana that Malik might be dead, so he said, "Malik is missing."

"Missing?" Dana asked with raised brows. "What do you mean?"

"I went by his apartment, and the police were there."

Dana's eyes flew open from shock. "What do you think happened to him?" she asked, as tears poured down her face.

"I don't know. That's what I plan to find out. In the meantime, your brother asked me to drop you and Cassie off at the hospital."

"Why?"

"He wouldn't say."

Chapter 31
Life Near Death

Where am I? Alex silently asked himself, after he felt something sticking in his arm and air being pumped through his nostrils. He struggled to open his eyes but they felt heavy, like lumps of coal. Then he heard mumbling sounds of machines and people around him. *Why can't I open my eyes or move my limbs? Everything is so pitch black. Is this what 'life after death' feels like?*

Desperate to find out what was going on, Alex zoomed in on the voices. One of the voices sounded familiar. He tried to open his mouth to call out Guy's name, but his lips never moved. Feeling frustrated, Alex drifted off to a dark place, believing he heard his brother's voice for the last time.

Regine and Guy were in the room when the doctor walked in. They stood back while the doctor took Alex's vitals. Guy turned to the doctor, and asked, "Is he going to be okay?"

After checking Alex's heart rate with the stethoscope, the doctor said, "We won't know anything until he comes out of the coma."

Overcome with fear of losing Alex, Guy broke down crying. "Come on, Alex," he sobbed. "You've got to pull through."

Although Regine was visibly upset, she stifled her tears to console her husband. Lovingly, she rested her hand on the back of his shoulder, and said, "He's going to pull through."

Noticing their fragile state, the doctor turned to Regine, and said, "Maybe it would be a good idea for both of you to go to the chapel and pray. Right now, Alex needs a miracle."

"I think it's a good idea," Regine replied.

Guy nodded in agreement as his eyes remained focused on Alex. "Hang in there, little brother. I love you." Then he grabbed Regine's hand and headed to the chapel.

In the chapel, Guy and Regine prayed for God's divine intervention. Guy also reflected on what he could have possibly done to protect his brother. When they returned to the hospital room, they were surprised to see Rhaunda standing next to Alex's bed with her parents, Elizabeth and Pastor Coleman.

"What in the *hell* are you doing here?!" Guy hollered while glaring at Rhaunda.

Rhaunda turned to Guy with tears in her eyes. When she arrived at the hospital, she was overwhelmed with guilt and had been crying ever since. "We got here as soon as we found out," she said between sniffles. "How is he?"

"How dare you come here after you shot my brother?!" Guy shouted, while looking at Rhaunda with disdain.

After observing the scene, Pastor Coleman stepped in front of Rhaunda to confront Guy. "You have some nerve blaming my daughter," he spouted with flared nostrils.

"I don't want her here!" Guy sharply announced.

Realizing the situation was getting out of hand, Elizabeth intervened using a soothing voice, "Now, now, let's simmer down. We all know Rhaunda did not have anything to do with Alex getting shot. She's a sweet girl. She loves Alex. That's why we're here."

"Mrs. Coleman," Guy said through clenched teeth, "with all due respect, I think it's best if you all leave."

Elizabeth gasped from Guy's response. "Honey," she said as she moved closer to her husband, "say something."

"There's nothing to say," the pastor muttered, as he stood toe-to-toe with Guy. "It's obvious that he doesn't want us here. Let's go."

With pleading eyes, Rhaunda turned to Regine for support. "Please talk to Guy. I love Alex. I would not hurt him."

Regine peered at her husband, who looked like he was about to have a conniption. "I think Guy is right. There are so many accusations floating around, some we cannot ignore."

"What are you saying?" Rhaunda asked in disbelief. "You think I shot Alex?"

Careful not to sound accusatory, Regine cautiously said, "I mean we should refrain from blaming anyone, until the police finish their investigation."

Rhaunda nodded. "I understand. I'll come back tomorrow."

"Not if I can help it," Guy countered.

"Let's go!" the pastor barked, as he grabbed his daughter's hand and rushed out of the room." His wife quickly followed suit.

As soon as Rhaunda and her parents left, Billy walked in Alex's room with the twins in tow. He looked at Alex lying in the hospital bed, and instantly felt sorrow. Realizing the family needed some privacy, he decided to step outside the room.

Dana broke down crying as soon as she walked in the room. "What happened?" she asked, as she approached Alex's bed.

"Alex is in a coma," Guy said, as he stood next to her with his arm wrapped around her shoulder.

Holding back tears, Cassie asked, "Who did this to our brother?"

Guy did not want to outright accuse Rhaunda without knowing all the facts, so he simply said, "Someone shot him."

Dana looked to Guy for answers as tears flowed down her face. "Is he going to be okay?" she asked, her voice filled with worry.

To comfort Dana, Regine said, "All we can do right now is pray that Alex pulls through. Let's hold hands and pray together." She led the prayer while everyone else bowed their heads.

Then Guy turned to Regine, and said, "I'll stay up here with Alex for a little while longer. Tell Billy to take you all home."

"Are you sure you don't want us to stay longer?" Regine asked.

Guy briefly looked at Alex before responding. "I'm sure."

Regine grabbed her purse, then gave Guy a warm embrace. "What do you want me to tell your mother?"

"Nothing," he said, after pondering her question.

Regine frowned. "Don't you think you're being unfair by keeping this from her?"

"She's been through enough already," Guy explained. "I don't want her to worry, needlessly."

"I hope you know what you're doing," Regine said, before turning to the twins. "Come on girls, we're leaving." Looking sad, Dana and Cassie followed her out of the room.

Alex's neighbor strolled into Alex's room right after they left. "How is he?!" Brian asked Guy, sounding as if he was almost out of breath. Driving like a maniac, he had rushed to the hospital after the police left Alex's condo.

"He's comatose."

"*Damn!*" Brian balked, as he briefly lowered his head. "I couldn't help but notice Rhaunda and her parents leaving the hospital. I hope they weren't here to see Alex."

Guy grimaced. "Unfortunately, they were."

"What in the hell are they doing up here?" Brian inquired. "The way Rhaunda's parents threatened Alex; it wasn't right."

"What are you talking about?" Guy inquired, eagerly seeking an explanation. He remained speechless as Brian gave him specific details about what happened between Alex and Rhaunda's parents.

"When did this happen?" Guy asked out of curiosity.

Brian sighed. "Her father showed up yesterday, and her mother showed up early this morning. I feel bad for what happened to Alex."

Feeling the same guilt, Guy rested his hand on Brian's shoulder. "Alex was my responsibility, not yours."

"You don't understand," Brian said, as he glanced at Alex.

"But I do. Alex is my brother, not yours. I appreciate the way you've been looking out for him."

"I would like to stay with him tonight, if you don't mind."

"No I don't. I'd appreciate that."

Shaken up by Guy's allegation, Rhaunda and her parents left Alex's room in silence. They did not notice Brian when he stepped out of the elevator before they got on it. As soon as the elevator door closed, Pastor Coleman turned to Rhaunda, and asked, "What was that all about?"

"I don't know what you mean?" Rhaunda innocently replied.

He looked at Rhaunda with narrowed eyes. "I believe you do. What happened between you and Alex? I thought you two were over."

Elizabeth intervened. "Honey, you remember I told you Rhaunda and Alex made up."

"That's not what I recall. You told me Rhaunda was over Alex."

Caught in a lie, Elizabeth was rendered speechless.

Probing further, the pastor asked his wife, "Why did you insist that we come to the hospital to visit Alex? And why does his brother think Rhaunda shot Alex?"

"Honey," Elizabeth said in a syrupy voice, "you know how Rhaunda feels about Alex. And his brother is probably repeating what Alecia told the police."

Pastor Coleman eyed his wife as he thought to himself, *I smell a rat.* He looked over at Rhaunda and wondered if she knew more than she let on. "We'll discuss this later," he said, as the elevator door opened on cue.

Elizabeth waited until they got in the car before she turned to her husband and suggested that they go to the police station.

"Why?" the pastor asked with furrowed brows.

Elizabeth buckled her seatbelt before stating, "I told the police that we will bring Rhaunda in for questioning."

"What are you talking about?"

"The police called after Alecia accused Rhaunda of shooting Alex. I figured she would pull a stunt like this," Elizabeth snarled.

The pastor was trying to control his anger as he turned to Rhaunda before pulling out onto to the highway, en route to the police station.

Guy returned home from the hospital worried sick over whether Alex would come out of the coma. As soon as he walked into the bedroom, Regine rolled over in bed and turned to him with questioning eyes. "How is he?"

"He's still in a coma," he solemnly replied. "What did you tell mother?"

"When we came home, Mimi told me Jeanine found out about Alex, because it was on the news."

Guy winced. He had hoped to delay telling Jeanine about Alex. "How did she handle the news?"

"According to Mimi, not well."

Sighing, Guy sat at the foot of the bed to remove his shoes. "I'll talk to her in the morning. How are the girls?"

"You know Dana, she's an emotional wreck. And Cassie, she's quiet but I think she's holding everything inside. I think all of us need to go to therapy, to learn how to cope with this."

"Maybe you're right," Guy admitted, as he prepared for bed. "You were supposed to meet with your business associate this morning. Did you get ahold of him, to reschedule your meeting?"

"Yes, I contacted Lamar Greene as soon as I returned home."

"When will I get a chance to meet him?" Guy curiously asked with a flicker of jealousy.

"You can meet him tomorrow, if you'd like. We will be meeting at the restaurant in St. Petersburg."

"That won't work. I have a lot of running around to do in the morning. Then I'm going to the hospital to see about Alex."

"Okay, whenever you have time, I'll arrange the meeting around *your* schedule."

Quietly, Guy got in bed and turned away from Regine. He did not want her to see that he was scared and vulnerable. After he left the hospital, he went to the police station to report that Rhaunda's parents made threats to kill Alex. Guy felt deflated when they told him they could not do anything, unless Alex pressed charges. Of course that was impossible, considering Alex's comatose status. He was also disappointed to discover he could not get an injunction that would prevent Rhaunda from going near his brother without Alex's signed statement.

Chapter 32

On the Run

After Billy took Regine and the twins home, he returned to Malik's apartment complex and continued questioning any and everyone who had seen Malik before he went missing. Unfortunately, he did not find any leads, so he returned home to discover Sapp was nowhere in sight. "Sapp, are you here?" he asked, after checking all the rooms. He did not see anyone but heard a slight movement coming from the closet in his guest bedroom. With his gun drawn, Billy warned, "Whoever you are, come out now with your hands up."

"Don't shoot," Sapp said, as he opened the closet door with his hands up. "It's me." He was trembling, and his fair complexion had turned almost ghostly.

Exhaling, Billy withdrew his gun. "What are you doing in there?"

Shivering, Sapp stood in one place, as he fearfully stated, "He's going to kill me."

"Who?"

"Abdul, Malik's father."

"But you're safe in my apartment. No one knows you're here."

"They know who you are." Sapp muttered under his breath.

"How?"

Sapp paused, before he explained, "Abdul wanted to know who Malik was hanging out with, so I gave him some information about you."

Billy cupped his chin, mulling over Sapp's confession. "So Abdul knows where I live, huh?"

Sapp nodded with his eyes averted to the floor.

Earlier, Abdul had requested the names and addresses of everyone that was in Malik's life. At the time, Sapp did not think he would be relying on Billy's assistance, or his residence to hide out.

Pacing back and forth, Billy tried to think of an alternate escape plan for him and Sapp. He pulled out his cell phone and called his employer. "I need your help."

"Where are you?" Big Mike curiously asked, as he sat up in his office chair.

"I'm home. Can you arrange to have a helicopter pick me up?"

"Why?"

"Malik's friend is in trouble."

"Who? Sapp?"

"Yes, his life is in danger," Billy explained, as he briefly looked at Sapp, who was on the verge of a nervous breakdown.

Meditatively, Big Mike thought about Billy's request. He knew Billy would not have called if it were not serious. "Where does he need to go?"

"He needs to leave the country."

"This sounds serious."

"It is. I wouldn't have contacted you, otherwise."

"I'll make some phone calls, and…."

"Sir," Billy interrupted, "this is serious. Sapp is with me, so my life is also in danger."

"Well if that's the case, I think we should get the police involved."

"Sir, based on what Sapp told me, we cannot rely on the police to protect us."

"I understand," Big Mike said, after a brief pause. "Where do you want me to send the helicopter?"

"Behind the YMCA, off Washington Avenue in Tampa, there's a baseball field under construction. The helicopter can land there. Then we will need a jet once we touch down in New York."

"I'll make the arrangements. Be careful."

"Thanks boss."

"Call and let me know when you've arrived at your final destination."

"Will do."

"Don't worry about the twins. I'll call Guy and tell him you're dealing with a family crisis. I'll get someone else to watch over them."

"Thank you for everything."

After Billy disconnected the call, he looked over at Sapp and saw fear written all over his face. Then his eyes honed in on Sapp's thuggish appearance. "You need to change into something less conspicuous. You look to be about Malik's size. Look in the guest closet and find something."

A while ago, Billy had purchased some clothes for Malik, so whenever he spent the night, he would have something to wear the next day. Malik did not like Billy's selections, so the clothes remained in the guestroom closet with the new tags still on them.

In the guest room, Sapp had changed into a pair of jeans and a plaid dress shirt. Then he strolled into Billy's bedroom and noticed Billy was packing a small suitcase.

Billy looked at Sapp and laughed. "We look like twins, huh?"

Sapp snickered after noticing Billy had changed out of his black two-piece suit and tie to a pair of jeans and a plaid shirt. "Yeah, something like that."

"Wear these," Billy insisted, as he threw Sapp a baseball cap and a pair of dark shades. "I have a plan, follow me."

Sapp put on the cap and shades, grabbed his overnight bag and stayed close behind Billy. "Where are we going?"

Billy briefly turned back, and said, "Just trust me." He did not want to take any chances at being followed, so he and Sapp went to his neighbor's to borrow their car. His neighbors were a young hip couple. They were also newlyweds and free spirits. Billy was relieved the couple did not ask any questions, especially when he told them exactly where to find their car in one hour.

During the drive to the YMCA, Sapp sat in the front passenger seat with his head hunched low. Billy, who also sported a baseball cap and shades, peered over at Sapp, and wondered if he was hiding something. "Is there something you haven't told me?"

Slowly, Sapp turned to Billy, and said, "I told you everything I know."

"If you have something to say, now is the time to tell me. I'm here to protect you."

Pondering Billy's question, Sapp toyed with the idea of coming clean. He looked at Billy, then turned away as he spoke. "I returned to Malik's apartment the night he got killed."

Nodding his head, Sapp had confirmed Billy's suspicions. "What happened?"

"One day, I walked into Malik's apartment and caught him snorting cocaine. I tried to talk some sense into him, but he freaked out on me. In fact, he consistently indulged in drugs and alcohol, which made him violent and unmanageable. When Malik hit Dana, I lost it," Sapp admitted, while choked up. "No woman should ever be disrespected like that."

Billy nodded in agreement.

With uneasiness, Sapp looked out of the window as he recounted what happened that infamous night. "I entered Malik's apartment with his key. Malik never moved. He was still passed out on the sofa from his drunken state. I walked over to the sofa and hovered over him with a thirty-eight. I was getting ready to fire the gun, but I saw blood seeping out of his mouth. He was already dead. Someone had put a hole in his chest, and another one in his head."

"Why didn't you call the police?" Billy asked, struggling to contain his anger.

"Dana's brothers were looking for Malik after I discovered his body. I was afraid that they would be implicated for murder. For what it's worth," he said as he looked at Billy, "I'm sorry for your loss."

Swallowing hard, Billy asked the one question that had been haunting him. "Where did you hide Malik's body?"

"I didn't touch it," Sapp defensively replied. "I never moved his body."

Billy remained quiet. He was still having a hard time trying to digest everything Sapp had told him. "Was that your first time seeing a dead body?" he asked out of curiosity.

Sapp nodded his head, confirming that it was.

"Do you have family?"

"Yes," Sapp said after deep thought, "but I'd rather not get them involved. It's a long story," he added, to discourage Billy from probing further. He was afraid his family's lives could be in imminent danger, if their identities were ever revealed.

Billy glanced at Sapp, deciding not to probe further. When he parked in front of the YMCA, he and Sapp quickly climbed out of the car and rushed around the back where they discovered the helicopter landing on the baseball field.

After climbing into the helicopter, the pilot asked, "Where to?"

"The JFK airport in New York," Billy explained.

"Why New York?" Sapp asked, once they buckled up.

"We're going to take a private jet to Ireland from there. I figure we can hide out there with some of my family members. That is, unless you have another destination in mind."

"Ireland sounds fine to me." For the first time in a long time, Sapp seemed to relax. He had been to Ireland several times before. In fact, he had traveled the world with his grandparents in his younger days.

Billy nodded as he pulled out his cell phone to call Big Mike, but his call went to voicemail. "Boss, I'm calling to let you know we're okay. I'll call you when we land."

When Officer Ratcliff received Abdul's initial request to find Malik, he was at Malik's apartment investigating the scene of the crime. He had purposely held off on telling Abdul he was there, and that he believed Malik was dead. He thought it was best to wait for the DNA results from the blood samples taken from Malik apartment. "Hello, this is Officer Ratcliff from the Tampa Bay police department."

"What's up?" Abdul gruffly answered.

"I have some bad news for you. Are you sitting down?"

"Don't worry about me," Abdul grumbled. "Have you been able to locate my son?"

"I'm sorry to report that your son is missing."

Abdul was rendered speechless, upon hearing the news of his son's disappearance. Everything around him seemed to freeze in place. He had been estranged from Malik for most of his life. Because Malik rejected him, he needed Sapp to discreetly look after him. It was the best he could do at the time. Now he was second-guessing his decision.

Officer Ratcliff was not sure if Abdul was still on the phone, so he asked, "Did you hear me?"

"Yeah," Abdul somberly replied. "Do you have any leads?

"No. I'm in the process of contacting Malik's friend, Billy Hampden. He wanted an update of Malik's whereabouts?"

"Why?"

"I think he's looking for Malik."

Nodding, Abdul was not shocked to hear about Billy's intentions. "I need another favor," he said after deep thought, "find Sapp Burger, and bring him to me."

"Who is that?"

"Malik's friend."

"I'll let you know as soon as I find him," Officer Ratcliff eagerly replied. He had been on Abdul's payroll for the past two years, and was looking forward to a bonus.

After disconnecting the call, Abdul buried his face in his hands. He had a hard time grasping the idea that his son was missing. With grave concern, one of his henchmen, Chico, approached him. "Yo boss, are you okay?"

Overcome with anger, Abdul looked at Chico with a scowl on his face. "Do I look like I'm okay?! My boy is missing!"

"Damn," Chico whispered under his breath, "that's messed up. What do you want me to do?"

Abdul stood up and faced his men, including Chico. "We're going to Tampa to find Malik." He banged his fist on the table, "Someone's gonna pay if they hurt my son!"

Chapter 33
Woe is Me!

Locked up behind bars was not something Alecia would have ever imagined. She dreaded calling her father, the well-regarded and distinguished Dr. Anthony Kellam. Using her one phone call, she dialed the number to the man that helped shape her life. She held her breath as the phone rang, then paused when her father answered on the third ring.

"Hello," Dr. Kellam repeated, "is anyone there?"

"Hi dad, it's me," Alecia replied in a soft whisper.

The doctor smiled at the sound of his daughter's voice. "Hi baby, how are you?"

Alecia hesitated before she spoke. "Dad, I'm in jail."

Dr. Kellam paused for five seconds before responding in an eerily calm manner. "Why are you in jail?"

"Attempted murder," she softly answered, "but I didn't do it."

"First-degree," he thought aloud, while gripping the phone close to his ear.

Alecia started crying. Her father seemed so cold and distant. She knew he was worried about his reputation, and the impact it might have on his pharmaceutical company.

"Calm down," he instructed, "and write down every detail leading up to this incident. In the meantime, I'll find a way to get you out of this mess."

Between sniffles, Alecia wiped away her tears with her fingers. "Okay daddy."

"Hang in there," her father encouraged. "I'm in London right now, but I'll see you soon." Dr. Kellam disconnected the call, then phoned his personal pilot, to fly to the United States on his private jet.

That was two days ago. Alecia was eagerly waiting to see her father for the first time in six months. Dr. Kellam's busy travel schedule made it impossible for him to see her on a regular basis.

The guard escorted Alecia to a windowless room with one table and four chairs. Fifteen minutes later, the guard opened the door and Dr. Kellam walked in with his attorney in tow.

"Hi Daddy!" Alecia cried out, as she ran into her father's arms. Painstakingly, she looked into his sad eyes. "You've got to believe me. I didn't shoot anyone."

"I know, baby," Dr. Kellam said, after kissing her on the forehead. Then he briefly turned to his attorney. "You remember Michael Weinberg, don't you?"

Alecia nodded as she extended her hand to the attorney. "It's nice to see you, again."

"Let's have a seat," Weinberg suggested, after shaking her hand.

After everyone was seated, the attorney opened up his briefcase, then pulled out a document and put on his reading glasses. He looked at Alecia after reviewing the document. "Ms. Kellam, why did you confess to shooting Alex Simmons?"

"But I didn't," Alecia replied in her defense.

The attorney held up the document he was reading from. "The State Attorney obtained a copy of your recorded phone call to the 911 operator. You told the operator you killed Mr. Simmons."

"I was coerced!" Alecia sharply retorted. "Rhaunda told me if I didn't call, she would kill me."

Her father intervened, by asking, "Why didn't you just pretend to dial the wrong number?"

Alecia lowered her head before responding in a soft whisper. "I wasn't thinking clearly."

Weinberg probed further. "What about the deal you wanted to make with Alex?"

"What deal?" her father questioned, as he turned to Alecia for answers.

"Well...I...," Alecia stammered for an explanation, avoiding her father's piercing glare. "I...uh...told Alex I would make sure his stepmother received the experimental drug. She has stage-four cancer," she added, hoping that her father would understand.

Dr. Kellam's eyes grew bigger from shock. He was furious. "Who gave you permission to do that?!"

Fidgeting with her hands, Alecia stuttered, "Dad... I...uh." She paused as she briefly turned to her attorney to intervene. "Dad, Alex was desperate. I...wanted to help him."

"What did you get in return?" Dr. Kellam asked, knowing his daughter expected to gain something for this gracious deed.

"A commitment," she said in a soft whisper.

Shocked by his daughter's response, Dr. Kellam felt the hairs standing up on his skin. He moved his chair closer to Alecia and got up in her face. When their eyes connected, he grumbled, "What type of commitment?"

"Marriage," she mumbled, wishing she could crawl under a rock and hide.

Sighing, Dr. Kellam sat back in his chair with crossed arms. "Let me get this right," he said in a condescending manner. "You promised Alex's stepmother the cancer drug in exchange for his hand in marriage?"

Alecia felt foolish now that her father put it that way. She did not even know if Alex's stepmother would be a good candidate for the drug. She now realized she may have made the biggest mistake of her life.

Weinberg intervened after realizing Dr. Kellam's anger was not helping matters. He turned to Alecia, and asked, "Did you and Alex sign a statement agreeing to your terms?"

"We signed the contract the same day Alex was shot," Alecia answered.

"Who drew up the contract?" Weinberg inquired.

"Well," Alecia nervously said as she briefly glanced at her father, "I downloaded a blank contract from the internet after you refused to help me."

"What?!" Dr. Kellam shouted, directing his gaze at Weinberg. "You knew about this and didn't tell me."

"When your daughter came to me," Weinberg said in his defense, "I asked her to discuss it with you first." Then he turned to Alecia, and asked, "Where's the contract?"

Alecia shrugged her shoulders. "It's in Alex's condo, I guess."

"Good!" Dr. Kellam excitedly replied. "Do you know what this means?"

"Dad, what are you talking about?" Alecia inquired, as she turned to her father, confused.

"It proves you didn't have a motive to shoot Mr. Simmons," her father concluded. "Now we have to find that contract."

Dumbfounded, Alecia asked, "What good is that going to do?"

"A lot of good," Dr. Kellam made clear, before turning to Weinberg. "What if I gave Mrs. Benedict the drug?"

Weinberg shook his head. "Sir, I don't think that's a good idea. You could put your practice in legal jeopardy if you got involved at this point. Further, you could be arrested for obstruction of justice."

"How else is this going to work?" Dr. Kellam questioned. "We need to find a way to try to keep his stepmother alive. When or if Mr. Simmons comes out of the coma, I want to make sure he knows Alecia has fulfilled her part of the bargain."

Grimacing, Weinberg doubted the doctor's strategy. "Without a contract," he reiterated, "we have nothing." Then he turned to

Alecia, and asked, "Do you know exactly where Mr. Simmons put the signed contract?"

"I'm not sure," Alecia weakly admitted. "I know Alex was getting ready to make a copy of it when Rhaunda showed up, unexpectedly."

Weinberg jotted some notes on his pad before responding. "I will submit a request to the courts, to search Alex's condo for the signed contract."

"And what about Rhaunda?" Alecia asked.

The attorney thoughtfully replied, "We're going to try to persuade her to take a lie detector test."

"And if she doesn't?" Dr. Kellam countered.

"We have to plan a solid defense to create reasonable doubt. That's the only way we can prove that your daughter did not shoot Alex Simmons."

"Rhaunda shot him," Alecia countered with an attitude, "because she's a crazy lunatic."

Weinberg explained, "If Ms. Coleman didn't display this type of behavior prior to shooting Alex Simmons, her lunacy will not be questioned."

"Rhaunda was jealous," Alecia spouted. "She wanted Alex all to herself." Mentioning his name compelled her to change her focus. "How are we going to find out when he comes out of the coma?" she asked her attorney.

Weinberg said, "I told the detective to call me if Mr. Simmons' prognosis changes."

"Alex will tell you the truth about Rhaunda," Alecia stated with confidence. "I'm sure of it." Then she pitifully looked around the room and realized it was cold, like her cell. "When will I be able to get out of this place?"

The attorney briefly looked at Dr. Kellam before responding. "During the preliminary hearing, there's a chance the judge might not release you, especially since this is a high-profile case. The Simmons family is highly regarded in the Tampa Bay area."

Dr. Kellam sat up in his chair and glared at Weinberg. "What does that have to do with my daughter?" he grumbled.

"There is no room for error," Weinberg replied. "The State Attorney is going to be very careful with how they handle this high-profile case. If there is a bond, it could be as high as one million dollars."

"No problem," Dr. Kellam said, as he pulled out his wallet to write a check.

The attorney put his hand on top of Dr. Kellam's checkbook. "We have to first wait for the judge's decision," he said, before he turned to Alecia. "I need you to refrain from talking to the media."

Alecia threw her hands in the air as she looked around the room. "How's that possible when I'm locked up twenty-four/seven like a caged animal?!" she squealed.

"They have their ways," Weinberg explained. "Just keep to yourself." He put the documents in his briefcase and closed it before he stood up to leave. "Our visitation has come to an end. In the meantime, I'll see if I can get you into a better facility."

Alecia turned to her father with teary eyes. "Daddy, I don't want to stay here," she whined. "I'll die if I spend one more night in jail."

Dr. Kellam embraced Alecia before cupping her face. "Baby, I need you to be strong until we get you out of this jam." He retrieved his handkerchief from his suit pocket and dried her eyes. "I promise, I'm going to get you out of here." Heartbroken, the doctor slowly pulled away from his one and only child. He wished Alecia's mother was still alive, especially during times like this.

When the doctor stepped outside the prison gates, he turned to Weinberg and said, "Make sure the judge sets my daughter free. Also, I need the contact information for Jeanine Benedict's doctor. Whatever costs, and whatever it takes. Am I clear?" he asked, extending his hand.

"Loud and clear," Weinberg said, as he shook Dr. Kellam's hand. "I'll do my best."

Weinberg stood still as he watched the doctor walk away with his head hung low. Feeling overwhelmed with doubts about Alecia's case, he decided he needed help. He was hopeful that his new private investigator, Craig Marshall, would be able to shed light on his new client's case.

One of Weinberg's colleagues referred Craig to him months earlier, and had insisted that he hire him on the spot. After a short trial run, Weinberg was impressed with Craig's search and discovery skills. On the way to his car, he retrieved his cell phone from his suit jacket and called him.

"Hello Craig, I'm working on a new case. I need you to drop everything and help me out."

"Give me the specifics," Craig requested, eager for this opportunity.

"This is a high-profile case, involving Alex Simmons and Alecia Kellam. Allegedly, she shot him but there's no motive."

"I know this case. The news reporters are having a field day with this story. *Daughter of a millionaire shoots another millionaire.* What are the odds?" Craig rhetorically questioned.

"Yes, that's the case. I was hired to defend Ms. Kellam. She's claiming she didn't shoot Alex Simmons."

Craig whistled before responding. "But all the evidence is pointing in her direction. The nine-one-one recording with Ms. Kellam's confession is all over the news."

"I know, but she claims her friend, Rhaunda Coleman, shot him. I need you to conduct some research to see if you can find evidence that would corroborate her story. I also need you to locate Jeanine Benedict's doctor. She is the former owner of Trowne Key Estates."

"Who is she, and what does she have to do with this case?"

"I'd rather not say."

"I understand."

"And Craig, try to be discreet. Call me if you find anything."

"Gotcha!"

In less than twenty-four hours, Craig discovered more than he bargained for. He located Jeanine's physician with ease. That was the easy part.

Now about Rhaunda, Craig uncovered a big surprise. During the morning Alex was shot, Rhaunda was pulled over for speeding. The ticket was written thirty minutes before Alecia called the nine-one-one operator to confess to shooting Alex. The gap in time was just enough to support Alecia's account of what happened, and prove her innocence.

Chapter 34
The Unexpected

Jeanine woke up in the middle of the night, worried about Alex. She suddenly found it difficult to breathe. After pressing the panic button, she cried into the attached microphone, "Mimi, come quickly! I need your help!"

Mimi rushed into Jeanine's room and found her breathing erratically. "Mrs. Benedict," she said as she shook her shoulder, "open your eyes if you can hear me."

Jeanine opened her bloodshot eyes, and said in a hoarse voice, "I want to go to the hospital. I don't want to die in this house."

Quickly, Mimi darted to Guy and Regine's bedroom and knocked on their door. "Mr. Simmons!" she yelled through the door. "It's urgent! I need to see you right away!"

Guy shot up in bed after hearing Mimi's panicky voice. "Give me a second," he said loud enough for her to hear him. "I'll be right there." He rushed to get out of bed and put on his robe before opening the door. "What's the matter?" he asked, after noticing Mimi's teary-eyes.

"It's Mrs. Benedict," she weakly replied. "She wants to go to the hospital."

"Okay, give me a few minutes to get dressed." When Guy turned around, Regine was standing in front of him, crying.

He embraced her, and softly said, "Mom has fought a long battle."

"I know," Regine said between sniffles, "but it still hurts that she's suffering."

"Regine, we have to be strong. I'm going with Mom to the hospital. I want you to stay here."

Regine nodded in agreement.

Thirty minutes later, Jeanine's doctor met her at the hospital. After checking her vitals, he gave her some codeine to ease the pain. Within minutes, Jeanine was sedated, but fully alert.

"Mrs. Benedict," the doctor happily announced, "I have some good news for you."

"What do you mean?" Guy interrupted, standing next to Jeanine's hospital bed.

The doctor turned to Guy with a wide grin. "Mrs. Benedict has been selected to receive the drug I told you about earlier."

"I thought you said the drug was still in its testing phase."

"It is, but it may be your mother's only hope. It could possibly extend her life."

"But you also told me the drug has not been approved by the Food and Drug Administration."

"Which is why I recommend that Mrs. Benedict be flown to London tonight," the doctor explained.

Perplexed, Guy glanced at Jeanine before he turned to the doctor. "What are the chances this drug would work?"

"There's no guarantee she'll be cancer-free, but there's a greater chance that the cancer might go into remission."

Guy turned to Jeanine, and asked, "What do you want to do?"

Jeanine coughed a little before responding. "You make the decision."

Guy thought long and hard before he looked into Jeanine's eyes. "It's worth a try," he thought aloud. "I'll call Regine and tell her our plans. Then I'll arrange to have a private jet to fly us to London."

"Good," the doctor interjected. "I'll notify the doctors in London."

"Can I ask you one more question?" Guy asked, as he walked with the doctor outside of Jeanine's room. "How was my mother selected to be a candidate for this drug?"

"Beats me," the doctor said, shrugging his shoulders.

"Who contacted you?"

"Someone from Kellam Pharmaceuticals."

"Kellam," Guy said with scrunched brows. "Why does that name sound familiar?"

"Don't worry about a thing," the doctor said, to calm Guy's worries. "I'm going to call the doctor in London, and tell them Mrs. Benedict will be flying out tonight."

Guy returned to Jeanine's room and held her hand. "Mom, I believe in my heart that this drug is going to save your life."

Jeanine smiled. "Son, whatever happens, know that I love you. You've made me so proud."

Guy blushed before he kissed Jeanine on the cheek.

"I want you to stay with Alex," Jeanine explained. "He needs you here when he comes out of the coma."

Protesting, Guy shook his head. "I need to be with you."

Before responding, Jeanine looked over at Mimi, who was on the other side of her bed. Her pale complexion was void of color, and she was barely one hundred pounds. "I want Mimi to come with me to London."

Torn between a rock and a hard place, Guy wanted to be with Jeanine, but he also knew Alex needed him. Reluctantly, he agreed with her request.

After Guy left, the nurse walked into Jeanine's room, inserted the tip of a needle in her arm for IV therapy to prevent dehydration. Later on, the IV bag was injected with the cancer drug, per Dr. Kellam's instructions. The doctor did not think Jeanine would have survived the trip to London, otherwise.

On pins and needles, Guy stayed up all night and morning, waiting by the phone. He could not sleep until he knew Jeanine had arrived in London, safely. When Mimi finally called, Jeanine was in the hospital being admitted. Her attending physician had requested to speak to Guy.

"Hello Mr. Simmons. I am Dr. Daniel, the attending physician at the hospital. I want you to know that your mother will be receiving the very best of care."

Guy smiled. "That's reassuring. How soon will we know if the drug worked?"

"In the next week or so, we should see a sign," Dr. Daniel said with certainty.

"Please keep me posted."

"Will do."

Guy exhaled after disconnecting the call. He silently prayed the drug would work. He never understood why or how Jeanine was selected to be a candidate for the drug, but did not care at this point. He was looking for a miracle.

After disconnecting the call, Guy called Trowne Key Estates, and asked to speak with Sidney McKinley. He wanted to make sure the company continued thriving in Alex's absence.

"Hello Mr. Simmons," Sidney said with surprise in his voice. He wondered what prompted Guy's phone call.

"Hi Sidney. I have bad news to share with you."

"What is it?" Sidney asked, fearing Guy found out about his connection to Bryce Jennings.

"Alex is in the hospital," Guy replied with sadness in his voice.

"I heard about it on the news. Is he going to be okay?"

"We don't know," Guy said, while keeping his emotions intact. "I need you to step up and be in charge for now."

"Most certainly," Sidney replied, while trying hard to control his excitement. "You don't have to worry about the company. I will make sure things run smoothly until Alex returns."

"I'm happy to hear that. You'll be compensated for your efforts."

"Thank you, sir. I won't disappoint you."

Guy nodded. "I know. I'll contact you as soon as Alex's condition changes."

"Godspeed," Sidney said, before disconnecting the call. His disposition changed within a split second. He no longer hated Alex, or resented Jeanine for not making him part owner of Trowne Key Estates. He wanted the company to strive and remain highly competitive in Alex's absence. Now was the time for him to shine, even though he believed that he rightly deserved partnership.

Two days later, Bryce contacted Sidney to ask about the merger deal, after learning from a business associate that Sidney was temporarily appointed the President of Trowne Key Estates. It was not a well kept secret. Sidney had announced his new position to everyone and anyone who would listen.

Five minutes into their conversation, Bryce asked, "What is your problem? We had a deal, remember?"

"Yes," Sidney sarcastically replied, "but you were trying to cut me out of the deal."

"I don't know what you're talking about."

Sidney chuckled before turning serious. "I am not an idiot. I know all about your outings with Alex."

"Is that what this is about? Your feelings are hurt because I didn't invite you?" Bryce's voice was filled with surprised.

"No, my feelings aren't hurt!" Sidney sharply replied. "At least, not any more. And for the record, *I* call the shots."

"Good," Bryce said. "Let's make the merger deal happen." When Sidney laughed in response, he asked, "What is so *damn* funny?!"

"You, my friend," Sidney said in a dignified manner. "I don't know why I ever associated myself with the likes of you."

"You don't know who you're dealing with," Bryce threatened. "What if I told Alex's brother about the deal you made with me?"

"Without a paper trail," Sidney snapped, "you have nothing. On the other hand, I wonder how Guy Simmons would feel if I told him your true intentions," he said, before disconnecting the call.

Feeling double-crossed, Bryce had no one to blame but himself. Sidney was right. He was so busy trying to go after the big fish, he did not foresee his biggest obstacle: *Guy Simmons.*

Chapter 35

Secrets and Lies

*P*rior to going to the hospital, Elizabeth had psyched Rhaunda into believing she did not shoot Alex. She had even coached her daughter on what to say to her father and the police detectives. To make sure her daughter was ruled out as a potential suspect, she thought it was best to cooperate with the police, under the condition that she and her husband remain present throughout the interrogation process.

Upon arriving at the police station, Rhaunda was fingerprinted and her hands were checked for gun residue. Afterward, Detective Hines took Rhaunda and her parents to a private room, to address Alecia's allegations. He waited until they were seated before asking Rhaunda about her whereabouts at the time Alex was shot.

Rhaunda looked to her mother first before responding. "I was home. Earlier, I was at his condo. We were discussing our wedding plans."

"Did you see Alecia Kellam enter Mr. Simmons' condo?" the detective asked.

"No," Rhaunda lied, "but she drove up as I was leaving."

"Were you on good terms with Mr. Simmons?"

Rhaunda smiled. "Yes, we're in-love."

The detective paused, after realizing Rhaunda's statements were in conflict with Alecia's. "Are you sure you two weren't fighting?" he probed.

Shaking her head back and forth, Rhaunda adamantly said, "No. We never fought."

"Never?" the detective quizzed.

"Well," Rhaunda said with a wide grin, "we had a little dispute about our wedding colors. I wanted blue and white, but Alex wanted black and white."

Elizabeth lightly chuckled as she rubbed her daughter's back. She wanted to assure Rhaunda that her performance was superb.

Detective Hines reviewed the document with Alecia's lie detector results, which showed Alecia had told the truth when she stated she and Alex were supposed to get married. She also told the truth when she stated Alex was going to break up with Rhaunda. He did not know who to believe, so he asked Rhaunda, "Would you be willing to take a polygraph test?"

"That's not necessary!" Elizabeth sharply interjected. "Alecia Kellam has already admitted to shooting Alex."

Pastor Coleman nodded. "I agree. Don't you have Alecia's confession? What more do you want?"

"Ms. Kellam told us Ms. Coleman forced her to confess to shooting Alex."

"That's absurd!" Elizabeth cut in. "My child wouldn't kill a fly!"

"She's right," the pastor added. "Rhaunda has always been a good, decent young woman."

The detective turned to Rhaunda, and asked, "Do you know anything about the contract Mr. Simmons and Ms. Kellam signed?"

"What contract?" the pastor interrupted.

Detective Hines turned to the pastor, and explained, "According to Ms. Kellam, she met with Mr. Simmons to make arrangements to give his stepmother a drug used to cure stage IV breast cancer or stop the cancer growth in exchange for his hand in marriage."

"That's crazy!" Elizabeth shouted out.

Rhaunda's mouth flew open in surprise.

"Have you seen the contract?" the pastor asked the detective.

"No," Detective Hines confirmed.

"Well, that settles it," Elizabeth said, as she grabbed Rhaunda's hand and stood up. "Alecia is making things up to get off the hook. Can't you see that?"

The detective ignored Elizabeth as he looked at Rhaunda, and asked, "Would you be willing to take a lie detector test?"

"What part of *no* don't you understand?!" Elizabeth hollered, as she quickly grabbed her purse and nudged Rhaunda toward the exit.

The pastor sternly looked at Detective Hines before he followed Rhaunda and Elizabeth out of the precinct.

When they arrived home, Elizabeth went with Rhaunda upstairs to her bedroom. She embraced her daughter, then asked, "How are you feeling?"

"Ma, I still love him."

Elizabeth shook her head. She knew Rhaunda was referring to Alex. "I know honey, but sometimes people are only meant to be in your life for a season and a reason. You need to get Alex out of your system, so you can move on."

"He wanted to marry me, but Alecia...."

"Don't ever mention that woman's name again," Elizabeth interrupted. "She's the reason you're in this situation in the first place."

"I suppose you're right, Mom," Rhaunda glumly replied. She averted her eyes, when she softly said, "I want to go see Alex, again."

After they left the police station, the pastor had convinced Rhaunda that it was not a good idea, but Elizabeth knew her daughter was determined to see Alex, with or without their permission. "Okay," she reluctantly agreed, "but do not bring up the past. You should focus on the future."

Rhaunda smiled as she nodded in agreement.

Elizabeth returned to her bedroom where she found her husband getting dressed for bed.

"How is she?" the pastor asked.

"Rhaunda's okay, but she still wants to be with Alex."

The pastor grunted, shaking his head in disbelief. "I hope you told her it wasn't a good idea."

"You know Rhaunda. She's stubborn, just like her father."

Pastor Coleman groaned. "Don't start, Elizabeth. It's been a very stressful day."

Elizabeth stifled her response. She was afraid to tell her husband that Rhaunda was very much like her biological father, a man she had a fling with over twenty years ago.

After Rhaunda was born, the pastor never questioned his wife about his paternity, nor did Elizabeth let on that he was not Rhaunda's biological father. She did not think it was necessary, especially since her daughter possessed most of her physical features.

Sitting on the edge of her bed, Elizabeth thought about the one time she cheated on her husband. It was basically *tit-for-tat*. When the pastor cheated on her, she kicked him out of the house but did not feel vindicated. She wanted to hurt him just like he had hurt her.

By chance, Elizabeth ran into Abdul Mitchell one night on her way home from church. She had a flat tire in the middle of a thunderstorm. When she pulled over on the side of the highway, a truck pulled up behind her. She saw Abdul out of her rearview mirror.

Ready to offer assistance, Abdul got out of his truck and walked toward her car. He knocked on Elizabeth's window before peering inside. "Ma'am, are you okay?"

Partially rolling down the window, Elizabeth lied, "Yes, I'm fine. My husband is on his way." When she took a closer look, she realized Abdul was absolutely breathtaking.

Actually, Elizabeth had called for roadside assistance. The phone operator told her that it would be an hour before they would be able to get to her.

"Are you sure?" Abdul probed.

Elizabeth was captivated by Abdul's thuggish appearance. At six four and two hundred-seventy pounds, he was built like a professional boxer. His sideburns and chiseled nose were prominent on his oval shaped face and caramel brown complexion. Without shame or guilt, Elizabeth checked out the way Abdul's jeans grabbed his big buff thighs.

He blushed after he caught Elizabeth gawking at his crotch. "Miss?"

"Uh...yeah," Elizabeth stammered, deciding to change her focus. "Can you help me?"

"Sure."

After he changed her tire, Elizabeth had asked him to sleep with her. "That is, if you're not busy," she added.

Abdul frowned. He was not sure if Elizabeth was serious, so he teased, "Do you want to go to a hotel?"

"Yes," Elizabeth said with a sly grin.

Abdul was surprised by her answer, but readily agreed. "Follow me."

That night of passion with Abdul was the first time Elizabeth was sexually satisfied. Abdul dissected her body as if he was building a house. His tongue was like magic, especially when he used it in all the right places. Elizabeth was taken by surprise when he revealed his manhood, all eight inches of pure luck.

"Don't worry," Abdul assured her, "I'll take my time with you."

Elizabeth squirmed and moaned while Abdul kissed every inch of her body. When she had an orgasm, her world seemed to spiral out of control. Instantly, she felt a strong connection to Abdul and could not understand why, until it dawned on her that he did not use a condom.

After that night, Elizabeth and Abdul spent a lot of time together. She was not put off when he told her about serving time in prison for murder. In fact, she found herself growing closer to him.

During their short union, Abdul had taught Elizabeth the tools and trades for surviving the streets. He had also taken her to a gun range and taught her how to shoot, then showed her how to remove residue by scrubbing her hands with comet and bleach. This was the same remedy she used on Rhaunda's hands.

A month later, Elizabeth realized she could never have a stable relationship with Abdul. He was constantly on the move, and missing in action. She decided to cut all ties with Abdul, then begged her husband to come back home. Elizabeth and the pastor reunited, deciding to put the past behind them.

Nine months later, Elizabeth gave birth to Rhaunda. For twenty-six years, she had been living a lie; afraid to tell her husband the truth about Rhaunda's real father. When Abdul found out Elizabeth was pregnant, she tried to lie, but he knew better. He had agreed to stay out of his daughter's life as long as no one ever caused her harm. The other condition Abdul imposed: Elizabeth had to keep him updated on Rhaunda's life. Their agreement had worked up to this point.

Initially, when Rhaunda started dating Alex, Elizabeth was more worried about what Abdul was capable of doing to Alex than her husband. Now she was wrestling over whether to tell Abdul about Rhaunda's recent ordeal.

Chapter 36

Awakening

*O*n the seventh day, Alex was still in a coma. The doctor told Guy the longer Alex stayed in a coma, the slimmer his chances were of recovering. Guy had spent the night at the hospital, looking for a miracle. When he woke up, he tried to shake his brother awake. "Can you hear me?" Guy whispered next to Alex's ear. He was disappointed, when he did not receive a response.

The doctor came in shortly after. "Good morning, Mr. Simmons. I see you stayed here all night," he said, as he observed the cot next to Alex's bed.

Guy nodded.

"Why don't you go and get a bite to eat?" the doctor suggested. "I'll stay here until you return." With apprehension, Guy stood up and slowly walked out of the room.

Minutes later, Rhaunda snuck into Alex's room. She had patiently waited for Guy to leave, avoiding another confrontation.

The doctor eyed her suspiciously. "May I help you?"

"I'm Alex's fiancé. Rhaunda Coleman."

The doctor peered out of the rim of his glasses. "I didn't know he had one."

"How is he?"

"He's still comatose. We're getting ready to run some tests. You can come back later."

"Can I just see him for a second?"

"Uh…sure," the doctor said as he looked at his watch. "I'll give you some time to spend with him. I'll be back soon."

"Alex, baby," Rhaunda said next to his ear, "I love you." She lightly kissed Alex on the lips, then sat in the chair next to his bed. Against her father's wishes, Rhaunda had been sneaking to see Alex. She was relieved that the judge refused to let Alecia out on bail. She could not believe the story Alecia had concocted about arranging to give his stepmother some type of miracle drug if Alex agreed to marry her.

"Baby," Rhaunda pleaded as she held Alex's hand and looked at his closed eyes, "give me a sign to let me know you can hear me."

Alex's pupils moved around before he finally opened his eyes.

Rhaunda's heart throbbed from excitement. "Alex, baby, do you know who I am?!"

He looked at Rhaunda as if she were invisible.

"Alex, I'll be back. I'm going to get the doctor." Rhaunda ran out of the room, calling out for the doctor, who was standing near the nurses' station. "Doctor! Come quickly!" she urged.

"What's going on?" the doctor asked, as he rushed to Alex's room with Rhaunda on his tail.

"He's awake!" she boasted.

Within seconds, a team of nurses along with Alex's doctor were at his bedside. "Step aside Miss," the nurse said to Rhaunda.

"Can I stay?" Rhaunda asked with a pleading voice.

The doctor nodded, agreeing to let Rhaunda stay, before turning his attention to Alex. "Mr. Simmons, if you can hear me, squeeze my hand."

Alex complied with shaky hands.

Next, the doctor looked into Alex's eyes and shined a tiny flashlight in his face. "Mr. Simmons, keep your eyes open and follow my finger." Alex blinked several times before he rolled his eyes from side to side, following the doctor's instructions.

The doctor pulled out his stethoscope, to check Alex's heartbeat. Satisfied with the results, the doctor asked, "Do you know where you are?"

Alex shook his head, confirming the doctor's suspicions about his memory loss. "Mr. Simmons, you are in the hospital," the doctor said, as he motioned for Rhaunda to step closer to the bed. "Your fiancé is here."

Cautiously, Rhaunda approached the bed. "Hi, Alex," she said as she lowered her head and moved closer to his face. "How are you?"

When Alex did not respond, the doctor asked, "Do you know who this is?"

Alex shook his head. He did not remember her.

"This is your fiancé," the doctor clarified.

Alex turned to Rhaunda with a blank expression. He grew frustrated with himself, as her face did not register. Then he turned to the doctor, and asked in a soft whisper, "How did I get here?"

The doctor said, "You were shot. We performed surgery, and were able to remove the bullets and repair the damage."

Alex stared at the doctor as if he had six eyes.

"Mr. Simmons," the doctor explained, "some detectives were here to see you, earlier. They need to ask you some questions about what happened, but it looks like they're going to have to wait a while longer. Just relax. Your brother should be returning any moment."

"My brother?"

"Yes," the doctor said, before he glanced at Rhaunda. "Your fiancé is going to stay here and keep you company. I have to make some calls, but I'll be back to check on you."

Rhaunda waited until the doctor left the room before she leaned over and kissed Alex on the cheek. "I'm so happy you're okay."

Stone-faced, Alex looked at Rhaunda, and asked, "Who are you?"

"I'm Rhaunda, your fiancé," she said with conviction. "We're supposed to get married this year."

Alex's brows shot up. "We are?"

"Yes, silly," Rhaunda said with a nervous giggle.

Guy had returned to Alex's room when Rhaunda leaned over and kissed Alex. Initially, he was upset because Rhaunda was in Alex's room, but his anger subsided after witnessing Alex's reaction to Rhaunda.

"Hi Alex," Guy said, as he slowly walked into the room.

"Do I know you?" Alex asked, totally dumbfounded.

Noticing Alex's reaction, Rhaunda said to Alex, "This is Guy, your older brother. Actually, he's your only brother. You also have twin sisters, Dana and Cassie."

Slowly, Guy approached Alex's bedside, opposite of Rhaunda. "Alex, buddy," he said, sounding upbeat. "I'm glad you came through."

"When can I get something to eat?" Alex asked with a dry mouth. "I'm hungry."

Rhaunda and Guy laughed in response.

Guy said, "As soon as you get the okay from the doctor."

Minutes later, the nurse stepped in the room with a tray of gauze and other medication. "If you don't mind," she said to both Rhaunda and Guy, "I need both of you to leave the room for a few minutes, so I can give Mr. Simmons his meds and change his bandages."

Guy and Rhaunda stepped out of the room and stood next to each other. There was awkward silence, until Guy spoke up first. "Maybe I was wrong about you," he explained. "Maybe you didn't have anything to do with Alex getting shot, but what I can't understand is why Alecia would lie on you?"

Rhaunda sighed before facing Guy. "Alecia has always had a thing for Alex, ever since she first laid eyes on him."

"But why did she shoot him?"

"I'm not sure, but I think it had something to do with me and Alex getting married."

Guy was getting ready to respond, until he spotted Bryce, Alex's friend, walking up the hallway toward him.

"How is he?" Bryce asked, turning to Guy for an answer.

"He pulled through," Guy replied, curious to know why Bryce was there.

"Good," Bryce said with relief. "Can I go in to see him?"

"Now is not a good time," Rhaunda interjected. "Alex is having a hard time remembering anyone."

Bryce looked at Rhaunda suspiciously before responding. "I'm Bryce Jennings, and you are?"

"I'm Alex's fiancé," she excitedly declared.

Eyeing Rhaunda suspiciously, Bryce asked, "When did that happen?"

Agitated with Bryce, Rhaunda withdrew her hand. "I don't know what you mean."

"I've been hanging out with Alex for the past few months," Bryce explained, "and he never told me he had a fiancé."

"Oh, but recently we made up," Rhaunda quickly explained. "That's when he proposed to me."

"This is news to me," Guy chimed in with a bewildered gaze.

"Maybe Alex didn't get a chance to tell you about us yet," Rhaunda spouted with an attitude. "Do you want to ask him?" In her mind, she truly believed every word she said.

"No," Guy interjected, "now is not a good time."

Skeptically, Bryce looked at Rhaunda as he spoke to Guy. "Tell Alex I stopped by. I'll be back tomorrow."

"Wait," Guy asked Bryce. "Is there any way you and I can talk briefly?"

"Sure. We can go to the coffee house on the first floor."

Guy hesitated. He was not sure if he should leave Alex with Rhaunda.

"Don't worry," Rhaunda said, after sensing Guy's reluctance to leave. "I'll stay with Alex until you return."

Guy turned to Rhaunda, and said, "That's not necessary."

Rhaunda smiled. "But it is necessary. I plan on staying by my fiancé's bedside until he's released from the hospital."

Bryce sensed that Guy was uncomfortable leaving Alex. "Rhaunda," he intervened, "we'd appreciate that. Come on, Guy."

Guy briefly looked at Rhaunda before following Bryce to the coffeehouse. Over a cup of coffee, he eyed Bryce suspiciously. "Can I ask you a question?"

"Sure," Bryce eagerly replied.

"Why are you here?"

"To see about Alex. Your brother and I have formed a good friendship, and I care about him. Is there anything wrong with that?"

"No," Guy slowly replied. "Are you sure your visit isn't business related?"

Bryce laughed. "Come on, Guy. I have my own company."

Guy put his cup of coffee on the table before responding. "Alex told me about your business proposal. Trowne Key is not for sale, nor are we interested in relinquishing a percentage of the company."

Bryce sat up in his chair, slightly leaning toward Guy. "I'm not here to convince you to change your mind, if that's what you think."

Smiling softly, Guy let down his guard. He was convinced that Bryce was telling the truth. "Okay, I believe you."

"Good. Have you heard any more about the investigation?"

Guy shook his head. "No, not yet. The police believe they arrested the right suspect."

"What about Rhaunda?"

"What about her?"

"Do you trust her?"

"That's a tough question. I believe she's the reason Alex pulled through." Guy checked his watch before he stood up and extended his hand. "Thanks for coming by. I'll tell Alex you stopped by."

Bryce stood up and shook Guy's hand. "I'd appreciate that. You take care."

"Thanks."

When Guy returned to his brother's room, Rhaunda was nowhere in sight. She had to leave after her father called and ordered her to come home. The pastor was livid after he drove by the hospital, on a whim, and discovered his daughter's SUV parked in the hospital garage. He suspected she was visiting Alex.

Guy walked up to Alex's bed and smiled. "How's it going?"

"My head is spinning," Alex explained, as he placed his hands on his temples. "Other than that, I'm okay."

"Don't push it," Guy encouraged. "Take one day at a time."

Alex turned his head toward the door, and asked, "Where's Rhaunda?"

Guy looked toward the door before he turned back to Alex and shrugged his shoulders. "I guess she had to leave." Then he hesitantly asked, "Do you remember what happened?"

Alex shook his head. "Can you tell me?"

"Alecia Kellam was arrested for shooting you."

As soon as Guy said her name, it was as if a light bulb went on. From his earlier research, he had learned that the experimental drug his stepmother was taking came from Kellam Pharmaceuticals. It was a long shot, but he made a mental note to find out if Alecia was affiliated with that company.

Perplexed, Alex scrunched his forehead, when he asked, "Why did she shoot me?"

"I'm not sure," Guy thoughtfully replied. "Do you think Rhaunda had anything to do with it?"

"But that's my fiancé," Alex answered, remembering what Rhaunda had told him. "Why would she have anything to do with it?"

"Alecia is Rhaunda's best friend."

"She is?"

"You sort of have a playboy past," Guy cautiously admitted. "You might have been seeing both women at the same time."

Shocked to hear this, Alex lowered his head, feeling ashamed.

Guy smiled, trying to lighten the mood. "You have a big future ahead of you; a chance to redeem yourself."

Alex bore a thin smile, even though he was frustrated because he could not remember Guy, Rhaunda, or Alecia. He closed his eyes before he slowly drifted off to sleep.

Chapter 37

Desperate Measures

*C*urious to see how Jeanine was doing, Dr. Kellam took a private jet to London, to get a personal look at her prognosis. Upon arriving at the hospital, he entered Jeanine's room and found her sound asleep. He acknowledged Mimi and the attending physician, Dr. Daniel, with a nod.

Eagerly, Mimi stood up and approached the doctor. "Hi, I'm Mimi Kirkland, Mrs. Benedict's private caretaker. We met in the States."

Dr. Kellam smiled. "It's nice to see you again."

"Do you really think this drug is going to work?" Mimi curiously asked.

"There are no guarantees," Dr. Kellam acknowledged, "but there is a good chance that she will pull through."

Mimi breathed a sigh of relief, before muttering, "You're her only hope."

Dr. Kellam smiled. "Let's keep our fingers crossed. We're not out of the woods yet. Within the next week or so, we'll know if the drug was successful." He walked over to Jeanine's bed and looked at her chart, which hung from a holder at the foot of the bed. "What's her prognosis?" he asked, as he directed his gaze to his colleague.

"It's hard to say," Dr. Daniel stated. "We haven't seen any negative reactions to the miracle drug."

Dr. Kellam's chuckled at his colleague's reference to Humercin, the drug responsible for saving a little more than one thousand lives to date.

Gently touching Jeanine's arm, Dr. Kellam turned to his colleague, and said, "I'll be in my office upstairs. Call me as soon as you see an improvement."

"Most certainly," the attending physician replied.

Dr. Kellam walked out of Jeanine's room feeling conflicted. He was happy she had agreed to try the experimental drug, but was disappointed to learn that the grand jury indicted his daughter for attempted murder. Soon after, Alecia's bail request was denied. The judge believed she would pose a flight risk, because she had access to her father's fortunes.

Sighing, Dr. Kellam walked to his office and turned on the computer monitor. Minutes later, his secretary walked into his office in a cheery mood. "Welcome back, doc."

The doctor turned to his secretary and smiled. "Hello Sherry, how are you?"

"I'm fine. I've been holding down the fort in your absence," she teased.

Dr. Kellam chuckled, before asking, "Do I have any messages?"

"No, but you have a couple of letters. This letter had no return address," Sherry indicated, as she held the envelope in the air.

The doctor reached for the envelope and opened it, after noting that the letter was mailed from Florida. As he read it, his eyes grew bigger and his hands began to tremble.

Dr. Kellam,

I know what you're trying to do. It's not going to work. I wonder what would happen if I informed the proper officials that you administered an illegal drug to Jeanine Benedict, while she was still in the U.S. While it is admirable that you did this to get your daughter out of jail, you've also put yourself in legal jeopardy. So, if I were you, I would convince Alecia to accept whatever plea deal the State Attorney recommends, and abandon any efforts to go to trial. Otherwise, you will end up being your daughter's cell mate.

Yours Truly,

John Doe

The doctor became uncomfortable thinking about the consequences of his actions. Everything he had worked so hard for was on the line. He assumed the letter was from Guy Simmons. As owner of Kellam Pharmaceuticals, Dr. Kellam was aware that he could potentially face a huge malpractice suit, aside from being in legal jeopardy. His daughter's attorney feared this would happen. Suddenly, sweat beads began to form along the top of his bald head as he sat back in his chair, finding it difficult to breathe.

"Dr. Kellam, are you okay?" Sherry asked, after noticing that the doctor looked as if he had seen a ghost.

Experiencing sharp pains in his chest, Dr. Kellam keeled over, falling out of his chair.

Quick on her feet, Sherry phoned the hospital operator before performing CPR. "Come on, Dr. Kellam!" she shouted, after pumping his chest and breathing into his mouth. "You have to pull through!"

Within seconds, Dr. Kellam's colleague, Dr. Sue, and her staff came rushing in his office with CPR equipment.

"Stand back!" Dr. Sue barked at Sherry. Then she used the CPR machine to pump his chest. Seconds later, Dr. Kellam started breathing again.

"Dr. Kellam, can you hear me?!" Dr. Sue hollered.

He opened his eyes and nodded, affirming that he could hear her.

"Okay," Dr. Sue said to her staff, "let's get the doctor to the ER, to see what's going on with his heart."

Alecia was sitting in her cell when the guard called for her. She was not expecting any visitors. She stood up and waited for the cell gate to open. "Am I getting out?" she anxiously asked the guard.

"Not today," the guard somberly replied, "but you do have a visitor."

"Is it my dad?"

"No, it's your attorney."

Alecia was disappointed. She was looking forward to seeing her father, whom she had not seen in two weeks. When she walked into the visitor's room and saw her attorney's gloomy face, she had a feeling something was wrong. "Where's my dad?"

"Ms. Kellam, please sit down," Weinberg insisted.

"No, tell me," Alecia persisted, "where's my dad?!"

"He's in the hospital, in London," Weinberg sadly announced. He hated being the bearer of bad news. "Your dad had a massive heart attack."

"Oh God! No!" Alecia hollered out, as tears flowed down her cheeks. "I want to see my dad!" she screamed, as she slouched in her chair.

"I wish it were possible," the attorney said, as he touched Alecia's shoulder. "You have to be strong, so we can get you out of this mess. Your dad is getting the very best of care. Besides, we have more pressing matters to discuss."

Drying her eyes, Alecia softly asked, "What are you talking about?"

"The State wants to send you to prison for a long time."

Alecia rose up out of her slumped position. "Repeat what you said," she instructed, while looking at her attorney in disbelief.

"You heard me correctly. I asked the State Attorney to search Alex's condo for the contract. They were unable to find it."

"So what are you saying?" Alecia asked in a whisper.

"It means we don't have a leg to stand on."

"Did Rhaunda take the lie detector test?"

"No."

"Why not?" Alecia incredulously asked.

"That was her choice."

Coincidentally, Alecia recognized the chances of getting out of jail soon bordered on zero. "What's going to happen now?"

"We go to trial." Weinberg paused before continuing, "The State will try to prove that you've been stalking Alex for the past six months."

Alecia frowned. "How?"

Weinberg tightened his lips as he stared at Alecia. "Is it true that you conducted extensive research on Alex Simmons prior to relocating to Florida?"

Alecia winced. It was true, but she did not want to admit it. "I met Alex in college," she offered.

"You never answered my question."

"I researched a lot of people."

"Your laptop and desktop were confiscated. The police detectives also have proof that you hired a P.I. firm to investigate Alex."

Alecia's mouth flew open. Her little scheme was busted. "That doesn't mean anything," she weakly replied.

"It means you have a motive. The State Attorney is going to paint you as a crazy, obsessed woman. In their opening statement, they're going to tell the jurors that you shot Alex Simmons because you couldn't have him."

"That's not true!" Alecia sharply argued.

Sighing, the attorney sat up on the edge of his chair with clasped hands. "I knew it was a long shot, but I told the State Attorney that you conducted research on Alex Simmons to help his stepmother."

"What did they say?"

"Without a contract, my explanation sounded unbelievable."

"But my dad has already given the drug to Alex's stepmother."

"Which makes us look bad," Weinberg pointed out. "Again, without a contract, the State Attorney is going to view your father's gesture as a last ditch effort to get his daughter off the hook. Your father might be charged with bribery and obstruction of justice." The attorney bit his bottom lip before he looked into Alecia's eyes. "Mr. Simmons is no longer comatose, so the State Attorney offered us a plea deal."

"A plea deal?!" Alecia exclaimed. "But I didn't shoot him!"

"I believe you, but all the State's evidence is pointing to you."

"Since Alex is out of the coma, why don't you ask him who shot him?" she spouted with an attitude.

"Unfortunately, he's suffering from memory loss."

Alecia shook her head. "What are the chances of Alex regaining his memory?" she asked with sadness in her voice.

"It's hard to say. If you take the plea deal, you will be sentenced to fifteen years for intentional murder."

"Fifteen years!" Alecia cried out.

"I believe the State is trying to make an example out of spoiled rich kids, and you just happen to be in the limelight."

Alecia sat back in her chair with crossed arms. "I'm not going to prison for a crime I didn't commit," she gruffly replied.

Weinberg said, "I gave the State Attorney a counter offer of ten years. If you take it, you'll be out in five."

"Let me make myself clear," Alecia firmly stated, as she uncrossed her arms and sat up in her chair. "I'm not interested in a plea deal."

Sighing, the attorney thought it was useless to reason with Alecia. "Fine, I'll tell them we're going to trial. If we lose, you will be given the maximum sentence of twenty years in prison."

"Well, you better make sure that doesn't happen," Alecia snapped. "I don't care what it takes. You better make sure I walk out of here a free woman."

Refusing to be talked down to by a snotty-nose brat, Weinberg gathered his documents and placed them in his briefcase. Then he turned to Alecia, and said, "I'll be in touch."

"Yeah, you do that," Alecia said with an attitude. In a way, she did not want her attorney to leave. She was relieved to be outside her cell. If it were not for her attorney, Alecia realized her temporary living conditions could have been worse. She was grateful to Weinberg for his role in getting her relocated to a private jail with modest amenities. Of course, her father was footing the bill for her comfort.

Scared and lonely, Alecia returned to her cell, thinking about her father. She sincerely prayed for his speedy recovery. There was no one else that she could trust, not even his wife, whom she fell out with years earlier. She missed him so much, her heart ached.

Chapter 38

Bamboozled

Feeling jubilant, Rhaunda walked into Alex's hospital room with a vase of roses. "Good afternoon, honey," she said in a syrupy voice. "These are for you."

"Roses?" Alex asked in surprise.

Rhaunda smiled. "I figured you needed some color in this room." She sat the vase on top of the shelf, opposite of Alex's bed, before turning around to face him. "Roses are my favorite flower," she explained. "You used to buy them for me all the time."

"I did?"

"Yes," Rhaunda replied with confidence. "You even showed up at my house with a dozen roses when you proposed to me."

Alex smiled. "How long have we been seeing each other?"

"Two and a half glorious years!" Rhaunda happily announced, as she moved closer to his bed. "I cannot wait to spend the rest of my life with you."

Feeling Rhaunda's love, Alex realized she was always at the hospital and very attentive to his needs. Every day, she would remind him that she was his fiancé. In fact, she told the entire hospital staff about their upcoming nuptials.

"Do you still want to marry me?" he asked, wondering if Rhaunda had changed her mind about him, especially considering his current condition.

"Of course I do," Rhaunda said with a wide grin. "I would love to be your wife."

"Okay," Alex thoughtfully replied, "we'll get married as soon as I get out of the hospital." Even though his memory was still fuzzy, he believed he loved Rhaunda. He wanted to make her happy.

"Are you sure?" she felt compelled to ask. "What about your memory?"

"We can make new memories. I know I love you," Alex admitted with dreamy eyes.

Rhaunda began crying tears of joy. "I love you too," she said with teary eyes. "You just made me the happiest woman in the world."

Alex smiled in response. "When I get out of here, we can plan our wedding."

Rhaunda cupped Alex's face and looked into his sexy eyes. "You just worry about getting better. I'll take care of our wedding plans."

"Are you sure?" he asked with worry in his voice.

"Yes," Rhaunda said, before kissing Alex on the lips. "I look forward to being your wife, for better or worse, until death do us part."

When Guy walked into the room moments later, he was surprised to see Rhaunda and Alex cuddled up. "What's going on?" he asked with jitters in his stomach.

Alex glanced at Rhaunda before facing Guy with a wide grin, and announced, "We're getting married."

Troubled by this news, Guy looked at Rhaunda before turning to his brother. "Are you sure this is a good idea? Maybe you should wait until you fully regain your memory."

Alex held Rhaunda's hand and looked into her eyes. "We're sure," he answered. "I love her."

"We love each other," Rhaunda added, envisioning little hearts in her eyes.

Guy treaded lightly as he fumbled for the right response. "But this is so sudden," he pointed out.

"I know what I'm doing," Alex said with assurance. "Rhaunda has been telling me about everything we've been through these past two years." Then he turned to Rhaunda, when he said, "Seeing the glow in her face as she recalled our past is enough to prove that we belong together, on a more permanent basis."

Guy did not know how to respond, so he forced a smile. "I'm so happy for both of you," he pretentiously said, before hugging Alex. Then he turned to Rhaunda, and uneasily said, "Welcome to the family."

Grinning from ear-to-ear, Rhaunda embraced Guy. "Thank you. Hearing this from you means so much."

Still forcing a smile, Guy offered, "I'm sure Regine will be happy to help out with the wedding plans."

"I got it covered," Rhaunda replied with confidence.

Guy looked at the way Alex was fawning all over Rhaunda. To him, it looked like his brother was bitten by the love bug.

Rhaunda smiled as she turned to Alex. "I'll give you some time to spend with your brother. I'll be back tomorrow," she said, while directing her gaze at Guy. Then she gave Alex a smack on the cheek before leaving the room.

As soon as Rhaunda left the hospital, she started making wedding plans right away. She decided to delay telling her parents the good news. In the meantime, she went to the bridal shop to pick out a wedding dress.

Guy placed his right hand on the back of his neck, thinking about how he could convince his brother to hold off on marrying Rhaunda. "Alex," he cautiously said, "I can't tell you what to do, but I think you and Rhaunda need to slow things down. At least, until your memory comes back."

"That's not necessary," Alex countered with confidence. "I know enough to know that Rhaunda is the woman for me."

Guy sighed. "Alex, there are some things you should know about Rhaunda."

"What is it?" Alex asked with raised brows.

Guy slowly said, "I don't think she is who she seems to be."

Alex grimaced. He was put off by his brother's response. "Will you at least be happy for me?" he begged. His voice was filled with a mixture of anger and anxiety. "Right now, I need something positive to look forward to. Please don't try to take that from me."

Suddenly, Guy felt ashamed of his behavior. He thought he may have misjudged Rhaunda. With a soft smile, he said, "I'm sorry. From now on, I'll try to be more supportive."

"Thank you."

"I'm headed to work. I'll be back tomorrow to check on you."

Alex nodded. "I'd appreciate that."

Shortly after Guy left the hospital, Alex drifted off into a deep dream with Rhaunda on his mind. He smiled as he dreamt of how he and Rhaunda met during graduate school at Florida International University in Miami, Florida. After discovering they were both from the Tampa Bay area, they had quickly bonded. Soon after, they became study partners. The more time they spent together, the more Alex realized Rhaunda reminded him of his brother's wife, Regine.

At first sight, Alex recognized Rhaunda's beauty. He also noticed how she had always put God first in her life, and did not have any qualms with displaying her religious beliefs in public. To him, Rhaunda was a *diamond in the rough*.

Suddenly, Alex's dream became sharper when he zoomed in on the day he and Rhaunda were in the library studying together. He looked up from his book and stared at her. He knew he could have any woman of his choosing, but Rhaunda was special. Alex wanted what no other man had been able to conquer: *her heart.*

"How do you feel about us dating?" he asked, holding his breath for her answer.

Rhaunda frowned as she looked up from her book, pushing strands of her shoulder-length hair from her face. "I don't think that's a good idea. You're nice, but you have issues."

"No I don't," Alex spouted, offended by Rhaunda's remark.

"Are you serious?" she asked in disbelief. Aware of Alex's sexcapades, Rhaunda detested the idea of becoming one of his girls. "I gotta go," she said, as she grabbed her book bag.

Alex lightly touched Rhaunda's hand as he faced her with pleading eyes. "Give me a chance," he insisted. "I think we could be good together."

Rhaunda twisted her mouth as she blankly stared at Alex. "What if I told you that I'm still a virgin?" She figured he would be turned off, and would think twice about asking her again.

Alex opened his mouth to respond, but was thrown off balance by Rhaunda's confession. "Well, um….," he stuttered, "that doesn't …matter to me."

"Really?" Rhaunda asked, as she eyed him, skeptically.

Clearing his throat, Alex acknowledged that he would be treading on new territory. "Yeah, that's a minor detail."

"Actually, it's major," she said with certainty. "I plan on staying this way until I'm married."

Alex rolled his eyes and exhaled in response.

"Now, do you still want to date me?" she asked, expecting Alex to say *no*. Because my status is not going to change, until I'm married."

Lightly scratching his head, Alex fumbled for the right words. "Um…wow," he muttered. "I…don't…know what to say."

"If you say you can't handle it, I'll understand. But I won't compromise," Rhaunda stated with heart-felt conviction. "I'm saving myself for my husband. My body is God's temple."

Alex chuckled. "Sort of like the Virgin Mary," he teased.

"Forget you, Alex!" Rhaunda exclaimed, as she darted for the exit.

Alex ran to catch up with Rhaunda, then blocked her from leaving. "Come on," he said with a wide grin, "you know I was just kidding. I think we can make this work."

Because Alex was five inches taller, Rhaunda had to look up to see if he was sincere. His dark-brown sparkling eyes, deep dimples, and heart-throbbing smile blew her away. "Okay," she reluctantly agreed, "but if you can't handle the kitchen, get out of the fire."

Alex laughed in response. "You mean, if you can't handle the heat, get out of the kitchen."

Rhaunda giggled. "Yeah, something like that."

"It's okay, cliché buster," he teased.

A month into their relationship, Alex respected Rhaunda's wishes to remain a virgin until marriage, but he also realized remaining celibate was a lot harder than he could have ever imagined. He asked himself, *What was I thinking, by messing with a saved and sanctified woman?* Even his best friend, Brian Lancaster, laughed when he found out Alex was going steady with Rhaunda.

"Why don't you just marry the chick?" Brian asked him one day when they were leaving class. "You know she's not going to let you pass first base without a ring and a prayer."

"Don't worry about me," Alex replied with his chest poked out. "I get mine."

"You're selfish, Alex. Rhaunda's faithful to you, and you're faithful to every female that comes your way."

"I keep it clean; trust me. I give Rhaunda nothing but respect."

Sighing, Brian shook his head. "Alex, you're playing with fire. Chicks like Rhaunda have been known to do some crazy things. Be careful."

"Okay, daddy," Alex teased with light laughter. "I'll chat with you later."

Brian threw up the peace sign and walked away.

Alex had dismissed Brian's argument, figuring he and Rhaunda could have the best of both of worlds. *He would honor her wishes to remain a virgin; and he would satisfy his sexual appetite with other women.*

One day, the waters were tested when Alex ran into Cyprus Wilson, a blonde-haired, blue-eyed knock out. He had seen her around campus a couple of times, and thought she was *hot*. Cyprus was walking to her car when she spotted Alex. Her smile was contagious, and everything about her screamed, *I want you, Alex!* "Hello sexy," she cooed, looking at him like a piece of cake. "You want to come home with me?"

Thinking with the wrong side of his brain, Alex took the bait, and followed her to her apartment. As soon as they entered her apartment, they quickly stripped down and got busy, like dogs in heat. They failed to ensure that the door was locked.

Ten minutes later, his relationship with Rhaunda fell apart. She walked in on Alex and Cyprus while they were in the act. To make matters worse, Cyprus' boyfriend, Danny DeSoto, showed up seconds later and kicked Alex's butt.

After getting caught, Alex tried to apologize to Rhaunda but she would not give him the time or day. She had even gone out of her way to avoid him through the remainder of the school year. They saw each other during the graduation ceremony but it was not a friendly union. That was the last time he saw her.

Long after graduate school, Alex had longed to be reunited with Rhaunda. She constantly monopolized his thoughts. One night, he searched the internet, and was relieved to discover she had returned to her parents' home in Tampa, Florida. Soon after, he had called her repeatedly, but she did not return his calls.

Eager to make amends, Alex took a chance by going to visit Rhaunda at her parents' house with a dozen red roses. He knocked on the door, but no one responded. So he called Rhaunda, and breathed a sigh of relief when she finally answered. "Please give me a chance to explain."

Rhaunda rolled her eyes toward the ceiling as she remained in bed. "There's nothing to talk about."

"I screwed up," Alex confessed. "Please come to the front door, so we can talk."

Wondering if she heard Alex correctly, Rhaunda sat up in bed and turned on the light on her nightstand. "Where are you?"

"I'm right outside your parents' front door."

Rushing to her bedroom window, she was stunned to see Alex on her front porch. She picked up the phone and said into the mouthpiece, "Give me a few minutes."

With reservations, Rhaunda put on her robe and slippers, and walked to the front door. "Why should I waste my time with you?" she asked, after she opened the door.

"Because you're a good person," he wearily commented, "and I don't want to lose your friendship. Will you forgive me?"

Rhaunda leaned against the door, pondering Alex's question. "How would you like it if a man mistreats your sisters the way you mistreated me?"

Alex stammered for a response. "I wouldn't...like it, but I've changed. Would you give me another chance?" he asked in an almost pleading voice.

"No," Rhaunda replied with certainty.

"Why not?"

"Do you want me to pretend as if I never witnessed you sleeping with that woman?" She found it difficult to say Cyprus Wilson's name without getting sick to her stomach.

"It was a mistake."

"You were making a lot of mistakes, because you slept with several women besides Cyprus." Rhaunda did not have proof, so she had recited what Alecia told her. "My only saving grace," she sassed, "is that I did not sleep with you."

Alex opened his mouth to respond but was temporarily speechless. Based on Rhaunda's harsh demeanor, he believed he had lost the battle to recapture her heart. "I promise," he said with pleading eyes, "if you give me a second chance, you won't regret it. I love you."

"Are you sure this is what you really want?" she asked, as she looked into Alex's eyes for clarification

"I've learned from my past mistakes. Losing you was the worst thing that has ever happened to me."

Rhaunda was captivated by Alex's heart-felt words. She decided to follow her heart. "If you screw up again," she firmly said, "don't think twice about asking for another chance."

What happened next rendered Rhaunda speechless. Alex gave her the roses, pulled a small box out of his pocket and knelt down on one knee. "Will you marry me?"

"Are you serious?" Rhaunda asked in disbelief, as she stared at the heart-shaped engagement ring.

"I'm as serious as a heart attack. I know you're a good woman. I can't stand to lose you. I love you. Please say you will marry me."

Rhaunda became teary-eyed as her emotions took over her soul and mind. Her mind said *'no'* but her heart said *'yes'*.

"Say you'll marry me," Alex said, as he held the ring box closer to her hand.

"I don't know, Alex," Rhaunda muttered. "This is all too sudden. Let's work on mending our relationship first."

Disappointed, Alex closed the ring box and returned it to his pocket. He had a bittersweet moment. He did not get the answer he wanted, but he was satisfied Rhaunda had given him a second chance to redeem himself.

Suddenly, Alex snapped out of his dream, feeling confused over whether he was actually engaged to Rhaunda. He tried to remember if she had accepted his proposal later on, but came up empty.

Chapter 39
School Daze

*G*uy thought it was a good idea for the twins to return to school after being absent for over a week. He understood they were dealing with a lot of stress over Alex and Jeanine's medical status. Though, he was particularly concerned about Dana. Guy knew she wanted answers about Malik; answers that would probably devastate her. After waking the twins, he asked them to meet him downstairs.

Slothfully, Cassie came downstairs in her pajamas. "Good morning Guy," she said, after yawning.

"Where's Dana?" he asked, looking upstairs.

Cassie smirked. "You know Dana. Sleeping beauty will be down soon."

"I heard that!" Dana hollered from the top of the stairs.

"C'mon, Dana!" Guy called out.

Dana stomped downstairs, grumbling, "I don't know why you woke us up so early anyway."

"If you follow me in the family room," Guy firmly replied, "I will tell explain it to you."

Dana bore questioning eyes before she followed Guy and her sister to the family room. After she flopped down on the sofa, she asked, "What was so urgent that it couldn't wait until we woke up?"

Guy sighed, choosing to ignore Dana. "I decided it's time for you to go back to school," he cautiously said. "I know it's been hard on you girls with Alex and Jeanine in the hospital, but I think returning to school will help lessen the stress. Besides, don't you miss your friends?"

"No," Cassie answered. "I don't care if I ever go back to school."

"Speak for yourself," Dana countered, looking at Cassie with piercing eyes. "I miss my friends."

"Let's try it out for a couple of days," Guy said, as he directed his gaze to Cassie. "If it ends up being too much for you, I'll arrange to have you home-schooled." Then he shifted his eyes between Cassie and Dana. "In the meantime, I have asked your new bodyguard to be here in thirty minutes, to take you to school."

"What happened to Billy?" Cassie asked.

"Billy had to go out of town to tend to a family emergency," Guy stated, reciting what Big Mike had told him earlier.

Rolling her eyes, Dana said, "Do you really think it's necessary for us to have a bodyguard?"

"Yes," Guy simply said, "and I don't need any backtalk. Effie will be here soon."

Without saying another word, Dana and Cassie darted upstairs to get dressed for school. An hour later, they ran outside to greet Effie. "Good morning," the twins said in unison. Then Dana introduced her and her sister. Instantly, they felt safe in her care.

"It's a pleasure meeting you," Effie announced, as she opened the door for them.

Effie stood six four and weighed over two hundred pounds. As a former police officer, she was committed to protecting the twins at all costs.

When they arrived at school, Dana felt anxious to see her friends, but Cassie seemed unsure as she made her way to her first period class. She stopped after she heard someone call out her name. Turning around, she noticed Tabatha Williams, who sported a short afro, an oversized t-shirt, and baggy jeans.

"Yo!" Tabatha hollered, walking briskly to catch up with Cassie. "Wassup?"

Cassie turned around to face Tabatha. "Excuse me?" she asked with scrunched brows.

"Can I talk to you for a bit?" Tabatha asked, after catching her breath.

After witnessing Cassie and Tabatha's interaction from afar, Dana ran up from behind them, then forcefully pulled her sister away from Tabatha. "C'mon, Cassie," she said, while rolling her eyes at Tabatha. "Let's go." As Dana walked with Cassie to her next class, she asked, "Why were you talking to that girl?"

"She was being friendly."

"Yeah, right," Dana said, hinting she had doubts about Tabatha's intentions. "Listen, Pam invited us to a frat party tonight, at the University of Tampa. You want to go?"

Actually, Pam was dating a guy at the university, and decided to invite Dana, who in turn, invited Cassie.

Afraid Dana would try to match her with another boy, Cassie adamantly said, "No. Besides, Guy would never give us permission."

"Why don't you want to go?" Dana griped.

"Come on, Dana. We've been through this already. I'm not attracted to boys."

"Please say you will come with me," Dana begged, holding Cassie's hands.

Cassie knew her sister would never accept 'no' for an answer. "Fine, I'll go," she conceded. "But what about Guy?"

"While he's at the hospital visiting Alex," Dana explained, we'll sneak out of the house. I have a pair of skinny jeans you can borrow, so you can show off your sexy legs," she added, hoping to win Cassie over.

"Oh brother," Cassie grumbled, as she shook her head, trying to imagine her pencil thin legs in skinny jeans.

After Guy left to go to the hospital, Dana and Cassie initiated their plan to sneak out of the house. Unlike Cassie, Dana was eager to go to the party, to get her mind off Malik. She could not believe he was still missing after all this time. He occupied her thoughts day and night. Slipping into her blue sling back V-neck dress, Dana was looking forward to brighter days.

She called her friend, Pam, and told her to pick up her and her sister near the gate entrance. After they ran down the driveway, Pam arrived minutes later.

"Thanks for picking us up," Dana said as she climbed in the front seat while Cassie climbed in the back. "Let's get this party started!" she cheered.

"That's what I'm talking about!" Pam excitedly replied, giving Dana a high-five.

At the party, blue and white dominated the scene, clearly indicating that it was sponsored by the Phi Beta Sigma fraternity. Rap music blared from the speakers as Pam and the twins walked through the entrance. All eyes were on them. Pam and Dana welcomed the attention, but Cassie shied away from it, slightly covering the side of her face with her hand. She felt uncomfortable and overwhelmed at the same time.

When Pam met up with her boyfriend, Dana nudged Cassie with her arm, in the direction of the dance floor. "Come on, Cassie. Let's dance."

Cassie shook her head, protesting. "Not now. I'll sit this one out."

"Are you sure?"

Cassie nodded before she walked to a vacant table and sat down.

Unlike her sister, Dana had easily acclimated to the scene. As soon as she stepped on the dance floor, a young man came up to her from behind and fell in sync with her dance moves.

Sitting alone, Cassie felt a pair of eyes glaring at her from the next table over. She turned around and came face-to-face with Tabatha Williams.

Tabatha was at the frat with her girlfriend, Sammie. She was invited by an older cousin, who was a member of the Phi Beta Sigma fraternity. Tabatha spotted Cassie and her sister as soon as they walked through the fraternity hall.

While Sammie was on the dance floor dancing with her cousin, she walked over to Cassie's table, pulled out a chair and sat down. "Hey Cassie. How are you?"

"I'm okay," Cassie shyly admitted. Mentally, she was happy to see Tabatha.

"I need to ask you a question."

"What do you want to know?"

"What was your sister doing messing around with Malik?"

Cassie shrugged her shoulders. "You know him?"

Tabatha nodded. "Yeah, I know that clown," she gruffly answered.

"Have you seen him?" Cassie asked on behalf of her sister.

Tabatha briefly averted her eyes before she shook her head. "Nah, I haven't seen him. The sooner your sister gets Malik out of her head, the better." She paused before changing the subject. "Cassie, you're a good person."

Cassie smiled. "Thanks."

Dana frowned when she looked over and saw Tabatha talking to her sister. Then she left the dance floor and walked over to their table with an attitude. "Why are you talking to my sister?" she asked Tabatha.

Tabatha did not reply. Instead, she bore a wide grin, which infuriated Dana even more.

"Dana," Cassie calmly interjected, "we're just talking."

"Talking about what?!" Dana exclaimed, eyeballing Tabatha.

Cassie spoke up first. "Why are you getting bent out of shape?"

Dana looked at Tabatha with contempt, then looked at her sister and shook her head. "She knows why."

"I don't," Tabatha said with an attitude, "so why don't you explain it."

Dana exhaled before turning to Cassie. "You can't be that naïve."

Before Cassie could respond, Dana's dance partner approached the table. Shifting his eyes from Tabatha to Dana, he instantly picked up some bad vibes. "Hey there," he said to Dana, "is everything okay?"

Dana nodded. "Yeah, everything is straight." She lied because she did not want anyone in her business, or her sister's.

"Good," Dana's dance partner said, as he extended his hand. "Can I have another dance?"

With slanted eyes, Dana studied Tabatha before she took her partner's hand and followed him on the dance floor.

As soon as Dana left the table, Tabatha pulled her chair closer to Cassie. "What's up with your sister?"

Cassie glimpsed at Dana on the dance floor before responding. "She knows I have issues."

"What kind of issues?"

"I'd rather not say."

"You don't have to tell me. I know all the signs."

"What are you talking about?" Cassie asked with alarm.

"I was in denial for years before I finally came out."

Cassie frowned. "I still don't know what you're talking about."

"I believe you do," Tabatha said, before she stood up and walked away from the table.

Suddenly, Cassie was overcome with fear. She figured Tabatha could see through her. She began to cry as she stood up and bolted out of the fraternity hall.

Dana noticed her sister leaving, and followed suit. "Cassie!" she called out. "Hold up!"

Emotionally distraught, Cassie continued walking.

"Cassie!" Dana hollered repeatedly, before she managed to catch up with her sister. That was when she noticed her sister crying. "What's the matter, baby sis?"

Cassie was choked up. "She knew about me."

"Who?"

"Tabatha."

Dana frowned. "That dyke?"

"Don't say that ever again!" Cassie scolded. "The only difference between me and Tabatha is that she's not afraid to be true to herself."

"But you're not like her."

"I'm worse," Cassie conceded with a shaky voice. "I'm a coward."

"Don't do this to yourself. You're still young. All of us are just experimenting with life."

"Dana, I need some time alone," Cassie explained between sniffles. "Go back to the party. I'll be okay."

"I don't want to leave you like this."

"I'll be fine," Cassie said with certainty. "Please leave me alone, for now."

Dana did not want to leave, but she also wanted to respect Cassie's wishes. "I love you, Cassie."

"I love you too."

With Cassie on her mind, Dana slowly walked toward the fraternity hall. She wanted to support her sister, but was having a hard time accepting the fact that Cassie might be gay.

"Is she okay?" Tabatha asked, standing near the entrance of the fraternity hall.

Dana copped an attitude. "Why do you want to know?" she sassed.

"Because I'm afraid for your sister."

"She's fine."

"But she's not, and you know it. When are you going to accept that your sister is gay?"

"You don't know what you're talking about."

Tabatha shook her head in disgust. "It's because of family members like you, gay people live secret lives. Sometimes they marry the opposite sex because their family can't accept them for who they are. Do you want your sister to live like that?"

Dana thought about what Tabatha was saying, but she did not reply. She knew Cassie was possibly struggling with her sexual identity, but did not realize the severity of her sister's dilemma.

"Some people are miserable," Tabatha continued, "trying to live up to their family's expectations. Sometimes young people, who discover they're gay, commit suicide because they can't handle being judged, teased and bullied by their peers."

Dana's eyes grew bigger. Fearing the worse, she turned around to look for Cassie, who was in the same place she left her. Dana panicked when she noticed Cassie was getting ready to open a bottle of pills. She ran to her sister with Tabatha on her heels. "Don't do it!" Dana pleaded, when she approached her sister.

Cassie frowned. "What are you talking about?"

"What are you doing with those pills?" Dana asked with fear in her voice.

Cassie held up the bottle of aspirin. "I have a headache." Then she looked over at Tabatha, and asked, "What do you want?"

Tabatha did not want to let on that she picked up on Dana's vibe. "I just wanted to check up on you."

Perplexed, Cassie looked from Tabatha to Dana. "I'm okay."

"Good," Tabatha said, staring at the bottle of pills. "How many of those pills did you take?"

"Two," Cassie answered. "Why?"

Tabatha wanted to make sure Cassie was being truthful, so she asked, "Can I have two? I think I'm also coming down with a headache."

Dana remained silent, waiting for a signal from Tabatha to confirm whether Cassie had overdosed. Tabatha took the bottle and shook it; it was practically full. She nodded as a gesture for Dana.

Breathing a sigh of relief, Dana sat next to Cassie on the stoop. "You sure you're okay?"

"I told you, I just want to be left alone for now."

Unbeknownst to Cassie, Tabatha slipped the bottle of pills in her pocket before she turned to Dana. "I think we need to give your sister some space."

Dana noticed that Tabatha kept the pills. She was somewhat relieved as she walked with Tabatha toward the fraternity hall. "Is she going to be okay?" she asked, worried sick about Cassie.

"Yeah, she'll be fine," Tabatha replied with a wave of her hand. "Just so you know, I have a girlfriend. I'm just trying to school your sister for what she's about to go through to live this type of life. To be black is one thing, but to be black, gay and young, that's a whole different story."

Dana sighed as she absorbed what Tabatha was saying.

"Your sister is vulnerable. Cassie needs your strength and your support. You need to start listening to her when she conveys her concerns, and do not discount her true feelings."

Dana nodded. "Thank you for your advice."

"No problem."

When Tabatha walked inside the fraternity hall, her girlfriend, Sammie, approached her with an attitude. "I saw you talking to the rich girl. *What?!* I'm not good enough for you?"

"Nah baby," Tabatha said, as she reached out to Sammie, "it's nothing like that. I have nothing but love for you."

Sammie folded her arms and grunted. "Yeah, right."

Frustrated, Tabatha sighed as she shook her head. "I'm tired of this!" she snapped. "You accuse me of cheating every time you see me talking to a female. What's your problem?"

"Just forget it!" Sammie hollered, before turning her back to Tabatha.

"Yeah, that's our best bet!" Tabatha yelled to Sammie's back. "Let's just squash this whole relationship. It's not going to work."

Sammie turned around and reached for Tabatha with pleading eyes. "Don't do this. I'm sorry, okay?"

Tabatha ignored Sammie's outstretched arms. "No, I think it's best that we go our separate ways."

Sammie's eyes began to tear up at the thought of losing Tabatha. "I'm not going to let you leave me."

"You don't have a choice!" Tabatha retorted. She briefly looked at Sammie one last time, before leaving the party.

"Fine!" Sammie yelled. "I don't need you anyway!"

Tabatha turned back to Sammie with a serious look, and said, "Trust me; you're going to thank me in the long run." Then she walked away from Sammie without regret.

Several months earlier, Tabatha had grown tired of Sammie's childish and possessive ways. She was certain their break up was for the best.

Chapter 40

Crystal Clear

*W*hen Abdul and his men arrived in Tampa, he knew there would likely be some friction between him and the local police. Several years earlier, a police officer had gunned down one of his henchmen. In response, Abdul killed the police officer and set his corpse on fire. His actions never made it to the news, because the police officer in question was a loose cannon. Instead of arresting Abdul, the police commissioner told him to leave the city and never return. Abdul had honored the commissioner's request, until his son was reported missing.

As soon as Abdul arrived in Tampa, he contacted his informant, Officer Ratcliff. They met in a vacant alley behind an abandoned home in downtown Tampa.

"What did you find out?" Abdul gruffly asked the officer.

Officer Ratcliff told Abdul how he had questioned everyone in the community about Malik. One of the neighbors told him they spotted a silver Mercedes Benz in the area around the time Malik disappeared. The officer also went to the Roundtree Bar and Club, not too far from Malik's residence. It was the same club Malik frequented. The officer paused, before he explained, "A couple of patrons told me that two black men came to the club looking for Malik around the time he went missing. I also learned that Malik was on a date with one of his girlfriend's Dana Simmons."

Abdul frowned. "What does that have to do with anything?"

"After doing further research, I discovered that the men looking for your son were possibly her brothers, Guy and Alex Simmons."

"What makes you think that?"

"Her older brother, Guy, drives a silver Mercedes Benz, which happens to match the witnesses' description."

Abdul started pacing back and forth as he pondered the officer's findings. "Have you spoken to these men yet?"

"Not yet. We're still investigating other possible suspects."

"Who?"

"Malik's friend, Sapp Burger."

Abdul nodded, remembering the last conversation he had with Sapp. Mentally, he ruled out Sapp as a potential suspect. "I appreciate you're looking into this," he said to the officer. "Call me if you have further information.

"Will do. In the meantime, I need you and your men to lay low, so we can do our job."

Abdul turned to Officer Ratcliff with a scowl on his face. "I want you to find out what happened to my son. Otherwise, I'm going to take matters into my own hands."

The offer grimaced. "Idle threats are not necessary."

"It's not a threat, it's a promise." Abdul stomped over to his car and sped away. He did not know who he was more furious with: Sapp, who suddenly disappeared; or the officer, who seemed to be dragging his feet with his son's case.

Officer Ratcliff was left to ponder Abdul's allegations. He wondered if Abdul found out about the blood that was discovered in Malik's apartment. Based on Abdul's angry demeanor, he made a mental note to interview Guy and Alex Simmons.

Against Officer Ratcliff's wishes, Abdul decided to take matters into his own hands. He was convinced Dana's brothers knew something about Malik's disappearance. Then again, he thought about all the enemies he created behind his criminal activities, and determined the situation could be worse than he thought. He did not want to take any chances. He called his daughter's mother, and asked her to meet him.

Elizabeth freaked out when Abdul called and explained that he was in town. He would not go into specifics over the phone, so he asked her to meet him at a discreet location. Curious to know why he had returned to Florida, she readily agreed to meet Abdul at a local restaurant. She hung up the phone, then grabbed her car keys and headed toward the front door.

Pastor Coleman thought it was strange when his wife hung up the phone and did not tell him the identity of the caller. His gut feeling told him Elizabeth was seeing another man. He wanted answers, so he discreetly followed her.

When Elizabeth walked into the restaurant, she barely recognized Abdul sitting at the bar, sporting a mustache and goatee. Suddenly, old feelings with her one and only fling came back in full force. Compared to twenty years earlier, Abdul no longer wore baggy jeans, wife beaters and Timberland boots. He looked like a business man in his Armani suit and Stacey Adams shoes. "Is that you?" she asked, as she stood in front of him, beaming.

Abdul stood up to greet Elizabeth with a kiss on the cheek. Even though she looked conservative in her red two-piece suit, the intimate times they shared in the past brought a smile to his face. "How are you?" he asked, as he stood back and stared into her brown eyes.

"Wow," she said while ogling Abdul's new appearance, "you've changed."

"I could say the same about you," he said with a sly grin. "How's my daughter?"

Elizabeth sighed, unsure if she should tell him the specifics about Rhaunda's latest predicament. "She's fine. What brings you to Tampa?"

"Have a seat," he suggested.

As soon as Elizabeth sat down, he sadly said, "My son is missing."

"You have a son?" Elizabeth asked with raised brows.

Abdul nodded. "Yes, I came here to find him."

"Did you contact the police?"

"Sort of," Abdul half-heartedly answered, not wanting anyone to know Officer Ratcliff was on his payroll.

"Is this why you wanted to see me?"

Abdul sighed. "You know what I do for a living," he stated without giving Elizabeth all the gory details of his criminal acts. "I wanted to make sure Rhaunda is safe."

"She's fine," Elizabeth said with assurance.

"Well, I have already ordered that a couple of my men watch over her, just in case."

Elizabeth frowned. "This sounds serious."

"It is. Until I find my son, I'm not taking any chances."

"I understand."

Abdul went on to explain that he was not leaving town until he located his son. He also told her that Rhaunda's life may be in danger. They chit-chatted a while longer before Elizabeth stood up and walked out of the restaurant, while Abdul stayed seated, nursing a beer. She was visibly upset.

An hour earlier, the pastor had parked his car in back of the restaurant, then walked inside and sat in a corner booth. Using the menu to shield his face, he had spotted his wife sitting next to Abdul. Watching closely, the pastor noticed they appeared friendly. He stood up and dropped some bills on the table, when Elizabeth exited the restaurant. Then he glared at Abdul before following his wife to her car.

With her eyes closed, Elizabeth was in a daze as she stood next to her car. She was finding it difficult to digest what Abdul had told her about his son, Malik. Consumed with fear for her daughter's safety, she did not hear or feel the pastor's presence.

"Is there anything you need to tell me?" the pastor asked.

When Elizabeth turned around, her mouth flew open from shock. "Thomas, what are you doing here?"

"I asked you a question first," he solemnly replied.

"I was getting a bite to eat," Elizabeth lied.

The pastor eyed his wife with disappointment. "Who was that man you were sitting next to in the restaurant?"

"He's an old friend."

"An old friend?"

Elizabeth hesitated before she admitted, "He's Rhaunda's biological father."

"That thug back there is Rhaunda's father?!" the pastor angrily asked in disbelief.

After a short pause, Elizabeth's voice cracked when she spoke. "Several years ago, when you had an affair, I wanted to get even."

"I can't believe this!" the pastor exclaimed. "You had a baby with another man to get even with me!"

Elizabeth nodded. She was overcome with shame and guilt.

The pastor was fuming mad, until he remembered what the doctor had told him about his sperm count, or lack thereof. He and Elizabeth had been trying to have a baby for fifteen years, without success. After ruling herself out as the cause, Elizabeth had begged her husband to get tested. The pastor was too embarrassed to tell her he was not capable of getting her pregnant.

When Elizabeth became pregnant, the pastor thought God had answered his prayers. Rhaunda was his miracle baby, or so he thought. Now he realized the desperation his wife must have felt to go to this extent. He blamed himself for driving his wife into the arms of another man. "I'm sorry," he finally said, after deep thought.

Elizabeth batted her eyes to stifle her tears. "I am too."

"What is his name, and what does he want?"

"His name is Abdul Mitchell. He's here to find his son."

"I see," the pastor said, as he cupped his chin. "Does Rhaunda know about him?"

"No," Elizabeth muttered, as she lowered her gaze.

"Good, we're going to keep it that way," the pastor determined. "As far as I'm concerned, Rhaunda has one father, and that's me."

Elizabeth looked at her husband with misty eyes. "Do you mean that?"

The pastor embraced Elizabeth, before whispering in her ear, "I love you and Rhaunda. You two are all I have. I'm sorry for everything I put you through."

At that moment, the pastor made up his mind to end his affair with Sister Hadly. He decided his family needed him the most. He looked into his wife's eyes, and sincerely said, "I will always love you."

Elizabeth beamed, before confessing, "I love you too." Then she asked, after a brief pause, "What are we going to do about Rhaunda? I don't think she's mentally stable. What if Alecia tries to fight her conviction and go to trial?" Her questions were filled with worry.

"You don't have to worry about a trial," the pastor said with assurance. "I've already taken care that."

"I don't understand."

"Just trust me."

The pastor became concerned after learning that there was a contract to give Alex's stepmother the cancer drug. He believed this key piece of evidence could possibly be Alecia's alibi. Without anyone else's knowledge, he had called the hospital to inquire about Jeanine's status. Then he pretended to be her pastor, claiming he wanted to come up to the hospital to pray for her. The nurse believed him, so she went out of her way to give him the contact information for Jeanine's regular doctor in the United States. That doctor, in turn, referred him to the doctor in London.

Without arm twisting, Dr. Daniels told the pastor Jeanine was taking the experimental drug. He had even mentioned that Dr. Kellam illegally gave her the drug while she was still in the United States, to save her life. Cleverly, the pastor had planned on using the information to make sure Alecia Kellam remained the primary and sole suspect for shooting Alex.

Craig Marshall, Attorney Weinberg's assistant, had been following the entire Coleman family for the past week. Rhaunda was pretty consistent. She went to church and to the hospital every day to visit Alex. Pastor Thomas Coleman was also consistent. Three nights in a row, Craig followed the pastor from his church to the same three-star hotel, which was an hour outside of town. Like clockwork, the pastor met up with a beautiful dark chocolate queen with big bold eyes and a curvy body. Based on the way they kissed, Craig did not think the pastor was going to the hotel to pray. After further investigation, he was shocked to discover this woman, Sister Hadly, was a member of the pastor's church.

But nothing prepared Craig for what he found out about the pastor's wife. He followed Elizabeth to a restaurant in St. Petersburg, where she met up with a man, who looked hard and tough; the complete opposite of the pastor. Craig tried to get a closer look but the man was surrounded by four burly men. Using his iPhone, he secretly took pictures of them before he snuck out of the restaurant. Then he phoned his friend, Detective Tom Hines. "Hi Tom, this is Craig."

"Hey buddy, what's going on?"

"I'm working on a special case, and I need your help. Can you meet me at the Family Diner in Tampa?"

"Sure, I'll be there at six o'clock."

"Thanks."

Next, Craig headed to Alex Simmons' condo. He was looking for any witnesses that were possibly in the area the day Alex was shot. He hit the jackpot when he spotted Brian Lancaster walking out of his front door. Eagerly, Brian told Craig everything that transpired between Alex and Rhaunda's parents. He also described Rhaunda and Alex's relationship as rocky.

Two hours later, Craig met up with Detective Hines at the diner, as scheduled. He greeted the detective with a smile and a handshake. "Hey buddy, good to see you."

Detective Hines smiled. "Same here. What can I do for you?"

Craig pulled out his iPhone and clicked through the photos before he held it out to his friend. "Do you know this person?"

Detective Hines looked at the picture of Abdul, then seemingly froze in place. "Where did you get this picture?"

"I took it today, in St. Petersburg. Do you know the man in the picture?"

"Yeah, that's Abdul Mitchell," Detective Hines acknowledged with a slight nod. He remembered when Abdul had gotten away with shooting a fellow police officer in cold blood. "What do you want to know?"

"I'm investigating a case."

"Does your case have anything to do with Malik Mitchell?" he asked, after realizing his colleague was investigating Malik's disappearance.

Craig raised his brows, as he asked, "Who is Malik Mitchell?"

"A young hothead, who's missing. My colleague told me that his father, the man in the picture, is looking for him."

"Wow," Craig muttered under his breath. "I'm not investigating that case. I was hired to find out some information, involving a millionaire, Alex Simmons. He was allegedly shot by my employer's client, Alecia Kellam."

Detective Hines nodded. "I'm familiar with that case. The perp was caught red-handed with the gun, and a recorded confession."

"Ms. Kellam is alleging that it was actually his girlfriend who shot him."

"What do you believe?"

"I'm not sure, which is why I'm searching for any evidence that could prove Ms. Kellam's innocence."

"So why did you take this picture?" the detective asked, pointing to Craig's iPhone.

"I am investigating the victim's girlfriend, Rhaunda Coleman, and her parents, Elizabeth and Pastor Coleman. I spotted the man in the picture with Elizabeth at a restaurant outside of town."

"Are you serious?" the detective asked in disbelief.

Craig nodded. "Yeah, I thought it was strange. They looked like they've known each other for quite some time."

Detective Hines looked at his watch and stood up. "I'm sorry buddy, but I can't help you. Keep me posted on what you find out."

"Oh, one more thing."

"What is it?"

"Can you search Alex Simmons's apartment for a key piece of evidence? I'll make it worth your time."

Slowly, Detective Hines sat back down. "Give me more information."

Craig explained the case he was working on, and the contract he was looking for. He also stated that his employer, Attorney Weinberg, had submitted a request to search Alex's apartment, but the police investigators claimed that they did not find anything.

"What do I get out of the deal?" the detective asked.

"Name your price."

The detective looked at Craig with wide eyes. "It's like that?"

Craig nodded. "Sure, if you can find the contract."

The detective smirked after thinking of ways to spend the money. "I'll do it," he said, after deciding to spend the money on an engagement ring for his fiancé.

"Please let me know as soon as you find it."

"Will do," the detective said, as he stood up to leave.

Chapter 41

Crossed

When Sammie spotted Cassie sitting alone in the school library, she approached her with an attitude. "So, you're the rich *heifer* that stole my woman!"

Cassie looked up from her book, confused. "What woman?" she asked, unable to determine the reason behind Sammie's hostility.

"Don't act like you're all innocent," Sammie griped. "I know your type. I used to be your type."

With furrowed brows, Cassie asked, "Who are you?"

"I'm Sammie," she sassed, leaning on one leg with her arms crossed. "Tabatha's my girlfriend."

Still perplexed, Cassie simply said, "Okay."

Suddenly, Dana came up behind Cassie. She instantly felt the tension. "What's going on?" she asked her sister, while rolling her eyes at Sammie.

"It's nothing," Cassie interjected, as she threw her hand up to silence Sammie. "She was just asking me for directions to the science lab."

Mentally, Dana asked herself, *"What did I miss?"*

"I'm going to escort her," Cassie said as she stood up and stood beside Sammie, "so she won't get lost." Then she looked at Sammie with pleading eyes, hoping she would go along with her ploy.

Sammie grimaced while staring at Cassie with slanted eyes.

"You want me to go with you?" Dana offered.

"Uh…that's not necessary," Cassie stammered, as she put her books in her book bag. "We can manage." Then she gestured for Sammie to follow her.

"Okay," Dana said to Cassie, as she glanced at Sammie. "I'll see you later." She had a feeling her sister was lying, but was not sure why.

As Sammie walked away with Cassie out of the library, she put two and two together. "Does your sister know you're gay?"

"I'm not gay!" Cassie defensively replied.

Sammie bore a sly grin before responding. "I wonder how your sister would react if I told her we were lovers."

Cassie stopped walking and turned to Sammie with wide eyes. "You wouldn't," she fearfully stated.

With a mischievous grin, Sammie said, "Oh yes I would. I'll be sure to tell her the sordid details of our sexual encounter."

"Please don't!" Cassie begged.

A wicked smile formed on Sammie's face, before she said, "My silence can be bought."

"What are you saying?" Cassie asked. Though, she had an idea what Sammie was hinting.

"You're not stupid. Figure it out."

Cassie's mouth flew open as it dawned on her that she was being blackmailed. She dreaded the idea of Sammie spreading rumors about her, but she also had issues with being taken advantage of. Shaking her head, Cassie spouted, "I'm not going to give you anything."

"Fine. I'll just tell the whole school you're gay."

"Oh no!" Cassie screeched. "Don't do that."

"The ball is in your court. What are you prepared to give me?"

"What do you want?"

"Surprise me," Sammie replied, as she looked at Cassie with a smug grin. "Meet me in front of school tomorrow morning, in the library, before the first period. If you don't show up, I'm going to pass flyers all over the school, announcing your coming out party." She walked away from Cassie with a look of satisfaction, but briefly turned back, and yelled, "Stay the hell away from Tabatha!"

After school, Dana questioned Cassie about her run-in with Sammie. "What did she want with you?"

Averting her eyes, Cassie said, "I told you, she just needed directions to the science lab."

"I'm not stupid. That's Tabatha's friend. I've seen her around campus since the beginning of the school year."

"She was looking for the lab," Cassie repeated, as they approached the limo.

When their new bodyguard, Effie, opened the door for them, the twins climbed in and rode home in silence. Dana knew Cassie was hiding something. She turned to her sister, and asked, "Do you trust me?"

Thrown off by the question, Cassie jerked her head in Dana's direction, and said, "Of course I do."

"Would you ever lie to me?"

"I would lie to keep from hurting you," Cassie thoughtfully replied.

"Don't do me any favors," Dana grumbled. "Tell me what's going on."

Cassie exploded as she turned to face Dana. "Would you just drop it?! And stay out of my business!" she shouted, before she turned toward the window in a huff.

Dana was surprised by Cassie's reaction. She had never seen her sister so bent out of shape. "Why are you so angry?"

Cassie ignored Dana, opting to look out the window at the passing cars.

When Effie pulled in front of their home, Cassie climbed out of the limo and ran inside the house, leaving Dana behind. Then she went to her bedroom, sat at her vanity table and opened her jewelry box. She eyed the one-karat diamond necklace Regine had given her for her sixteenth birthday. It brought tears to her eyes at the thought of giving it away.

The next morning, the twins barely said two words to each other as they climbed in the limo. After Effie dropped them off at school, they parted and went their separate ways. But this time, Dana skipped her first period class and decided to follow Cassie. Discreetly, she stayed ten feet behind her sister, and was alarmed when Cassie met up with Sammie, again.

When Cassie gave Sammie the necklace, Dana came up from behind them. "What's going on?" she asked, as she shifted her eyes to Sammie. She did not get a response, so she turned to Cassie, and asked, "Why did you give her your necklace?"

Cassie's voice was shaky after thinking of a good excuse. "Because...," she stammered, "Sammie wanted...to borrow it."

Seeking confirmation, Dana turned to Sammie, and asked, "Is that true?"

"Yeah," Sammie nonchalantly replied, turning to Dana. "Your sister was being nice." She smirked as she put the necklace around her neck. Before walking away, she said to no one in particular, "I'll see you later."

Dana rolled her eyes at Sammie before she turned her attention to Cassie. "Tell me what's going on."

Fidgeting under Dana's glare, Cassie searched for a better explanation but came up empty. "I got to go," she finally said. "I'll catch up with you later."

Dana stood still, stunned by what just happened. She knew something was up, and made it her business to find out.

Later on, she ran into Tabatha in the hallway. "Hi Tabatha. I need to talk to you."

"Hey Dana. What's up?"

"We need to talk. Please follow me."

Dana walked outside and found a place for them to talk in private. Although they were alone, she used a hushed voice to discuss her concerns. "My sister met with your friend this morning. I need to know what's going on."

Tabatha's brow shot up, as she asked, "What friend?"

"Sammie."

"Sammie?" Tabatha asked, to be sure she heard correctly.

Dana nodded. "Yeah. I need to know why you introduced her to my sister."

"What are you saying? You think I tried to hook Sammie up with your sister? I don't roll like that."

"But...."

Tabatha held up her hand to interrupt Dana. "First of all," she said with an attitude, "I would never introduce Sammie to Cassie. Secondly, I broke up with Sammie."

"I'm sorry, I didn't mean to imply that you set Sammie up with my sister, but there's something going on between them."

Tabatha twisted her mouth, pondering Dana's concerns. She was also curious to know why Sammie and Cassie were all of a sudden communicating with each other.

Dana bit her bottom lip before she thought of a clever plan. "Can you arrange for me to talk to Sammie?"

"I don't think that's a good idea," Tabatha stated, after deep thought. "Let me talk to Sammie first." She walked away wondering what Sammie was up to. She called her ex on her cell phone, but there was no answer. So Tabatha decided to go to Sammie's home after school.

She made sure her emotions were in check before she drove to Sammie's house. When she knocked on the door, Sammie's mother came to the door.

"Hello Tabatha," Mrs. Doristein greeted with a warm smile. "It's so good to see you."

"Hello, Mrs. Doristein. Is Sammie here?"

"No, she went to the mall. I'm surprised you didn't call before you came all the way over here."

"I tried, but Sammie is not answering her phone. Can I come inside and wait for her?"

"Sure," Mrs. Doristein said, as she stepped back to let Tabatha inside her home. She became concerned when she noted the scowl on Tabatha's face. "What's going on with you girls?"

Before responding, Tabatha sat on the edge of the sofa with her legs spread apart, rubbing her hands on her jeans. "Nothing. I just need to talk to Sammie about a problem I have."

"Sammie told me you broke up with her."

"Yes, I think it's for the best." Tabatha knew Sammie's mother could not hold water, so she thought it was best not to give any details of their break-up.

"You both are so young," Mrs. Doristein explained. "When you meet the right person, you'll know." She smiled, before she said, "I'm going to start dinner. Do you want anything to drink?"

Tabatha shook her head. "No thank you."

Thirty minutes later, Sammie came home and found Tabatha sitting on the sofa. "What are you doing here?"

Tabatha stood up, and cut to the chase. "What did you want with Cassie?"

"I don't know what you're talking about," Sammie replied, pretending to act innocent.

"Now you want to play games. Okay, let me spell it out. I heard you met up with Cassie at school. What did y'all talk about? "

Sammie smiled as she fingered the diamond necklace around her neck. "Cassie is a good friend."

Tabatha looked at Sammie's neck, and asked, "Where did you get that necklace?"

Sammie flinched before she thought of a good lie. "I bought it."

"Stop lying," Tabatha accused.

"Why do you care?!" Sammie snapped. "We're not together anymore, remember?"

Tabatha stood up to leave, but first she went toe-to-toe with Sammie. "Leave Cassie alone. If you don't, your *ass* is mine."

Sammie shivered at the thought. She knew Tabatha was a woman of her word. She had witnessed her ex-girlfriend in action. The last guy who put his hands on Tabatha's sister ended up regretting it. She had beaten the crap out of him, making sure he was incapable of putting his hands on anyone else. "I can't help that she's afraid to admit she's gay," Sammie said in a huff.

"So that's it. You're trying to blackmail her."

"I don't know what you're talking about."

Tabatha yanked the necklace off Sammie's neck, and said through clenched teeth, "As of today, the *B.S.* stops. Otherwise, you're going to have to deal with me," she added, before she turned and walked out of the house, hoping Sammie did not force her to follow through with her threat.

Chapter 42
Reflections

*A*lecia had just gotten off the phone with her attorney, who informed her that her father was gravely ill. He had suffered another heart attack. Crying nonstop, the pain was too much for her to bear. She returned to her cell, feeling as though the world was coming to an end. Alecia could not help but feel partially responsible for his physical condition. "It not fair!" she hollered, as she stretched out on her cot, bursting out in tears.

While whimpering, Alecia reflected on the unsuccessful attempts to try and win Alex's heart in graduate school. When he ignored her, she tried talking Rhaunda into breaking up with him. "Take away Alex's good looks and smooth talking," she said to Rhaunda while they were watching TV, "then you'll have the perfect man for you."

"But people change," Rhaunda explained.

"Not men like Alex."

Rhaunda sighed. "Alecia, thanks for your concern, but I know what I'm doing."

With a smug grin, Alecia turned to her friend, and asked, "Are you going to break your religious rule?"

Rhaunda frowned. "What are you talking about?"

"You know," Alecia egged on, "give *it* up before marriage?"

"Of course not!" Rhaunda rebuffed, put off by Alecia's question.

That was the response Alecia was counting on. *Good,* she thought to herself, *just maybe there's a chance for me.*

Six months later, Alecia spotted Alex talking to her classmate, Cyprus Wilson, whom she had secretly referred to as the blonde, blue eyed Barbie doll. She noted Cyprus was fawning all over Alex. Then she looked at Alex, who was captivated by her classmate's beauty. Alecia suspected they were up to something when Cyprus got in her car and Alex jumped in his, and followed her. A mischievous grin crept across her face as she maneuvered her car onto the road to follow them. Then she retrieved her cell phone from her purse and called Rhaunda. "Where are you?" she asked, trying with great difficulty, to contain the rush of excitement in her voice.

Rhaunda sat up on the edge of the sofa after closing her bible. "I'm home. Why?" she asked, suspecting something was wrong.

"Hurry up and get dressed!" Alecia demanded in a screeching voice. She assumed Rhaunda was home and still in her pajamas, because she did not have class that day. "I have something to show you."

"What's going on?" Rhaunda asked, balancing the cordless phone to her ear as she ran to her bedroom to change clothes.

"Get dressed!" Alecia ordered. "I'm on my way to pick you up."

"Okay, but where are we going?"

To savor the element of surprise, Alecia abruptly hung up on Rhaunda. She gasped when Alex pulled into the parking lot in front of Cyprus' apartment complex, not too far from where she and Rhaunda lived.

"That dawg!" Alecia yelled aloud. "Well, I'll fix him for choosing that slut over me!"

Alecia was so focused on where Alex was going, she almost ran into the car in front of her. She slammed on the brake pedal, jerking forward. "Damn it!" she hollered at the other driver. "Watch where you're going?!"

Regaining her composure, Alecia hunched over as she drove by Alex's car at a snail's pace. She looked in her rearview mirror and grew furious when Cyprus greeted Alex with a wet sloppy kiss. Shaking her head, it was just as she suspected; Cyprus lured Alex to her apartment to have mind-blowing sex with him. Quickly, she drove to her and Rhaunda's apartment, climbed out of her car, and rushed to the apartment to retrieve her friend.

When Alecia busted through the front door, Rhaunda stood up, noting Alecia's crazed appearance. "What's going on?" Rhaunda nervously asked.

"Hurry up!" Alecia barked, as she grabbed Rhaunda's hand and pulled her toward the front door. "We have to go!"

Rhaunda yanked her hand from Alecia's grasp. "I'm not going anywhere until you tell me what's going on?"

Alecia bit her bottom lip, trying to think of a good excuse. "I have to show you something."

Rhaunda crossed her arms and stood in one place. "I'm not going anywhere until I know what is going on."

"It's about Alex," Alecia simply replied.

"What about him?"

"He's in the next building over," Alecia blurted out, hoping this piece of information would be enough to satisfy Rhaunda's curiosity.

Still confused, Rhaunda stared at Alecia, waiting for her to elaborate.

Alecia became annoyed with Rhaunda's response. Things were not going as she had anticipated. "Um...well...," she mumbled, "I spotted Alex with Cyprus Wilson."

Rhaunda's eyes narrowed as she caught on to what Alecia was hinting. "That Jezebel!" she hollered, her heart pounding from rage. "Where does Cyprus live?!"

"Bel-air Apartments, around the corner from here," Alecia answered, trying hard to conceal her smile.

"That buzzard!" Rhaunda exclaimed, dashing out of the front door, on her way to her car. She waited until Alecia jumped in the passenger seat, before heading to Cyprus' apartment.

Hyped up and ready to see a fight, Alecia escorted Rhaunda to Cyprus' apartment. She was still upset with Alex for rejecting her. She wanted to hurt him, at Rhaunda's expense.

Rhaunda took a deep breath before she knocked on Cyprus' apartment door. When she did not get an answer, she turned the knob and was surprised it was unlocked. She turned back to Alecia with a puzzled expression. "What should I do?"

"Go on in," Alecia insisted, nudging Rhaunda toward the door. "I'll be right behind you."

Without further prodding, Rhaunda opened the front door and looked around the apartment. Alex and Cyprus were no-where in sight. She followed the muffled sounds. Rhaunda walked in the bedroom, and was shocked to find Alex and Cyprus in bed getting busy. Suddenly, she felt someone breathing down her back. She thought it was Alecia until she spun around and discovered an angry young man, rubbing his fists like he wanted to hurt someone.

The young man looked past Rhaunda, and yelled, "Cyprus! What in the *hell* are you doing?!"

Cyprus sprung out of bed and covered up with a blanket. "Danny! What...are you... doing here?!" Her voice was shaky from hysteria.

"I would ask you the same question," Danny sarcastically replied, "but the answer is obvious."

Ignoring Danny, Alex was surprised to see Rhaunda standing before him. He covered his manhood with his hand while looking at Rhaunda with pleading eyes. "Uh...Rhaunda," he stuttered, "um ...baby...I'm sorry."

Rhaunda remained quiet as she turned around and walked out of the apartment. "Come on, Alecia," she ordered, darting to her car.

Incensed, Alecia could not get over the fact that Alex rejected her for the likes of *Cyprus Wilson*. "Rhaunda," she said as she climbed in her friend's car, "we should kick Cyprus' behind for messing with your man."

Rhaunda shook her head. "He's not worth it." She did not need further proof of Alex's unfaithfulness. She drove back to their apartment in silence.

"What are you going to do?" Alecia asked, as soon as they returned to their apartment.

Seconds went by before Rhaunda responded. "I'm going to forgive him."

Unsatisfied with Rhaunda's response, Alecia tried to instigate matters. "I told you Alex was no good. Pretty boys like him can't be trusted, even if you were the last woman standing. On second thought, ugly boys are dogs too," Alecia added, cracking up over her last comment.

Rhaunda held up her hand to silence Alecia. "Don't do this. Alex is a good man. His only flaw is his weakness for women."

Alecia rolled her eyes skyward. "You need to open your eyes and realize he was playing you."

Rhaunda did not agree with Alecia. Prior to this incident, Alex had never disrespected her. She had seen his gentler side. He was the kind of guy who would call her in the middle of the night just to say 'I love you.' *With God's help*, Rhaunda silently prayed, *Alex can be healed of his sex addiction.*

Shortly after getting caught, Alecia knew it would be a matter of time before Alex called Rhaunda to apologize and beg for forgiveness. When he finally called, Alecia answered. Earlier, she lied and told Rhaunda she needed to borrow her cell phone because hers was broken.

Alex was thrown off course by the sound of Alecia's voice. "Hi, may I speak to Rhaunda?"

Alecia smiled. "Is this who I think it is?"

"I'm not sure," Alex mumbled. "Is Rhaunda there?"

"No, but I am."

Alex frowned. "I don't have time for games. I need to talk to Rhaunda."

"So, I hear you're a free man," Alecia replied with a smug grin. "I can fix that issue *if* you give me a chance."

"No thanks!" Alex barked, before he hung up on her.

Alecia was baffled when she heard the dial tone. Despite Alex's rejection, she had vowed to capture his heart. That was then. Looking back, Alecia wished she could turn back the hands of time,

Chapter 43

Fear Factor

*D*espite Tabatha's threat, Sammie was determined to make Cassie's life a living hell. She approached her in the hallway the next school day, taunting her from behind, and shouting, *"Loser! Slut! Cunt!"*

Cassie became angry as she turned around, and yelled, "What do you want from me?!"

Sammie smirked. "You got something else for me?"

"No! Will you please leave me alone?!"

Enjoying the cat and mouse game, Sammie said, "We had a deal, remember?"

"I gave you my necklace," Cassie made clear. "I'm not giving you anything else."

From afar, Tabatha had witnessed Cassie and Sammie engaging in an animated conversation in the hallway. Curious to see what was going on, she approached them while massaging her fists, ready for a fight. "Is there a problem?" she asked, while eyeballing Sammie.

Suddenly, Sammie was overcome with fear. She took a step backward, stuttering, "This has…nothing to do…with you."

Tabatha looked at Cassie, and said, "Go on to class. I'll take care of this."

Cassie walked away, dumbfounded. She could not understand why Sammie was not satisfied with the necklace she had given her.

With slanted eyes, Tabatha redirected her attention to Sammie. "So, you're the type of person that has to learn the hard way. Do you really want me to put my foot up your behind?"

"No," Sammie replied with fear in her voice. "Why can't we go back to the way things used to be? Don't you still love me?"

Tabatha shook her head. "I can't deal with your jealousy."

Sammie reached out to Tabatha with misty eyes, before announcing, "I love you."

Deep down, Tabatha still loved Sammie, but she was no longer interested in having a relationship with her. "Maybe your mother was right," she thoughtfully stated. "We're still young. If it's meant to be, we'll be together in the future." Tabatha walked away but briefly turned back. "Leave Cassie alone. I don't want to have to hurt you."

Sammie stood there, sulking. "How dare Tabatha threaten me?" she asked herself. "After all the things I've done for her. I'll fix her. She can't toy with my emotions and get away with it. She's going to regret dissin' me."

An hour later, Dana saw her sister in the hallway walking to her next class. She became concerned when she noticed her sister crying. "Cassie, what's wrong?"

Cassie looked around to see if Sammie was nearby before she spoke. "It's nothing."

"You don't have to worry about Sammie anymore," Dana said with confidence.

Drying her eyes, Cassie asked, "What are you talking about?"

Dana crossed her arms as she faced Cassie. "I know all about the deal you made with Sammie. You no longer have to give her gifts to keep quiet about being gay."

"But I'm not gay!" Cassie snapped.

"I don't care if you are. I love you no matter what," Dana said, before she dug inside her purse and retrieved Cassie's necklace. "Tabatha gave this to me to return to you."

Cassie retrieved the necklace from Dana and eyed it. "How did Tabatha know?"

"Don't worry about that. You got your necklace back, and that's all that matters."

"Did you mean what you said, 'about loving me no matter what?'?"

Dana smiled. "You're my little sister. I will always love you."

Cassie lightly chuckled. "You're older by a few minutes."

"But in dog years, that's a long time," Dana teased.

Cassie smiled. "I love you too."

"You better, because I love you more," Dana said, as she playfully nudged her sister with her shoulder.

Dana was relieved Cassie's problem with Sammie was resolved. She was beginning to relax when the unexpected happened. She was walking to her next class when a man, posing as a janitor, approached her.

"Hey, Ms. Lady," the man said in a friendly manner. "Can I talk to you for a second?"

Dana frowned. "I don't know you," she sassed.

"But we have a mutual friend," the man said with a sly grin. "Does Malik Mitchell ring a bell?"

"Oh God! Where is he?!" she cried out. "Do you know what happened to him?"

The man shook his head. "I don't know. That's why I'm here."

Dana looked into the man's eyes, and asked, "Who are you?"

"I'm Malik's father. My name is Abdul. I heard you and my son were dating."

Dana nodded in affirmation.

Abdul said, "Some people told me your brothers were looking for Malik around the time he disappeared."

"My, my…brothers?" Dana stammered.

Abdul nodded. "Yes, that's the word on the street."

"But that's not true," she said in her brothers' defense.

Abdul gave Dana a business card with his phone number written on it. "Tell your brothers to call me. If I don't hear from them, I'll know what time it is," he added, before walking away.

Dana panicked. She was worried sick over whether Abdul would hurt her brothers. Quickly, she pulled out her cell phone to call Guy, but there was no answer. Then she went to Cassie's class to ask that she be excused.

Out of earshot of other students, Dana gave her sister an account of what Abdul told her about Malik, and their brothers' involvement.

"What are we going to do?" Cassie nervously asked.

"I'm not sure. I haven't been able to reach Guy."

"I'm sorry to hear that Malik is still missing."

Dana became misty-eyed, again. "I miss him so much."

Cassie embraced Dana before looking into her eyes. "Does Malik's father know Alex is in the hospital?"

"I don't think so."

"We have to leave school now," Cassie said, as she retrieved her cell phone. "I'll call Effie to pick us up."

Chapter 44
Second Chances

*A*fter the cancer drug was administered, there was marked improvement in Jeanine's health. The doctor ordered that she undergo chemotherapy treatments, after noticing signs that the cancer had gone into remission. Jeanine's reaction to the treatments was positive. Regaining fullness in her face, she was glowing and looked healthy.

Mimi was ecstatic with Jeanine's recent prognosis. She called Guy and told him the good news. "Mr. Simmons! You're not going to believe it, but Mrs. Benedict is doing much better."

"This is wonderful news!" Guy cheered. "Is Mom there? I'd like to speak with her."

"She's in chemotherapy right now."

"I understand. I wanted to tell her the good news about Alex."

"Is he out of the coma?" Mimi asked, but feared Guy would not be as forthcoming with her.

Guy smiled. "Yes, Alex is out of the coma. He plans on getting married," he announced with uneasy feelings.

Mimi fell silent before she spoke. "Sir, may I ask who he's marrying?"

"His longtime girlfriend, Rhaunda Coleman."

"I remember her. Ms. Coleman called the house several weeks ago, and asked to speak with Mrs. Benedict."

"I didn't know that," Guy softly whispered.

"Their conversation didn't last long. Mrs. Benedict hung up on her."

"Do you know what they discussed?"

"No, I'm afraid not."

"When did this happen?"

"A couple hours before we found out Alex was hospitalized."

Jerking his head back in surprise, Guy asked, "Are you serious?"

"Yes, according to Mrs. Benedict, Ms. Coleman was unstable."

"Why didn't you tell me?"

"Mrs. Benedict asked me not to."

Sighing, Guy shook his head in disbelief. "Please tell mom to call me when she feels up to it."

"Most certainly. Tell everyone I said hello."

"Will do." Guy hung up the phone in a daze. While on the phone with Mimi, he noticed two missed calls from Dana. He dialed her cell number, and was elated that she answered on the first ring. "Dana, I'm sorry I missed your call. Is everything okay?"

"No, Guy," Dana replied, while glancing at her sister. "Malik's father came to my school."

Guy tightened the phone to his ear, as he asked, "What did he want?"

"He wanted to know if I had seen or heard from Malik."

"Did he hurt you?" Guy's question was filled with fear.

Dana shook her head. "No, but he asked me about you and Alex."

"What about me and Alex?"

Dana ignored Guy's question and posed a question of her own. "Did you hurt Malik?"

Guy shook his head. "No, Dana."

"Do you know who hurt him?"

"No I do not," Guy uneasily replied. "Where are you?"

"Cassie and I are on our way home."

Guy looked at his watch. "So soon?"

"Yes, after we couldn't reach you, we thought it was best to head home."

"Good thinking. I'll see you when you get here." After Guy hung up, he heard a knock at the front door.

"I'll get it!" Regine yelled from the kitchen.

No!" Guy shouted, as he ran out of his office and beat Regine to the front door.

Regine frowned. "What's wrong with you?"

Guy stood next to the front door with his hand on the doorknob. "Uh...nothing, honey." He glanced at KC playing with his remote control car before he turned to Regine. "Please go to our bedroom and take KC with you."

"Why?"

"Please, Regine!" he pleaded a little louder. He was still shaken by Dana's phone call. "Don't argue with me."

Regine was put off by Guy's attitude. Sulking, she grabbed KC and stomped off to her bedroom.

As soon as Regine was out of sight, Guy opened the front door to Tim Carter, Jeanine's private investigator. "Tim," he stammered, "what a surprise."

Tim bore a thin smile, before asking, "Can I come in?"

Guy nodded. "Sure," he said, as he opened the door wider and stepped aside for Tim's entry.

"I heard about Alex," Tim said, as he walked inside the house. "Is he going to be okay?"

"Yes, thanks for asking. I think he's on the road to a full recovery. Did you hear about my mother?"

"Not since she left for London."

"I'm happy to tell you that Mom's cancer is in remission. Hopefully, I'll get a chance to talk to her soon."

Tim smiled. "That's great news! Do you know when she will return home?"

"I'm not sure, but I'll be sure to tell her you stopped by."

"Good," Tim said with a warm smile. "I'll wait until she gets home to talk to her."

"Talk to her about what?" Guy asked out of curiosity.

Tim hesitated as he mulled over whether to tell Guy about his findings. "Mrs. Benedict asked me to do some research for her a while ago."

Guy frowned. "She did?"

"Yes. She became worried about Alex after he started getting into trouble."

"Let's go into my office to talk privately," Guy said, after looking around to see if Regine was nearby.

Tim nodded before he followed Guy's lead.

Closing the office door behind them, Guy sat behind his desk while Tim sat across from him. "Tim, what's going on?" he probed.

"Mrs. Benedict asked me to find out what Bryce Jennings was up to."

"Why did she do that?"

"She was concerned with Alex's association with Mr. Jennings. For some reason, she doesn't trust him."

"She's not alone," Guy said under his breath. "What did you find out about him?"

"I discovered Bryce Jennings had some dealings with Sidney McKinley in the past."

"He did?" Guy asked in amazement.

Tim nodded *yes*.

"Do you know what type of dealings?"

"From what I gathered, Bryce may have propositioned Sidney to work for him."

Guy swatted the air, downplaying Tim's findings. "I'm not surprised. Sidney is a good employee. What else did you find out?"

"I think Mr. Jennings is interested in Trowne Key Estates. I'm not sure in what capacity."

Guy nodded. He made a mental note to confront Bryce.

"Mrs. Benedict had also asked me to find out what happened to Armando Gomez."

"Who is he?"

"Alex's former secretary, Maria Gomez's husband."

"I remember that incident," Guy said with a nod. "Alex came by the house not long after her husband had threatened him."

"Her husband, Armando, no longer poses a threat."

"What do you mean?"

"He's dead, but I'm not sure who killed him."

Stunned, Guy sat up in his chair, and asked, "Are you serious?"

Tim nodded. "I've been following one of the men that may have been involved with Armando's demise. His name is Philipo Rijos. Strangely, Philipo met up with Bryce Jennings the same day Armando was killed."

Guy stared at Tim in disbelief, before asking, "Come again?"

"I'm only guessing, but I believe Bryce Jennings may have put a hit on Armando Gomez. I haven't been able to figure out his motive."

Cupping his chin, Guy thought there was something about Bryce that he did not like or trust. Tim's update had confirmed his suspicions about Alex's new friend.

Tim continued, "I'm also having a hard time trying to find out what happened to Danny DeSoto, the young man Alex had an altercation with in graduate school."

Confused, guy stared at Tim. "I don't understand."

Tim explained, "Mrs. Benedict wanted assurance that Danny DeSoto and Armando Gomez would not pose a problem for Alex in the future."

"Why would they be a threat?"

"Both men had threatened Alex's life. Mrs. Benedict wanted to make sure Alex did not get hurt, or worse. Besides, I think her concerns had a lot to do with *loose ends* in her past."

"Loose ends?"

"I don't know if I should be telling you this, but your father was seeing another woman."

Guy nodded before responding. "I know, my mother...."

"No," Tim interrupted. "I said another woman. This woman tried to blackmail Mrs. Benedict for years, up until your father's death."

Guy exhaled as he sat back in his chair.

Tim further explained, "Your father had a child with this woman, a son."

"He did?"

"Mrs. Benedict paid the woman hush money to keep quiet about the baby, but the woman was relentless. The more Mrs. Benedict gave, the more she wanted."

"What happened to the woman?"

"She disappeared after she had the baby."

"Do you know what happened to the baby?"

Tim shook his head. "No. Mrs. Benedict was going to find him, so she could raise him, but your father told her it wasn't a good idea."

"Why?"

"I'm not sure. I think it had a lot to do with guilt."

"Is the child older or younger than me and Alex?"

"He's about your age."

Shaking his head, Guy could not believe he had another sibling. "Do you know his name?"

"No. It's as if his mother disappeared in thin air."

"More secrets," Guy acknowledged in a soft whisper.

"I'm afraid so." Tim stood up to leave, then pulled his business card out of his wallet and handed it to Guy. "Give me a call as soon as Mrs. Benedict returns home."

Guy took the card and stared at it. "I thought you were retired."

Tim grinned. "I am, but I'll do anything for Mrs. Benedict."

Guy smiled as she shook Tim's hand. "Thanks for being a good friend, and investigator."

"No problem. I'll let myself out."

Guy returned to his office, feeling overwhelmed by what he had just learned from Tim Carter. Even in sickness, he realized Jeanine was still pulling strings to make sure the family was safe from harm. What shocked him more was what Tim told him about he and Alex's estranged brother. Though, he thought it was best to refrain from discussing this issue with Jeanine and Alex.

Five minutes later, the twins arrived home. As soon as Dana spotted Guy, she recited the conversation she had with Malik's father. "I'm worried about you and Alex," she explained.

"Don't worry, Dana," Guy said, as he placed his hand on her shoulder. "Malik's father is not a threat."

"But he sounded scary."

"Trust me," Guy said with a plastered smile, "everything is going to be fine. I want you and Cassie to stay home until we can get this cleared up." He tried to pretend as if he was not worried but internally, he was shivering in his pants. Not taking any chances, Guy picked up the phone to call Big Mike. He decided to hire more bodyguards, to watch over their home twenty-four/seven.

When Jeanine came out of her chemotherapy session, Mimi told her she had spoken with Guy. She also told her Alex was no longer in a coma. Jeanine was elated, but her smile turned upside down, when Mimi told her that Alex was getting married.

"To whom?" Jeanine asked, hoping it was not who she thought it was. Mimi bit her bottom lip, before acknowledging that it was Rhaunda Coleman.

Jeanine shook her head in disgust. "I'm ready to go home."

"I know, Mrs. Benedict, but the doctor is recommending that you stay here a little longer for observation."

"Not if I can help it," Jeanine firmly said, as she sat up in her hospital bed. She was determined to stop Alex from making the biggest mistake of his life. Ever since she regained her strength, she became a force to be reckoned with, especially when it came to her children.

Chapter 45
Cry Wolf

$\mathcal{E}$ ver since Abdul confronted Dana, Guy kept a tight reign on the twins. He refused to let them return to school, and even told them to stay away from the windows and doors. He had pulled out all the stops, to make sure his family was safe. In the process, Guy began drinking, excessively. He was in his office nursing a glass of vodka, when two police officers showed up at his house and rang the door bell.

Against Guy's wishes, Dana answered the door after the bell chimed. She was surprised to see the police officers standing on the other side. "Hi," she said with reservations, "may I help you?"

"Hi, I'm Officer Ratcliff, and this is my partner, Officer Kelly" he indicated, while pointing to the female officer standing next to him. "We're here to see Guy Simmons."

"Why do you want to speak to my brother?" Dana asked, as she eyed the officers with squinted eyes.

"We have a pressing issue that we'd rather discuss with your brother," he emphasized, after Dana mentioned her relationship to Guy.

Curiosity got the best of Dana as she opened the door and told the officers to follow her. She led them to her brother's office, where she found him sitting behind his desk, drinking. "Hi Guy, these police officers are here to see you."

Guy placed his drink on his desk as the police officers came from behind Dana and stood in front of him. Officer Ratcliff retrieved his writing pad and pen from his shirt pocket before he spoke. "Sir, where were you on Saturday, September 1st, between six pm and twelve midnight?"

Guy briefly averted his eyes downward. "What are...you talking...about?" he asked, clearly remembering it was the same day he and Alex went looking for Malik.

"We are investigating Malik Mitchell's disappearance," Officer Kelly made clear. "You and your brother have been named as persons of interest."

Guy's heart beat rapidly as he tried to think of an alibi.

"He was here!" Dana blurted out, after observing the worry lines on her brother's forehead.

Officer Ratcliff turned to Dana, and asked, "How do you know?"

Dana explained, "That was the same day my sister and I went out on a date with Malik and his friend, for our birthday. When we came home, Guy was up waiting for us," she added with certainty.

"What time did you and your sister get home?" Officer Ratcliff asked, realizing Dana was establishing Guy's alibi.

"Around eleven p.m.," Dana offered.

"I see," Officer Ratcliff said, as he massaged his chin with his right hand. Then he turned to Guy for clarification. "Is she telling the truth?"

Shifting his eyes between Dana and the officers, Guy stammered, "Yes....yes."

After closing his writing pad, Officer Ratcliff turned to Guy, and said, "We'll call you if we have further questions."

"No problem," Dana interjected. "I'll see you out."

As soon as the officers left, Dana returned to Guy's office, slamming the door behind her. "Did you hurt him?!" she screamed.

"No," he simply replied. He knew Dana was referring to Malik.

"Do you know what happened to him?"

"Yes."

"Is he dead?"

After Guy did not respond, Dana knew the answer. Her eyes watered, as she asked, "Who killed him?"

Guy placed his elbow on the desk, and spread his hands across his forehead. "I don't know," he said, feeling remorseful. "He was already dead when *we* got there."

"We?"

"Alex was with me."

"Why did you and Alex go see Malik?"

"To threaten him," Guy answered. "Malik hurt you, and we wanted to protect you."

"Why can't you just stay out of my business?!" Dana yelled, before storming out of the office.

Guy felt bad for his sister. He knew she was convinced he did something to Malik. He thought, with time, she would forgive him for a crime he did not commit.

Reflecting on the past, Guy remembered that night like it was yesterday. When Alex refused to help him dispose of Malik's body, Guy was determined to go at it alone. That was the same night he ran into Regine's father, Kevin. He tried not to think about that night, but ever since the police showed up at his door, he was beginning to think he was going down for murder.

Regine was in her bedroom sulking and stressing over her marriage. Her thoughts were interrupted when Dana came into her bedroom and told her about the police officers' visit.

"Do you think Guy hurt Malik?" Dana asked. She had assumed her brothers were the sole culprits.

Any other time, Regine would have said '*no*'. Nowadays, she was not sure. "I don't know," she finally said, after deep thought. "Did the police say that Guy was a suspect?"

"No. He said Guy and Alex are persons of interest. What does that mean?"

"It means the investigators don't have enough evidence to charge them with a crime."

"Oh."

Regine hugged Dana. "Don't worry, honey. Nothing is going to happen to your brothers."

With a thin smile, Dana looked into Regine's eyes. "Thank you, for always being here for me when I need you. I love you."

Regine smiled. "I love you too."

When Dana stood up and walked out of the bedroom, Regine laid in bed. She felt as if she could not leave Guy, even if she wanted to. She loved Dana and Cassie, and wanted to be there for them. Also, Regine wanted to make sure her husband remained a constant figure in their son's life, especially since she did not have a relationship with her own father, until later on in life.

With his head held low, Guy walked into their bedroom minutes later, and found Regine in bed with her eyes open. He remained quiet as he walked over to the bed and sat down next to her.

Regine noticed Guy's somber mood. "Is everything okay?"

"No," Guy truthfully stated. He did not want to discuss Malik, so he offered another problem that kept him awake at night. "I'm worried Alex is making the wrong decision by marrying Rhaunda."

Regine refrained from asking Guy to explain why he felt that way. His vague response told her that she would not get more information than he provided. She noted their hearts were not as one.

As of late, she had become unsure of herself and her marriage. She could not explain how easily her heart had yearned for her new business partner, Lamar Greene, every time Guy dismissed her. She turned to her husband with sadness in her eyes. "Have you once considered that Rhaunda and Alex are truly in love?"

"Listen Regine," Guy harshly replied, "just because you believe Rhaunda didn't have anything to do with shooting Alex, it doesn't mean I feel the same way. You said yourself that Rhaunda acted like a woman scorned."

"But...."

Guy held up his hand to silence Regine. "You also told me Rhaunda said she wanted to kill Alex and Alecia."

"But Alecia is the only one that admitted to shooting Alex. Do you really want to discount her admission of guilt?"

"No, but I don't trust Rhaunda. I don't want her near my brother; not until Alex can remember who shot him."

"But Guy...."

"Don't do this Regine," Guy said in a hushed but strict tone. "Not now."

Regine refrained from speaking further. She wanted to tell Guy that he should be appreciative of Rhaunda's willingness to help out with Alex, but knew it would cause another argument.

In the middle of the morning, Alex tossed and turned in the hospital bed before his eyes flew open. His mind was cluttered with memories of his relationship with Rhaunda; some good, some bad. His head was spinning out of control as reality hit him like a ton of bricks. Suddenly, Alex remembered being shot, but could not recall who pulled the trigger. He sat up in bed, pressing his fists against his head, trying hard to remember specifics about that infamous day.

"Mr. Simmons," the nurse said as she walked into his room, "are you okay?"

"I remember."

"What do you remember?"

"I was shot."

The nurse asked, "Do you remember who shot you?"

Alex nodded. He had been racking his brain, trying to find the answers, to no avail.

With a soft smile, the nurse lightly patted Alex's hand, and said, "Why don't you lie down and try to relax. This is a good sign that you're regaining your long-term memory," she added, before she darted out of the room to alert the doctor.

With reservations, Alex rested his head on his pillow, following the nurse's advice. The doctor returned to Alex's room minutes later, sounding chipper. "Mr. Simmons, the nurse told me your long-term memory might be returning. This is great news!"

Alex struggled to sit up. "I have to get out of here," he insisted, grimacing from pain. "I have a company to run."

The doctor stood in front of Alex to block him from getting out of bed. "No, I don't think that's a good idea."

"You don't understand," Alex tried to explain. "I am part owner of Trowne Key Estates," he pointed out, after remembering clearly. "I have to get out of here."

"Can you wait until we call your fiancé?"

"Fiancé?" Alex asked in disbelief.

"Yes, Ms. Coleman. She left me her number in case there was an emergency."

"Oh," Alex said with surprise in his voice. Based on his last clear recollection, Rhaunda was upset with him, but he could not understand why. "When is she coming up here?"

"She should be here in a couple of hours."

"Where's my brother?"

"Your brother was up here last night. He should be here soon. Try to lay back and relax, until they get here."

Chapter 46

Silver Lining

*A*ttorney Weinberg reviewed Alecia's case over a dozen times, and came up with the same results. She had confessed to killing Alex twice; once the nine-one-one tape, then on the polygraph test. Though, the polygraph test had also proven that Alecia's confession was coerced, and she was telling the truth about Alex signing a contract to marry her in exchange for giving his stepmother the cancer drug. Unfortunately, the polygraph was inadmissible in court.

Without a contract or gun, however, Weinberg knew he was fighting an uphill battle. He sat at his desk in a daze but perked up when his private investigator walked into his office minutes later. "Hi Craig," he greeted with a warm smile, "What did you find out?"

Craig smiled as he sat in the chair across from Weinberg's desk, and retrieved a document from his briefcase. "Rhaunda Coleman received a traffic citation twenty minutes before Alex was shot."

On pins and needles, Weinberg asked, "Do you have proof?"

Gloating, Craig slid a copy of the traffic ticket across the desk.

Weinberg's mouth flew open after he picked up the document and read the time on the ticket. It was just what he needed to corroborate Alecia's account of what happened.

"I have more news for you," Craig boasted, as he handed the attorney another document.

Weinberg put the traffic ticket aside, then glanced over the document before looking at Craig with wide eyes. "Is this what I think it is?" he quizzed, finding it hard to conceal his excitement.

Craig nodded with a wide grin. "Yes, that's the signed contract."

Weinberg almost jumped out of his chair, feeling rejuvenated. "Where did you get this?!"

"I have connections," Craig smugly replied.

"But the State Attorney claimed the investigators searched Alex Simmons' condo, and couldn't find it."

Craig said, "The State Attorney has enough evidence to convict Ms. Kellam. They are not trying to help you get her off the hook."

"Point taken," Weinberg said, as his eyes remained focused on the contract.

Detective Hines had told Craig how he had asked the condo association to let him in Alex's condo. After searching Alex's home from top to bottom, the detective found the contract under the copy machine.

"What does your source want in exchange for the evidence?"

"Ten thousand," Craig answered. He had upped the ante to include his own cut. Detective Hines had only asked for five grand.

"No problem," Weinberg replied, as he pulled out his checkbook and made out a check payable to cash. As he was writing the check, he asked, "Did you find any witnesses?"

"Alex's neighbor, Brian Lancaster, revealed some telling information about Rhaunda's parents."

"What about Rhaunda's parents?" Weinberg questioned, as he handed the check to Craig.

Craig put the check in his wallet before responding. Grimly, he stated, "Mr. Lancaster told me Rhaunda's father paid Alex Simmons a visit, and assaulted him the day before he was shot."

"He did?" Weinberg asked in surprised.

Craig nodded, before continuing, "Hours before Mr. Simmons was shot, Rhaunda's mother also paid him a visit and threatened to kill him with a gun. Luckily, he was not there."

Weinberg raised his brows from shock. "Are you serious?"

"These facts possibly prove Alecia's case. Alex may have broken up with Rhaunda, which would explain why Rhaunda's parents went to such extremes to hurt him."

"Good point," Weinberg said. "The missing pieces of the puzzle are coming together."

"Rhaunda's parents have their own set of issues," Craig added with a smug grin, "but it has nothing to do with this case."

"What do you mean?"

Without responding, Craig slid a manila envelope full of pictures across the desk.

Weinberg looked at Craig in disbelief, then perused through the pictures. "The pastor and the first lady of the church?" he asked with wide eyes.

"Yep," Craig confirmed with a slight nod. "It seems that the pastor has had many flings with his female parishioners. I guess his wife wanted to share in his excitement. But she took it a step further when she had a baby with a big time drug lord, Abdul Mitchell," he said, remembering the conversation he had with Detective Hines.

"This sounds like a freakin' soap opera," Weinberg stated with a light chuckle. "Is Brian Lancaster willing to testify?"

"Yes."

"Excellent!" Weinberg shouted with approval. At the present, he was feeling one-hundred percent sure that he could win Alecia's case. With his eyes casted downward, he thought aloud, "Alecia told me she communicated with Rhaunda's mother, Elizabeth, prior to relocating here. She said Elizabeth had encouraged her to go after Alex." Weinberg paused, before looking up to face Craig. "Can you get a copy of Alecia and Elizabeth's phone records?"

"That's a great idea!" Craig stated, as he sat on the edge of his chair. "I'm certain Rhaunda doesn't know her mother tried to sabotage her relationship with Alex."

Weinberg cracked a smile. "Craig, you are a genius!"

Craig smiled. "Thank you."

"How soon can you get those phone records?"

"Within twenty-four hours."

"Good, we have to hand over our evidence to the prosecutors by Friday. You have two days."

"I'm on it, boss," Craig said, as he stood up to leave.

As soon as Craig left his office, Weinberg went to visit Alecia, to give her an update on her case. Last week, it had pained him to tell Alecia that her father had passed away. Dr. Kellam had another heart attack following heart surgery. The attending physician was present when Dr. Kellam said to no one in particular, "Set my daughter free," before he took his last breath.

In light of the new evidence, Weinberg had planned on making Alecia's father's last wish a reality. He was already seated in the visitation room when Alecia walked in, flanked by two security officers. Weinberg almost did not recognize her.

Alecia looked sad. Her hair was loose and wild, she had lost a lot of weight, and her fiery spirit was nonexistent. The guards guided her to the chair across the table from Weinberg.

"Alecia," the attorney said as he reached for her hand, "I have good news for you."

She never looked up. Instead, tears started pouring down her face. The attorney became misty-eyed watching Alecia mourn her father's death. "Alecia," he slowly said, "you have to be strong."

Looking pitiful, Alecia muttered, "I have nothing to live for."

"I'm going to get you out of here," Weinberg firmly stated.

Still weeping, she asked, "How?"

"We have a witness, and we found the contract."

"You did?" she weakly inquired, feeling a glimmer of hope.

"Yes. Even if Alex does not remember signing the contract, we can hire a signature expert to verify his signature."

Alecia smiled for the first time since being locked up. She listened closely as her attorney outlined his strategy to win her case.

Chapter 47

Premonition

*O*fficer Ratcliff sighed before he picked up the phone to call Abdul. He just found out that a dead body was discovered in a landfill in downtown Tampa. When Abdul answered his call, the officer did not speak right away.

"Who is this?!" Abdul yelled after he heard silence on the other end of the phone.

"It's me," Officer Ratcliff reported.

"What's going on? Did you find my son?"

"No, I'm afraid I have bad news for you. Are you sitting down?"

"Damn all that! Give it to me straight!"

"Your son is dead."

Abdul went silent as his heart ached.

"Are you there?" Officer Ratcliff asked.

Abdul took a deep breath, before asking, "How did he die?'

"His body was discovered in a landfill but the autopsy report showed he was shot three times; twice in the heart and once in the head."

Casting his eyes to the floor, Abdul could not believe what he had just heard. He knew what he had to do. "Did you interview the Simmons's brothers yet?"

"Yes, Guy Simmons agreed to come to the police station to give his fingerprints."

"Where is he?"

"Sir, please, whatever you're thinking, let us do our job."

"I'm going to do whatever it takes to find my son's murderer."

"Please Abdul," Officer Ratcliff urged, "let us do our job."

Abdul hung up on the officer, then rounded up his henchmen to set his plan in motion. He vowed to not sleep or eat until he found out why his son was murdered.

Back in Ireland, Sapp and Billy had settled into a quaint little cottage out in the middle of nowhere. Billy had assured Sapp that they were safe. However Sapp experienced many sleepless nights, worrying about what was going on in the United States. He had a bad feeling Abdul was taking drastic measures to find his son. He could only imagine what Abdul would do once he found out Malik was dead. Curious to find out what was going on, Sapp called his friend and ally, Chico, one of Abdul's henchmen. "Hey Chico, it's me, Sapp."

"Hey Sapp. You a'ight?"

"Yeah, I'm cool."

"Good," Chico said with relief. "Abdul is going crazy. Ever since he found out Malik was dead, he has been stomping the pavement looking for his son's murderer. He even questioned Malik's girlfriend at her school."

"He did?" Sapp asked in disbelief.

Chico nodded. "Yeah, man. Whatever you do, don't come back. Abdul is also looking for you."

"I assumed he would be."

"What happened to you?" Chico asked out of curiosity. "You were supposed to look out for Malik."

"I couldn't handle Malik after he started using drugs."

"I hear ya. Just lay low for now. Peace out."

Suddenly, Sapp was afraid for Dana's life. He knew Abdul was on the verge of killing anyone and everyone he suspected of killing his son, even innocent bystanders, if necessary. Sapp could not stand by and let that happen. He knew what he had to do. However, he was in dire need of money. Picking up the phone, he called the one person he detested the most, to ask for help.

"Hello," the proper sounding voice answered on the first ring.

Sapp grimaced at the sound of his father's voice. The last time he heard from Bobby Toil was during his high school graduation. Seeing the smile on his mother's face, when he walked across the stage to receive his diploma, had meant the world to Sapp. That was, until his father showed up. She started crying, begging his father to be a part of her life. As in the past, Bobby had rejected Sapp's mother, quickly distancing himself from her.

"Hi Bobby," Sapp flatly replied.

"Son," Bobby said after recognizing his voice, "are you okay?"

Sapp's body tensed up when his father referred to him as his son. "I need your help," he admitted.

"Anything," his father said. "What do you need?"

"I need money to fly back home."

"Where are you?"

"Out of the country," Sapp answered, choosing to be vague about his exact location.

"Why didn't you claim your inheritance?"

"I don't want anything from your parents. I'll never forget the way they treated my mother. She died of a broken heart."

Bobby's parents did not like the fact that Sapp's mother, an African American, was dating their son. The hell his mother went through after she became pregnant took a toll on her health. His grandparents had warmed up to him, but continued to ostracize his mother. She was not allowed to step one foot inside their home.

"Son," Bobby said after deep thought, "your grandparents died years ago. They were ignorant," he conceded. "Blacks and whites didn't mix in that era."

"What about the way *you* treated her?" Sapp harshly countered. He remembered she had refused to marry anyone unless it was his father, the one and only man she truly loved.

Bobby sighed. "I was young back then. I'm wiser now. I'm sorry. Will you ever find it in your heart to forgive me?"

Sapp did not respond. He found it easier to remain upset. He was not ready to forgive his father, or let go of the past.

"Would ten thousand be enough?" his father asked, to change the subject.

"More than enough," Sapp answered with assurance. "I'll repay you when I return home."

"You don't have to repay me. Do you want me to meet you at the airport?"

"That won't be necessary."

"Please son," Bobby urged, "give me a chance to make amends."

"Okay, fine," Sapp said in short. "I'll fly into Miami this afternoon, then I'll take a connecting flight to Tampa. You can meet me at the airport there."

"Are you sure you don't want me to send one of the private jets to pick you up from where you are?"

"I'm sure." Sapp hung up the phone with misgivings about seeing his father for the first time in five years. He turned around, and came face-to-face with Billy.

"Are you going somewhere?" Billy asked with his head cocked to one side.

Sapp averted his eyes, as he said, "I need to return to the States."

"You know what will happen, if you do that."

"I can't live with myself if Abdul hurts Dana."

Perplexed, Billy asked, "Why would he do that?"

"One of my acquaintances told me Abdul had recently questioned Dana about Malik."

"He did?" Billy asked, surprised by this revelation.

Sapp nodded. "Yes. Now that Malik's corpse has shown up, I believe Abdul is putting all of his energy into finding his son's murderer."

Billy flinched. Even though he had suspected Malik was dead, he was still hanging on to hope that he was still alive. "What are you going to do?"

Sighing, Sapp thought of the only solution to this problem. "I'm going to tell Abdul that I killed Malik."

"No you're not!" Billy said in defiance.

"You don't understand. I can't take a chance that Abdul won't hurt my sisters."

Billy frowned. "Your sisters?"

"Dana and Cassie. They're my half-sisters. I'll die if something ever happened to either of them."

Exhaling, Billy was in a temporary trance from hearing this revelation. "Why didn't you tell me this before?"

"I recently found out myself."

Billy sighed. "Out of curiosity, is Sapp Burger your real name?"

"Sapp is my nickname and Burger is my mother's surname. My birth name is Michael Toil."

"Toil," Billy thought aloud. "Why does that name sound familiar?"

"Toil and Day Paper Company," Sapp dryly announced.

Billy raised a brow, after recognizing that the company in question was worth billions. "That's your family?"

Sapp nodded. "Yes."

"I'm confused. Why would an heir of one of the biggest companies in the world be associated with a crime lord?"

"It's a long story."

"Give me the short version," Billy insisted.

Sapp paused as he put the past two months of his life in perspective. He explained how his job with Abdul was a source for his college thesis on the drug and gang world. He paused before he continued, "Discovering my sisters was the only good thing about this assignment."

"Wow," Billy said in disbelief.

Sapp nodded. "Yeah, I know."

"When are you leaving?" Billy asked, after sensing he could not stop Sapp from leaving, even if he wanted to.

"Now."

"I'll drive you to the airport."

Chapter 48
All Hell Breaks Loose

*T*he next morning, Guy and Regine woke up early, and decided to go visit Alex at the hospital. They drove to the hospital in silence. Unfortunately, Guy chose to keep quiet about the ongoing investigation against him and Alex, and Regine was at her wits end trying to keep her marriage together. However, they changed their focus when they walked into Alex's room, and discovered Rhaunda sitting next to his bed.

"Hi Rhaunda," Regine greeted with a warm smile. "It's good to see you."

Rhaunda stood up and hugged Regine. "Hi Regine, how are you?"

"I'm fine." Regine smiled as she glanced at Guy, who had a scowl on his face. "We appreciate you visiting Alex."

Rhaunda beamed as she looked at Alex. "Not as much as I do."

Regine peered over at Alex before she approached his bed and gave him a warm hug. "How are you?"

Alex smiled as wonderful memories of Regine flashed before his very eyes. "I'm happy to see you, sis."

Regine smiled. "You haven't called me that in a while."

"How can I forget my favorite sister-in-law?" Alex asked, as fond memories of Regine became fluid.

"I'm your only sister-in-law," Regine teased.

Alex grinned. "I know."

Regine briefly turned to Guy before responding to Alex. "I see you're getting your memory back."

"Yes, he is," Rhaunda answered for Alex. "He's been telling me how much he misses your food."

"When you get out of the hospital," Regine said to Alex, "I'm going to personally make your favorite dishes."

"Alex and I would love to come over for dinner," Rhaunda butted in. "Besides, that would be the perfect opportunity to discuss our wedding plans."

"Whoa," Guy interjected, as his eyes connected with Rhaunda's. "I don't think we need to talk about wedding plans, until Alex gets out of the hospital."

Rhaunda hovered over Alex, as she said in a syrupy voice, "You remember me, don't you, honey?"

With flushed cheeks, Alex looked at Rhaunda, grinning from ear-to-ear. "How can I forget my fiancé?" he asked, not expecting an answer.

Guy was rendered speechless. His gut feeling told him Rhaunda was guilty even though Alecia had confessed to shooting Alex. Though, he acknowledged Rhaunda's charm may have contributed to Alex's recovery. Guy approached Alex's bed, and asked, "Is it true? You have your long-term memory back?"

"It's still kind of fuzzy, but I remember some things."

"Do you remember me?" Guy asked, pointing to himself.

"How can I forget the man that practically raised me?" Alex asked with a light chuckle.

"The doctor will be running some tests today," Rhaunda inserted, as an effort to be included in their conversation.

"Thanks," Guy dryly replied. "You can go home now. Regine and I will stay here with Alex."

"I don't mind staying longer," Rhaunda said, as she moved closer to Alex's bedside and kissed his forehead. "I want to take care of him."

After noticing Guy's tense reaction, Regine intervened with care. "Rhaunda, I think you should go on home and get some rest."

"I really don't mind," Rhaunda insisted.

Regine glanced at Guy, who looked like he was about to explode. "Rhaunda," she cautiously said, "can I talk to you outside for a moment?"

"Sure." Rhaunda kissed Alex on the cheek. "I'll be back, sweetheart," she made clear, before she followed Regine outside the room.

Purposely monitoring her tone and words, Regine said, "Rhaunda, we appreciate you being here for Alex, so don't take this the wrong way."

Rhaunda frowned. "What are you saying?"

"Guy loves his brother as much as you do. Since Alex is getting his memory back, they need time to bond. You understand?"

"No problem," Rhaunda solemnly replied. "I can come back later," she quickly added. "I'll go tell Alex I'm leaving."

"That's not necessary," Guy said, as he stood in the door entrance holding Rhaunda's handbag.

"Oh…I see," Rhaunda said with an attitude. While eyeballing Guy, she retrieved her handbag from his extended hand. "I'll be back tomorrow," she said to no one in particular, before heading down the hallway to the elevator.

Regine waited until Rhaunda was out of sight before she turned to Guy, and sternly asked, "Why were you mean to her?"

"Regine," Guy defensively replied, "I told you how I don't trust her. There's nothing you can do or say to change how I feel," he added, before he returned to Alex's room. Regine shook her head as she followed suit.

Ten minutes later, Officer Ratcliff walked into Alex's room, and approached Guy. "Mr. Simmons," Officer Ratcliff said as he briefly looked at Regine, "I need to talk to you and your brother alone."

"For what?" Alex asked.

"I don't think this is an appropriate time," Regine interjected. "Alex is just now getting his memory back, so whatever you have to discuss with him, will have to wait."

Perplexed, Alex turned to the officer, and asked, "What do you want to know?"

Officer Ratcliff walked around Regine and approached Alex's bed. "Do you know Malik Mitchell?"

"Malik Mitchell?" Alex repeated, trying with great difficulty to remember.

"Officer," Guy interrupted, "can we talk in private?"

"What's going on?" Alex asked, before Guy walked with the officer on his heels.

"I promise," Guy said, as he turned to face his brother. "I'll talk to you when I return."

Guy followed the officer to the waiting room down the hall from Alex's room, where he was questioned, relentlessly. "Where were you on the night in question?" Officer Ratcliff asked, while peering into Guy's eyes for a response.

"I told you, I was home," Guy replied, his nervousness showed. "Both my sister and I submitted a statement to that affect," he added, to convince the officer.

Officer Ratcliff looked at his notepad before responding. "We checked out the dates and they don't add up. Your sister failed to tell us she went on a date with Malik Mitchell the night before he went missing."

"It doesn't matter. I'm sure I was home," Guy countered, breaking out in sweat.

"Where was your brother?" Officer Ratcliff probed.

"I don't know," Guy replied, clearly frustrated. "Why are you asking me all of these questions?"

Officer Ratcliff pondered Guy's question, before stating, "We found some new evidence that may shed light on Malik Mitchell's case."

"What new evidence?" Guy curiously asked. He was eager to know the details.

"Malik Mitchell's body recently showed up in a landfill."

"Oh...I understand," Guy stammered. "But why are you questioning me?"

"Are you sure you don't have anything to tell us?" the officer asked, hoping Guy would come clean.

Guy shook his head. "No."

The officer said, "A witness told me they spotted a silver Mercedes near Malik's apartment the night he disappeared. You drive a car that matches that description, right?"

"Yes I do, but do you realize how many cars are similar to mine?" Guy argued.

Officer Ratcliff nodded. "You have a point, but we have to investigate all leads. We also found a set of fingerprints." He paused, before asking, "Is there a reason you never made it to the police station to get fingerprinted?"

"I have a lot on my plate," Guy countered, defensively. Actually, he had purposely held off on this request for fear he would be implicated. "I have to fly to London today to see about my mother," he added to garner sympathy. "She's in the hospital."

Jeanine had called Guy two days earlier, and told him she was ready to come home. After getting the doctor's approval, Guy had arranged to fly to London to retrieve her.

"Cancel your plans," Officer Ratcliff ordered. "We need you to come to the police station ASAP."

When the officer walked out of the waiting room, Guy buried his face in his hands. He felt as though his actions were coming back to haunt him. Minutes later, he returned to Alex's room in a daze. "If you don't mind," he said to Regine, "I would like to talk to my brother, alone."

Perplexed, Regine asked, "Why? What's going on?"

Guy twisted his mouth as he considered Regine's question. "I'd rather not say," he finally said. "Can you give me and Alex time to talk in private?"

Regine hesitated before she grabbed her purse and darted out of the room. She was tired of being shut out of Guy's life. Crying nonstop, she headed for the hospital exit.

As soon as Regine was out of his sight, Guy sat next to Alex's bed. "Alex, a while ago, Dana was involved with a young man named Malik Mitchell. When Malik hit Dana, we went to his apartment to confront him. Do you remember that night?"

Alex shook his head, confirming he did not.

"Think long and hard before you answer," Guy urged, before he asked the next question. "When we got to Malik's apartment, we found him on the sofa, dead. I suggested that we move his body. Do you remember when you asked me not to?"

"No." Alex slowly answered, as he shook his head in disbelief. "What happened to his body?" he curiously asked.

"It recently showed up in a landfill."

"Who killed him?"

"I don't know. That's why the police officer came here earlier. He wanted to question us about what we knew."

"Why?"

"Someone spotted a car that looked like mine."

Alex closed his eyes trying to remember. He was disappointed when he came up empty. "I wish I could help, but I don't remember."

Exhaling, Guy hunched over in the chair. He knew it was senseless to ask Alex if he had returned to Malik's apartment to remove Malik's body.

"Tell me what's going on," Alex insisted.

Guy sat up on the edge of his chair, pondering Alex's request. "I'm not going to lie to you," he slowly said. "We're in a bad situation. The police are investigating Malik's murder. We have been listed as persons of interest. To make matters worse, Malik's father questioned Dana about Malik."

"Why?"

"I think he suspects that we murdered his son."

"What are we going to do?" Alex fearfully asked.

"I'm going to see if I can find Malik's murderer. In the meantime, I'm going to leave a bodyguard up here to protect you," Guy said, as he pulled out his cell phone to call Big Mike to make the arrangements. He was relieved when his friend had agreed to send a bodyguard to the hospital right away.

"This sounds serious," Alex acknowledged.

Guy nodded. "It is. Hang in there," he said, as he stood up to leave. He walked down the hall to the waiting room, looking for Regine. His heart began beating like a drum when he did not find her. Guy ran up and down the hallways, looking for Regine, to no avail. With shaky hands, he dialed her cell phone number. He was disappointed when his phone call went to her voicemail.

Fifteen minutes later, Guy was still unable to find her. He decided to call the house. He was relieved when Dana answered on the first ring. "Hi Dana. Is everyone okay?"

"Yes, Guy, we're fine."

"Have you seen Regine?"

Dana frowned. "No, I thought she was with you."

"She was, I mean, she is, he stammered. "I'll call you back." Guy disconnected the call, and phoned Regine again, without success. He rushed to the limo, to see if she was waiting for him there. "Have you seen Regine?" he asked the limo driver.

"No sir."

Guy brushed his hand across his forehead, wiping away the sweat beads. "Where are you Regine?" he said aloud.

Reluctantly, he called Regine's father. He vividly remembered when Kevin had threatened to kill him if something ever happened to his daughter.

"What's up?" Kevin gruffly answered.

"Hi Kevin...uh...this is Guy."

"How's my baby?"

"Uh, I don't know," Guy replied.

"What the hell do you mean, 'you don't know?!'"

"She was here at the hospital with me, but now I can't find her. Should I call her mother?"

"No. I'm on my way. Don't call the cops either!" Kevin barked, before he hung up the phone.

Guy returned to his brother's room, to see if his wife was there. "Have you seen Regine?" he asked Alex in a breathless voice.

"No, why?" Alex asked, noticing the sweat dripping off Guy's forehead. "What's going on?"

"I can't find her."

Alex quickly sat up in bed. "Did you call her?"

"Yes, but she's not answering."

Guy looked at his watch, remembering he had to go home to meet with Regine's father. "I gotta go. I'll be back to check up on you," he said, before he ran out of the room.

"Please tell me what's going on!" Alex yelled out.

Guy never heard Alex. He was on a mission to find his wife.

Chapter 49
Web of Deception

*A*lex thought long and hard, pondering the information Guy had told him about Malik. He was frustrated because his memory was still fuzzy, so he changed his focus to Rhaunda. Suddenly, he remembered seeing flashes of Rhaunda's face on the day he was shot. Closing his eyes, Alex allowed his subconscious to walk him through past events that lead up to him being shot. He envisioned kissing Rhaunda, passionately. His heart melted as he reflected on how she had submitted to him, willingly.

Rhaunda whispered, "I love you," in his ear, before he heard the gun cock. With his eyes still closed, Alex strained to see who held the gun near his face. His eyes flew open when it dawned on him that Rhaunda shot him. He rushed to buzz the nurse, then struggled to get out of bed.

"What are you doing?" the nurse asked, as soon as she walked into his room.

Alex's whole body trembled. "I have to call the police," he said in a hurry. "I know who shot me."

"Who?" the nurse asked with raised brows.

Alex hated to admit that the woman, whom he referred to as his fiancé for the past several weeks, was the culprit. "Rhaunda Coleman," he confessed, void of any emotional connection.

"Ms. Coleman?" the nurse asked for clarification. "Are you sure?"

Alex nodded. He felt foolish to have been caught up in Rhaunda's web of deception. "I have to notify the police."

"Please sit tight. I'll go call the police," the nurse said, before she ran out of the room.

Filled with anxiety, Alex picked up the phone in his room and dialed his brother's number from memory. He was disappointed when he received Guy's voicemail. "This is Alex. Please give me a call as soon as you receive this message. I know who shot me," he said, before disconnecting the call.

Detective Hines arrived twenty minutes after the nurse contacted him. "Mr. Simmons," he said as he entered Alex's room, "your nurse told us you remembered who shot you."

"Yes," Alex said with a nod. "It was Rhaunda Coleman."

"Do you know why Ms. Coleman shot you?"

Summing up Rhaunda's motive, Alex said, "She thought I was having an affair with her best friend, Alecia Kellam."

"Are you sure Ms. Coleman shot you?"

"Yes, why?"

Detective Hines pondered Alex's response before responding. "Ms. Kellam has already confessed to shooting you. She's in jail, currently awaiting trial."

"But you have it all wrong," Alex adamantly replied. "Alecia didn't shoot me. Rhaunda did. Besides, Alecia and I had an agreement," Alex added, remembering he and Alecia signed a contract to have the cancer drug administered to his stepmother, in exchange for her hand in marriage.

"What kind of agreement?"

Briefly, Alex averted his eyes downward. "I'd rather not say. It was a private matter." He turned to the detective, and asked, "What's going to happen to Alecia?"

"I'm going to notify the State Attorney to see what they can do about releasing her."

"And Rhaunda?"

"I'm going to arrest her for attempted murder."

"I'd appreciate that."

Alex breathed a little better, knowing Rhaunda would be brought to justice. Then he looked at the detective's gun, and envisioned flashes of blood. His eyes blinked as he remembered Malik's lifeless and bloodied body. "I have to get out of here!" he shouted hysterically, while trying to get out of bed.

"Whoa!" Detective Hines said, as he blocked Alex from getting out of bed. "You can't go anywhere in your condition."

"But I have to go help my brother."

"Maybe I can help. Tell me what's going on."

"Not until I talk to my brother first."

"Okay. We'll see if we can reach him for you. You don't have to worry about your safety. I see there's a bodyguard standing right outside your room," the detective stated, before exiting Alex's room.

Alex remembered Malik Mitchell's father was the reason Guy had hired the bodyguard to watch over his room.

Minutes later, Bryce attempted to walk into Alex's room, but the bodyguard blocked him from entering. "Alex!" Bryce called out from the hallway. "What's going on?!"

"Let him in!" Alex demanded of the bodyguard, after he clearly remembered Bryce was his friend.

The bodyguard stared Bryce up and down before he stepped aside to let him through.

"Hi Alex," Bryce said, as he rushed in the room. "Do you remember me?"

Alex smiled. "How are you, Bryce?"

"I should be asking you the same question," Bryce said with a light chuckle. "I'm glad you got your memory back. You had us all worried."

Alex nodded. "It felt like an out of body experience."

With caution, Bryce glanced at the bodyguard standing near the door entrance. "What's up with the guard?"

"It's a long story," Alex thoughtfully replied, as he began to put the pieces of his life together.

Pulling up a chair and sitting next to Alex's bed, Bryce said, "You can trust me. Tell me what's going on."

Alex sighed. "My memory is still a little fuzzy, but I'll tell you what I remember." Mapping out the latest events in his head, Alex told Bryce about his and Guy's role involving Malik Mitchell. He also told Bryce why he thought Malik's father was looking for them.

"Wow, that's deep," Bryce replied in disbelief.

"If you think that's something, I know who shot me."

Bryce's eyes widened. "It was Rhaunda, wasn't it?"

Alex frowned. "How did you know?"

"I didn't. I had a bad feeling about her ever since I met her. Did you contact the police?"

Alex nodded. "Hopefully, she's on her way to jail."

Bryce smiled. "I'm glad to hear that."

"Me too, but I'm still concerned about Malik's father. I haven't been able to reach Guy."

"Don't worry, I'm sure Guy has everything under control."

"I hope so."

Bryce sighed. "Alex, I know this is not a good time to talk to you about business, but I was wondering if you remembered agreeing to a merger deal."

"What merger deal?" Alex asked, clearly confused.

"You know, the one you and I discussed."

Alex put his hand over his forehead trying to remember, but found it difficult. "I'm sorry, but I don't know what you're talking about."

Exhaling, Bryce was frustrated with Alex's response. He realized his chances of ever owning Trowne Key Estates was becoming grimmer by the day. He checked his watch before he stood up to leave. "I have a business meeting. I'll return tomorrow, to check on you."

Alex nodded with a thin smile. "I'd appreciate that."

"Take care," Bryce said, before he left Alex's room.

Kicking himself, Bryce had a feeling the merger deal with Alex was a lame duck. To make matters worse, Sidney had severed all ties with him. Bryce thought it was odd that he did not flinch when he had threatened to kill him. Instead, Sidney laughed hysterically, before stating he was not afraid to die. Tabling this issue for now, Bryce was on his way to meet up with a potential investor.

Detective Hines called his friend, Craig Marshall, after he left the hospital. He knew Craig would want to know about the breakthrough in Alex's case. "Hey buddy," he said, after Craig answered his call. "You're not going to believe this, but I just met with Alex Simmons. He told me Ms. Coleman shot him."

Craig bore a look of surprise. "Are you serious?" He was sitting across from Attorney Weinberg's desk, trying hard to conceal his excitement. They were working on Alecia's case when the detective called.

The detective nodded. "Yes, I just left the hospital. I'm on my way to the police station to request a warrant for Ms. Coleman's arrest."

"Did Alex Simmons regain his full memory?" Craig asked loud enough to get Weinberg's attention. It worked because Weinberg looked up from the document he was reviewing with an open mouth.

The detective smiled. "Yes he has."

"Thanks for the update. How much do we owe you?"

"Nothing. This one is on the house," the detective said, before disconnecting the call.

"What's going on?" Weinberg asked, after checking the smirk on Craig's face.

"You're not going to believe this," Craig said in amazement. "Alex Simmons just filed charges against Rhaunda Coleman for shooting him."

"This is great news!" Weinberg excitedly announced, as he picked up the phone to call the State Attorney's office. He wanted to get Alecia released from jail as soon as possible.

At least five police cars showed up at the Coleman's home with sirens blaring. Detective Hines knocked on the door while two officers stood on each side of him. The other police officers stayed near their cars with their guns cocked and aimed at the house.

Pastor Coleman looked through the peephole and became alarmed at the sight of police officers on the other side of the door. "What do you want?" the pastor yelled.

"Sir," Detective Hines said aloud, "we have a warrant for Rhaunda Coleman's arrest. Open up!"

"What did she do?" the pastor asked through the closed door.

Detective Hines firmly replied, "If you don't open up, you will be arrested for obstruction of justice."

Feeling pressured, the pastor turned to his wife for help. She was standing behind him.

"No!" Elizabeth cried out. "We can't let them take her!"

Rhaunda was in her bedroom when she heard the commotion. She walked downstairs to find her parents barricading the front door with their bodies. "Mom, dad, who's at the door?"

Elizabeth's eyes shifted to the pastor before she turned to face her daughter. "No one, baby," she lied. "Go back to your bedroom."

"No Elizabeth!" the pastor retorted. "We can no longer protect her." He slowly approached Rhaunda, and lovingly put his arms around her. "Baby," he said as he cupped her face, "the police are here for you. They're here to arrest you."

"Why do they want to arrest me?" Rhaunda asked, as she turned to her mother for answers.

"For attempted murder," her father answered.

"Murder?" Rhaunda questioned. "But I didn't kill anyone."

"Rhaunda, baby," Elizabeth timidly intervened, "remember when you told me you shot Alex."

"But you told me not to worry. You told me God forgave me."

"I know baby, but this is more serious than I thought," Elizabeth admitted. Her voice was filled with sorrow. Then she looked at the front door after she heard the banging. "We have to let them in."

When Pastor Coleman opened the door, Detective Hines headed for Rhaunda. He handcuffed her while reciting the Miranda Rights, then nudged her toward the front door.

"Mom!" Rhaunda cried out. "What's going to happen to me?"

"Don't worry," Elizabeth tried to assure her daughter, "we're going to get you an attorney."

After Rhaunda was escorted outside to the police car, Elizabeth cried on her husband's shoulder. "Honey, what are we going to do?"

"We have to pray," he answered, "and ask God to fix this."

"I don't want Rhaunda in jail," Elizabeth sobbed. "She needs medical treatment."

Deeply troubled, the pastor looked at wife for an explanation. "What are you talking about?"

Elizabeth bit her bottom lip, realizing she almost let the cat out of the bag. "Nothing, honey."

Pastor Coleman frowned. "No more secrets," he said, as he looked in her eyes. "Tell me what's going on with our daughter."

Averting her eyes downward, Elizabeth said, "Rhaunda was diagnosed with schizophrenia several years ago." She was relieved to tell someone else about Rhaunda's mental condition.

Perplexed, the pastor scrunched up his eyes and looked at Elizabeth with a bewildered expression. "Why didn't you tell me?"

"Because she was getting treatment for her condition."

"You still could have told me!" the pastor shouted.

"I know, honey," Elizabeth said, as she grabbed the pastor's hands and looked at him with pleading eyes. "I'm sorry."

The pastor looked at his wife with disgust. "What else haven't you told me?"

"You must believe me," Elizabeth begged. "I don't have any more secrets."

The pastor was getting ready to respond, but his cell phone started ringing. He looked at the caller ID, then turned the ringer off.

"Was that Sister Hadly?" Elizabeth assumed.

He nodded. "Yes, I have to stop by her house this afternoon."

"Not today!" Elizabeth barked. "Our daughter needs us."

"I have to go." The pastor threw on his jacket as he headed out the front door. "You go on and meet with our attorney," he said, before he opened the door. "I'll meet you at his office later."

The pastor was furious as he walked out the front door and headed to his car. Sister Hadly was getting on his last nerves. When he tried to break up with her two weeks earlier, she had threatened to tell the congregation about their love affair. Now he found himself jumping at her every beck and call.

Chapter 50
Guilt by Association

Sapp's plane landed at Miami International airport as scheduled. After deboarding, he walked down the corridor on his way to board another plane headed to Tampa. He stopped in his tracks when he noticed a familiar face. It was easy for him to spot his father. With the exception of their skin complexion and hair texture, Sapp looked the spitting image of his father. Like his sisters, he had even inherited his father's vibrant green eyes and lightly freckled face. Sluggishly, he walked toward his father, feeling indifferent about their reunion.

Smiling, Bobby Toil approached his one and only son. He was unsure if he should hug Sapp or shake his hand. Choosing the latter, Bobby extended his hand. "Michael, it's so good to see you."

"Bobby," Sapp said with lackluster enthusiasm, "you're the last person I expected to see."

Swallowing hard, Bobby withdrew his hand after picking up on Sapp's curt response. "I guess I deserve that."

Sapp faced his father, and asked, "Why are you here?"

"I was worried about you."

"I'm fine," Sapp dryly announced.

Bobby was not convinced, so he asked, "Are you in trouble?"

Sapp winced. He was unsure if he should tell his father the truth. "It's nothing I can't handle," he said, after deciding to take matters into his own hands.

"Whatever is going on," Bobby stressed, "I want to help you."

"Why do you care?" Sapp grumbled.

"Because I owe it to you, and to them."

Sapp stared at his father with slanted eyes. "When you say them," he slowly said, "who are you referring to?"

"Cassie and Dana, your sisters."

"Why didn't you tell me about my sisters?"

Bobby was always waiting for the right time to tell his son about the twins but found it difficult to explain his past. "It's complicated," he finally answered.

"Why?" Sapp probed, pressing his father for an answer.

"Their mother was involved in a complex relationship with her sons' father," Bobby explained. "Their father begged me to let him raise the twins as his own."

"Just like that," Sapp griped. "You let another man take over your responsibilities."

"I knew they would be fine," Bobby said with a nod.

"At least they had a father," Sapp grumbled. "Mine has been MIA practically my entire life."

"I've always made sure you had the best of everything."

"Except your presence," Sapp rebuffed.

Bobby held his head down in shame. "I'm sorry for all the pain I caused. Give me a chance to make it right."

Sapp was not sure if he should trust his father.

"I may have been an absent parent," Bobby acknowledged, "but I've always tried to make sure my kids were safe."

Rolling his eyes, Sapp found it hard to believe his father.

A month earlier, Bobby was shocked when the twins' stepmother, Jeanine Benedict, called the Toils and Day Paper Company and requested to speak with the Executor of their grandparents' Estate. Reluctantly, Bobby answered her call.

Jeanine was surprised to learn that the twins' father was still alive. She did not know if it was a good idea to tell the twins about her conversation with Bobby, when he refused to meet with them. What she did not know was that he had someone check on the twins after receiving her phone call.

Bobby looked in his son's eyes and saw disappointment. He wanted to make it right between them. "I recently found out the twins' brothers were ruled as persons of interest in a murder case."

Sapp's eyes grew bigger in surprise. "Who's the victim?"

"I was told that it was someone named Malik Mitchell."

"Damn!" Sapp exclaimed, as he lowered his gaze.

"Son, tell me what's going on," Bobby insisted.

Sapp mumbled to himself, "I was supposed to protect Malik."

Bobby grabbed Sapp's suitcase. "Let's go. I think I know someone who can help you. We're going to take my private jet to Tampa. It's faster." Reluctantly, Sapp followed suit.

Bobby wondered why his son was affiliated with the likes of Malik, especially after learning that Malik was a street thug with a criminal background. After boarding the jet, he turned to Sapp for answers. "Son, I'm baffled. You go to school in New York. Why were you working for a criminal?"

Sapp glanced at Bobby before staring straight ahead. "To make a long story short, I was working on my thesis. I wanted firsthand experience on what it's like to a work for crime lord. I needed time to gather information to support my thesis, so I didn't take any classes during the summer and fall semesters. I figured six months would have been sufficient to do the research."

Bobby sighed. He did not think his son should have chosen this route, but kept his feelings to himself. "Why did Abdul send you to Tampa, to look after his son?"

"Like you," Sapp solemnly replied, "Abdul was not a part of Malik's life when he was younger. As Malik got older, he started wanted to be a part of his son's life, but Malik rejected him and everything he tried to do for him."

"Is Malik the reason you're headed to Tampa?"

Sapp nodded. "I'm here to make sure his father doesn't hurt anyone, while looking for his son's murderer."

"Why are you involved?"

"I'm responsible."

Bobby's brows shot up. "Come again?"

"I told you I was supposed to watch over Malik," Sapp pointed out. "But I was angry with him, after he put his hands on Dana."

"He did?" Bobby asked in surprise. "Is she okay?"

"Dana's fine," Sapp said with confidence. "I wanted to kill Malik," he said as he thought about that infamous night.

"Did you?"

"No, Malik was already dead before I got to him."

Exhaling, Bobby was having a hard time digesting everything Sapp told him, but it did not stop him from probing further. "Tell me how you found out about your sisters."

Sapp became choked up when he told his father about his discovery. "Malik was dating Dana," after sighing, "and I'm sure Dana begged him to set Cassie up on a date. So Malik asked me to go out with her. When I first saw the twins, I was struck by their features. We look so much alike. I knew we were related when Dana told Malik her deceased grandfather was the original owner of the Toil and Day Paper Company. Can you imagine how I felt when Malik set me up on a date with my sister?"

Bobby shook his head, feeling remorseful. He knew there was nothing he could say to make the situation better. "I'm sorry you found out that way," he replied, while averting his eyes.

"Were you ever going to tell me?" Sapp asked in a soft voice.

Bobby nodded. "Eventually."

Sapp grimaced, doubting his father's sincerity. Then it dawned on him that Abdul may be targeting Guy and Alex as his son's murderers. "I have to warn Dana and Cassie's brothers."

After retrieving his cell phone, Bobby said, "I think I know someone who could probably help us out." He called Kevin, whom he had met several years earlier. Kevin had intervened after he had gotten himself into an altercation with a local drug dealer. Afterward, they remained acquaintances.

"Hello Kevin," Bobby said, after picking up on his friend's voice. "I need your help."

"Wassup?" Kevin asked from the backseat of his sedan. He was en route to Guy and Regine's home.

Bobby told Kevin the little he learned about Malik Mitchell. He also explained how Sapp became involved. With pride in his voice, he told Kevin, "Sapp and the twins are my biological children."

Flustered, Kevin could not believe what Bobby had just told him. "You do know the twins are related to my son-in-law, right?"

"I figured that much out. Sapp told me Abdul might be looking for Guy and Alex."

Kevin had a knee-jerk moment. He thought this revelation possibly explained why his daughter was missing. "Put your son on the phone," he demanded.

Perplexed, Bobby handed the phone to Sapp. "My friend, Kevin, wants to ask you some questions."

Sapp frowned. "Who is he?"

"Guy Simmons' father-in-law."

"How do you know him?"

"Trust me," Bobby insisted, "he can help you."

With reservations, Sapp took the phone from Bobby. "Hello."

Kevin cut straight to the chase. "Tell me about the guy you worked for," he said in a harsh voice.

Put off by Kevin's harsh demeanor, Sapp turned to Bobby with a bewildered gaze.

"Trust him," Bobby urged.

Sapp's nervousness showed as he returned the phone to his ear and answered Kevin. "His name is Abdul Mitchell. He's from New York, but he travels all over the country."

When Sapp mentioned Abdul's name, Kevin knew exactly who he was dealing with. He had a run-in with Abdul several years earlier. "Do you have Abdul's phone number?"

"Yes." After Sapp recited the phone number by heart, he asked, "What are you going to do?"

"Don't worry about all that," Kevin grumbled. "Put Bobby on the phone."

Bobby retrieved the phone from Sapp's extended hand. "Kevin, what's going on?"

"How soon can you get to Clearwater, Florida?"

"In a couple of hours. Why?"

"My daughter is missing. If everything your son told me is the truth, I believe Abdul may have kidnapped her."

Shocked by this revelation, Bobby did not know what to say.

"Meet me at Guy's home," Kevin instructed, after he gave Bobby the address. "We'll figure out how to get your son off the hook, *and* get my daughter back."

Bobby nodded before disconnecting the call.

"Damn!" Kevin exclaimed, after he hung up the phone.

"What's going on?" one of his henchmen asked.

"They got her."

"Who?"

"Abdul Mitchell and his men," Kevin grumbled, as he dialed the number Sapp had given him. "Where is my baby girl?!" he yelled, as soon as Abdul answered his call.

Abdul knew who the caller was, but asked in a rough sounding voice, "Who is this?"

"Kevin."

"Why are you calling me?!" Abdul barked.

"My daughter is missing," Kevin gruffly replied. "She's married to Guy Simmons, the guy you're looking for."

"Nah man, you got it wrong. I didn't take your daughter."

Shaking his head, Kevin did not believe Abdul. "You messed with the wrong person," he threatened. "If you return my daughter, I'll give you a pass."

"You don't get it!" Abdul shouted. "I didn't touch your damn daughter! She didn't do anything to me. Now your son-in-law, on the other hand, gotta *pay the piper* for killing my son."

"I think you got it wrong."

"Let me be the judge of that!" Abdul shouted.

Kevin was so angry, his jaws twitched and every vein in his forehead was noticeable. "If you touch my daughter," he warned, "you're going to wish you were dead."

"Bring it!" Abdul yelled, before slamming his cell phone shut.

In a daze long after phone call, Kevin had more questions than answers. He was no closer to learning the whereabouts of his daughter.

Chapter 51

Chaos!

*A*fter Regine left the hospital, she caught a cab to a local hotel. Crying nonstop, she sat in the cab, thinking long and hard about her marriage. She needed a break from Guy and all his secrets. Six months earlier, her husband had made sweet love to her, and told her how much he loved her. She believed him. Now Regine was trying to get as far away from Guy as she possibly could.

When the cab pulled in front of the hotel, Regine was all cried out. She checked into the hotel, and found peace in the comfort of her hotel room. She was tempted to call Guy, but knew he would try to convince her to come home. After flipping open her cell phone, Regine turned off the ringer, and threw the cell phone on the bed. Then she went downstairs to the hotel restaurant to get a bite to eat.

By chance, she ran into her new business partner, Lamar Greene, who was sitting at the bar. Making sure her emotions were intact, Regine walked over to him with a forced smile. "Lamar, what are you doing here?"

Lamar turned to Regine and smiled. "I have a meeting with an associate in a few hours," he said, after checking his watch. "What are you doing here?"

Regine did not want to reveal the truth, so she provided a short explanation minus all the facts. "My brother-in-law is in the hospital."

"Is he going to be okay?" Lamar asked with genuine concern.

Regine nodded. "Yes, thanks for asking. It was 'touch and go' for a moment, but he's coming around."

"Good. Can I buy you a drink?"

Putting up her right hand to protest, Regine said, "No thank you. I don't drink."

"C'mon, Regine," Lamar urged, "alcohol is good for stress."

Shifting her eyes downward, Regine thought about whether she should try it.

Lamar sensed her reluctance. "I'll order something special for you," he egged on. "You won't even taste the alcohol."

Relaxing her shoulders, Regine smiled as she took a seat next to Lamar. "Okay, just one drink."

After motioning the bartender, Lamar ordered a pina colada with cherry rum. Then he moved the drink in front of Regine, and said, "You're going to like it."

"Hmmm," Regine moaned, after taking a sip. "This is good."

Lamar smiled. "See, I knew you would like it."

Regine felt the cool drink travel down her throat before responding. "I think this is going to be my last drink," she said, after suddenly feeling bubbly and loose.

"Just one more," Lamar insisted.

Regine shook her head. "No."

Lamar knew he could not convince Regine to change her mind, so he entertained her with light conversation. "How's the family?"

"They're fine."

"That's good to hear. What about your husband?"

Regine sighed, while fidgeting for an appropriate response. "Guy is…well, he's fine."

"What's wrong?" Lamar asked with genuine concern.

"Our marriage is on unchartered territory," Regine thought aloud, while casting her eyes downward.

Lamar picked up on her sorrow. He wanted to help her. "Regine, please tell me what's going on."

Fearing she said too much, Regine swatted at the air and pretended to laugh. "You don't want to know about my problems."

"I don't mind."

After sighing, Regine explained her and Guy's marital problems in great detail, including Guy's obsession with his siblings. She began to tear up, as she admitted, "I don't know what to do. I love him so much."

While listening to Regine talk about her marital woes, Lamar was captivated by her soft-spoken voice and big beautiful brown eyes. He felt as if he could look into her soul. He eased his hand on top of hers, and said, "I'm so sorry to hear about your troubles. Is there anything I can do?"

"No," Regine said, as she slipped her hand from under his. "This is my problem, not yours." When she stood up to leave, Lamar grabbed her hand, then planted a kiss on the back of her hand. "I care about you. You are beautiful. If you give me the opportunity, I will never hurt you."

Regine's heart fluttered. This was the first time, in a long time, since she heard those heart-felt words. She recognized it could have been the alcohol that was making her feel all warm and fuzzy inside. Suddenly, she snapped out of her spell as she looked into Lamar's eyes. "I'm flattered, but I'm married."

"I don't care," Lamar made clear. "It feels right, when I'm with you."

Regine smiled. "Thanks for the drinks," When she turned to leave, she bumped into Lamar's associate, Bryce Jennings.

"I'm sorry," Bryce said, as his eyes shifted to Lamar. "Am I interrupting something here?"

Lamar shook his head. "No, my new business partner was just leaving."

"Business partner?" Bryce asked, as he stared at Regine.

Lamar stood up to introduce them. "Bryce Jennings this is Regine Simmons, owner of three five-star restaurants. Together, Mrs. Simmons and I will introduce the world to fine cuisine and superb service."

Regine chuckled as she turned to Lamar. "Wow, you make me sound like I've conquered the world."

"It's just a matter of time," Lamar commented with a sly grin.

Regine laughed as she turned to face Bryce. "It was nice meeting you Mr. Jennings," she said with a warm smile.

"Same here," Bryce said as he undressed her body with dreamy eyes. "Maybe you and I could get together to talk about a joint venture."

"I don't think so," Lamar intervened, after noticing the way Bryce was flirting with Regine. He wanted to protect Regine from the likes of Bryce, aside from the fact that he was jealous.

Bryce backed off after checking out Lamar's protective stance. "My bad," he said, as he raised his hands. "I didn't know."

"It's not like that," Lamar said, after catching on to what Bryce was hinting.

"Well, if that's the case," Bryce said as he looked at Regine with a wide grin, "I'll see you soon."

"Possibly," she said, before she turned to Lamar. "Good evening gentlemen."

Bryce tilted his head. "Good evening, Mrs. Simmons."

Regine walked away thinking there was something familiar about Bryce's face and name, but she could not put her finger on it.

Smirking, Bryce thought it was odd that Regine was not headed for the exit. He had a funny suspicion that she was staying in the hotel. Shortly after he and Lamar sat a table in the corner of the restaurant to discuss business, Bryce excused himself to go to the restroom. But he made a quick detour to the front desk of the hotel. He gave the hotel clerk a one-hundred dollar bill to confirm whether Regine was staying in the hotel.

When Regine returned to her hotel room, she started second-guessing her decision to leave Guy. Thirty minutes after meditating, Regine had made up her mind to go home and fight for her marriage. She grabbed her purse and bolted for the exit. She opened the door, and was surprised to see Bryce standing in the door entrance.

"Hello Regine," he said with a wicked grin. "Where are you going?"

"Home," Regine said, as she tried to walk past Bryce but he stood in her way. "Please move out of my way," she said with force.

"You're not going anywhere," Bryce firmly stated.

Regine was caught off guard when he pushed her backward, forcing his way into her room. "What are you doing?!" she screamed, as Bryce closed the door behind him.

"Your husband is playing hardball," Bryce said in a creepy voice, "so I figure his wife would get him to listen to reason."

Regine backed away from him, until she could not back up any further. She stood near the dresser, eyeing the lamp before she faced Bryce. "Have we met before?"

"You don't know me?" Bryce mocked. "I met you at the hospital. Remember, I was in Alex's room after he was shot."

After registering his face, Regine backed away from him. She was overcome with fear. "Why are you doing this?"

"I deserve full ownership of Trowne Key Estates, and right now, you're my secret weapon. All you have to do is convince your husband that a merger with my company would be in the best interest of his family."

Regine frowned. "I don't understand what you mean."

"You want to play ignorant, so I'll make it loud and clear. If you do not convince your husband to agree to the merger deal, your family members will disappear one by one, starting with your son."

"Please don't hurt my baby," Regine pleaded as her heart beat in overdrive. She believed she would die if something ever happened to KC. "I promise, I'll make sure Guy agrees with your terms."

"I don't believe you," Bryce determined, after his gut instincts kicked in.

"Regine!" Lamar called out, after knocking. "Is everything okay?"

Bryce rushed to Regine and put his hands over her mouth. Then he grabbed her around her neck, and threatened through gritted teeth, "If you scream, I will kill you. Do you understand?"

Regine nodded as her eyes watered from fear.

After Bryce dragged Regine to the door, he said in a hushed voice, "Tell Lamar everything is fine."

"Hi Lamar," Regine said with a trembling voice. "Everything is fine."

"Are you sure?" Lamar asked, sensing something was wrong.

As Bryce tightened his grip around Regine's waist, he said in her ear, "Answer him."

Regine nodded. "Yes…everything's fine."

"Call me if you need me," Lamar said, before turning to leave.

Certain that Lamar left the scene, Bryce shoved Regine away from the door and onto the bed. Then he stood over her with blazing eyes and malice in his heart.

"Why are you doing this?!" Regine shouted.

"Jeanine Benedict owes me. My father lost his company behind her scandalous tactics, to take over the hotel industry. After bribing the Mayor for contracts, Mrs. Benedict had built hotels next to my father's, making them twice as big. She had also given her customers a better rate than my father could ever offer. Six months later, my father died of a heart attack because of her," he added with hurt feelings.

Frowning, Regine said, "I don't have anything to do with this."

"But it has everything to do with you. If it weren't for your husband, I would have owned Trowne Key Estates by now. I saved your brother-in-law's life twice. I had men killed after they threatened to kill Alex, for messing around with their women," Bryce clarified, reflecting on the events leading up to Armando Gomez and Danny DeSoto's deaths.

Bryce continued, "After Jeanine was diagnosed with cancer, I found out she turned over the company to Alex. I've been following him ever since. Had I done my homework, I would have known your husband was also part owner. Alex was in graduate school when Danny DeSoto threatened to kill him. I made sure Danny did not live to see the next day. It was supposed to be an isolated incident. And Armando Gomez was an unsuspecting bystander. When his stupid wife lured Alex over to her house, things got out of hand."

"So you killed him," Regine asked in disbelief.

He nodded. "I figure I did him a favor. If it makes you feel better, I made sure my men made his death painless."

"Did you kill Malik Mitchell?" Regine asked, after remembering the last conversation she had with Dana.

Bryce shook his head. "No, I didn't have anything to do with that. I don't know how in the *hell* they got away with it," he said while directing his gaze to the floor.

Regine frowned. "What are you talking about?"

"Your husband didn't tell you?" Bryce inquired in disbelief. "Guy and Alex went to Malik Mitchell's apartment, to confront him about your sister-in-law. After they left, one of my men came in behind them, and discovered Malik had been murdered. I wonder what they did with the body," he whispered, but loud enough for Regine to hear him.

Regine was speechless as she tried to make sense of Bryce's confession. She could not believe he went to great extents to protect Alex, even resorting to murder.

Bryce sat on the bed, thinking aloud, "If only Sidney was able to convince Alex to go along with the merger deal."

"Sidney McKinley was in on this?" Regine asked in disbelief.

"It was supposed to be a ploy to get Alex into signing over Trowne Key Estates to me," Bryce explained. "After Alex was hospitalized, your husband appointed Sidney as the Acting President. But Sidney turned on me."

"I still don't know what you want from me."

Bryce bore a wicked grin, before confessing, "I want *vengeance*."

Regine began reflecting on how Guy had been mistreating her the past two months, now Bryce was trying to do the same. For the first time in a long time, she found the inner strength to fight back. She was no longer afraid as she sat up in bed, gazing into Bryce's eyes. "Do you know who you're dealing with?" Her voice was void of fear.

Bryce nodded. "The wife of the man that's going to help me dominate the hotel industry," he said with conviction.

"Not only am I Guy's wife," Regine said with an attitude, "but I'm the daughter of one of the most dangerous men in the country. You have no idea what you've just done."

He laughed but it was forced. "Come on, Regine. Am I supposed to be scared?"

Looking at Bryce with piercing eyes, she warned, "You should be, because after my father gets through with you, you're going to be scared to *death,* literally."

"Woooooo," Bryce sang with a ghost-like voice. "I'm shaking in my pants. Trust me, your father will not survive my bullets," he pointed out, as he aimed the gun at Regine's face.

"Is that gun supposed make you feel like a man?" she asked, while fearlessly staring down the barrel of Bryce's gun.

Bryce became nervous. He was unsure of how to respond to Regine's sudden boldness. He thought he could pressure her into doing whatever he wanted her to do. Now he was not so sure.

"Who's shaking in their pants, now?" Regine asked, after noting Bryce's trembling hands.

Chapter 52

Free at Last!

*I*n light of Alex's testimony, the State Attorney dismissed all charges against Alecia, ensuring her immediate release from jail. Her attorney was present when she walked through the gates of freedom. "Hi Alecia," Weinberg said, as he approached her. "How does freedom feel?"

Alecia was emotionally drained. She sighed before responding. "It feels empty without my father."

Weinberg embraced Alecia, to comfort her. "I understand."

"What's going to happen to Rhaunda?"

"Instead of spending the next twenty years behind bars for attempted murder," he explained, "she will likely be committed to a mental institution for a couple of years."

"Are you serious?" Alecia asked with raised brows.

Weinberg nodded. "I discovered through the court records that Ms. Coleman pleaded guilty with temporary insanity as her defense."

"Can she do that?"

"I'm afraid so. After Ms. Coleman was arrested, her mother provided medical history that supports her claim."

Alecia shook her head in disbelief.

"Let's get you out of here, so you can put this whole ordeal behind you." He drove her home, then left after Alecia insisted that she would be fine.

After getting settled in her apartment, she went to her mailbox to retrieve her mail. It was filled with mostly junk mail, but there was an envelope that took her by surprise. It was mailed from her father's office in London. She looked at the postage seal and realized it was dated two days after her father passed away. With shaky hands, Alecia sat on her bed and opened the letter.

Dear Ms. Kellam,

Attached is a letter that was in your father's possession when he had the first heart attack. It did not have a return address, so I didn't know what to make of it. I thought it was strange when I received a phone call from Mr. Thomas Coleman three days after your father died. He asked me if your father received the letter attached. Then he proceeded to describe its contents. I'm only guessing, but I believe this letter triggered your father's heart failure.

After Alecia read the attached letter, it dawned on her that Pastor Coleman was blackmailing her father. Shaking her head, she believed that the entire Coleman family did everything in their power to break her. First, Elizabeth used her to break up Rhaunda and Alex, even though she knew Rhaunda had mental problems. Then, Pastor Thomas Coleman attempted to blackmail her father. And Rhaunda was going to let her remain locked up behind bars for a crime she did not commit.

Alecia thought the Colemans had always acted holier than thou. In public, they put on this facade, fooling everyone into believing they were the perfect family. She had a burning desire to make them suffer for the hell they put her through. She wanted vindication. She picked up the phone to call her attorney.

Halfway to his office, Attorney Weinberg answered his cell phone on the first ring after looking at the caller ID. "Hello Ms. Kellam. Are you okay?"

"I'm okay. I have another problem."

"What is it?"

Alecia explained the letter she received from her father's secretary. Then she read the attached letter from Pastor Coleman. "What do you make of this?"

"It sounds like Mr. Coleman has crossed the line."

"Can I press charges?"

"I'm not sure. Meet me at my office in an hour, and make sure you bring the letters with you. In the meantime, I'll contact the State Attorney to see what they have to say about this."

"I'll be there this afternoon."

As soon as Alecia got off the phone, she felt dizzy and nauseous. She had a gut feeling she knew the cause of her sudden illness but wanted to be sure. She went to her bathroom and retrieved her pregnancy kit from the medicine cabinet. Five minutes later, the results had confirmed her suspicions. She was pregnant with Alex's baby.

In good spirits, Alecia arrived at her attorney's office two hours later. She walked into Weinberg's office and noted he was on the phone. So she took a seat across from his desk.

Weinberg acknowledged Alecia with a nod. After cutting his conversation short, he hung up the phone and turned to face Alecia with a wide grin.

"What did you find out?" Alecia asked. Her question was rushed and filled with anticipation.

Weinberg said, "Not only is the State Attorney going to pursue charges against Pastor Coleman for blackmail and obstruction of justice, but they have just issued a warrant for his arrest."

Alecia wanted to leap for joy, but she was still faced with the reality that she would never see her father again.

"What is it?" the attorney asked, as he noted sadness in her eyes. "I thought you would be happy to hear this news."

Alecia pondered Weinberg's comment before responding. "What about Rhaunda's mother?"

"What do you have in mind?"

"I want her to pay for what she did to me."

"I think she's already suffering. Her daughter is locked up in a mental institution, and her husband is on his way to jail. What more do you want?"

"Justice."

Against Weinberg's better judgment, he pulled a manila envelope out of his desk and handed it to Alecia.

"What is this?" Alecia asked, as she retrieved the envelope from Weinberg.

"Something that'll make you feel vindicated."

Alecia opened the envelope and pulled out five pictures of Pastor Coleman in a hotel room with another woman. Then she looked at a picture of Elizabeth and Abdul, sitting at a restaurant making goo-goo eyes at each other. She looked up at the attorney with surprise in her eyes. "This man," she said as she looked at Abdul, "looks familiar."

Weinberg nodded. "My investigator discovered he is Rhaunda's biological father."

Alecia eyes almost popped out of its sockets.

Weinberg grinned. "You can keep the pictures. Do whatever you want with them."

Alecia smiled as she devised a plan to get even with Rhaunda's mother. She put the pictures in her purse, then extended her hand to Weinberg. "Thank you."

Weinberg shook her hand. "I hope this has brought you closure."

Alecia nodded "It has."

Chapter 53
Fired Up!

*L*amar walked away from Regine's room with reservations. He thought it was strange that she did not open the door for him. *Maybe she was just being cautious*, he thought. *After all, we are just acquaintances. But she did not sound well. Her voice was shaky; it sounded like she was in fear of something.*

When he returned to the restaurant, it dawned on him that her strange behavior probably had something to do with his new business associate, Bryce Jennings. Bryce had asked him several questions about Regine, before excusing himself to go to the men's restroom. That was more than a half-hour ago. He checked with the female receptionist to see if a room was listed in Bryce's name. After she told him *no*, his gut instinct told him to ask for Regine's room number.

Lamar retrieved his cell phone from his pocket and dialed Regine's home number. She had given him the number in case of an emergency. "Mr. Simmons," he said after Guy answered on the first ring, "I'm your wife's business partner, Lamar Greene."

"What do you want?" Guy said with an attitude. It was quite clear that he was jealous of Lamar. He was also in a bad mood because the twins had asked him about Regine's whereabouts as soon as he arrived home. Not wanting them to worry, he told them she would be home soon.

"I'm calling to let you know that your wife might be in trouble."

"Oh God!" Guy cried out. "Where is she?"

"She's at the Casatango hotel in Tampa."

"I'm on my way."

When Lamar returned to the restaurant, Bryce was still MIA. He decided to wait for Guy in the lobby.

Kevin walked in the house just as Guy was returning the phone to its cradle. "Who was that on the phone?" he sternly asked.

"It was Regine's business partner," Guy explained. "He told me Regine might be in trouble. She checked into the Casatango hotel in Tampa."

"Let's go!" Kevin ordered, as he bolted for his car and called his henchmen, who were holed up in a hotel not too far from Regine's.

He told his men to find his daughter and kill anyone that got in their way.

After Guy and Kevin climbed into the backseat of Kevin's sedan, Kevin instructed the driver to take them to the Casatango hotel. Then he turned to Guy, and angrily asked, "Do you have anything to say?"

"I'm not sure what you're asking," Guy replied, trying with great difficulty to avoid Kevin's glare.

"Why didn't you protect my daughter?"

Guy's voice cracked, when he said, "I tried."

Shaking his head, Kevin did not like Guy's response, so he decided to wait and get the specifics from his daughter. As they made it to the hotel, he shifted his focus. He spotted three black sedans parked in front of the hotel. "It looks like my men are already here. You stay in the car," Kevin said, as he turned to Guy. "I'll go see what's going on."

"No," Guy insisted, "I need to go."

"I'm letting you know now, somebody might get killed. Are you sure you can handle that?"

"Yes, I love Regine. I would die for her."

"Okay, let's go.'

When they walked into the lobby, Lamar was standing near the entrance. "Mr. Simmons!" he called out, after spotting Guy from the pictures Regine had displayed in her office. "I'm Lamar Greene, Regine's business associate."

"Thanks for calling," Kevin interrupted, "but you can go on home. We'll take care of her."

"But sir," Lamar persisted, "you don't understand."

"We do," Kevin firmly stated. "Trust me, when I tell you we got it from here."

Lamar looked at Guy, then he turned to Kevin, who bore a scowl on his face. Taking a deep breath, he believed Bryce Jennings was about to get exactly what he deserved. "Please tell Mrs. Simmons to call me as soon as possible."

By the time Kevin and Guy made it to Regine's room, Kevin's henchmen had Bryce pinned to the floor. Earlier, they had beaten him so badly, his face was bloodied and barely recognizable.

Kevin's nose was flaring and his eyes were on fire as he looked at Bryce in disgust. Then he looked across the room, and spotted his daughter sitting on the bed.

Although Regine was unharmed, her blouse was ripped open from wrestling with Bryce earlier. "Hi Daddy," she said with outstretched hands.

Kevin quickly went to Regine. "I'm here for you, baby," he said, as he embraced her. Tears welled up in his eyes as he thought the worst. "Did he?"

"No dad," Regine answered. "He didn't rape me. Those men saved me," she said, as she pointed to Kevin's henchmen.

"Kevin," Guy said as he stood behind him, "can I talk to Regine?"

While eyeballing Guy, Kevin stepped aside. He had a bone to pick with his son-in-law, but realized this was not the appropriate time or place.

Guy wrapped his arms around Regine, and sincerely said, "I'm so sorry this happened to you," as a river of tears flowed down his face.

Regine forced a smile. "I'm okay."

Guy watched Kevin's men drag Bryce out of the room. Then he turned to Kevin, and asked, "What are they going to do with him?"

Kevin paused before responding. "Don't ask, if you don't want to know the truth. I'll meet up with you and Regine later. "

On the drive home, Guy told Regine everything from beginning to end. "I thought I was protecting you," he explained. "Please forgive me."

Regine looked at Guy with sadness in her eyes. "I forgive you, but I wish you would have been honest with me. When you started shutting me out of your life, I didn't know what to think."

Guy held Regine's hand, as he said, "I know, and I'm sorry. I promise things will be different this time."

Regine lifted her head as she looked into Guy's eyes. "How do I know this won't happen again?"

"Because I'm going to be honest with you from now on. I love you. I didn't mean to hurt you." He cupped her chin, then brushed his lips across hers.

Kissing him back, Regine breathlessly whispered, "I love you too," but deep down, she questioned the future of her marriage.

When they arrived home, the twins bombarded them with questions of their whereabouts. They were especially troubled with Regine's disheveled appearance.

"Girls, I'm okay," Regine tried to assure them.

"What happened?" Dana asked.

Regine looked to Guy for help with a response.

"Girls," he said to the twins, "it's been a long day. We'll explain everything tomorrow," he added, before heading upstairs with Regine. Then he guided Regine to bed.

"I know what you're thinking," Regine said, as she sat on their bed. "I didn't go to the hotel to meet Lamar. I went there because I was angry with you."

Guy was relieved Regine had answered the question that had been puzzling him since Lamar called. "I was wrong," he said with remorse. "Lie down and get some rest. I'm going outside to wait for your father."

Chapter 54

Love and Honor

Guy was in front of the house when Kevin arrived an hour later with his henchman. Kevin was calm, cool and collective as he climbed out of the backseat of his sedan. However, his men were on guard with their hands clutched to their guns, looking around for any sign of trouble. Seconds later, Bobby and Sapp, drove up behind Kevin.

Kevin acknowledged Guy with a nod, then he walked over to the other car to greet Bobby and Sapp.

Bobby smiled as he shook Kevin's hand. "Hey buddy, I'm glad you agreed to help us out. This is my son, Michael Toil," he said, while pointing to Sapp.

Kevin acknowledged Sapp with a nod.

Guy became alarmed when he spotted Sapp. He slowly approached the trio, and asked Kevin, "What is he doing here?"

Kevin said, "This is my friend, Bobby, and his son."

"Sapp is his son?" Guy asked in disbelief.

"He's also the twin's brother," Kevin explained.

Perplexed, Guy's eyes shifted to Bobby before turning to Kevin. "Come again?"

"Long story," Kevin pointed out. "Let's talk about this in the house."

"Sir," Sapp said as he walked along side Guy in his home, "thanks for helping me out earlier. If it weren't for you and Billy, I'm sure Malik's father would have killed me by now."

Guy looked at Sapp sideways, before stating, "I don't know what you're talking about."

"I thought you arranged for me and Billy to leave the country."

"No, it wasn't me," Guy said as he shook his head. "Why is Malik's father looking for you?"

Sapp said, "I used to work for him."

Guy looked at Kevin and Bobby as he sought clarification.

Kevin nodded. "It's true."

"Wow," Guy said, as he walked through the foyer. He found it hard to believe everything he had just learned. He walked to the staircase, and yelled, "Dana! Cassie! Come on down. I want you girls to meet someone," he added, as Sapp came up from behind him. Bobby and Kevin remained in the guest room, to give Sapp time to get reacquainted with his sisters.

Dana peeped out of her bedroom from upstairs. Then she looked closer. "Sapp?" she questioned with surprise in her voice. "What are you doing here?"

"Where's Cassie?" Sapp asked, ignoring Dana's question.

"Why do you want to know?" she asked with an attitude.

"Go get her," Sapp instructed. "I don't want to have to repeat myself twice."

In response to Sapp giving her orders, Dana tilted her head to one side, twisted her mouth, and rolled her eyes. "Who are you to tell me what to do? You're not my daddy!"

"I'm sorry," Sapp said with pleading eyes. "I didn't mean anything by it. I'd like to speak with you and your sister about a private matter."

"Fine," Dana said, as she turned around and knocked on her sister's bedroom door. "Cassie, someone is here to see you." Then she walked downstairs with her arms crossed and a scowl on her face.

Guy laughed and playfully nudged Sapp with his shoulder. Then he whispered in his ear, "Welcome to the family."

Sapp shook his head, laughing.

Seconds later, Cassie came out of her bedroom. She looked down stairs and was surprised to see Sapp. "Hi," Cassie said, remembering their last awkward encounter.

"Hi Cassie," Sapp said with a warm smile, "please come downstairs. I need to talk to you and Dana."

Although she was nervous, Cassie complied with Sapp's request. She walked downstairs and stood before him. She did not know what to think or how to react to his presence.

"Now that we're here," Dana sassed, "what did you want to talk about?"

"I'm your brother," Sapp replied with a photo op smile.

Dana's eyes grew bigger. "You are?" she asked with disbelief.

Sapp nodded. "Thanks to you, I was able to figure it out."

"Me?" Dana asked, unsure of what Sapp was suggesting.

"If it weren't for you telling Malik about your inheritance," Sapp explained, "I wouldn't have known."

Cassie turned to Sapp with questioning eyes. "What are you talking about?"

Sapp smiled. "The original owner of the Toils and Day Paper Company is also my grandfather."

Dana's mouth flew open while Cassie stood in one place, stunned.

"Can I hug my sisters?" Sapp pleaded with outstretched arms.

Snapping out of their shock, the twins rushed into Sapp's open arms. "I love you girls so much," he said while embracing them. Still smiling, he looked into their eyes. "I have another surprise for you."

The twins looked at each other before turning to Sapp with questioning eyes.

Sapp purposely remained silent, knowing the suspense was killing Dana.

"Well?" Dana said with an attitude.

"Dad!" Sapp called out, to beckon Bobby's presence.

The girls gasped when Bobby Toil entered the room. They instantly believed he was their father.

"Hello girls," Bobby said, as he approached the twins.

"Are you our father?" Cassie asked, for confirmation.

Bobby nodded and smiled. "Yes."

Cassie ran into Bobby's arms, crying tears of joy. She had dreamed of this day ever since she was a little girl.

Sizzling mad, Dana remained in one place. "I thought you were dead," she spouted, as she looked at Bobby with hatred in her eyes. "Where have you been?"

Bobby reached out to Dana with his free hand, but she crossed her arms and stared at him with an attitude. "It's a long story," he said, after withdrawing his hand.

"We have time," Dana grumbled, as she looked at the invisible watch on her wrist.

Bobby looked at Dana's wrist, and realized she was being mean. Though, he understood her anger.

"We have to tend to some business," Kevin interrupted. He had just gotten off the phone with Abdul. They agreed to meet at a club in downtown Tampa. Abdul had specifically asked to meet with Guy. "I promise," he said as he turned to the twins, "your father will talk to you when he returns."

Tears welled up in Dana's eyes as she stomped upstairs to her bedroom, slamming the door behind her. After diving in her bed, she wondered why her father decided to show up seventeen years later.

"She'll be okay," Cassie tried to assure her father.

Bobby's heart ached as he held Cassie's hand. "I never stopped loving you and your sister."

Kevin looked at his watch again before turning to Bobby. "We have to go!" he barked.

Bobby cupped Cassie's face before kissing her on the forehead. "I'll be back, Sweetheart."

As agreed, Kevin met with Abdul at a bar they used to frequent in their younger days. They became enemies when Abdul murdered one of Kevin's best friends. Now they were working together for the sake of their families. In preparation for the meeting, Abdul had asked the owner to clear the bar, so he and Kevin could have some privacy.

When Kevin walked in with his henchmen, Abdul's men stood up with their hands clutched on their guns. Their actions caused a chain reaction, because Kevin's men drew their guns.

"Chill out!" Abdul and Kevin sharply ordered their men in unison.

Following orders, the men lowered their guns but kept their hands on the trigger, just in case.

With slanted eyes, Abdul looked over and spotted Guy standing behind Kevin. "Did you kill my son?"

There was complete silence as everyone stared at Guy.

"I did not kill your son,' Guy said with assurance. "Malik was already dead before my brother and I went to his apartment."

"Why did you go to his apartment?" Abdul probed.

"We came here to help you find your son's murderer," Kevin interjected, after realizing this question and answer session was pointless.

Abdul was getting ready to respond, but he spotted someone he never thought he would see again. "What is he doing here?" he asked, while eyeing Sapp with contempt.

"He works for me," Kevin lied, to ensure that Sapp was protected from this day forward.

Abdul walked over to Sapp with fire in his eyes and steam coming from his ears. "I hired you to look after my son!" he grumbled. "Where in the *hell* were you?!"

With a shaky voice, Sapp said, "Your son was getting out of control."

"What in the hell do you mean?!" Abdul barked, as he balled up his fist, ready to knock Sapp into the next life.

Sensing things might get out of hand, Kevin walked over and stood next to Sapp.

Sapp's voice trembled as he provided an explanation. "Malik was drinking and doing drugs. When he hit my sister, I lost it."

"Your sister?" Abdul asked with squinty eyes and his head cocked to one side.

"Malik's ex-girlfriend, Dana," Sapp explained, "is my sister."

Abdul frowned. "Why didn't you tell me?"

Shrugging his shoulders, Sapp figured this fact would not have mattered to Abdul.

"Do you know who killed my son?" Abdul asked, choosing to deal with what was important to him.

Sapp shook his head. "No."

"So we're back to square one," Abdul said, as he stared at Guy. When his cell phone rang, he was going to ignore it but the caller ID showed the call was from his informant. "Talk to me," he said, after flipping open his cell phone.

"We have a suspect in custody," Officer Ratcliff said to Abdul. "Does Tabatha Williams ring a bell?"

Abdul shook his head. "No, who is she?"

"The sister of one of the girls Malik used to date."

"Are you saying she killed my son?"

Officer Ratcliff nodded. "We interviewed the perpetrator's ex-girlfriend, Samantha. She told us Tabatha murdered Malik because he assaulted her sister. We're getting ready to question the perpetrator. If you want to, you can come to the police station and watch the interview from another room."

"I'm on my way."

"No problem," the officer said. "I'll see you soon."

Abdul's frown softened as he looked at Sapp and Guy. "Both of you are off the hook."

In response, Guy and Sapp breathed a sigh of relief.

Abdul put on his hat before walking out of the bar with his henchmen behind him. He was too ashamed to admit that his son was killed behind something as senseless as domestic violence.

Afterward, Bobby shook Kevin's hand. "I owe you."

"No you don't," Kevin replied, after pondering his own situation. "I'll see you around."

Two years earlier, his daughter, Regine, was led to believe he was deceased.

Bobby nodded before he turned to Guy, and asked, "Do you need a lift?"

Guy nodded. "Yes, thanks."

During the drive to Guy's home, Sapp retrieved his cell phone from his pocket and called Billy. He was happy to hear his friend's voice. "Hi Billy, I'm calling to let you know that I'm safe, and the issue with Abdul has been resolved.

"How?" Billy asked out of curiosity.

"I'd rather not share the details, but know that Abdul no longer poses a threat."

Billy smiled. "That's good to hear."

"Do you plan on returning to the States?"

Billy shook his head. "No, I think I'm going to stay put for a while. I'm getting older, and I'm thinking about retiring early."

"Well I appreciate everything you've done for me."

"You take care of yourself."

"You too."

Regine and Cassie were sitting in the living room waiting for Bobby, Guy and Sapp. Regine was shocked when she found out the twins' father was alive. She could not help but think about her own situation, when she found out her father was alive two years earlier.

When Bobby, Guy and Sapp walked through the front door, Regine ran into Guy's arms. "Honey, is everything okay?"

Guy nodded. "Now it is. I promise, I'll explain everything to you later on. I want to introduce you to someone," he said, before beckoning Bobby and Sapp's presence.

Sapp and Bobby came from behind Guy and stood next him. After the introductions, Bobby looked around and noticed Dana was not present. He assumed she was in her bedroom. He turned to Guy, and asked, "Can I go upstairs to talk to her?"

"Sure," Guy said, "but it's going to take some time before you get through to her."

Bobby's heart was beating in overdrive as he walked upstairs and knocked on Dana's door. "Dana," he said in a soft voice, can we talk?" Dana did not respond. She was in bed, sulking.

Cassie approached her father from behind, and said, "Let me talk to her."

Bobby stepped aside while Cassie knocked on Dana's door. "Dana, it's me, Cassie. Please open the door."

Seconds later, Dana cracked the door open. "I have nothing to say to that man!" she shouted, as she spotted Bobby in the background. "He made us both bastards!"

"Don't say that," Bobby admonished. "You had a father. His name was Charlie Smith. Your mother, Dottie, did not want me in your lives because she was afraid it would cause confusion."

"What about after they died?" Dana griped. "You could have at least contacted us to let us know that you were alive."

"I was not stable at the time," Bobby explained. "Please give me a chance to make it right."

Dana rolled her eyes in response.

"Please Dana," Cassie interjected, "give him a chance."

Dana looked at her sister with a shocked expression. "Aren't you the least bit angry with him?"

Cassie shook her head. "No, because Guy has always looked after us, making sure we had everything we needed. But what we needed most was our father."

Bobby reached out to Dana. "I promise I'll never betray you again. I love you."

Dana teared up upon hearing Bobby's confession. Deep down, she wanted him in her life. Her tense shoulders relaxed as she allowed her father to embrace her. Feeling Cassie's presence, Bobby reached for her, embracing his daughters at the same time. He also cried tears of joy.

Chapter 55

Vindicated

*P*astor Coleman and Elizabeth were relieved after learning Rhaunda would be locked away in a mental institution instead of prison. The pastor, however, was more worried about his congregation's reaction. He was in the bedroom sitting at his desk, preparing a sermon that would explain Rhaunda's transgressions. Elizabeth was sitting in front of her vanity mirror brushing her hair. Looking out of her bedroom window, she was shocked to find policemen surrounding her house. "Honey," she said to her husband, "why are the police here?"

"What are you talking about?" the pastor grumbled, as he stopped writing and looked at Elizabeth with a frown.

"What should we do?" Elizabeth's voice trembled.

Incensed, the pastor walked over to the bedroom window before responding to his wife. "Go see what they want."

When there was a knock at the door, Elizabeth stomped downstairs to the front door and threw it open. "What do you want?!" she yelled, after recognizing Detective Hines. She was still upset with him for arresting her daughter.

Detective Hines held up a document, as he said, "We have a warrant for your husband's arrest."

Elizabeth gasped. "My husband?" she asked, clearly confused.

The detective nodded. "Is he here?"

"Why is he being arrested?"

"Ma'am is your husband here?" the detective repeated.

"What's going on down there?!" the pastor shouted from upstairs.

Overcome with sadness, Elizabeth looked up at her husband. "The police are here to arrest you."

"For what?" the pastor scoffed. "I didn't do anything."

"Sir," Detective Hines said as he barged through the front door, "we need you to come downstairs, or we will be forced to come get you."

"That's not necessary. I'll be down soon," the pastor replied, before returning to his bedroom to get dressed. Minutes later, he came downstairs with his suit on. "Now, what is this about?" he demanded to know.

Within a split second, the detective turned the pastor around and snapped handcuffs on his wrists. "Sir, you are being arrested for blackmail and obstruction of justice."

"What the hell?!" the pastor spouted, struggling to free his hands.

Elizabeth grabbed the detective's arm, and started screaming, "Set my husband free!"

Detective Hines pushed Elizabeth backward before he turned the pastor around and shoved him out of the front door. Then he read the pastor the Miranda Rights before throwing him in the backseat of his police car.

As the police car drove away, the pastor spotted Alecia sitting in her Sports BMW across the street from his house. She was smiling and waving her hand. Sighing, the pastor figured out Alecia had something to do with him getting arrested. *It was the letter I wrote to her father*, he thought to himself. He was chiding himself for being so stupid.

Elizabeth also noticed Alecia. She stood still as Alecia climbed out of her car and walked up the pathway to confront her.

"Mrs. Coleman," Alecia greeted with a warm smile, "it's so good to see you."

Elizabeth looked down her nose at Alecia with an air of superiority. "What do you want?" she snapped.

Alecia smiled. "I wanted to see, firsthand, how it felt to see a rising family fall from grace."

"You witch!" Elizabeth barked, as she pushed Alecia. "Get off my property!"

Alecia braced herself from falling, then she cracked up laughing.

"What's so funny?" Elizabeth asked, confused by Alecia's wacky behavior.

"Let me get this straight," Alecia said, finding it difficult to control her anger. "Everyone in this family screwed me. And everyone except you, have gotten what they deserve. So I figured I need to do something about that." Then Alecia handed over the envelope that contained pictures the attorney gave her.

"What is this?" Elizabeth asked, before she opened the envelope and saw pictures of her and Abdul, and very risqué pictures of her husband with Sister Hadly at the hotel.

With a wide grin, Alecia took pleasure in watching tears roll down Elizabeth's face.

"Where did you get these?" Elizabeth asked, as she browsed through the pictures. She knew, the pictures alone, would destroy her *perfect family* image.

"I will never reveal my source, but I'm certain your church members will want to know why both the pastor and his wife are cheating on each other. I'm also certain that they would want to know why the first lady had a child from someone other than her husband."

Still in shock from the pictures, Elizabeth looked up at Alecia, frowning. "The church members?"

"Yes," Alecia said with a wicked grin, "I dropped off courtesy copies of the pictures at your church before I came to see your husband off to his new home."

"You bitch!" Elizabeth shouted with venom.

Alecia cracked up. "I know. Payback is a bitch!"

"Go to hell!" Elizabeth growled, before walking in her house and slamming the door in Alecia's face.

"Life is good," Alecia said to herself, as she climbed into her car. She was headed to her birthplace in Baltimore, Maryland, but made a detour to the hospital, to see Alex. She was nervous because she was not sure how Alex would react to her visit.

At a snail's pace, Alecia walked into Alex's room, and approached his bed. "Hi Alex.'

Alex smiled. "Hi Alecia. I'm happy to see you."

"You are?" she asked in surprise.

He nodded. "Of course. I hope you can forgive me for putting you in the middle of all *my* drama."

Alecia shook her head. "No, I owe you an apology. If it weren't for me interfering, you and Rhaunda would have been married by now."

"Things happened the way they should have," Alex thoughtfully acknowledged. "I didn't know Rhaunda had *problems*."

"Her whole family has issues," Alecia added, before she changed the subject. "What are you going to do when you get out of the hospital?"

"I look forward to spending time with my stepmother."

"How is she doing?"

Alex smiled. "Thanks to your father, she's doing quite well. I'm sorry to hear about your father," he stated, after Alecia fell silent. "Dr. Kellam was a great man."

She nodded. "Yes he was. I miss him so much."

After remembering the agreement he and Alecia signed, Alex said, "About that contract...."

Alecia held up her hand to silence Alex. "Don't worry about it. I thought long and hard about the deal I made with you, while I was in jail. It was stupid and immature."

"Don't be too hard on yourself. I think we both learned a lot from this." To change the subject, Alex asked, "What are you going to do, now that you're a free woman?"

Alecia smiled. "I'm going to get as far away from Florida as I possibly can. What are you going to do?"

"Go back to work, hopefully with my stepmother."

Alecia looked at her watch before kissing Alex on the cheek. "It was good seeing you. You take care of yourself."

"You too."

For a split second, Alecia thought about telling Alex about her pregnancy but changed her mind. She figured he had enough on his plate. As Alecia strolled out of the hospital, she rubbed her belly, feeling the small bump on her stomach. She wondered if her baby would ever forgive her for keeping its father a well-kept secret.

Alex also had a lot on his mind. He was relieved Alecia was not convicted for a crime she did not commit. He had also breathed a little better knowing Rhaunda was getting help for her mental problems. Though, he felt partially responsible for her melt down.

When Abdul arrived at the police station, Officer Ratcliff snuck Abdul through the back door, to let him watch the interrogation process in an adjoining room. He was surprised to learn that Tabatha was a seventeen-year-old kid.

Abdul tensed up when Tabatha angrily stated, "You damn right I killed Malik, and I hope he's rotting in hell!"

"Why did you do it?" Officer Ratcliff asked.

"Malik had already hurt my sister," Tabatha acknowledged. "When he put his hands on Dana, I lost it. I knew he wouldn't stop until he killed someone. Malik needed to be stopped."

"Why did you move the body?"

Tabatha frowned. "I didn't move his body."

"Do you know who moved his body?"

Tabatha shrugged her shoulders. "I don't know and I don't care."

Abdul became alarmed after hearing Tabatha's response. Shaking his head, he wondered if this mystery would ever be solved. He left the police station determined to see his only surviving child, to make amends.

Boldly, Abdul knocked on the door, and was shocked to find Elizabeth crying and distraught. "Where's my daughter?"

"She's not here," Elizabeth sobbed. "They took her."

Abdul asked, "Who took her?"

"The police. Rhaunda was committed to a mental institution for attempted murder."

"A mental institution? Why?"

Holding the door open for Abdul, Elizabeth stepped aside and said, "Come inside. It's a long story."

"Tell me what's going on," Abdul insisted.

"Rhaunda was diagnosed with paranoid schizophrenia several years ago," she solemnly explained.

Abdul frowned. "Why didn't you tell me?"

Elizabeth's eyes began to water and her lips trembled. "Because she was taking her medication. She was fine, until...."

"Until what?"

"She met Alex Simmons." Tears streamed down Elizabeth's face, as she cried out, "I don't know what I'm going to do without my baby."

Abdul felt her pain, but put up a strong front. "Where's your husband?" he asked, after successfully holding back tears.

"He's in jail. He tried to protect her."

Abdul sighed as he cupped his chin.

"What are *we* going to do?" she asked.

Abdul shook his head, honestly answering, "I don't know." This was a first for him. Typically, he would handle every situation with a gun or iron fist.

Feeling helpless, Elizabeth cried on Abdul's shoulder. "Please don't leave me," she begged. "I'm so lonely." Her life had crumbed right before her eyes. Her daughter was in a mental institution; her husband was in jail; and without her husband's income from church, she would soon be homeless. Overwhelmed with grief, she was about to topple over but Abdul grabbed her.

Abdul embraced Elizabeth. He was not sure how to respond to Elizabeth's request. He did not love her, nor did he know how to comfort her. To make matters worse, he was also hurting. Abdul wanted to seek vindication for his children, but realized there was no one to blame. He thought had he been a part of his children's lives, things may have turned out differently.

Chapter 56
Wild Card

Two Weeks Later....

The twins were still finding it hard to believe that their biological father was alive. They admired Bobby for stepping up to the plate, to try and make amends. On a routine basis, he called and visited the twins and spoiled them with gifts. Their half brother, Sapp had also remained a constant figure in their lives. He became the typical overprotective big brother, doting on them and giving them unwelcomed advice about life.

When Dana was not busy with schoolwork and socializing with friends, she often thought about Malik. She was finding it difficult to get him out of her heart and thoughts. Up until his body was discovered, she was still holding on to hope that he was still alive. She was shocked to learn that Tabatha was convicted of shooting him.

Cassie returned to school with a new disposition. She stopped being afraid of the possibility that she might be gay. She had opened her heart to new beginnings.

Regine and Guy began working on building a stronger relationship. Though, Guy was still jealous of Lamar, who seemed to be constant in Regine's life. He kept his true feelings to himself for fear of causing tension in his fragile marriage.

After being kidnapped, Regine had called her mother and assured her that she was fine. Sue paid Regine a visit shortly after. Their reunion was short but special.

Alex felt rejuvenated after surviving a near death experience. After he was released from the hospital, he and Sidney decided to squash their differences and work together. In fact, Alex had insisted that Sidney remain in charge, until he was able to return to work full time. Unfortunately, Alex still had a wandering eye for ladies, but he was on the hunt for a special lady.

Jeanine's recent test results showed the cancer was in remission. Though, her doctor thought it was too early to determine if she had been cured of breast cancer. Even though he wanted Jeanine to stay in London a while longer, she was eager to return to the United States. In response, Guy sent a private jet to London to retrieve her.

When Jeanine's jet landed at the Tama Bay airport, she thought it was strange that no one was there to greet her. Guy, Regine and the twins had flown to London to visit her a week earlier. Mimi told her that their absence was just a fluke, ensuring Jeanine's 'Welcome Home' party remained a surprise.

From the living room window, Dana was the first to spot the limo pulling up in the driveway. "She's here!" she yelled out.

"Okay guys," Guy said with great enthusiasm, "let's get ready to give mom a warm reception."

As soon as Mimi opened the front door and Jeanine walked in behind her, everyone yelled, "Surprise!"

Jeanine laughed. She was elated to discover colorful balloons and a *Welcome Home* sign hanging from the ceiling.

Smiling, Dana brought Jeanine a vase of red roses. "I'm happy to see you, Mother."

Jeanine kissed Dana on the cheek. "I'm happy to see you too!"

Cassie came up from behind Dana and hugged Jeanine. "Hi Mom. Welcome home."

Jeanine gave Cassie a warm hug. "Hi Cassie, how are you?"

"Fine," Cassie said with assurance, "now that you're home."

"And I'm glad to be home," Jeanine excitedly replied.

"Mom," Dana warmly interjected, "Cassie and I have a surprise for you in the family room."

"Is that right?" Jeanine sheepishly asked with a wide grin. Cassie, who was standing next to Dana, nodded. She and Dana had worked with Regine to do all the cooking for Jeanine homecoming party. "Give me a few minutes. I'll be down shortly."

After the twins walked downstairs, Jeanine walked over to Alex and gave him a warm hug. He had been released from the hospital a week earlier. "Son, I'm happy you're fully recovered."

"Mom," Alex said with misty eyes, "I've missed you so much. I'm so happy you're feeling better."

"I know what you did for me," Jeanine said, as tears welled up in her eyes. "I owe you my life."

Alex smiled. "No, you don't. If I had to do it all over again, I wouldn't change a thing."

Jeanine kissed Alex on the cheek, then she looked at Tim who was grinning from ear to ear. "It's so good to see you," she said with joy in her voice,

Tim held Jeanine's hand and kissed her on the cheek. "Welcome home, Mrs. Benedict. I'm elated to see you."

A week earlier, Jeanine had contacted Tim to ask about Danny Desoto and Armando Gomez. She was somewhat relieved when Tim told her the men were dead. He also recounted what Guy had told him about Bryce Jennings, including the events leading up to his demise. Jeanine heard on the news that Bryce was missing but suspected foul play.

Jeanine smiled as she looked into Tim's eyes. "Thanks, for everything." Next, she went over to her daughter-in-law, who stood next to Guy. "I love you so much," she said, as she held Regine's hand. "Thank you for remaining committed to Guy and your marriage."

Regine hugged Jeanine. "I love you too. It's been rough," she stated as she grabbed Guy's hand, "but we're managing."

"Every marriage has its rough patches. Hang in there," Jeanine encouraged. Then, she spotted her grandson, who stood in front of his mother. She bent down and gave KC a warm hug. "How's my grandbaby?"

"Hi Gramma," KC said, as he hugged and kissed Jeanine.

"Look at you," Jeanine beamed as she embraced KC. "You are so handsome, just like your father." He laughed in response. She gave KC another peck on the cheek before she stood up, and turned to her oldest son.

Jeanine gave Guy a warm hug. "Son, I'm so proud of you. Thank you for protecting this family."

Guy smiled. "I could not have done it without you."

Jeanine smiled as she turned to Big Mike, who stood on the other side of Guy. "I remember you."

Big Mike smiled. "It's good to see you again, Mrs. Benedict."

"I'm happy you're Guy's friend, and I'm ecstatic you're here."

"I wouldn't miss this reunion for the world," Big Mike stressed.

Suddenly, there was a knock at the door. Mimi's jaw dropped when she opened the door and saw that it was Sidney McKinley. "What are you doing here?" she asked in a hushed voice.

Sidney smirked as he brushed past Mimi, and walked over to Jeanine to give her a warm hug. "Welcome home, Mrs. Benedict," he said in an animated tone. "It's so good to have you home."

"Sidney," Jeanine excitedly said, "it's so good to see you."

"The pleasure is mine," Sidney announced with open arms.

Regine tensed up upon seeing Sidney. She suddenly remembered what Bryce had told her about Sidney's involvement in trying to take over Trowne Key Estates. In fact, she told Guy everything Bryce had told her, but had forgotten to mention Sidney. Regine could not stand by and pretend as if she did not know anything. "Sidney," she said as she approached him, "when was the last time you heard from Bryce Jennings?"

Sidney frowned. "I don't know him well," he murmured. "I thought he was Alex's friend and associate."

Alex and Guy stared at Regine, wondering where she was going with her question, especially since she was aware that her father was responsible for making Bryce disappear. However, she did not know Kevin's men buried Bryce while he was still alive.

"I was just wondering, that's all," Regine said to Sidney with slanted eyes. "He was fond of you."

"Really?" Sidney asked with surprise in his voice.

Jeanine frowned as she turned to Regine. "Why are you dredging up Bryce Jennings' name?"

"Mrs. Benedict," Tim interrupted, "I did some more research on Bryce Jennings. You may have known his father, James Jennings. He used to own Cascade Resorts."

"James," Jeanine said aloud, as she briefly looked skyward. "Yes I remember him. He died several years ago." Then she turned to Sidney, and asked, "How did you meet Bryce Jennings?"

"Through Alex," Sidney quickly replied.

"That's not true," Alex begged to differ, as he stepped forward and shifted his eyes to Sidney. "You initiated the meeting with Bryce, remember?"

Jeanine turned to Sidney, seeking clarification. "Why were you affiliated with Bryce Jennings?"

"It's a long story," Sidney said, after failing to come up with a good explanation.

"If I may," Regine interjected while directing her gaze to Jeanine, "I think Sidney's association had something to do with his desire to help Bryce Jennings take over Trowne Key Estates."

Standing still, everyone eagerly awaited Sidney's rebuttal.

Sidney turned to Jeanine, and shouted, "You forced me to do this! You owe me!"

"I owe you nothing!" Jeanine snapped.

Alex was shocked by Jeanine's sharp response. He had never seen her so bold and definitive.

Shaking his head, Sidney was boiling inside from anger. "I busted my *ass* to help you make Trowne Key Estates an international success!"

"And I paid you for your efforts!" Jeanine retorted in a harsh manner.

Guy and Alex were about to put Sidney in check for yelling at Jeanine, but she held up her hand to stop them. Then she turned to Sidney and glared at him with contempt.

Under intense scrutiny, sweat beads began to form along Sidney's forehead. Then he began fidgeting with his hands, trying to think of something to say, to save his job. "It's not what it seems," he weakly explained.

After standing back and watching this drama unfold, Mimi came up from behind Jeanine with tears in her eyes. "Mrs. Benedict," she sobbed, "I can't do this anymore."

"Do what?" Jeanine asked, as she looked at her caretaker with deep concern.

"Sidney McKinley is my cousin," Mimi admitted in a soft spoken voice. "He told me he and Bryce made arrangements to take over Trowne Key Estates. Sidney told me if I reported everything that went on in this house, he'd pay me fifty-thousand dollars."

Exhaling, it took a while for Jeanine to digest Mimi's confession. "You were a spy?" she asked in a soft whisper.

"I'm so sorry," Mimi said, as tears rolled down her face.

Jeanine shook her head in disbelief. "But you went out of your way to help our family. Why?"

"I fell in love with this family," Mimi declared, as she looked at Guy, Regine, and Alex with a sincere heart. "I never took Sidney's money," she said, as she directed her eyes to her cousin. "I stopped communicating with him shortly after I started working for you."

Glaring at Sidney with contempt, Jeanine said in a stern voice, "Your only saving grace is that my children did not fall victim to your scheme. So, I'm going to let you walk out of here with your tail between your legs. But, if you come near my children again," she warned through gnashed teeth, "I promise, you will regret it. Don't bother returning to the office. Your things will be packed and shipped to you."

Feeling deflated, Sidney walked out of the front door with his head bowed. He knew there was nothing he could say or do to repair the damage to his image and self-worth.

Jeanine turned to Mimi, and asked, "Can we trust you?"

"Yes," Mimi answered, while nodding her head. "I love this whole family."

Jeanine smiled. "I believe you."

Alex felt guilty when he approached Jeanine. "Mom, I should have known Sidney was up to something."

Jeanine held Alex's hand. "It was my fault for believing Sidney would be a great mentor for you."

"You had no way of knowing Sidney was a jerk," Alex countered, trying to deflect the blame.

After deep thought, Jeanine asked, "How do you feel about me returning to the office, to help out?"

Alex smiled. "I would love that."

"Mom," Guy intervened, "are you sure you feel up to returning to work?"

"Yes, I feel fine," Jeanine answered, before she briefly turned to Alex and winked. "I'll take things slow, I promise." Then she walked over to Guy and Regine. "It's time you and Regine go on a long vacation. I'll watch after KC and the twins while you're away."

"I don't know if that's a good idea," Guy nervously replied.

"Mimi will help me," Jeanine concluded. "You have your own family now. Now that I'm feeling better, the twins are my responsibility."

Guy shook his head. "Mom, you just got out of the hospital. And KC can be a hand full."

Jeanine smiled as she cupped the right side of Guy's face. "Son, don't argue with me. Please let me do this."

Nodding, Guy realized there was no sense in debating with Jeanine.

Next, Jeanine turned to Tim. "I appreciate your help, but I think we're going to be okay. This time, I want you to officially retire."

Tim smiled. "Mrs. Benedict, you can always contact me whenever you need me."

"Thank you Tim, but that won't be necessary."

Jeanine turned to everyone with a warm smile. "This is my welcome home party. Let's act like it. Where's my cake?" she teased with a light chuckle.

Everyone laughed except Big Mike, who was relieved after witnessing a good ending to his friend's dilemma. He loved Guy like a brother, and was willing to do anything to help him out of a bad situation. Unbeknownst to Guy, Big Mike was responsible for hiding Malik's body.

Big Mike had a feeling Guy was up to something when he called and asked for specifics about Malik Mitchell, the day after Dana was assaulted. Knowing how Guy felt about someone harming his siblings, Big Mike had instructed one of his employees to follow Guy. He was alarmed when his employee called him back and told him he spotted Guy and Alex leaving Malik's apartment. In response, Big Mike had instructed his employee to return to Malik's apartment to make sure there was no evidence of any wrong doing. He was shocked when his employee called and told him Malik's lifeless body was sprawled out on the sofa. Big Mike could not take the chance that Guy and his brother could end up in jail for murder, so he had asked his employee to hide Malik's body in the landfill. Looking back, if he had to do it all over again, he would not change a thing.

318

Epilogue

A year later....

Jeanine moved into her own mansion in Clearwater, Florida, taking the twins with her. It was only two blocks away from Guy and Regine's home. She thought it was best for her son and daughter-in-law to experience what it was like to raise their son, KC, as a separate family unit. Besides, Jeanine thought it would be a great opportunity to experience motherhood, which was her lifelong dream.

The twins had made up their minds to follow in their brothers footsteps. They had planned on attending University of Florida in Gainesville, Alex's alma mater for their undergraduate degree, and Florida International University in Miami, Florida, Guy's alma mater for their graduate degree. Though, they had different career paths. Dana wanted to become a lawyer, whereas Cassie wanted to become a psychologist.

The twins were preparing for their high school graduation, when Jeanine walked into Cassie's room and noticed the twins were standing in the mirror posing and giggling. "I'm so proud of you girls," Jeanine announced with excitement in her voice.

The twins smiled. "Thanks, Mom," they said in unison.

"Do you really want to go away to college? This house is not going to be the same without you," Jeanine acknowledged. The sadness in her voice was obvious.

"Mom," Dana whined, "don't start crying. Gainesville is just two hours away. We'll come home as often as we can."

"How do you feel about your father being a part of your lives?" Jeanine asked out of curiosity. When she was in the hospital, Guy told her the twins' father was making efforts to be a part of their lives.

"I love it!" Cassie gleefully admitted.

"It feels weird," Dana countered.

Jeanine nodded. "I can imagine. Give him a chance."

"Okay, Mom," Cassie replied. "Give us a few more minutes. We'll be down in a little bit. Mom, is it okay if I invite a friend to the graduation party?"

"Sure sweetie," Jeanine replied with a wide grin. "Who is it?"

Cassie bit her bottom lip. She was unsure if she was ready to disclose her friend's name. "I'd rather not say."

Jeanine looked at Dana for an answer, but Dana shrugged her shoulders. She was clueless.

Then Jeanine touched Cassie's shoulder with love in her heart. "Honey, any friend of yours is a friend of mine. Everyone is waiting. We have to get out of here if we're going to make it to the graduation ceremony on time," Jeanine added before descending down stairs.

Walking downstairs, Jeanine looked at the men who had remained constant in the twins' lives the past year. Guy, Sapp, and Bobby readied their cameras to snap pictures of the twins coming downstairs.

Cassie and Dana put on their cap and robe before they descended downstairs, hand in hand. They were bombarded with flashing cameras as they walked downstairs, striking funny poses.

Smiling, Guy walked up to the twins and hugged them. "I'm so proud of you girls."

Sapp stepped forward and stood next to Guy. "No, I'm prouder."

Then Bobby Toil stepped forward with a big grin. "No one could be more ecstatic than me," he added with soft laughter. "How would you girls like to be transported to your graduation?"

Dana frowned. She was confused by her father's question. "Aren't we taking one of the limos?"

While gloating, Bobby held up two keys, one in each hand. "Or you can drive yourselves."

Dana and Cassie looked at each other in amazement before they turned back to Bobby. "Dad," Dana slowly said, "did you buy us a car?"

Bobby looked at the twins with knowing eyes. "Well, there's only one way to find out."

Without further prodding, the twins rushed past their father and brothers, and out of the front door. They were elated to find two brand new BMWs parked in the driveway. Dana dashed to the red BMW and Cassie darted to the blue one. Bobby had ordered the cars after he had asked Guy about the twins' favorite colors.

After Dana and Cassie climbed in their cars, they were surprised to discover an envelope placed on the passenger seats. They did not know what to expect as they pulled a picture out of the envelope. At first sight, they knew it was a picture of them, taken when they were newborn babies. Then they looked at the man holding them in the pictures. Bobby had inscribed on the bottom of their pictures, *"I never stopped loving you, Your Dad."*

Tears welled up in Dana and Cassie's eyes as doubts about whether Bobby abandoned them before they were born evaporated.

They got out of their cars at the same time, then looked toward the front door to find Bobby standing there with outstretched arms. As if on cue, the twins ran into his arms, and said at the same time, "Thank you, Daddy!"

Everyone, including Regine, Mimi and KC congregated outside to congratulate them. Shortly after, Alex arrived with a young woman in tow. Regine and Guy's mouths flew open when they recognized Miss America sitting in the passenger seat of Alex's car.

"How did he pull that off?" Regine whispered to Guy.

Guy shook his head. "I don't know," he said with disbelief. "Hopefully, she's a keeper."

While Regine stood in one place, Guy approached Alex's car. "Hey Alex, how are you?"

Alex gave Guy a warm embrace, before he spotted the BMWs. "I see the twins' received their gifts. Do you think it was a good idea?"

Guy nodded. "Between all of us watching over them, including the bodyguards I hired from Big Mike's investigative firm, I don't foresee a problem," he explained, before glancing at Miss America, who remained seated in Alex's car. "What's up with your date?"

Alex smiled with pride. "She's a cutie, isn't she?"

"Is she coming with us to the twins' graduation?"

"No, I wanted to stop by and see the twins before I took her home. She spent the night at my place last night."

Guy looked at Alex in disbelief. He wondered if his brother would ever settle down. Deciding not to press the issue, Guy asked, "Will you be able to make it to the twins' graduation?"

Alex nodded. "Yes, I'll be there. I wouldn't miss it for the world. Let me go congratulate the twins." He walked over to the twins and gave them a warm embrace. "I'm so proud of my favorite girls."

"Thanks Alex," the twins said in unison.

Fifteen minutes into the graduation party, Cassie's friend knocked on the door. Before Mimi could reach for the door, Cassie beat her to it. "I got it!" she yelled out.

Grinning as she opened the door, Cassie was happy to see her friend, BJ, on the other side. Her friend's hair was styled with four braids going back. Based on the loose fitting clothes her friend wore, no one could tell if BJ was a boy or girl.

"Hi BJ, come on in," Cassie insisted. After they kissed and embraced, she guided her friend downstairs where the party commenced. "I want to introduce you to my family."

Cassie and BJ were the same age, and had been talking over the phone for the past few months. Every so often, they would sneak off to be with each other without anyone's knowledge.

When Cassie walked into the family room arm-and-arm with her friend, everyone seemed to freeze in place. Everyone was in shock, except Dana, who was the first to introduce herself. Dana looked at BJ with a smug grin. "So you're the best-kept secret. What is your name?"

Cassie's friend said, "Just call me BJ."

"I hope you like to dance," Dana said with excitement in her eyes, "because that's what we're going to do all night long." Then she pulled BJ on the dance floor.

Everyone stopped trying to figure out if BJ was a boy or girl, and noticed that Cassie seemed happy and in-love. It did not take long for them to join the festivities.

Coming soon....

Part III of the Fatal Trilogy

A fictional story about survival of the fittest. What would happen if your closest relative betrays you, but you need that same relative to survive? The question of *'What would you do?'* leaves you in suspense until the very end.

Visit dorothyjmorris.com for the excerpt

About the Author

Dorothy J Morris was born and raised in Fort Lauderdale, Florida. *Fatal Vengeance* is her sophomore novel. She is currently working on *Fatal Blow,* the final installment of the Fatal Trilogy.

She lives in Maryland with her husband and two daughters.

To learn more about the author and her upcoming novels, visit wwwdorothyjmorris.com. Or if you wish to provide feedback, send an email message to the author at contactme@dorothyjmorris.com.